*MAGIC
IN your
HEART.*

*Awesome To
see you
:)*

FORCED MAGIC

BY

JEROD LOLLAR

FORCED MAGIC

COPYRIGHT 2013 JEROD LOLLAR

PUBLISHER: JEROD LOLLAR

PUBLISHED: JANUARY 30, 2013

DEDICATION

I dedicate this book to all those who helped. To Peggy Hertel for editing and telling me that it was great! Troy and Djuana Berlin for their encouragement, love and all around support, to Bob and Sherry for just putting up with me .And to Lucas for the awesome cover.

I would also like to dedicate this book to all who spent their days in a fantasy world of their own. Hope you enjoy reading this as much as I enjoyed writing it.

Prologue

Do you believe in Magic? I'm not talking about what you see on TV or in the movies. I've seen them all. Trust me, I am a big fan of the kid with a scar on his forehead. I'm talking about a driving presence that can make extraordinary things happen in your life.

Any true fan of Science Fiction and Fantasy will tell you how they want to believe the stories can be true. H.G. Wells wrote so many tales of Science Fiction that ended up in some way coming true. Why not Fantasy? There has always been a hint of true history attached to all of the mythological creatures and stories. If you were to look online into the origins of a lot of the stories, you might be surprised at the grains of truth that are attached to them. Who is to say that they don't exist? I know for a fact that they do.

My mom used to tell me that I had my head in the clouds, my feet on the ground, and my heart in my comic books. She was right. But I never let it overwhelm me. I wanted to believe it was real, but I always knew it wasn't. I guess you could call me a practical Fantasy geek.

My name is Jack, Jack Dewitte. The best way to describe me is average, brown hair, brown eyes, and average height. Well, that's how I would describe myself. Others would describe me as odd, I guess.

One of those people would be my older brother Paul. He always took care of me. He was an anchor in my life.

Let me tell you a little secret. This story is being written by magic. Right now it is explaining, in my own words, what is happening to me. It may seem as if I am telling a tale as a survivor, but I'm not. I have no idea if I am going to make it through this. There are times that I feel that all of what I am now a part of is not real. That I have lost my mind and will wake up in a strait-jacket somewhere awaiting shock treatments. I guess in the end I'll let you decide if I'm crazy or not, unless, this story is part of the delusion. What a paradox.

One more thing before I begin my story, a kind of warning. This isn't a typical tale of fantasy. It goes down dark paths and, much like the true fairy tales written long ago, my story can get pretty horrific. I'll let you decide for yourselves. Just remember this one thing; Magic is real.

Chapter 1

A little over a year ago I was hit by a truck. I was crossing a street on my way to work when this jerk, who was in a hurry, tried to beat a light and hit me. My hip was broken. Nothing magical happened to me at that time. I remember lying in the street and seeing people bending over me looking at me with concern on their faces. I was rushed to the hospital and into surgery.

I was lucky enough not to have to have an artificial hip, just three pins holding my hip together and some pain. After a year of physical therapy, my body was healed to the point that I could go on with my life. I was lucky, but I didn't feel like it at the time. It was the last straw for me.

Physical therapy may have helped my body, but the damage to my spirit was my biggest problem. Basically my life sucked. I didn't really want to do anything. I was just going through the motions. I was living with my brother during this time and I couldn't help but feel like I was a burden to him. I knew I had to get out of there and be on my own again, but after a year of not working, I lacked the confidence to go back to what I was doing before the accident. The accident seemed to take more away from me than the use of my hip. It wasn't like I had the best job in the world before. Even though I worked in a restaurant as a waiter, it was hard for me to relate to people in general. I have always been a kind of misfit. I've never really fit in.

Going for long walks daily was part of my physical therapy. Starting at first with a walker, then graduating to a cane, and finally making my way without artificial help, I was getting better every day. I still had stiffness in my leg and a slight limp on my left side, but I was getting around fairly well. The walks got me out of the house and gave me time to think. During that time many of my thoughts turned to a nagging question I would pose to myself, *"What Now?"*

I was on my daily walk when my life changed. It was warm when I left the house that morning. I took the same route I always take. I had change in my pocket for a cup of coffee and I could hear it jingling against the rock I had found a few days before. I'm always picking up interesting rocks, and keeping them as good luck charms. This one looked cool. It was black with silver speckles. Eventually my rocks would end up on my dresser, forgotten. I would find another one to take its place. This kind of quirky behavior drove my brother nuts. He would walk into my room and see the pile of rocks on my dresser, shaking his head with a little frown on his lips. I really think my brother was disappointed in me. That bothered me.

I could feel the slight stiffness in my leg as I started my walk that day, the same feeling I always felt when I started my day. The warm weather would help ease that pain.

Tucson is a unique place to live in. You can go to any place in the city and it will give you a different view at which to look. All you have to do is stand in one spot and look around and you could swear you are in a different city. You can admire the stark beauty of the desert and then look up and enjoy the mountains that surround the city.

From that neighborhood you could look to the right and see nothing but a long stretch of desert. Kind of desolate, not much to see, unless you were lucky enough to see the beautiful flowers that bloom on the cacti. To the left you can find neighborhoods of desert colored houses all in neat rows. This is was what I would see every day as I took my walk. It was when I looked over at the desert across the street from my usual walking path that I saw her.

She was the most beautiful woman I had ever seen. Long blonde hair reached down past her waist. She had a perfect nose and mouth, the latter turned down in a small frown. She was wearing a white cotton summer dress that went down to her knees. Her eyes were a piercing blue. Even from the distance I could see them. She stared intensely at me.

It was love at first sight. Everything about her was perfect, from the top of her head to her slender bare feet.

She was floating, swaying gently side to side in the air. FLOATING! I thought I was losing my mind.

She reached out to me and moved a little toward the road, and that is when I saw how she was staying in the air. She had wings. She was flying. There was no doubt in my mind that what I was seeing was in fact a Fey, a beautiful fairy, an image of grace and beauty, right out of my fantasies. I am sure I had imagined her before. I had to be imagining her right at that moment. *"Is she* real?" I thought to myself. *"Am I just imagining her?"* No, she was better than anything I ever imagined. She was perfect.

She reached out to me again and moved toward me. I was mesmerized by her beauty. I took a step into the street toward her. She was trying to tell me something. She was getting ready to speak.

She pointed at my leg and said something. I couldn't hear her. The horn of the blue truck heading straight for me was too loud. I had stepped out into the middle of the street like I had been in a trance.

A blue Dodge pickup had come running down the street. Its brakes squealed and it swerved to keep from hitting me. I was standing in the middle of the street. The driver never stopped pounding the horn as it swerved to dodge me.

I saw a strange light. She led me into the street and disappeared. And I couldn't help but ask, "Why did she do that?"

As the truck screamed past me I felt air in my face, a sharp pain in my hip as the driver blasted the horn. A phantom pain as the memory of the accident that caused me to break it continued to flash in my mind.

As the truck continued down the road, I heard the driver screaming at me. That broke the spell and I backpedaled toward the curb, keeping my eyes on the pickup as it continued to make its way down the street. I hit the curb with the back of my heels and fell backwards, sitting on my butt hard, knocking the wind out of me, and still watching the truck disappear down the street.

Quickly turning my head, I looked across the street to the spot where my fairy had been. There was no sign of her. Did I imagine her? If she was real then she just tried to kill me.

Even as the thought formed in my mind, I began to feel foolish. Fairies do not exist. I let out a strange coughing laugh at this thought, as I sat there staring across the street at the spot she had stood. She seemed so real.

I sat there thinking over and over these same thoughts trying to piece it all together. None of it was making any sense to me. The only logical explanation was that I was losing my mind. This thought scared me but it seemed to be the right conclusion. When you see a fairy and you are convinced she is trying to kill you, you have lost it.

The panic that started to swell in my chest felt like someone had hit me with a baseball bat.

What a truly unique fear it is, when you convince yourself that you are losing your mind. You search your thoughts for something normal to latch on to. Something that would snap you back to reality and wake you up.

I did the most normal thing I could do, I started walking down the sidewalk again. I started feeling better. Another nervous coughing laugh. *"This was nothing more than an over active imagination."* I said to myself. With the massive collection of Fantasy and Science Fiction novels and DVD's spread across the room, I am definitely a fan. Add to that the boxes of comic books and graphic novels and you might even consider thinking I'm a fanatic. Years and years of reading those incredible stories have taken its toll a little. My fairy is nothing more than a wake-up call to get rid of it all. I made a vow that I would pack it all away when I got home.

I told myself that I was ok. *"I didn't see a fairy,"* I said to myself. *"It must have been some kind of reflection, from a car window, that I had seen out of the corner of my eye, and my imagination just took over for a second."*

I couldn't help but glance across the street every few steps as I continued my walk. *"Is she back?"* I would ask myself. *"No, she's not real. She was too beautiful to be real. What a face."* Then it hit me like a ton of bricks. *"That face, that beautiful perfect fairy face."* I had seen it before. I was sure of it. This thought stopped me in my tracks so suddenly that I almost fell over. I stumbled and my feet did a little awkward dance as I struggled to keep my balance. I somehow managed to keep from falling on my face as the words sunk in. I had seen that fairy before. Her face now familiar in my mind's eye, was so clear, that when I closed my eyes it was there like a photograph. A familiar face of someone I had seen before today. "But where have I seen her before?" I asked myself out loud. This thought that I had seen her face before today became very important to me. I knew that if I could remember where I had seen her before, I would understand why I had imagined her. I had stopped walking and had been standing there awkwardly as a car slowly stopped next to me. The window rolled down and a friendly voice asked "Are you ok?"

I jumped at the sound of that voice, realizing just how silly I must look. There was a little old lady sitting behind the wheel of a big Cadillac.

"Um, no, I'm fine. I just remembered something." I said in a shaky voice.

"It must be very important," she said. Giving her a weak smile, I mumbled "Just one of those days." She smiled at me, waved her hand a little and slowly pulled away. It was starting to get hot and I needed a place to sit down and try to piece this all together.

I finally made it to the store. Walking in, I felt the air conditioner hitting me with a gust of cool air that gave me an idea of just how hot I was. I walked up to the little coffee counter that was at the front of the store, trying to decide if I was too hot for my usual cup of coffee or not. Giving in to the idea of holding on to something normal, I went ahead and got my usual and sat down at a table close to the door. I kept seeing that fairy's face in my mind as I sat at the small table trying to piece it all together. I knew I could figure out where I had seen that face before.

As I sat there staring at my coffee, I heard a loud cough. I glanced up to see a man with a shopping cart full of groceries glaring at me. He had a scowl on his face and was griping the handle of his shopping cart so tightly his knuckles were turning white. He was mad, and the way he was glaring at me, I got the idea he was mad at me. I looked at him, trying to figure out exactly what I could possibly have done to him. I shrugged my shoulders and mouthed the word "What?"

He pointed at me and mumbled something. I couldn't hear what he was saying, but I knew that it wasn't nice. Then it hit me who he was. He was the driver of that truck I had walked out in front of. The look of realization on my face must have been very apparent. The little old man wagged his head in an exaggerated 'yes' and said, loud enough for me to hear the word, "Nut" as he wheeled his rickety shopping cart out the door.

My face felt hot with embarrassment as I looked down at my coffee. I sat there wishing I could have started this day all over again. If I knew how it was going to start, I would have stayed in bed. A bead of sweat fell on the table next to my cup as I let my mind wonder back to the question of the fairy and where I had seen her face before. Why could I not convince myself that it was all just my imagination? Why did I see her again today of all days? And why was I so hot?

My entire body was covered in sweat. I was breathing heavily. My hands, dripping with perspiration, started turning red. They started to shake and a tremor moved down my body. I started to spasm and I knocked my coffee off the table and across the floor. I grabbed the corner of the table, desperately trying to keep my body from shaking. The heat coming off of my body continued to rise. I wanted to call out for help but I was unable to form the words. Through all of this I started to feel a focal point for the heat. The heat was coming from my right leg, the same leg that the fairy had pointed to. I reached for my leg, trying to find the source, and felt a bump where my pocket was. I reached into my pocket and let out a yell as my hand touched the bump. It was my lucky rock. It had attached itself to my leg. I tried to pull it free as a white-hot pain shot up my body.

It felt like an electric shock. My body shook so hard that I tore the top of the table off of its base. People in the store, seeing I was in some sort of trouble, started to walk toward me. I sat there shaking uncontrollably. I could hear voices asking me If I was ok or if I needed help. There were several people on their cell phones talking to 911. Others were taking pictures and videos of me with their camera phones to show to friends the nut who had obviously lost it. The burning pain continued to climb and my right leg started to throb. I wanted this to end! I wanted help. I had no control over my body. I stood up knocking my chair over. I was still clutching the table. Pain shot through my body and another spasm shook me violently. In my head I saw the fairy pointing to the leg that now had the rock attached to it

"The fairy did it. The FAIRY did IT. THE FAIRY DID IT! THEFAIRYDIDIT!."

This thought kept screaming over and over again in my head. The pain was real. The rock that had attached itself to my leg was real. The fairy had to be real.

Chapter 2

I stood there shaking as a strange feeling started to enter my body. That feeling was to run. Escape. Flee. Fear and pain had totally taken over. Another spasm hit me and my head whipped back and with a clinching of my stomach I threw up my coffee. I heard people talking as I struggled with my body.

"Eww, he just threw up."

"Hey man, are you ok?"

"Someone call an ambulance."

The manager moved toward me. He wanted to help me but I knew I must have looked like a lunatic. I wanted his help but, when I tried to say something, another wave of pain overtook me. With a strangled yell of pain, I raised the table over my head and sent it crashing to the floor. The wood splintered and shattered and, with screams and yells of panic, I took off at a full run toward the crowd of people. They scattered in all directions as I ran toward the door. The manager stepped in front of me trying to stop me, trying to help me. I shoved him sending him skidding across the floor. I ran through the doors as the pain throbbed through my body. I didn't want to run, I wanted to stop but I couldn't. I screamed as the pain intensified. I bolted for the door.

As I stumbled through the parking lot foaming from the mouth, my vision going in and out, another wave of white pain hit me. I could hear sirens getting closer.

The rock pulsed a regular beat as it sank a little further into my skin. I wanted to claw at it and rip it out of my leg. I didn't care what damage that would do. I started to run.

Up ahead of me I saw a wash. Alongside of it next to the road was a bike path. I stumbled down to the path wanting to stop and lay down. But the pain wouldn't let me stop.

The pain was more intense than when I broke my hip. I stopped on the edge of the wash as I heard my pants rip. I looked down at my leg gasping in horror.

My lucky rock had fully attached itself to my leg. It had grown all the way down to the knee and all the way up my upper thigh. The silver specks glowed as it pulsed, bubbling like it was alive. I clawed at it in an attempt to rip it from my body. Another wave of pain sent me to my knees.

I tumbled head first into the wash, my body flaying around. Hitting the bottom with a loud thump I knew I had broken bones. There could be no way I could survive a fall like that. As I lay there in pain, I thought of my brother and how I would miss him.

My brain started to shut down. I welcomed the dark oblivion. My last thought as I started to fade was remembering where I had seen the fairy before. She was there when I got hit by the truck and broke my hip.

What did she want with me?

The rock pulsed once again. Then darkness.

Chapter 3

I am home, standing at the front door. I can feel the sun on my back and there is no pain. I look down at my leg and it is fine. No pulsing mass. No parasite thing draining me of life. I don't know how I got outside the door of my brother's house, and, to tell you the truth, I don't care. I am home and that is all that matters. I rest my head against the door as relief washes over me. It was a dream. It had to just be a dream. That was it. Just an over-the-top nightmare. I don't even care how I got outside. I am just glad I'm home. I take a second to shake off the last images of the nightmare. I reach into my pocket to get my keys. I feel the lucky rock as I dig around for the key. It feels warm. I pull my hand out of my pocket quickly. I'm breathing heavily and I break out in a cold sweat. I laugh at how silly I'm being. I dig in my pocket again getting out the key. I unlock the door. Before I open the door, I notice black smoke swirling around my feet.

"How weird," I think as I push open the door.

The door slowly swings open into a dark long hallway *"This isn't right,"* I think as I take a step back. But I can't step back. I try to turn away from the gloom of the hallway but I can't move. The dark swirling smoke is crawling up my legs to my waist. It starts to force me into the dark hallway.

As I step into the house, the heavy dark smoke surrounds my head. I see my parent's car. I hear the crunch and the crash and a scream. It's my mother. I can hear the cars crashing into each other as the speeding drunk T-bones into my parent's car. I run to the car hoping to somehow help this time, knowing it was hopeless. This was all just a dream, a vision, a twisted nightmare. I get to the car and looking in, I see my dad. His head is hanging down as blood drips across his face. His head turns.

He looks at me and says, "It's your entire fault, Jack. We were rushing home to you when we were hit. It's all your fault."

Tears stream down my face as the black smoke pulls me away from the scene.

I'm at school. The boys in my fourth grade class are holding me down forcing me to drink out of a can of coke that they had all peed in. I saw my teacher, Miss Rose, walk by. This time she doesn't stop them. She stands there laughing as they force my mouth open to make me drink.

"Take a long drink Jack," she says as she laughs, "take a good long drink."

The next step is me breaking my arm when I was eight. This is more than a memory as my arm starts to ache. I can feel the pain. I look up and see my friend Mike standing at the top of the stairs.

"I pushed you," he said smiling. "All these years you thought you tripped and fell but you didn't. I pushed you."

I am being forced to go through memories of pain, anger and sadness from my life. But all these memories are twisted. I am being dragged into despair. There is no hope in these images, no relief from the pain. I pull against the smoky blackness, fighting, trying not to take another step.

I am at the crosswalk where I am hit by that truck. I scream in pain as the pins that are still in my hip push their way out and fall to the ground. I lay in the street moaning in pain as a crowd of people gather around laughing. I beg for help but no one helps me. Everyone is laughing as I see my beautiful deadly fairy. She kneels down and whispers in my ear.

"You're not going to make it Jack. You won't survive this."

She smiles, stands, and kicks me in my bad hip.

Another forced step and I am back in the street from earlier that day. This time the truck speeds up hitting me, knocking me in the air. I hit the ground bones breaking. I see my fairy laughing at me as she gestures to me to cross the street.

I'm forced to move again. The living room is just ahead. I can make out a dark shape swinging back and forth. I know what is there and I don't want to see the horrifying reality of what is before me. It's my brother. He's hanging from a rope. His neck is broken and his head is tilted to the side. His lifeless body sways back and forth. I can hear a creaking sound from the rope as it moves across my brother's neck. A long low moan escapes me in despair of this horrific sight. This is not a memory but a dark hidden fear.

Suddenly, my brother opens his eyes and smiles. I try to back away as he reaches up and grabs the rope around his neck pulling himself up.

"You've always been a burden, Jack," he says in a strange rough voice, "You have failed at everything you've tried. I tried to help you but it never worked. I have given up because of you. All the dreams I had for my life are washed away because I had to take care of you. It's your entire fault."

With those last words I feel the parasite on my leg finally rip open. I scream in pain as thousands of spiders start pouring out of it. He laughs as the spiders crawl all over my body biting me and tearing at my skin. He is no longer dangling from the rope. He steps toward me, his broken neck making his head wobble and flap around his shoulders. He grabs my arm. His hand melts over my arm as the spiders continue to tear at my body. I am slowly being pulled into my brother as he melts around me. I try to scream but no sound comes from my mouth as I am slowly being pulled into my brother's body.

I hear laughing and the mocking voice of my brother saying over and over again, "It's your fault."

I feel strange warmth around my feet. It starts moving up my body, getting warmer as it rises. As it moves up my body, the spiders began to fall off. They disintegrate into a grey powder. The pain begins to melt away. As the warmth continues to cover my body, my brother releases his hold on me. He backs away, a look of confusion on his face. I start to fight. A strange new hope begins to well up inside me. I will not let my past fears destroy me. I will not allow my own doubts bring me to despair anymore. I am better than that. I am not useless. I am not a burden.

I pull myself away from the living room, the black smoke fighting to keep me there. I break free. The thing that looks like my brother makes a last attempt to grab me. This time I am ready. I turn the tables on it. Grabbing the thing that looks like my brother by the throat, it begins to dissolve in my hands. The final thing I see in its face is surprise as it melts away.

I feel stronger. More confident. I am going to get away. The black smoke grabs at me again and as it touches me I feel flashes of pain. It's trying to get me to return to that feeling of despair. I kick and swing at it, beating it down. I am mad! Mad at this blackness, mad at the way my life has turned out, and mad at myself! I'm not going to take it anymore!

I stomp the black smoke to the floor. As I run for the front door, the house stretches and twists back on itself. This dark evil thing in my dream isn't done with me yet. There's a screeching sound behind me and I turn to see the black smoke coming down the hall. It pours itself down like spilt water. A stretching dark clawed hand moves all around the hallway trying to find me. In the blackness I can see images of the nightmare twisted memories that it had tried to get me to believe were true. I could feel its frustration as it tries to get into my mind again. Creeping down the hallway that was now impossibly long, I was now somehow hidden from it. It can't see me and is blindly searching for me. I have my back up against the door now, trying to open it and escape. There's a roar, a loud triumphant sound.

"Is that part of the dream?" I ask myself. The warmth spreads up my body and a strength fills my heart. I stare at the darkness and know I have won. It doesn't matter if I get away or not. I will fight it. I will not let it take me away.

I can feel its presence searching for me. Feel the anger swelling up like a giant wave as it comes closer. Its frustration thumping in my mind has replaced the twisted nightmare memories.

Something is wrong. This is not supposed to happen. I am not supposed to get away. It is impossible. Something is supposed to happen, something that will allow this dark evil thing to take me. But it isn't happening. Fumbling with the door, I finally get it opened, falling backwards into a sunlit day. I hear one last scream from the darkness as I fall backwards, and then I wake up.

I opened my eyes, a yell stuck in my throat. Tears of relief ran down my face as I lay in the dark. It's over. "Where am I?" I said out loud.

Chapter 4

Wherever it was, it was dark and smelled. It smelled like rotten fruit and meat. I wanted to throw up.

I tried to sit up and was hit with a wave of nausea. A dull ache penetrated every muscle in my body. I was lying on my back and I could see only a faint gloom. There was a ceiling I could just make out about twelve feet above. I was in some sort of a cave. A cement floor scratched at my back as I tried to sit up again. Big mistake. Dizzy and weak as I was, my mind was fuzzy and I was having a hard time concentrating.

Trying to break through the fuzziness, I started to go over the day. Remembering the pulsing bubble that had formed on my leg, I grabbed for it to check if it was still there, slapping at the imaginary spiders that poured out of it in my nightmare vision.

That move was a little too much for me. The throbbing ache flared up and became a burning sharp pain. It shot through my entire body. Slowly it faded away and was replaced by the throbbing heartbeat ache that now seemed to be a relief compared to the other. I was definitely hurt, was in a place I didn't recognize. I tried to make sense of it all. Back to the moment I saw the fairy on my walk, to everything that happened after. I wanted it to be a dream. None of it could be real. But here I was in a dark cave of some sort. Something had to have happened to me. I must have gone on a walk and fallen into the wash and hurt myself. Everything else was just a dark and twisted dream. That made sense to me, except, how did I get in this smelly cave?

I had no answer that made any sense to me; the only thing that seemed correct was it all really happened. The fairy, the parasite thing, and the fall. All of it happened. A strange rumbling sound passed over my head as a vibrating sensation passed through the cave. There was something familiar in that sound. A comforting sound. If I could just place it, I would be ok. A small bubble of panic was forming in my mind. I took a few deep breaths and realized that my ribs were fine. Another wave of relief washed over me. It had to have all been a dream. I remembered falling down into the wash and feeling my bones break. If I could breathe without pain, I must be ok. But I remembered the pain. I felt it. I tried to wrack my brain to see if I remembered anything I had ever read or heard regarding someone feeling pain in a dream as if it was real? Why was I so weak and hungry? I had to get ahold of myself and get out of this cave if I could.

I started a check list in my mind. I could breathe without difficulty. Check. I could see even if there was not much to see in this gloomy dark cave. Check. Another rumbling sound passed over the cave. I checked off hearing.

I knew I had to move to get out of here. Even though it seemed like I had no broken bones I wanted to be sure. First, I wiggled my toes. Check. They seemed to be ok. Now I checked my fingers. Not too bad. Now I checked my feet. I went down the list moving every inch of my body carefully. When I got to the point of bending my knees, I was beginning to think that I was ok. I was fine. By the time I reached my head and moved it carefully, I had convinced myself that I was going to be ok.

"Take that, you stupid fairy. I'm going to live," I mumbled to myself. I was sure the fairy had something to do with all of this.

"It's always the pretty ones," I said.

I laughed a little and the dull sound of it brought me back to the reality of my situation. If this day was all just a fevered dream, I had to figure out what had really happened and I had to get out of this cave. Slowly I started to roll over.

"No pain. Good," I mumbled as I moved. I saw daylight. That was the way out of the cave. I didn't think I had the strength to stand up. As I looked to the light, I heard a sound that made me realize where I was. It was a car horn. I was still in the wash. I must have crawled under the road into the tunnel under the street. But what happened? I had convinced myself that all the fairy and rock stuff was a dream. I must be sick and needed help; psychiatric help.

Puzzling over the day, I was reminded of the old line from the Sherlock Holmes books." Eliminate all the other possibilities and whatever is left, no matter how improbable, that is the answer." I had to find out the truth. A dream or truth?

Ok, first I needed to see if that thing was still attached to my leg. I slowly moved my hand toward my right leg. I had to fight to keep it from twitching at the idea that the spiders would be crawling over what I was sure would be a gaping hole across my right side. The ache in my entire body had diminished, making this task of moving much easier than it would have been just a few minutes ago. Reaching my leg I felt skin, smooth skin. No cuts or damage. The bubble was gone. My "lucky" rock was no longer attached to my leg.   Another sensation of relief washed over me as I let out my breath   I had been holding it in without realizing it.

Was this just a dream? I felt around my leg. Then I felt something that was a little alarming. It was my clothing along the right side of my body. My clothes had been ripped, torn to shreds. I moved my hand up the right side of my body. Just shreds of jeans and T-shirt.

"That was one of my favorite shirts," I groaned.

I moved my hand all around my right side, not even trying to figure out what kind of nightmarish thing that could have happened. Putting my hand down by my side again, I gasped as I put my hand into something sticky. It squished and that horrible smell hit my nose again. I dry heaved. I raised my hand away from it and moved my back a little. I felt a strange squishing sensation. The smell intensified. It took all of my concentration to keep from retching again. I was lying in this smelly stuff and I had no idea what it was. With a groan of pain, I rolled over onto my stomach covering myself completely in this mess.

"Could this be blood?" I thought. *"Is it my blood?"*

There was so much of it. If it was my blood, I would probably be dead. I found no comfort in that thought. I reached my hands in front of me, and with my whole body screaming at me in protest, I began to half crawl, half drag toward the sunlight.

The same thought played over and over in my mind. *"What is this stuff? What is this stuff?"*

My imagination started to kick into overdrive. This had to be the cave that the fairy brought her victims to. The sticky stuff was the blood of countless others, and soon she would be there to finish me off and add my own blood to the mess. I could almost hear the spiders crawling out of the darkness to swarm over me, tearing the flesh from my body and eating me alive. I had to get out of that tunnel. It was the only way I was going to survive. That fear gave me the strength to crawl. Now covered in the sticky, smelly mess, I had to peel my hand from the floor of the tunnel to keep moving. The soreness in my muscles seemed to be fading in my panicked state, just a dull ache that kept time with my heartbeat and ragged struggling breath.

The black darkness of the tunnel started to become less and less as I actually made progress toward the end. I saw my hands and I got a look at the sticky mess. There was a yellow look to it and in this gloom it seemed to shine. There were black specks and a cockroach had gotten stuck in it. The roach moved. This sent a new wave of nausea through my body. I yelled out and clawed at my hand causing me to land hard on the floor of the tunnel. I hit my chin so hard on the ground that, if I had been sticking out my tongue, I would have bitten right through it. I lay there shaking and listened to my gasping breath. I rolled over onto my back. My sore muscles throbbed.

"This is it," I said to myself, *"I'm either going to die here or wake up in a hospital somewhere."*

I stayed there breathing through my mouth to keep from smelling that awful stuff. Eventually the pain started to drain away from my body.

Another car drove overhead and I could hear the music from the stereo as it zipped by. I yelled out hoping someone could hear me. I stayed still for a few minutes hoping to see someone or hear someone call back to me.

Then it hit me, my cell phone. How could I have been so stupid? I never even bothered to check and see if I still had it. I reached into my left pocket and there it was. Now things were going right for me. One look at the cell phone showed me it was impossible. The phone was covered in slime, completely unusable. There was no way I could make a call and get help. I had to get out and flag someone down for help.

I looked up toward the light at the end of the tunnel; it was starting to get dark. Had I been down there all day? At the edge of the tunnel I saw the shape of a small animal. A dog? Someone's pet? Yes! The owner of it would come down to see what it was looking at and I would be saved. I was too relieved to even speak or I would have yelled for help. I moved a little closer. It wasn't a dog. It was a cat, a big cat. I blinked and took another look. It was a bobcat.

It sat there staring at me. Its ears twitched and it opened its mouth. I could see sharp teeth as it yawned. I didn't dare move. Not even dared to make a sound. I had no idea if this bobcat would attack me. I might be in its den for all I knew. I was too weak to fight it off if it did attack. Finally it got up looking as if it saw something behind me. It took off running. Another moment of irrational fear griped me as I looked behind me expecting to see spiders. That bobcat had to be looking at something. I began to crawl toward the exit.

As I got closer to the end of the tunnel, I started to hear the sounds of traffic. This calmed me down. I was going to get out of this mess. I was almost there. My breath was ragged and my head was feeling light. As bad as I wanted to get out of that tunnel, I knew if I didn't calm myself and take it a little easy, I would run the risk of passing out. I decided to give myself a little break. Rolling over I put my back against the wall. Sitting up I closed my eyes and listened to my breathing. As I sat there I made the decision that, when I got out of this mess, the less I told anybody about what happened to me, or what I imagined happened to me, the better.

A warm breeze gently hit my face followed by a strange smell, different from the sticky smell. I couldn't place it as the breeze kept time with my own breathing. It wasn't a breeze. There was something else in this tunnel and it was now breathing on me. I slowly opened my eyes thinking that the bobcat had come back to eat me after all. It wasn't the bobcat. It was something that made me realize that what I had seen and experienced had to have been real. It wasn't the fairy finally finding me, ready to finish me off. This was even more fantastic than that. I was face to face with a dragon!

Chapter 5

The dragon's body was about the size of a German shepherd. Its long neck curved up like a snake about to strike. There were black and silver scales covering its body, with a snout that looked like a horse's face ending in two nostrils that had smoke gently coming out as it breathed in and out. The two front claws were as thick as my legs. The back ones were twice as thick. There was a strange movement on either side of it. It had wings. The dragon moved them in a twitchy way, as if it was not sure what I was going to do. Its eyes glowed and changed color as it stared at me. I was on my hands and knees staring into the face of a dragon! I was now convinced I was losing my mind. This was too fantastic. First a fairy, now this. A cold sensation crept up my spine. The fey must have sent the dragon when she realized the parasite lucky rock thing didn't turn into spiders and kill me. The dragon must be here to finish me off.

In the dragon's mouth was a bag from the local fast food restaurant down the street. I could smell hamburgers and realized how hungry I was. If I wasn't so terrified at that point, I would have found this whole situation funny. I mean, here I was covered in slime, clothes torn, weak and helpless, staring at a dragon and I was feeling hungry. The dragon moved and I sat back quickly moving against the wall of the tunnel. It growled a little. Moving slowly, it set the bag down. Keeping its eyes on me, it stuck its snout in the bag and pulled out a burger. Instead of eating it, wrapper and all, the dragon took the burger in its front claws and carefully unwrapped it. Never taking its eyes off me, it put the whole thing in its mouth and began to chew carefully. I could see flashes of its sharp teeth as it finished chewing. There was a loud gulping sound and a look of satisfaction on its face. Smoke poured out of the snout and a sigh rumbled up from the back of its long throat.

My stomach growled. The dragon stopped eating for a second. Placing a claw over the bag of burgers in a protective way, it growled and showed sharp rows of teeth. This creature was not going to share. It reached back into the bag and pulled out another burger, unwrapped it and shoved the whole thing in its mouth. As it chewed quickly, my stomach rumbled again. The dragon stopped chewing and swallowed loudly. Staring at me, it seemed to come to a conclusion. With another obvious sigh and a rolling of its fantastic, ever-changing eyes, it picked up the bag and moved toward me.

I was pinned up against the wall unable to get away. It put the bag of burgers down in my lap and nudged them with its snout. This dragon was offering me food. I was consumed with hunger.

It was hard for me to believe that I could actually think of anything except the dragon that was staring at me. I reached into the bag, pulled out a double cheeseburger, removed the wrapper and started eating. I never took my eyes off the dragon as I ate. I was so hungry that I ignored the slime that covered me. I finished the burger. The dragon moved his head slightly in my direction.

"Thanks," I said not knowing what else to say.

The dragon motioned with its head toward the bag, pointing at it with a clawed hand. The gesture seemed so human. I reached in and pulled out another burger. I held it up showing the dragon I had got another one. It nodded in a satisfied way. Reaching over and taking the bag out of my lap, it pulled out another burger for itself.

The dragon had a pleased look on its face as I quickly devoured the second burger. The food seemed to help me. The soreness of my muscles was beginning to drain away. It was like someone had pulled a stopper in a bath tub full of water. Starting from the top of my head the muscle ache was leaving my body. I was exhausted. I could have gone to sleep in that cave covered in slime right then and there, if it wasn't for the fact that there was a dragon chomping down on hamburgers right in front of me.

I never took my eyes off the dragon as it sat there looking at me. A sense of wonderment filled my heart. I was actually face to face with one of my favorite fantasy creatures come to life. A Dragon! It seemed to be just as curious about me as I was about it.

This whole day was a fantasy straight out of a book. A horror filled fantasy, twisted and weirder than anything I had ever read, but still fantastic.

I thought of the dream I had woken up from. I wondered if it was a dream at all. Maybe it was some sort of vision. Did the fairy have something to do with it? It made sense that she did. After all, my crazy day had started with her appearing across that street. The dragon must be here to keep me from leaving until the fairy could get here. I wasn't sure if I liked that thought, the dragon seemed friendly. If it wanted to kill me then why would it feed me? What did the fairy want with me anyway?

I relaxed a bit as the food I had eaten settled in my stomach. I took a good look at the dragon. It was enjoying another burger when I saw its silver scales shimmer. They had a kind of rippling effect. The black scales even seemed to glow. Black and silver scales that looked strangely familiar to me. Then it hit me. The dragon's scales were black and silver, the same colors as my lucky rock. This dragon was from my rock. It was the parasite. Spiders didn't come out of the bubble like in my dream. This dragon did!

I didn't know what to do. All of my life experience, all of the fantasy books I have read, never could have prepared me for this. My rock, which I thought of as a good luck charm, had somehow been transformed into a dragon. In my mind's eye I saw the fairy pointing at my leg. She had cast a spell that created this creature that was now looking at me with the strangest expression. Its head was tilted to the side as if it was studying me, trying to figure me out. It seemed to have realized that something was wrong. My heart felt like it was pounding out of my chest. I didn't dare move, out of fear that the beast would attack. All wonderment gone, I just wanted to get out of that tunnel. The problem was the dragon was blocking the way.

Chapter 6

We sat there staring at each other. The dragon began to move cautiously toward me, looking me over. Its eyes were really creepy, constantly changing colors, red, blue, yellow, green, and purple. Every once in a while they would go black. It moved in closer, smoke coming out of its nose so thick I could feel it in the air. The dragon stopped about a foot from my face, its mouth curled up in a snarl.

"This is it. I'm dead now. " I thought as a growl started rumbling from the dragon.

I panicked. Yelling at the top of my voice I took my fist and hit the dragon underneath its chin. It moved its head back and made a choking sound. With all my strength I swung again hitting it right on the nose. A growl rose up from the dragon's throat and its front paws went up to hold its snout. I bolted for the exit.

A new feeling started to form in me. It started in the pit of my stomach and slowly spread throughout my entire body. It was anger. I was mad and I wasn't going to take anymore.

"Well. Come on!" I yelled at the dragon. I sat up a little. "Are you going to kill me? You going to eat me? What?!! What?!! Don't just stare at me, do it! DO IT!"

I started cursing at the thing yelling insult after insult at it. The whole time it just sat there glaring and growling at me. It crouched like it was about to attack.

"COME ON!" I screamed, "DO IT! TAKE A BITE!"

All of a sudden the dragon disappeared. One second it was there and the next it was gone. But, before I could run, I was pushed up against the wall. The dragon had reappeared. It had pinned me up against the wall. Its sharp glistening fangs were inches from my face. Smoke poured out of its nose and the silver scales on its body glowed. The smoke smelled like a charcoal barbeque. The burgers must have been an appetizer and I was going to be the main course. Its low growl vibrated all the way through my body.

I sat there frozen waiting for the worst. The anger drained out of me. *"This is it,"* I thought, *"I'm dead for sure now."* I thought of how unfair it all was. Why was this happening to me? Why was this dragon doing this? Was it because it hatched on my leg? Was the fairy involved in some way?

With the last of my resolve, I gritted my teeth, looked the dragon in the eye and said, "Do it! Eat me! Kill me! Just do it you stupid fat lizard!"

Its claws dug into my shoulders, scratching through the torn pieces of my ruined T-shirt. I could feel blood running down the front of my chest and I let out a moan. The dragon stopped growling. It loosened its claws from my shoulders and backed up just a little. I could feel his hot breath on my face. It looked down at the blood that was forming on the front of my shirt. Its eyes changed to a deep glowing green. It opened its mouth slightly and smoke, matching the color of its eyes, began to pour out of its mouth. The smoke smell changed from a charcoal smell to one like cinnamon and vanilla. Heat was starting to come from its snout. The dragon was about to breathe fire. The dragon opened its mouth wider. I could see two rows of sharp teeth and a forked purple tongue.

"So I guess you are going to eat my face before you burn me? I guess you win."

I closed my eyes and waited for the chomp. I could hear the dragon take in a deep breath and then I felt a rush of hot air. I knew the fire was coming next and I braced myself, saying a little prayer, hoping it would be quick and painless. The dragon's breath continued to get hotter. I felt my torn clothes ripple as the dragon's breath ran up and down my body. As hot as it seemed, I was not burning. I cautiously opened my eyes to the biggest shock of the day. My body was completely engulfed in flame, but I was not burning.

The dragon was blowing a steady stream of fire. This fire was not a normal looking flame. It started as the same green color as the smoke, but it began to change from yellow to blue, to purple, to deep red, to jet black, to silver, constantly changing colors. As the dragon continued to breathe out this amazing beautiful flame, it made a strange humming sound that vibrated throughout the tunnel. As crazy as it seemed, it was humming some sort of tune.

My whole body was covered in this strange flame. I don't know if it was because I was in shock, or it was part of the magic of this flame, but I was unable to move. I just sat there as this fire burned up and down my entire body. I started feeling great, better, more relaxed, simply fantastic. I felt energized and strong. Any pain I had left in my body seemed to be stripped away by this flame. The dragon's song continued to get louder and the flame continued to change colors until all I could see was the flame. Its color pattern got faster and faster and then; it stopped. My eyes had spots in front of them, like I had been staring at a bright light, and it took a while before I could see again. As my vision came into focus, I could see the dragon sitting on its hind legs staring at me. Its eyes were now wide and blue. The only sound now was the sound of a car occasionally going over the street above us.

I sat up and moved to put my back against the wall. My butt scraped the floor and I realized to my embarrassment that I was naked. The fire that seemed to heal me burned away the remainder of my torn up clothes. Being naked in a tunnel, under a street, with a dragon staring at you, is quite a unique experience. I had the most embarrassing image of the fairy finding me here like this. I absentmindedly raised my hand to my head and got a second shock. I was now bald, no hair at all on my head. I felt down my face and discovered that I had no eyebrows either. Feeling around I quickly discovered that along with my clothes all the hair on my body had been burned away. I was truly and completely naked.

Despite the fact that I was naked and bald, I had to admit to myself that I felt pretty good. No aches or pains. If I had actually broken any bones, the way I thought I had, they seemed to be fine now. I felt like I could take on the world. Maybe I could even escape from this dragon and get home. I stood up and faced this beast, determined to get the upper hand. It looked at me unmoving, the eyes back to changing colors.

"Ok, look. You need to let me go now. I'm not afraid of you."

The dragon looked at me, its eyes returning to the glowing green color. Before I could make another move, its tail whipped around and slapped me on the side of the head. I fell over from the impact. I sprawled there naked, my head on the ground and my butt in the air.

"Huh" rumbled the dragon deep from within its throat.

"You're laughing at me," I said.

I felt my face grow warm at the embarrassing idea that, not only had I been slapped down by a dragon, I was now mooning a dragon. Slowly I got to my feet. I could feel a breeze coming from the end of the tunnel and fought to keep from shivering.

"Ok, you scaly lizard. I'm gonna tell you one time and one time only. Never smack me with your tail again."

I surprised myself with these words. I was angry, but to tell a dragon, who could breathe fire and easily tear me apart, what to do and then call it a stupid lizard was entering a realm of idiotic bravery that could easily get me killed.

The beast stopped laughing, it's now green eyes narrowed into slits. The tail came whipping around. This time I was ready. Bracing myself, I reached up my hand and caught the end of the tail before it connected. The dragon's eyes widened. I had just caught the dragon by the tail. Not knowing what else to do, I did the first stupid thing that came to mind. I bit it. I opened my mouth and just chomped down as hard as I could. The dragon tilted its head back and let out a terrible sounding howl. I giggled maniacally. Instead of a dragon biting me, I was biting a dragon. How ironic. It whipped its tail out of my mouth and again disappeared from view. I made a mad bolt for the end of the tunnel again.

"It's going to kill me. It's going to kill me. It's going to kill me," I repeated over and over again.

The beast reappeared right on top of me twisting me around. It was mad. The smoke pouring out of its mouth was red and I knew this time it was not going to be a healing flame. I wasn't going down without a fight. I punched and kicked and scratched blindly, trying to get it off of me. A finger ended up in one of its nostrils. The dragon put a claw in my mouth, pulling my lip to the side. As we scuffled, there was a strange chattering sound coming from the end of the tunnel. We froze in our position, and looked toward the tunnel entrance. I was drooling from the dragon's claw in my mouth. The dragon made a strange whistling sound around my finger that was thrust up its nose.

At the end of the tunnel, standing on its hind legs, was a big red squirrel. One of its tiny paws was clutching its chest. The other was pointing at the two of us. The chattering sound we heard was unmistakable laughter. A squirrel was laughing at us.

 We scrambled to get off of each other. How embarrassing! The dragon hung its head and sheepishly looked anywhere but in the direction of the laughing squirrel. The little fur ball continued to laugh and point, falling over backwards with uncontrollable chattering hiccups of mirth. Finally, it got control of itself. It sat up and rubbed its beady little eyes. It looked at us again and, with a little squeal of delight, fell over laughing again.

 "Shut up you stupid squirrel."

 I looked around the floor of the tunnel hoping to find a rock to throw at the little beast. The dragon took care of it by letting out a small burst of purple flame, catching the end of the squirrel's tail on fire. With a squeak, the squirrel jumped and started running around in a circle. With the end of its tail singed and holding it carefully, the squirrel looked at the both of us and jabbered angrily.

 "BAH!" I yelled.

 Shrieking and jumping into the air, it took off running. You could still hear it jabbering at us as it ran out of sight.

"Ha!" I laughed.

The dragon grunted, pleased with it as well. We looked at each other, cautiously. Neither one of us wanted to attack again as we sat there in the tunnel.

The dragon stretched its neck out, and took the now slime-covered bag of burgers in its mouth. It immediately spit it out it with a look of disgust on its face and, looking down at the now ruined bag of burgers, it growled at me.

"What? You think that's my fault?" I asked.

I sat there looking at this dragon, not knowing whether to be grateful for it not eating me, or angry for it getting me in this mess.

"This morning you were just a cool looking rock. Then you had to grow on my leg and turn my life upside down. So I guess the rock was an egg with you inside. You used me to hatch didn't you? You kind of fed on me and hatched."

The dragon just sat there staring at me as I talked, its eyes continuing to change colors.

"Well let's get one thing straight dragon. I'm not your mommy. "

Again it just sat there staring. A little puff of red smoke came out of its snout.

"I never heard of a dragon hatching like that before. I've read a lot of stories about dragons and I have never heard anything like that."

The dragon looked down at the now discarded bag of burgers. It began to poke at the bag as if it was hoping one burger made it out of the mess.

"Are you with that fairy? Is she part of this? Did she a cause you to hatch?"

No response.

"Ok then. Thanks for nothing," I said, annoyed with the dragon.

Picking up the ruined bag of burgers, the dragon threw them at me, hitting me in the chest. I got the message. I felt a little embarrassed.

"Uh, thanks for the food," I said, "It really helped me."

The dragon nodded its head.

"Can you talk?" I asked.

The dragon tilted its head to the side and huffed. A thrill of excitement went through me as I realized I was actually communicating with a dragon. I smiled and to my surprise the dragon smiled back. Its wide toothy grin was almost comical, if not for the rows and rows of sharp looking teeth. It opened its mouth and let out a little puff of green smoke. I had no doubt in my mind that it could easily bite through a car tire with those teeth and jaws. I counted myself lucky that, in our little scuffles, it had not torn me apart.

I began to look at my new companion. Its whole body radiated power and strength, from its short front paws, to the powerful back legs. Each claw was equipped with curved talons. A perfect fighting force of nature. I felt a little stupid at the thought of how I yelled at it earlier and he didn't tear me apart. But I still didn't know why. The only thing that I could think of, is that in some way, this magnificent creature felt some kind of gratitude. After all, it did attach itself to my leg and, in some way I didn't understand, used me to hatch.

The dragon was unfolding its wings as if trying to get used to them. The tunnel was too small to let them out completely. I reminded myself that it wasn't more than a few hours old. I wanted to think of it as friendly. At least I wanted to believe it didn't want to kill me. But with a shiver down my body, I remembered that I was naked, bald, and stuck in a tunnel under a busy street, not to mention the incredible pain I experienced when the dragon hatched. I shuddered again and thanked God that I must have been knocked out as the dragon hatched out of my leg. The nightmare must have been a reaction to the dragon tearing itself from my leg.

I put all these thoughts aside and decided I needed to get out of here. Not sure if the dragon would let me leave, I decided that by just talking to it I might get it to let me go.

"Sorry about the burgers," I said.

The dragon looked at me. Its head nodded slightly. Having nothing to lose, I asked the most important question I could think of.

"Um, do you know what is going on?"

The dragon's head tilted slightly to the side. Its shoulders moved up and down. It had just shrugged its shoulders. It was amazing. This creature could understand everything I was saying to it. I gave it a little thought and then went for broke.

"Were you trying to kill me? " It stared at me, its eyes changing color again. It was almost like watching two big Christmas lights changing colors at a very fast pace. After a few moments its eyes went back to green and its head shook a slow 'No'. It seemed as if it was not sure of what it was supposed to do.

"You're just as confused by all of this as I am?"

Its head looked down at the ground.

"You both seem to be a little confused," said an amused voice. "I think I can help."

The dragon and I jumped. We quickly turned to the mouth of the tunnel, and from the remaining light of the day, I could make out the bobcat from earlier. Another one had joined him. They were both laying on a duffle bag. The voice had come from one of them.

Chapter 7

"Did you just talk?" I asked.

The bobcat opened its mouth again and the amused voice came out.

"If you mean the bobcat, then the answer is no," said the voice, "I am talking through the bobcat. It's kind of like a speaker right now. My name is Johnathen. I am a wizard and I have been looking for the dragon all day. Not until my bobcat friend here reported to me about you, did I realize I was searching for you as well, my friend."

The bobcat closed its mouth as the voice of Johnathen the wizard stopped talking. It was quiet now in the tunnel. The only sound I could hear was the sound of the dragon's breath. I took a guess that Johnathen was waiting for me to say something.

"Why were you looking for the dragon?" I asked. The dragon looked at me, its eyes changing to blue for a second. I guessed it was grateful to me for asking the question.

"Well, my friend, that is actually a long and complicated story. I can sense when a dragon is about to hatch. I try to locate them and keep them from harm. They are not seen much in this part of the world. Unfortunately, I can only detect them when they are emerging from the host. It is amazing that you survived the experience. It must have been very painful. I have never heard of a host surviving before,"

"What do you mean? I was supposed to die?" I asked.

The bobcat laughed. "I can see you are having a hard time with all of this. It would be easier to explain if I could see you in person. I will tell you that you have been changed. You are now part of the magic world. There are however, those in the magic world when they discover you are still alive will not be happy."

"Wait, what? What are you talking about? Changed? In what way? Who won't be happy?"

"You survived a dragon hatching. You have changed. Haven't you noticed that you are able to see my bobcat messengers? You are in a dark tunnel and the sun has gone down. "

He was right. I was able to see in the dark. I looked over at the dragon. Not only could I see it, but I could see the smoke coming out of its nose. It was green. I could even read the graffiti on the walls of the tunnel.

"Amazing," I mumbled to myself. This was like my comic books and fantasy novels. I had gained some kind of power. My heart was pounding. I was geeking out.

"Take my advice and come see me," said the bobcat, "Both you and the dragon will need my help."

I looked over at the dragon. It looked at me for a moment and slightly nodded its head. I breathed a sigh of relief. I wouldn't have to go see this guy alone.

"Ok, we will come see you, but before I do, I have to go home and get some clothes. I have to explain to my brother where I have been all day."

"I'm sorry friend," said Johnathen, "you can't go home. You won't be welcome there now. Understand that your life is completely changed and it can be very dangerous for your loved ones to even be around you."

"Why?" I asked.

The excitement at my new night vision faded away as the wizard's words sunk in.

"What is going on? I never asked for this. First the fairy . . ."

"You saw a fairy?" the wizard interrupted. "When did you see a fey?"

"Yes, it started with a fairy, that led to me being here naked and bald, talking to a bobcat, with a dragon that won't let me leaves this tunnel!"

By the time I got to the end of my sentence I was yelling. I was tired, still hungry, and trying to maintain a grasp on reality.

"Are you sure it was a fairy?" asked the wizard.

"She had wings and she was flying. Yes I am pretty sure she was a fairy!" I yelled.

The bobcat sat there for a second. "You should have told me this before. You need to see me right away. You both are in great danger. I will give you as much protection as I can. Take the dragon and fly to where I am. "

"Where are you?"

The bobcats stood up. "At Reid Park. Go to the pond and I will meet you there. Keep your head down and talk to no one. I don't think the fey realizes you are still alive."

The first bobcat nudged the bag it was carrying, toward me. "There is a gift for you in the duffle bag, now hurry."

The bobcats turned and ran off into the night, leaving me and the dragon staring after them as they ran off. I approached the bag hoping it would have some clothes in it. Opening the duffle bag I discovered a collar made of leather with silver and gold studs. Obviously it was for the dragon. Cautiously, I showed it to the dragon. It took the collar and studied it for a second, then dropped it.

"You don't want it? I think you should take it."

The dragon just stared at me with green eyes.

"You might offend him."

Again the dragon stared. I wondered if it understood anything I was saying. I had no idea how I could convince the dragon to do what I thought it should do. I shrugged my shoulders and looked in the duffle bag again. There was a note, which read:

"It is an old tradition for a wizard to give a gift of great value when introducing himself to someone for the first time. I hope this seven million dollars will help you adjust to your new life. Sincerely Johnathen"

Looking in the bag I could see it stuffed with money.

Chapter 8

So, let's go down the list.

One: a fairy from my past may be trying to kill me. Two: A dragon hatched while attached to my leg. Three: A wizard has just given me a bag full of cash. Yup, this was officially the strangest day of my life.

I stood there in stunned silence. One shocking blow after another, in such a short time frame, took its toll on me. Everything from the fairy, to the dragon, to a bag of money from a wizard seemed too much for one day.

I looked around the tunnel. There was a cold breeze and my body shivered a little. I felt very tired and a little freaked out. The last words of this wizard were a warning. There must still be a fairy out there waiting for me to show myself, and, as soon as I did, I would be dead. I knelt down and looked out of the tunnel. I heard a dog bark. I jumped at the sound and the dragon let out a grunt. It moved restlessly, head swaying side to side as it made its way to the exit. It had fought me to keep me there, but after hearing what Johnathen had to say, seemed eager to leave. It was if it had been waiting for some kind of information to decide what to do.

It walked out of the tunnel and turned to look at me. I stepped toward the exit feeling very vulnerable. I felt exposed. I didn't know what would be worse, the fairy finding me and killing me, or the fairy finding me and seeing me naked. My face flushed at the idea and I knew I wasn't going anywhere without clothes. The dragon was out of the tunnel, stretching its wings, getting ready to fly. It seemed much bigger with its wings spread out.

"Hey! Wait a minute! I can't go anywhere like this."

The dragon looked at me with its green eyes glowing. As silly as it seemed, I knew the dragon could understand me. The way it listened to the wizard, the way it reacted to my anger, how it had unwrapped those burgers *("How did it get those burgers?")* I knew it could understand what I was saying.

"Come on, you need to get me something to wear. You burned my clothes off so you have to find me new ones. Do that invisible thing you did and swipe some. Oh! "

I had a moment of inspiration. I reached into the duffle bag and pulled out a handful of money. I was hit with amazement at the idea of how much I had now. Seven million dollars! It felt strange having all this money given to me. I made a promise to myself to return it to Johnathen as soon as I could. I felt weird using any of it, but this was an emergency.

"Leave this money behind when you grab some clothes, ok?"

The dragon continued to stare at me, unmoving. I was wondering what it was waiting for. Then it hit me. I didn't want to believe that was what it was waiting for, but I didn't know what else it could be.

I gritted my teeth and said "Please."

The dragon stepped over to me and took the money. It should have struck me as odd that it would understand what money was. He looked at me and disappeared. No, it wasn't that it disappeared, it was that its scales changed color. They became the same color of the dark night skyline. It didn't have the ability to disappear, it had the ability to camouflage itself. Like a chameleon.

With a rush of air and a moment of silver flashing of its wings, it flew off into the night.

As soon as the dragon left I regretted it. I stood at the mouth of the tunnel and held the duffel bag to my body. I was not feeling particularly brave and I felt very alone. Every sound was intensified and I jumped every time a car drove past me on the street above. As I was just about ready to abandon the whole idea of waiting for clothes, I prepared myself to run out to the street and flag down the first car I saw. That is when the dragon returned, carrying a garbage sack in its claws. It had another bag of burgers in its mouth. After dropping the garbage bag in front of me, it took a burger out of the fast food bag and tossed it to me with its mouth. I caught it in midair, the whole time amazed at what this dragon could do. I ripped the paper off of the burger and practically crammed the whole thing into my mouth. It was a little surprising to me that I was so hungry again.

"Thanks," I said to the dragon through a mouthful of burger.

I reached into the garbage bag to see what was in there. I pulled out a pair of purple sweatpants, two mismatched flip-flops (one yellow, one blue), a blue t-shirt with "It's all good" written across the chest, and a red stocking cap. I started to put the clothes on. It wasn't until I put the stocking cap on that I remembered that I was now bald. My hand went up to my face feeling the lack of eyebrows. I moaned a little bit and wondered if my hair and eyebrows would ever grow back. I looked down at the clothes the dragon had picked out for me. The sweatpants were twice my size. The shirt was too small, stretching tightly across my chest. And the red stocking cap had a fuzzy ball on the top. The dragon seemed to be laughing at me. It had picked this ensemble on purpose. I knew I had to look ridiculous. The jerk had played a joke on me.

"This is what you got for me?"

The dragon chuckled. Blue and green smoke came out of his snout. I was not going to let this beast get the best of me.

"I guess it's too much for me to think you would have any sense of style. You probably can't even see colors."

The dragon stopped laughing. Its eyes narrowed and the smoke started to look a little red.

"And this stupid hat? Only an idiot would wear this."

I took off the hat and threw it at the dragon. It landed right on its snout. With eyes changing color to purple and crossing to look at the red fuzzy balled cap, the creature looked so comically surprised that I started laughing.

"Yeah," I laughed, "I think you should wear it dragon. It looks much better on you."

It walked over to me slowly, staring me in the eyes. The red cap still dangled on the end of its snout. I was standing behind the duffle bag, the dragon now on the other side, its eyes turned green. Reaching up, the creature pulled the stocking cap off of its nose and handed it to me across the duffle bag. I had stopped laughing not knowing what to expect next. A smile played across its face. You could see all the teeth in that smile. My blood ran cold. I had reached the end of my rope with this beast. I didn't dare move out of fear of what it would do to me next. Its mouth opened a little bit and a short jet of green flame shot out, straight at the money in the duffle bag. It caught fire and before I realized what I was doing, I was beating it out with my hands. I got the small fire under control quickly. By the time the flames were out, the dragon had walked down the wash a little way, and before I could stop it, the dragon launched into the air, not even bothering to camouflage, and flew off into the night.

I could have kicked myself. I was alone again and I got the idea that the dragon was not coming back. I stood there searching the night sky for any sign of the dragon. It was no use. I was on my own.

Chapter 9

I had decided to leave the wash. I needed to get moving. I knew that Johnathen wanted me to stick with the dragon but I blew that.

"What is wrong with me?" I mumbled as I made my way to the side walk. *"I shouldn't have lost my temper. Not like me. I needed that dragon."* I thought as I walked. *"That dragon could have killed me at least four times over and I still pushed it."*

As I started walking down the sidewalk, I noticed I was getting some strange looks from people. Who could blame them? I looked like a clown in these clothes. Dumb dragon. I stopped walking and stood there, just out of sight of the grocery store where earlier I had made such a mess of things.

"What am I going to do?" I mumbled to myself. "I have to get past the store. If I'm recognized as the guy who caused the damage I'm in deep trouble."

I quickly looked around when I realized I was talking out loud to myself, embarrassed by my mumbling, even though no one was there to hear me. I took a deep breath and decided to move forward. I hoped I looked different enough that no one would recognize me. It was a long shot but it was all I had.

Walking as normally as possible, I walked past the front of the store. *"Maybe they won't recognize me."* I thought. *"I'm bald now and my goatee and eyebrows are gone."*

Looking up at the darkening sky, I hoped I would catch a glimpse of the dragon's silver scales in the night sky.

Getting near the store front, I saw my brother's car. He was probably looking for me. My cell phone was destroyed so I never got to call him. Sometimes, when he would get off work, he would look for me at the store coffee shop and give me a ride home. I started to head toward my brother's car and then stopped. I stood there trying to figure out what to do. Johnathen's words of not being able to go home came back to me. There might be a chance that my brother could be in danger if I tried to get in contact with him. I looked up at the night sky wishing the dragon would return. It could be helpful to have a dragon on my side. Like it or not, I knew it was better to have the dragon with me.

I didn't know what to do. I wanted to let my brother know I was ok. But I didn't want to put him in danger. I wandered into the parking lot trying to stay out of the overhead lights. I saw a silver flash up on the roof. It could be the dragon. I moved back toward the front of the store, waving my arm and staring up at the roof, when my brother walked out of the store. He was pushing a cart right toward me. He didn't seemed concerned or in a hurry. I guessed he hadn't heard about the earlier excitement and probably thought I was home. I had to talk to him and warn him. I didn't know what trouble it might cause, but he is my brother. I couldn't just disappear without telling him something. I decided to get a ride home from him. I could say goodbye and get some different clothes before meeting the wizard.

He wheeled the cart over to his car, totally distracted by the music he was listening to. He had the music turned up so loud on his iPod I could hear it myself. He didn't notice me until I walked up next to him.

"Hey Paul," I said trying to sound as normal as possible, "I need a ride home. It's been a strange day."

Paul's eyes drifted up to the red stocking cap on my head with an odd look on his face. I had to look crazy. I decided that the direct approach would be the best. I had to tell him as much as I could. Make him understand somehow. If I could show my brother the dragon, he would have to believe me. Looked like I was out of luck. I glanced up, trying to spot the dragon when my brother held his hand out toward me. He had a dollar in it.

"Do I know you friend?" he said. "Can I help you?"

Did I really look so different? He seemed not to know who I was. I stepped more into the light, being careful that the store manager didn't spot me and call the police.

"Paul, it's me!" I said, "It's Jack."

Now that I was standing in the light he had to recognize me.

"I'm sorry; I don't think I know you," Paul said taking a small step backwards.

"Very funny Paul. It's me, Jack, your brother," I said trying not to panic.

This was really scaring me. After everything that had happened to me today, the last thing I needed was my own brother not recognizing me.

"Look," He said, "You obviously know who I am but I don't know you. I don't have a brother. If you are trying some kind of scam, I really don't appreciate it. "

I felt like I'd been slapped. I backed away from the car as my brother got in. I kept on backing away and bumped into a parked car behind me. The car's alarm started beeping as I watched my brother drive away. He really didn't recognize me. He had no idea that I was his brother. Trying to take all of this in, I didn't notice the store manager coming up behind me until I heard his voice.

"Is everything ok?" he asked me.

That seemed to be the question of the evening. I turned around to face him and saw that he was the man I had knocked down earlier that day. He seemed unhurt, which surprised me. I had knocked him down hard. He also acted like he didn't know me.

The car alarm had stopped blaring as the manager asked me again, "Is everything ok? You seemed confused. "

I was sure this guy would recognize me. I had torn through a table, knocked him down making a public nuisance, and I was sure I remembered him shouting out to call 911 when I ran out of the store. This thought gave me some hope. I could find a kind of acceptance at my brother not knowing who I was if I looked completely different. But if that was it, then why did he say that he didn't have a brother at all? I cursed the dragon I was so willing to apologize to just moments before. This was its fault. I needed to get to a mirror. I needed to see what I really looked like. I found myself wanting the dragon back. No such luck, I was alone.

"Do you know me?" I asked.

The manager smiled and stuck out his hand to shake mine. I shook his hand wanting him to recognize me.

"My name is Jack. I was here earlier today."

He smiled and said, "That's nice Jack. I'm afraid I am going to have to ask you to not ask people for money in the parking lot. We have a strict policy against panhandling on our property. I could give you information for a shelter if you need a place to stay for the night."

He thought I was a homeless person. And if my brother didn't recognize me I guess I was.

"I'm not homeless and I didn't ask anyone for money." I reached into the duffle bag and pulled out some money.

"I am going to shop now," I said, "Did you get that mess cleaned up from earlier today?"

He gave me a blank look. He had no idea what I was talking about.

"Sorry dude," I said, "Look I just need to pick up a few things in the store. I won't be any trouble."

I stuck the money back into the duffle bag, slung it over my shoulder, and with one quick look around in the sky walked quickly into the store as the manager stared at me. I got the shock of my life. Everything was normal. The table I had ripped off of its base was fixed. What was going on? My hand shot up to the top of my head rubbing the hat back and forth. I could hear the store music playing gently in the background. I swayed back and forth trying to piece it all together.

"What if I don't look the same? What if the dragon hatching on my leg and his dragon fire that he used to clean me and heal me changed how I looked?"

I needed a mirror so I could get a good look at myself. Making my way to the back of the store to the restroom I kept my head down. I knew I needed to buy something in the store before I left. I knew that the manager had to still be watching me. But I had to see if there was any change to me other than the fact I had no hair. I decided to go to the bathroom to see what I looked like. I was having a hard time finding the courage to walk in the bathroom.

"What if I was some hideously deformed person now. What if all that had happened to me today had changed me into some kind of monster?"

I resolved to find out the truth, no matter how gruesome. I pushed open the bathroom door. My heart was pounding and at first I kept my head down not wanting to look in the mirror. Then I looked up. Yes, I was bald with no eyebrows. I looked tired. But it was the same face as always staring back at me. My face was filthy with black dust and soot. I took off the stocking cap and rubbed my smooth hairless head. I mourned my hair. But it was the same brown eyes that I had always had looking back at me in the mirror. I washed my face in the sink and took another look at myself. I could see my belly button. Stupid shirt was too short.

"Why didn't Paul recognize me?" I asked my reflection.

My brother had no idea who I was. I had to go home. I had to make him recognize me in some way. If I didn't, I would be alone. The wizard can wait. My brother was more important. After splashing more water on my face I walked out of the restroom. The store manager was still keeping an eye on me so I decided to do a little shopping. After grabbing some 'Top Ramen', an energy drink and some turkey jerky, I headed for the cashier. As she rang up the items, she gave me an awkward look.

"Not nice to stare," I said to her through gritted teeth.

She stammered an apology. I gave her some money and left the store. I felt a little guilty at my reaction to the cashier, then a thought hit me. I turned around and walked back into the store, straight to the table I destroyed earlier. It was fine. It was not a new table but the same one. There was the letter "H" that some kid had put there in an attempt to write his name. I had thrown down that table so hard that it had broken into a million pieces. Weird. I turned and walked out the front doors again.

I paused outside of the store, not sure what to do next or where to go. I had the invitation from the wizard and I knew I had to eventually go see him. His sense of urgency all but forgotten, I wasn't sure I was ready to do that yet. Looking around in the sky for the missing dragon once again, I finally spotted the glowing silver scales in the sky. It was back. It hovered over the parking lot. It must have been camouflaged in some way. All I could see was the silver from its scales. It floated down, resting about four feet off the ground.

Chapter 10

I headed toward the dragon, but the light didn't seem right. It was blue. As I got closer, the blue light washed over me. It wasn't the dragon. The light was about the size of a baseball and pulsed brighter as I walked closer. I stopped dead in my tracks. Could this be from the fairy? I took another step toward the ball and it grew a little bigger. I stopped again, trying to figure out what I was looking at. It began to pulse and seemed to be getting bigger. I took a step back and the ball seemed to move toward me. I tried to walk around it and it followed me. It was not going to let me pass.

"Maybe I'll go back to the store."

I turned around and saw just how many people were there. A growing group of shoppers and the store manager were standing there staring at the blue orb. Some of them had camera phones and were taking videos of what was going on. It was probably already on "YouTube" and going viral. Every eye was fixed on the floating ball of light. I took a step toward the crowd and the blue orb shot through the air and stopped at eye level directly in front of me. The crowd gasped and someone actually screamed.

I didn't know what to do. This ball of light seemed to be interested in me. It hadn't tried to hurt me. But that didn't mean that it wouldn't. The wizard's words came back to me. *"Man I wish I hadn't made that dragon mad. We should have flown straight to the wizard."* I wondered if the dragon was strong enough to carry me and the duffle bag all the way to Reid Park. I guessed that I would never know now.

The blue ball stayed in front of me. I had no idea what it was. I moved to the left and there it was. I moved to the right and it was still there. I started to sink to my knees hoping I could crawl underneath it. It slowly sank down to the ground always staying in front of me. The fairy must have sent it to finish me off. Johnathen had left me the image that fey were not good.

"What if it was some sort of bomb? All these people could get hurt."

I looked back to the crowd and saw phones pointed in my direction. I needed to lead the orb out of the parking lot and away from people. If it was a bomb, it could hurt not just me, but all these people. All of a sudden the ball started to hum. At first it was a low thrumming that I could feel in my chest. It quickly got higher in pitch and started to intensify in brightness. I took a step back away from it. I looked back at the gathering of people.

"RUN!" I yelled.

The ball started to grow to about the size of a small car. I could hear more gasps from my audience. I couldn't tell if anyone had run. The humming stopped abruptly and before I could move, a big, hairy, green arm shot out of it and grabbed me by the throat. I grabbed at it trying to pull it off me as I gasped for air. It had a slimy feel to it and was very strong. I raised my hands, and with all the strength I could muster, sent my hands crashing down on this monstrous arm. My blocking, smashing hit was enough to break the hold the arm had on me. But before I could get away, another arm shot out of the ball and hit me in the face. I could feel the crunch as the pain shot through my broken nose. The wind was knocked out of me as the thing shot out of the orb, tackling me to the ground. It pounded on me, stomping me into the asphalt. I could hear a strange growling voice chanting over and over again.

"Smash! Smash! Smash! Smash!"

As I was being pummeled, I could hear the crowd screaming and the sound of running feet. Finally they started to take my advice. Squeaks and grunts were coming from the smelly green monster as it hit me. I continued to try and fight this strange, green, hairy, slimy thing. It was now on top of me, jumping up and down on my chest, laughing as it clobbered me. I was afraid I would lose consciousness and then I would be dead. A burning sensation started in my chest as blood poured out of my nose. A strange pressure was building up in my stomach. I waved my arms wildly trying to hit this thing and knock it off of me. I got lucky with a hit and with a squeal this thing jumped from my chest.

I scrambled to a sitting position getting my first good look at my attacker. It was green and hairy all over its body. Its short squatty body couldn't be more than a foot long, but its massively muscled arms were at least twice as long as its body. It stood on them like they were legs. The creature's hand dug into the asphalt of the parking lot, tearing it up. Its whole body had a slimy glow to it. This thing was lethal. His head was almost a perfect round ball with black beady eyes, a smashed nose and twisted mouth. I couldn't help but think of this thing as a demon from a nightmare come to life. There was a scurrying commotion behind him and I realized there was more than one of these things.

My attacker smiled at me, showing rows and rows of sharp, crooked teeth. He reached behind his back and pulled out a cigar. Lighting it with a match struck off of its forehead, it took in a deep drag of smoke, smiled another twisted hideous smile and spoke.

"Hey ya freak. We're here to destroy you. You should have died today. We're here to make sure you do," he said with a twisted grin.

He took another drag from his cigar then tossed the rest to the side. He charged me, knocking me to the ground again. The pressure in my stomach was growing as I lashed out, trying to knock this thing off of me. It laughed at my week attempt to hit it again. The pressure in my stomach popped and my body was filled with power. Reaching up I grabbed this creature by the throat. A squeak and wheeze came from his mouth. Its beady black eyes grew wide with surprise at my speed and strength. I stood up holding this thing by the throat.

"I'm not going to die at the hands of a giant booger like you," I yelled as I shook it.

The creature hit me with a right hook causing me to let it go. He jumped up to its hands and looked at me, his face twisting in rage.

"No one calls me Booger!" it screamed, "You stupid flap! I'm gonna kill you!"

Throughout the parking lot you could hear the other green things running around. They all started chanting "Booger! Booger! Booger!" Over and over again. My attacker looked around the parking lot and shouted for them to shut up. He turned back to me, screaming in rage and charged again. This time I was ready for him. With a speed that surprised me, I grabbed Booger's arm. I swung him around my head as he squealed like a pig. Another one came after me. It charged and I swung Booger like a club, knocking the new one over a car. It landed crashing through the windshield of a nice looking convertible. The alarm started blaring around the parking lot.

To my amazement I could still see a crowd of people gathered around with camera phones clicking. They were watching this battle like it was a movie or something. Only a few had run away. The others had either stood there in shock and disbelief, or run around trying to get a better angle with their camera phones. I wanted to yell at them to run, but another attacker charged from behind and almost grabbed me. I swung Booger around just in time, smacking it upside of the head and sending it into the back of a truck. Booger hung limply in my hand.

"Stop it freak," he said, "I'm gonna to be sick."

A retching sound came from his throat. This made me want to puke too. I threw him as far as I could. He skidded and smashed into a light pole about ten feet away from me. Standing up slowly, he shook his head. He looked at me and to my surprise looked unharmed. It was as if I hadn't touched him at all. He reached behind his back again pulling out another cigar. Chomping down on this one he made a strange grunting sound. All of the other creatures began to come out of their hiding places. There were dozens of them. Behind them the crowd finally started to back up. Booger looked over his shoulder at the store and the crowd of people. With a wicked smile on his face he said to his companions.

"Half of you stay with me, the rest start raiding the store."

They all smiled crooked twisted smiles. Now the crowd was really in danger. All of them moved as one, taking off toward the store and the rapidly retreating crowd. Booger forgot to tell which half was supposed to stay with him. He turned and yelled at them.

"Not all of you, you stupid flaps! Come back!"

That was the distraction I needed. I knew I had to get to those people. Someone was going to get hurt. Booger turned around just in time to get my foot planted right in his ugly face. He grunted and fell to the ground and I ran past him. I headed for the hooting, squealing mass of the snot brigade that was heading for the front of the store and the people who were scrambling to get out of there. I was half way there when Booger recovered from my kick and grabbed me by the foot, tripping me. I landed hard on my newly broken nose and pain exploded in a fresh wave.

Booger started climbing up my back as I kicked and tried to fight him off. That strange pulling sensation started in my stomach again, as I reached out toward the running creatures. I realized that, even if I could get Booger off my back, I wouldn't reach the others in time.

I yelled out at the top of my lungs, "Run you idiots, run!"

Booger was now whispering in my ear "I'm gonna spit right in your face freak," he said.

I had begun to lose hope that I would get out of this. That was when the dragon returned.

Chapter 11

It came crashing out of the sky with a roar. No longer camouflaged, it wanted these creatures to see it. Booger stopped clawing his way to my face and sat on my back in stunned silence. I took this opportunity to roll over, knocking him off, but he jumped on top of me again. The other creatures ran squealing and screaming as the dragon dived after them. It grabbed three of them with its back claws, as it swooped down and knocked two more tumbling with its tail. Booger had begun beating on me again. I lay there trying to figure out how to get this thing off of me. I saw a strange red glowing thing next to my head. I realized it was one of Booger's cigars. I grabbed it and twisted around to face him as I plunged the lit cigar into the side of his face. A bloodcurdling howl came from Booger's mouth. He fell off of me, writhing in pain, and holding the quarter shaped burn he now had on his face. I took off towards the front of the store, dodging people right and left. There was blind panic. Some of the creatures must have made it into the store. One was running on its stubby little feet, holding a case of beer over its head. Another had a bottle of soda in its mouth. It had bitten through the bottle and was sucking it dry. Then it began to eat the plastic bottle.

A lot more of these green nightmares had come through the ball portal. Running back and forth, going in and out of the store, running with everything from 'Top Ramen' to toilet paper. It was total chaos. It amazed me that no one had been hurt. There was still one dummy standing by the front of the store, filming on his camera phone. A green guy stopped in front of him and spat at him. The guy jumped back just in time. The spit hit the sidewalk and started sizzling. At the sight of this, the guy took off. Seeing the smoke coming from the sidewalk, I realized why Booger wanted to spit in my face. These creatures' spit must have some kind acid in it.

I was being kept away from the front of the store as green guy after green guy jumped on me and tried to beat me down. I had no idea where the strength was coming from, but I continued to fight them off. After knocking one over a car trying to leave the parking lot, I had a moment to rest. I jumped into the back of a truck and watched the whole scene.

The dragon was fantastic. Swooping down it bowled them over. It seemed to be everywhere at once. Any time one of the nightmares got close to a panicky person trying to get away, the dragon was there, protecting them, sending the little beasts one way or another. But more and more kept appearing and it was becoming clear that we were fighting a losing battle. I heard a baby cry and a scream and I saw a woman with a stroller backed up against the side of the building. Two creatures had them trapped. I jumped up to help them when Booger came out of nowhere, grabbed my head, and pulled me back down into the truck. We rolled around with neither of us getting the upper hand. I heard the baby crying as the mother screamed for help. The strange pulling sensation from my stomach had returned. I kicked at Booger and must have hit a tender spot. He rolled off of me groaning in pain. I stood up in the back of the truck ready to help as the two beasts moved closer to the young mother and baby.

Booger jumped on my back tearing his claws into my flesh. As Booger continued to scratch at my back, I saw the dragon flying straight toward me. It didn't see the cornered mother. The pain was intense and the pressure grew inside of me. It was some sort of strange buzzing energy. My breath came out in short gasps. As the buzzing grew inside of me, I reached behind me and pulled Booger off my back and flipped him over my head, smashing him into the ground. I looked at the dragon and pointed toward the mother and baby.

"FETCH!" I yelled at the top of my lungs.

The dragon turned its head and saw the problem. With a roar, it dove down toward the creatures. Picking them both up by its tail, the dragon flung them into the air. They landed at least twenty feet away. The dragon was between the mother and baby, and the two green things. The creatures screeched and made a strange gargling sound in their throats. More and more green beasts ran to join the two who were now beginning to charge the dragon. It looked like there were at least twenty running at it. I jumped out of the truck and started running through the parking lot to help. I didn't know how I could help, but I had to try. But, before I could take two steps, a hand shot out and grabbed my ankle sending me sprawling on the pavement. It was my old friend Booger.

A fresh pain hit my chest as I slid across the asphalt. I could hear Booger running at me from behind as I skidded down the parking lot. My chest was now a raw mess and the wind had been knocked out of me. I lay there waiting for the next attack from Booger, when the dragon roared. I looked up to see the most amazing thing.

The dragon had raised its head back as a jet of red flame left its mouth. It sprayed the flame at the charging green things like a stream of water shooting out of a fireman's hose. The entire hoard of beasts that had charged the dragon caught fire. They squealed and screamed running into each other. At first they ran around trying to beat the flames out, running in all different directions. But then something pulsed from the portal and, as one, they ran for it, jumping into it and disappearing. There was a strange high pitched humming sound as they disappeared. When all of the ones the dragon had caught on fire had gone in, the humming stopped. I lay there in stunned silence. Spots were in front of my eyes from the fire the dragon had created. To my right I heard a voice.

"Whoa," said Booger.

He was standing next to me amazed too. I looked over at him, he looked up at me, and with a growl, he jumped on top of me, his feet twisted into freakish claws. I kicked at Booger knocking him off of me. I managed to get a good punch at his face and my hand went into his mouth. I felt a few sharp teeth break and when I pulled my fist back. I could see smoke coming off of my hand. The skin on my knuckles started to burn as I watched the flesh of my hand bubble and melt away. Booger knocked me down and barked a command at the remaining beasts left in the parking lot. Through the haze of pain I could see them all charging in my direction. I kicked at Booger, hitting him in the face where the cigar burn was. He let go of me and leaped back, holding his face and glaring at me.

I scrambled to my feet and faced my attackers. Behind them, flying low, was the dragon coming at them, hopefully coming to my rescue. Its flight looked a little wobbly. That burst of fire must have taken a lot out of it. It reared its head back ready to let out another fire burst. The red flame shot out of the dragon's mouth. It shot over the heads of the creatures, heading straight for my face. I threw up my hands to cover my face. I knew this wasn't the healing fire of before. This was an angry fire of battle. This was going to hurt.

I had closed my eyes waiting for the worst. I could hear the roar of the fire as it hit me. But there was no feeling of burning. Maybe he missed me. Opening my eyes, I was taken by surprise by what I saw. The fire had engulfed my hands. I felt the heat from the fire, but I could see that my hands were unburned. My hands were protected from the fire. The flame was red and had a weight to it. I was dumbfounded by the flame burning on my hands without damaging them. Just like the fire in the tunnel, this had healing qualities as well. I could see my hands healing from the damage of Booger's acid spit. It was like watching a burning candle in reverse. Within seconds my hand was healed, the damage from Booger's spit was gone. I opened and shut my hands, totally marveling at this incredible miracle. I looked up to see the dragon hovering in the air with an astonished look on its face. I looked at the remaining creatures. They were all staring at me with looks of shock and disbelief on their faces.

The flames began to burn brighter. I yelled and started to wave my hands around wildly, frantically trying to put the fire out. Small balls of flame began to fly off of my hands in all directions hitting the now panicky little green monsters. They scattered and ran away. They all ran toward the blue orb as it pulsed.

I finally got control of myself and stopped shaking my hands. The dragon had flown toward the creatures roaring in rage. It was trying to herd them all toward the blue light. There was a scattered fire throughout the parking lot. I watched the dragon swooping down at the snot brigade as they ran for the ball of light. It was busy keeping all of the things running. So busy that it didn't see the one creature with the wicked looking spear. It was Booger. I'm not sure where he had gotten the weapon. He had a twisted smile on his face as he pulled his powerful arm back aiming the spear at the dragon. I yelled out trying to warn it, but there was no way I could be heard over the screams and roars. The spear was going to hit the dragon and there was no way to stop it.

In a moment of mad inspiration, I raised my still burning hands over my head and flung them like I was throwing a heavy object. The fire shot away from my hands like a rock from a sling shot. It flew like a ball through the air and hit the spear, knocking it away from the dragon. It landed through the roof of a car and hit the horn. I didn't have a chance to be surprised at what I had just done. The dragon had looked back at me with a confused look on its face.

Not missing a beat, Booger began to bark a ruff growling shout. He was standing next to the blue ball of light. How did he get there so fast? All of the remaining creatures ran toward him, then they turned in a line to face me. The dragon had landed by my side. I was surprised that it would do this. I guess we had a common enemy. Whatever it felt about me, it wanted to stop these monsters from causing more destruction.

With a whooping sound, they charged us. The dragon crouched, ready to attack. The fire had finally burned itself out on my hands, so I had no idea how to fight off so many of them. I didn't want another fire burst from the dragon. Too many people still running through the parking lot could get hurt. Another burst of flame and our luck of no one seriously getting hurt would end. They were getting closer. I was at a loss as to what to do. I was too tired to attack like I did before, and I was sure I had lost the element of surprise, so I doubted that I would be able to do what I did before. They all stopped short of us, sneering and growling, waiting for us to make the first move. I could smell them. They really smelled bad.

The buzzing feeling I had this whole time intensified. It seemed to be feeding off my frustration and anger. It was the most uncomfortable feeling I had ever had. I started twitching and shaking my head trying to get the feeling away. The green things were about twenty feet from us now.

"Uh oh," I said, as a man, who was trying to escape from this nightmare, ran in between us and the creatures. He tripped over his own feet and fell flat on his face. As he struggled to get up, I could see the wicked smiles across the snot brigade's ugly faces. I could hear the dragon gather its breath, readying itself for another blast of fire. I had to get that guy out of the way before he got fried. If it let it loose, there was a good chance this guy would get hurt. The green things moved in closer as he covered his head and started yelling for help. The buzz took over my whole body. I couldn't see straight. All I could hear was the hum of this force, which had built up inside me, get louder. I had to get rid of this feeling. I closed my eyes, not even caring if this made me an easy target or not.

"Get out!" I shouted. I had to get this buzzing feeling out of my body. It was going to drive me crazy. For all I knew it would kill me. I focused on pushing it away, just relieving it, and somehow, without truly understanding what I did, I felt this buzzing force push itself away from my body. I felt like I was a piece of paper being torn in two. As the buzzing feeling escaped my body, it shimmered. I opened my eyes and yelled. It was an arch that passed over the head of the man on the ground and then it hit the green things. They all flew backwards, smashing into cars and crashing into each other. The arch, still flowing out of my chest, picked them all up, and pushed them toward the blue ball. I could see Booger trying to run away from it. He was knocked down by the wave then picked up, spinning around and around. He was the last one to be pushed through the blue ball. As he disappeared inside, the orb grew a little bigger, glowing brighter. With a loud pop, it collapsed in on itself and winked out of existence. I could have sworn I saw Booger pointing at me, giving me a rude gesture as he fell through.

The parking lot was full of panicked people running out of it or toward their cars. I heard sirens blaring down the street. I realized that the fight must not have been very long. I felt a rush of excitement as I realized that I had performed some kind of magic. Whatever had happened to me today had changed me. I could do magic! My legs gave out on me as all the energy in my body drained away. The dragon moved under me as I began to fall. I looked at it, allowing myself to see it as the magnificent creature it was, and not as the parasite that almost killed me. It turned its head and looked at me with concern.

"Dude," I said groggily, "You were incredible."

It looked at me and rolled its eyes. Unfolding its wings it knocked me off of its back. I hit the parking lot with a grunt and a dizzy giggle. I felt like I was drunk. I could hear the dragon sigh with frustration as it grabbed the remains of my shirt with its mouth and took off into the air with me dangling from its mouth. I could hear the remaining people in the parking lot gasp as we circled the lot. My feet dragged the ground, tearing off one of the mismatched flip flops, as the dragon hauled me toward my duffel bag. It grabbed it by its back claws and swooped clumsily up into the air. In my giddy exhausted state, I marveled at the strength of this beast as we took off in the air. I made a silent prayer of thanks for the strength of the now torn T-shirt I was wearing. Looking down, I could see the lights of the police and ambulances as they pulled into the parking lot.

"Hey dragon," I said with another giddy giggle, "looks like we're famous."

Then I passed out.

Chapter 12

I woke up to a strange, but familiar, sound I couldn't place. Then it hit me. Ducks. It was the sound of quacking ducks. I sat up.

The dragon had flown us to the pond at Reid Park. It was still dark. I looked at the pond and I could see the faint outline of ducks as they lazily floated. I found comfort in that sight and sound. They were normal ducks. After all I had just been through, It was nice to hear something as normal as ducks. At least, I thought they were normal. Remembering the bobcats and the laughing squirrel, I had no idea what animals might be tied to the magical world. I stood up, shivering as a cool breeze blew through my torn T-shirt and hit my skin. Looking down I could still see the letters that spelled out 'It's All Good' across the front.

"Yeah Right," I said softly to myself.

I heard a sound of paper being crumpled behind me and I quickly turned around, crouching, ready for another attack. It was the dragon. It was sitting on the duffel bag. It had another paper bag, full of tacos, it smelled like. I walked over to the dragon as he unwrapped one and began to eat. As it munched on the taco, the dragon reached into the bag again and tossed a taco at me. My stomach growled loudly as I unwrapped the taco. I ate it in a few bites, then a burrito was tossed at me.

"Thanks," I said in a scratchy voice.

My throat was dry. I walked over to a nearby water fountain. After I drank what felt like a gallon of water, I walked back toward the dragon. I surprised myself at the thought that I was so calm and accepting of the dragon now. I sat down on the bench next to it.

"Hey, uh, thanks for helping me out."

The dragon stopped chewing and looked up at me. Its eyes were green again. It turned its head away from me, almost snubbing me. I got the feeling it was upset at me still.

"Hey are you still mad about that hat? I would have never thrown it at you if you hadn't laughed at me. Besides, you burnt some of the money and flew off."

The dragon continued to ignore me.

"You don't have to get so mad."

I was beginning to get upset again. This stupid lizard had a knack for making me angry. The dragon reached down and picked up the end of its tail, then looked at me with its narrowed eyes glaring at me.

"You're mad because I bit your tail? You kept on smacking me with it! I told you to stop but you wouldn't listen."

The dragon pushed the tail at my face.

"I'm sorry," I said through gritted teeth.

At first the dragon stared, its tail still in my face. It was obvious that my halfhearted apology wasn't completely sincere, but after a few moments it put the tail down. It turned away, reaching into the bag, slamming a taco down on top of the uneaten burrito still in my hands. I was too hungry to be upset. "Thanks," I said again. I inhaled the food and sat there staring at the dragon.

Here I was, sitting next to this magnificent creature, while we munched on tacos and burritos. How did it get the food? If the food had been unwrapped, then I would have thought that the dragon just crashed into a restaurant, terrifying everyone in sight, as it scooped up burgers and tacos. But the food was wrapped. It was prepared. I had a sudden image of the dragon flying through the drive through, ordering food, paying for it with a twenty, and flying off as the drive through person shouts, "Thank you!" The absolute ridiculousness of this image started me laughing. Once I started laughing, I couldn't stop. It grew into hefty guffaws. I was breathless and lightheaded. I looked over to see a puzzled expression on the dragon's face. Its nostrils flared. This started me laughing again. My whole body was shaking and tears were streaming out of my eyes. As I finally started to calm down, I looked over at it. It had an enormous smile on its face. It opened its large mouth and let out a loud "HUH" sound followed by the rumbling growl of laughter. This started me up all over again. I fell off the bench I was laughing so hard.

The dragon stood there looking at me. A strange grumbling sound was coming from its throat. It grew louder, until finally, it opened its mouth and a loud "huh" came out. The grumbling continued. Short bursts of different colored smoke shot out of its nose, like party favors at a New Year's Eve party. I finally closed my eyes and, by breathing deeply, I began to calm down. The laughter was just what I needed. The dragon continued to laugh. Now puffs of colored smoke came out of its nose. It looked down at me and shook its head.

I thought back to the battle and felt a rush of pride at how well I did. My heart began to beat and I felt the adrenalin pumping through my body. I felt great. What an adventure. I felt like I could take on the world and win. Nothing could go wrong. I even felt like I could take on whoever wanted to kill me. After all, I had taken care of Booger and the snot brigade. If they were the best that could be thrown at me, then I would be fine. I and the dragon could handle them, no problem. If only my brother had been there to see. He left too soon. At the thought of my brother I stopped. My brother didn't know who I was. It wasn't that he didn't recognize me. He said that he didn't have a brother. The seriousness of the whole situation came rushing back to me. There were forces working here that I had no control over. I needed answers. Where was this wizard?

I looked around me. The park was quiet, dark and kind of eerie. I wasn't sure if this was the best idea, but, considering everything that happened, the idea of talking to someone who might be able to explain this craziness to me was a risk, at this point, that I was willing to take. I had a million questions about everything from the dragon to why my brother didn't remember me. I felt depressed. "What am I going to do?" I said out loud.

The dragon had been staring at me again. It seemed to sense my mood change. It reached into the bag and tossed a taco at me. I caught it and began unwrapping it. I decided to take this opportunity to ask some questions. I needed a distraction from thinking about my brother. I just didn't know where to start.

"Do you have a name?" I asked, as the dragon started eating tacos again.

It gave me a sideways glance. It had an annoyed look on its face as I realized how stupid the question was. The dragon was still new to the world no matter how smart it was. I sat there for a moment.

"Do you want a name?"

This question seemed to surprise the dragon. It stopped chewing and stared across the pond, its amazing eyes rapidly changing color. Finally the eyes went back to green. Slowly it nodded its head 'yes'. It wanted a name. The dragon got up and stood in front of me. I had its undivided attention now. Its tail was moving back and forth. I knew I had to do this right. One mistake, one bad name and I was sure I would get smacked again with that tail.

"OK, I guess what we have to think about is what is a good name for a dragon."

The tail twitched slightly then went back to swaying gently.

"You're not a pet, so Spot or Fido is out."

The tail swayed.

"Even though you did fetch those green things pretty well."

The tail swung at my face, I closed my eyes flinching for the smack that never came. I opened my eyes. The dragon was looking at me with a thoughtful look on its face. Something I had said got its attention.

"What? What did I say?"

Something I said had caught the dragon's attention. What was it? Was it a clue to what it wanted to be called?

"Green?"

The tail twitched. I flinched again. I pushed the tail away and got up.

"Look you stupid lizard. This is getting us nowhere. If you expect me to sit here, with the threat of being hit by your tail, as I try to guess what name you want, you are crazy. If it ain't green, then what? Fetch?"

The dragon nodded its head.

"Fetch?" I repeated, "But that's ridiculous that's not a...."

"Fetch." I thought. Looking at the dragon, it seemed to fit. It was a good name, Fetch.

"Ok, Fetch, that's now your name."

The dragon's eyes turned blue for a second and its silver scales glowed. Fetch's eyes went back to green and its tail twitched excitedly. It was great to see this dragon so happy. Fetch looked like a little kid who had just got news of a trip to a favorite amusement park. I had to smile a little.

"Ok," I said. "On to the next question. Are you a boy or a girl?"

I fell to the ground as the tail swung around and knocked me flat. I jumped up, my face stinging where the tail had hit me.

"What did you do that for?" I said, "How am I supposed to know the difference between a male and female dragon?"

Fetch swung his tail around again, but this time, I was ready for it. I jumped back. The tail swung by missing my head by inches.

"This isn't helping me learn, dragon."

Fetch stood there, muscles taut, ready to jump on me. I was ready for it, and, with a speed that surprised me, I wove to the right as he sprang. He jumped past me, and, before I realized what I was doing, I jumped on Fetch's back and wrapped my arms around his neck. I got close to the side of its face, trying to figure out where its ears were.

"Now you listen to me. I am just trying to figure this entire thing out. I never asked for you to hatch on my leg, but we are in this together and we've got to stop fighting each other. Maybe this wizard can explain things, Ok? I am just asking questions so I can learn what is going on. So please stop smacking me with your tail."

I could feel Fetch's muscles relax a little, and when I was sure it wasn't going to attack me, I let it go. When I got off Fetch's back, the dragon walked away. He stopped at the edge of the pond and looked across the water. What gave this dragon the right to be so sensitive and angry all the time? It had played jokes on me. Was it just a bad sport? I mean, I should be the one who was upset. After all, Fetch did fly off and leave me alone to face Booger and the snot brigade. Where was this dragon then? Where was Fetch when Booger broke my nose? My hand shot up to my face. My nose was fine now. In all the commotion I hadn't realized that Fetch had obviously healed it. I felt bad. I realized I really had no right to be mad.

I looked at the dragon. It sat perfectly still. It was hard for me to grasp that, just a few short hours ago, it was nothing but a lucky rock I had put in my pocket. Fetch didn't have any more idea as to what was going on than I did. No matter how smart Fetch was, it was new to this world. I walked up to Fetch, standing a little behind it.

"You know, I have always been embarrassed that I never learned to speak Spanish. I mean, here I am living in the southwest my whole life, and I never learned to speak a language that so many of my friends knew how to speak. I always felt dumb. That's how I feel right now. I always loved reading about dragons, but never learned enough about them to help me know what they were. So I guess what I am saying is, I am an idiot, Fetch. Could you help me out?"

Fetch looked back at me. Turning around Fetch nodded 'yes'.

"Ok," I said taking a deep breath, "Are you a male dragon?"

Fetch nodded 'yes'. Relief washed over me. A strange rumbling sound came from him and he opened his mouth, letting out a loud burp. It smelled like tacos. Fetch walked over to me and sat down next to me. We both looked over the pond. Across the pond, you could hear the animals at the zoo moving around and making noise. I guessed that was a sign that the sun would be rising soon. I had no phone or watch, so there was no way of telling what time it was. I began to wonder if the wizard was going to show. I remembered his cryptic words. I had to believe he had some answers for me. I looked up and scanned the park around us, looking for another blue ball of light, or my beautiful assassin fairy ready to pounce on me, finishing the job that the smelly snot heads had started.

"You fixed my nose?" I asked Fetch.

He nodded his head slightly as an answer.

"Thanks, great job on my hand too. You're getting better! I still have all my clothes this time."

He looked at me for a second as if trying to decide how to react to my teasing comment. He ducked his head down and placed it against my chest and gave me a playful shove backwards. I fell back, almost completely flipping over off the bench. I laughed and sat up and gently smacked his snout. It felt good to play a little like this.

I started worrying about this wizard. What was his name, Johnathen? We sat there for a while and I took time to take in everything that had happened today. My life had become a book. I think I would like this book if I was reading it, but it seemed a little different when you are living it. In the books you can say when a person is in pain. In life you feel it. The overwhelming sensation of pain. The gripping, strangling hold of fear. Just thinking about it gave me a new respect for the heroes in my favorite stories. A duck took flight across the pond. Fetch and I jumped, ready for action. Realizing it was a duck, I slowly sat back down on the bench. All the muscles in my body were stiff from tensing up ready to attack a duck.

"Man. I've got to calm down," I thought.

I was getting tired of waiting. Where was this wizard? I wanted answers from this Johnathen. That strange pulse that I had forced out of my body. Was it some sort of magic? Then the simple fact that I had caught Fetch's fire and was able to use it. All of these things were amazing to me.

"How could I fight like I did?"

I had actually faced green monsters. I hit them. I actually did pretty well. Heck, with some help from Fetch we won the battle. Up until that moment I had never truly been in a real fight. I always avoided confrontation. Pretty much ran away from fights. But now, in one day, I had more than one scuffle with a dragon and fought off an army of green snot creatures. I felt a swell of pride and felt like I could take on the fairy on my own at that point. This felt great, but it also felt wrong.

This was really happening to me. I never asked for any of this, even in my wildest dreams. Even at my excitement at beating the crap out of the green monsters, there was the feeling that this was some sort of mistake. My brother didn't remember me. There was a fairy that lured me into traffic too and, oh yeah, I was about to meet a wizard that had given me a duffle bag full of money. Seven million dollars. He had to be expecting something in return. It was all so confusing. I looked over at Fetch. He was staring across the lake. His mouth slightly open.

"Hey Fetch. Maybe I was supposed to find your egg," I said.

Fetch looked over at me with a blank green-eyed stare. He seemed to have no answers himself.

"But why? Why me? Was I picked?"

Fetch looked down shaking his head. He sighed. I had the feeling that he was asking himself the same questions. We needed answers. I hoped that this wizard Johnathen would provide them. I was beginning to wonder how much longer we would have to wait for this wizard. He never really gave a time. What if he came, waited, and thought we were not going to show, then left before we got here. What if there really wasn't a wizard? Maybe the bobcat was just some kind of magic animal I had never heard of. What if it was the fairy? She might have tricked me into coming here and was even now waiting to ambush us. But why would she have given me the bag full of money? I just remembered the collar that was left for Fetch. It had been left in the tunnel. I wondered if the wizard would be mad that Fetch had not accepted the gift. All of these thoughts swirled around in my head. I started looking around nervously. I jumped at every sound. Fetch looked at me annoyed at my agitated state. Time seemed to slow down as we sat there waiting for this wizard to show up.

I was starting to get impatient. I needed answers and I needed them now. The idea of waiting here until this Johnathen showed up was becoming less appealing to me. The sun would be up soon. How long could Fetch stay hidden? His camouflage abilities were an asset, but I had no idea how long they would last, or if he would be willing to stay hidden like that all of the time.

I thought of the fight and all of the camera phones. We had to be all over the news by now and must be viral on the Internet. Someone might recognize me if we had to wait here in the daylight. We were kind of like fugitives. I felt exposed. If he didn't show up soon, we would have to find a hiding place. I was lost in all of these thoughts when Fetch tapped me on the shoulder with his tail. I looked over at the pond and saw light in the middle of it. It looked like someone had just turned on a light bulb. I jumped up preparing myself for another fight with Booger. But this light looked different from the other. Then all of the sudden the wizard appeared.

Chapter 13

Standing in the middle of the pond, on a small island, was a man that I figured had to be the wizard. He was dressed all in black. His hands were clasped behind his back as he stood there looking at us. He motioned for us to come to him. I guessed that he wanted us to fly over to him. I was just about to turn to Fetch, and ask if he would take us out there, when I heard a strange rumbling sound. The water rippled out like someone had thrown a big rock in to agitate it.

Slowly a mist began to form across the water. It swirled around and then formed a thick line. It changed color from white to black and began to rise. As it lifted, a dry neat path appeared leading directly to the wizard and his small island. He was showing off. He could have met me easily next to the pond instead of in the middle of it. He wanted me and Fetch to know that he had power. He had established right away that he was in charge of this meeting; that we were here because he invited us. I looked at Fetch and saw how cautious he seemed. We got the message.

"Ok," I said turning to look at Fetch.

Even though I was not looking at him, I could feel the presence of this guy. He radiated power. There was a part of me that wanted to run away, but I needed answers and this seemed to be the guy who could give them to me. Besides, I had a feeling if I ran I wouldn't get very far away from this guy before he would catch up to us.

"Ok Fetch," I whispered.

Fetch was looking at the wizard as his eyes changed colors.

"This is it. We really need to stick together. Let's calmly walk out to this guy. We need to show him we are not afraid of him. We need to show him that we have some control and that we are in charge."

I put my hand on Fetch's shoulder. His tail twitched and he took off toward the pond at a galloping run. He had moved so suddenly that I lost my footing. I fell on my side with a clumsy grunt. Looking toward the wizard I saw what appeared to be the reason why Fetch had moved so quickly. Standing next to the wizard was a girl. She had on a tight, black, short dress and from what I could tell from this distance was very pretty. If there was any doubt in my mind that Fetch was male before it was now gone. I quickly got up and grabbed the duffle bag, running to catch up to Fetch. I paused for a moment before stepping onto the path. I looked up as I heard a gasp of delight coming from the girl. Fetch had made it to the small island and she was scratching him on the head. The wizard was watching this and laughing. No one was even looking at me as I made my way to the island.

When I reached the island, Fetch was sitting there looking up at the girl. She continued scratching his head. There was a strange humming sound coming from him. I swear he was purring. I gritted my teeth. So much for looking even remotely dignified. I dropped the duffle bag and turned to face the wizard.

To my surprise he didn't look much older than I did. Tall and lean with shoulder length hair, he was dressed in a black button up shirt and jeans. I was expecting him to be in flowing robes with a pointy hat and long white beard. His face was partly in shadow as he stood perfectly still. It bothered me that I couldn't see his whole face. His eyes were completely in the dark and I could only see the straight line of his mouth. Even though I couldn't see his eyes, I could feel them staring at me intently.

We stood there for a while. He seemed to be studying me. Taking measure of who I was. I was beginning to get uncomfortable at his unmoving silence when we both jumped at a strange rumbling sound. Fetch had finally gained some control over himself. He was now facing the wizard. The rumbling sound was coming from him. He was growling. He crouched down as if he was getting ready to pounce and the wizard, seeing this, cautiously took a step back.

"He is very protective of you," he said in that same pleasant voice we had heard from the bobcat.

The statement surprised me. It hadn't dawned on me, until the wizard said it, that the dragon growled as a protective instinct toward me.

"Sorry for staring at you, I have a tendency to do that. My name is Johnathen."

Johnathen had stepped more into the light and now I could see his whole face. He had a broad grin. At the sound of Johnathen speaking, Fetch stopped growling. He seemed to be satisfied by the fact that the wizard had spoken first. He went back to paying attention to the girl. I shook Johnathen's hand.

"I'm Jack," I said, "Jack Dewitte."

The wizard shook my hand enthusiastically. "It is great to meet you, Jack. Oh, I'm sorry, where are my manners?" He nods his head toward the girl, never taking his eyes off Fetch. "This is my friend and assistant, Michelle."

It struck me as interesting that a wizard would seem to be so amazed by a dragon. In story after story, wizards and dragons interacted all the time. The way he was acting, you would have thought he had never seen a dragon before.

I looked over at the girl. She was pretty with long black hair and blue eyes. She was kneeling down staring into the eyes of Fetch. Her hand was stroking his head. Fetch continued to purr. Any feelings of being cautious toward the wizard didn't seem to apply to this girl. She had a look of wonder on her face, as she stared at him. Fetch's eyes slowly changed from green to the same color blue as hers. She gasped and a tear ran down her cheek. Fetch smiled. He seemed quite pleased with himself and his little trick. The smoke coming out of his snout turned blue as well.

"Show off." I mumbled.

Fetch turned to me giving me a dirty look. The girl stood up. She must have heard me. She smiled at me and offered her hand.

"Hi Jack. It's nice to meet you."

She tried to look at me but her eyes kept wandering over to Fetch. I didn't blame her, after all Fetch was a dragon. I wondered what kind of magic creature Michelle was. A witch maybe? I wanted to ask, but I thought it might be rude. I looked down at her arm and saw a tattoo. She had them going up both her arms. It was very colorful and the design was really interesting. I couldn't tell exactly what it was but it was very beautiful. Some people have tattoos that stand out and just don't look right. My brother had a tattoo of a panther on his shoulder that kind of stuck out like a sore thumb. This tattoo seemed to fit perfectly with Michelle. It enhanced her beauty and seemed to tell a lot about who she was. I stared at it trying to figure out what the design was.

Johnathen cleared his throat. We both looked over at him. He was smiling at us, his eyebrows raised. He looked at our hands. We were still shaking hands. Michelle had been distracted by Fetch, I had been distracted by her tattoo. We quickly put our hands down, equally embarrassed.

"Hi, uh sorry, yeah, um I'm Jack . . . Dewitte, " I stammered.

I felt my face flush as I realized I told her my name, when she obviously heard me talking to Johnathen and knew it already. I always felt awkward around girls, never knowing what to say. I surprised myself that I was able to talk to Michelle at all. We stood there for a few silent uncomfortable seconds. What a picture we must have made, me, a dragon, a pretty woman, and a wizard, standing on a small island in the middle of a duck pond.

Finally Johnathen broke the silence. "Well, now that all the introductions have been made let's get down to business."

He clapped his hands together, rubbing them in an eager way. He was obviously very excited by all of this. There was a loud coughing "Harrumph" sound. We all turned and looked at Fetch. He was staring at me, eyes red and narrow. He was upset, and the way he was staring at me let me know that he was upset at me.

"What?" I asked.

He continued to stare at me, his tail thumping the ground impatiently. He was starting to annoy me. I guessed that he must be upset because he wasn't the center of attention right now.

"What did I do now?"

Fetch's tail whipped around slapping me upside the head. Johnathen jumped back a step and Michelle let out a little gasp. With my face turning red, and my patience growing thin, I rubbed the side of my face.

"I thought I told you to stop hitting me with your tail?"

Fetch took another swipe. I was ready this time, catching it before it connected with the side of my face. I held it tightly.

"I'll bite it again man, I swear I will. Now what is your problem?"

Fetch whipped his tail out of my hands. He rolled his eyes back in his head shaking it in frustration. He was upset by something, that was for sure, but I just couldn't tell what it was. Then it hit me. I felt bad.

"Oh man," I said to him. "I'm so sorry. That was stupid of me."

Fetch nodded his head in agreement.

"Sorry you guys. I forgot to introduce you. This is Fetch," I said, turning to face Michelle and Johnathen.

I stopped midsentence. Both Michelle and Johnathen were standing there with shocked looks on their faces.

"You named the dragon?" Jonathan whispered.

"Yeah," I responded "Well actually when you come right down to it he named himself."

Both Michelle and Johnathen stood there shocked expressions on their faces. Something I had said had really surprised them. I glanced at Fetch and saw the confusion on his face mirroring the confusion I was feeling.

"Yeah, I had to call him something, and, since he got the clothes and food for me, I joked about how he fetched them and it stuck."

This wasn't necessarily how it happened, but, just like anybody does when they meet people they want to impress, you make a story more interesting. I glanced over at Fetch again. He made no move indicating he disliked what I had said. Michelle and Johnathen continued to stare at us, mouths slightly open. They both seemed to be in shock.

"He presented you with clothes and food."

This was a statement, not a question. I found myself nodding my head "yes" anyway. He had a look of amazement on his face. The broad smile came back and he shook his head in disbelief.

"I think you need to tell me the whole story from the beginning," he said. "I need to know everything that happened to you. You can't leave out one detail. You are unique, Jack. As far as I know there has never been a person like you. And there has never been a Dragon quite like you Fetch."

"Why are we so special? "I asked.

"Simple," said Johnathen. He pointed at me and stated. "You are not supposed to be alive. No one, as far as I know, has ever survived a dragon hatching. Your friend Fetch here, according to his very nature as a dragon, should have killed you. He should have eaten you after he hatched."

I didn't know what to say to this. I thought back to when I was in the tunnel and how I was sure Fetch was going to kill me. I had been right all along. According to Johnathen, I was supposed to die. I could feel Fetch at my side but I couldn't bring myself to look at him. I was more confused than ever. The same paranoid feeling about the fairy trying to kill me came creeping into my mind. The fairy! I hadn't given her too much thought since the fight in the parking lot, but now the thought that she caused Fetch's egg to hatch and kill me came creeping back into my mind.

I turned to Fetch, looking at him. He gave me a level look waiting to see how I was going to react. His eyes had gone back to green. I looked at him standing there; I wanted to say so much. I couldn't be upset at him. Whether he was supposed to or not he didn't eat me. I had to thank him for that. The whole ridiculousness of this situation came rushing into my mind and I started to laugh. I didn't want to but I just couldn't help it. I laughed long and hard and pointed at Fetch.

"Dude!" I said, "You were supposed to eat me?"

Fetch turned his head away. He seemed confused. It must have been extremely hard to fight against his nature and spare me. I felt bad for laughing.

"I'm sorry Fetch, but this is all so confusing. I mean, you know that I thought you were part of some kind of plot by the fairy to kill me."

At these words, Johnathen grabbed me by the arm and spun me to face him. He looked like someone had drained all color from his face. His upper lip twitched.

"What fairy? Trying to kill you? What are you talking about? You mentioned a fairy in the tunnel Jack, what do you mean plot?"

He squeezed my arm tightly. He definitely was strong. I pulled away from him, not liking how his mood had changed. I could hear Fetch growling. He wasn't happy with the way Johnathen had reacted to the news of the fairy. Neither did I. He took a step back giving me some space.

"I'm sorry Jack," he said, "but the more I hear about this fairy, the more I am convinced you are in a lot of danger. I have a spell of protection in place at this park right now, but, if a fairy has tried to kill you, we will have to get moving soon."

Once again I started to feel frustration and anger swell up inside me. All of this seemed so unfair. I looked over at Michelle. She looked scared and angry.

"Johnathen, you didn't tell me anything about a fey being involved."

She stared at the wizard. Her voice had a slight tremor to it and her hands, clinched into fists, were visibly shaking.

"I didn't know all of the details," said Johnathen, "but does it surprise you that Jack here was targeted just like you were? "

Tears welled up in her eyes and she turned away. Fetch had stopped growling at Johnathen and was staring at Michelle. He was obviously concerned about her. I reached a boiling point. I was supposed to get some answers from this guy and now I seemed to have more questions.

"Ok man, what is going on?" I shouted. "You freaked in the tunnel when I mentioned the Fairy and now you've freaked again. I've been targeted by the fey now? Was this some sort of plot? Was I supposed to find Fetch? What is going on?"

Johnathen stood there staring at Michelle's back, as she had turned away from us and seemed to be crying. After a few moments he sighed and began to speak.

"There was a rumor going around the magic community about someone spreading Dragon eggs for people to find. No one had any idea if it was true or not. But me, and others who are sensitive to feeling the magic of a dragon hatching, have been searching to find answers. So far we have always been too late. By the time a hatched dragon has been located they had already consumed the host and disappeared. No one has had any clue as to who is behind this, until today. You, Jack, are the first host ever to survive. All other hosts die as a result of the dragon consuming the life force of its host to survive. Both you and Fetch are unique.

Neither one of you should be alive. You shouldn't have survived the hatching and Fetch should be dead because he never took your life force."

I stood there letting this all sink in. I seemed to be part of something big. Fetch and I were now right in the middle of some strange magic conspiracy.

"So the fairies have been killing people with these dragon eggs?"

"Yes, it would seem so," said Johnathen.

"Why?" I asked. "I mean, why are they doing this and why did they pick me?"

"I don't think they picked you on purpose Jack. Did anyone give you Fetch's egg?"

"No I found it on the ground. I just thought it was a cool looking rock and was keeping it as a good luck charm. Wait a minute, if she wanted Fetch to hatch and kill me, then why did she lead me out to the street where I almost got hit by the car?"

Johnathen looked at me in confusion.

"I think you better tell me what happened from the beginning Jack. There is a lot to your story

I don't know, and, the only way I can answer the questions that you and Fetch have is to hear what exactly happened to you both. But, what you need to know is that there is a world of magic all around you, Jack. So many of the stories you might have read about fantasy and magic is based in truth. What you need to understand is that there are forces in this magic world that would rather see you dead than let you be what you are now. There are creatures that would see all people, who are not magical, wiped off the face of the earth. The fey are part of that group. At best, they are mischievous causing difficulty for humans. At the worst, they can be evil and destroy lives."

At these words Michelle turned and walked away. A path leading in the opposite direction appeared behind us. Michelle walked that way toward a limo parked along the road. She stopped at a park bench and sat there with her head in her hands.

"She is a victim of the fey cruelty, Jack. They destroyed her family. Her parents and little brother were killed by them."

My blood ran cold at these words. It really brought home the seriousness of the situation.

"Why?" I asked.

"Because they could. They are cruel, Jack. "

I looked over at Fetch. He was staring in Michelle's direction.

"Ok," I said, "I will tell you everything."

Fetch looked at me. I don't think he liked the idea of me telling Johnathen everything.

"Hey Fetch, I know you don't want to kill me. If you did, you would have had more than one chance to do it. But you've got to let me know. Was I supposed to find you? Were you supposed to kill me?"

This just blurted out of me. It seemed silly as soon as I said it, but I felt I had to know. I was more confused than ever. I wondered at that moment if I would regret my question. Fetch looked at me, confusion in his eyes. I could tell that he didn't know. He needed answers just as badly as I did. He gave me a snort and, before I could react, he jumped into the air and started to fly off. I yelled at him to come back. It was starting to get light out and I could see him in the early light of dawn. He landed next to the park bench and I watched him walk up to Michelle. She sat up startled at his presence. He put a paw in her lap. They sat there staring at each other, then she wrapped her arms around him and buried her face in his neck. Even from this distance I could hear her sobbing gently. Johnathen put a hand on my shoulder.

"Come on. I've got some coffee in the limo."

We walked down the path together, not saying anything. I knew that Johnathen was anxious to hear mine and Fetch's story, but he wanted to give me some time to adjust to what I had heard and to what had happened to me. What he told me was taking a lot time to sink in.

"She is beautiful," said Johnathen.

He was staring over at Fetch and Michelle. I looked over at him my face turning red.

"Don't worry about it," said Johnathen smiling, "we're not together. I'm more like her guardian than anything. I do care for her and I had quite a fight to keep her safe and protected. The council wasn't too happy with me when I took her in, but she has proven herself to most of the magic community."

I looked at Johnathen. He must have seen the confusion on my face. He laughed and patted my shoulder reassuringly.

"I'll explain as much as I can to you, Jack. Don't worry."

I was beginning to like this guy. He seemed genuinely sincere, and was definitely down to earth.

"You are not like what I would expect a wizard to be," I said.

He laughed again. "I'm going to take that as a compliment," he smiled.

I looked back over at Michelle. "That's an interesting tattoo she has," I said.

"Ah yes, it is. When I first met Michelle, she just had the outline of it done. She has been working on it ever since. She is almost finished with it. Can you tell what it is?"

I shook my head no. "It's colorful and an interesting design," I said. "I couldn't tell what it is though."

Johnathen looked at me for a moment. "I think I'll let her tell you what it is."

We walked away from the pond, and Johnathen led me away from the park bench toward the limo. He seemed to want to give Fetch and Michelle some privacy.

"Do you have any tattoos?" he asked.

I looked over at him. He was trying hard to make small talk. Trying to relax me and put my mind at ease. I appreciated it.

"No," I said. "I don't have any. I've never found the right one for me. My brother got one and it just ended up looking ridiculous on him. So I wanted to give it a lot of thought as to what I would get if I were to get one."

At the mention of my brother, the memory of our meeting in the parking lot came back to me. I thought about asking Johnathen about this but I remembered how he told us to come see him immediately and I didn't want to get him upset. After all, he was a wizard and, even though I was beginning to trust him, I didn't want to make him mad.

We reached the limo. It hit me then that this guy had a limo. He must be rich. I remembered the duffle bag of money he had given me. My hand went to my forehead.

"O man," I said, "I left your money on that little island. I'll go get it."

"No need," said Johnathen.

He raised a hand to his chest and said a strange word. The duffle bag appeared outside the limo.

"It's not my money anymore, Jack. It is yours. This is your first lesson about the magic world. A gift from a wizard means that you have his protection. You cannot refuse the gift or return it to the wizard. If you do, it will just find you again. So you are stuck with the money. Don't even try to give it back. You're going to need it."

This last statement had me worried. More and more there seemed to be so much I didn't know.

Chapter 14

Johnathen opened the door to the limo and reached inside, pulling out two cups of coffee.

"Whoops," he said. "I didn't even ask if you liked coffee. I just took it for granted that you did."

I took the coffee out of his hands. "I love it Johnathen. Got any cream and sugar?"

He reached back into the car and handed me a handful of sugar and cream packets. I fixed my coffee. It tasted good. I remembered the last cup I had, and how I only got a few sips in before all this craziness happened. I thought back to the store and the table and then my brother again. Why didn't he remember me? Did the fairy have something to do with it?

I took a sip of the coffee. It was strong and sweet and helped me relax. I leaned against the limo and looked around the park. I had grown up in this area and had a lot of memories tied up in this park. Some were good, others bad. The past seemed to weigh on me in a heavy way and I stood there in silence. I looked over at Michele and Fetch. He was attempting to balance his whole body on his tail. Michelle was laughing. It was amazing to me how much my life had changed in just a short amount of time. I felt dizzy for a second at the idea of what was now my life. I looked at Johnathen as he leaned on the limo looking at the pond. He wasn't saying anything, but I could tell he was anxious to hear my story.

"Starting to get light out," he said softly.

I started to talk. I never meant to tell him everything. Just enough to maybe get some answers. But, before I knew it, I was telling him the whole story. From when I saw the fairy, to the egg, to the nightmare, everything. Every little detail I could think of came out of my mouth. I even described the details of Booger's face and the smell of his cigars. My whole adventure, so far, was laid out before him. When I was finished, he stood there in stunned silence. Michelle and Fetch had come over. I didn't even notice they were there until I had finished talking. I looked at Fetch.

"Sorry," I said to him.

I really didn't mean to tell Johnathen everything without Fetch being there. After all it was just as much his story as it was mine. Fetch seemed to understand my apology. He nodded his head. He seemed to believe that it was best to let Johnathen know it all. I let out a sigh of relief. I was glad that Fetch was beginning to trust Johnathen as much as I was beginning to trust him. Not just because he seemed to have answers, but also the fantasy geek in me was thrilled at the idea of having a wizard as a friend. Michelle just stood there, not saying a word. She had a hand on Fetch's back. They had shared a moment and were now good friends. In fact, he was treating her much better than he treated me. We turned to Johnathen waiting to hear what he had to say. My story had shocked him. He stared off into space thinking of what to say. Finally he spoke.

"You are an amazing person, Jack. I can't imagine too many people, going through what you went through, coming out of it without losing their minds. I can give you some answers, but, I doubt they will give you much comfort. You have been victimized. But, the simple fact that you have fought back, in the way you have, shows strength of character that I don't think you are fully aware you have. Both you and Fetch. I'm not trying to flatter you. Just simply stating a fact. For you two to survive, the way you have, shows a strength of spirit that few people possess. I hope what I can tell you will help. But, there are just too many unknowns to consider. I will try to answer everything I can. I hope it helps you."

"The fairy was trying to kill you, I have no doubt about that. They are a cruel race that finds pleasure in torturing and killing humans. They pick their victims randomly. I am not sure if you really saw her at your accident years ago. If you had, you wouldn't be here today. She would have definitely killed you then. Ironically, it was you finding Fetch's egg that saved your life. This is where it gets incredible. I have no doubt in my mind that it was the fairies that have been spreading the eggs around. They have the ability to detect when a dragon egg is about to hatch. Most can only feel it after it has begun."

"When she appeared to you, she sensed you had the egg. She probably wanted to watch you die. They can be cruel that way. In any other case the egg carrier would have died. That is how it has always been. She assumed that you would be killed by the dragon. Her luring you into the street would have just added to your pain as Fetch hatched. She could watch as you suffered through the hatching. It sounds like the sudden appearance of the truck, which almost hit you, startled her and she disappeared."

"Assuming that you would soon be dead from the hatching, she didn't bother finding you again. She waited until she felt the hatching process end and then cast a pulse spell. This is a type of magic that starts at a focal point, then moves outward. It's like when you drop a pebble into water and you get that ripple effect moving outward." I nodded my head to let him know that I understood. "This spell is a very powerful one that erases any and all knowledge that the victim of the fairy ever existed. That is why your brother didn't remember you. All memory of you ever existing was erased from the world. You no longer exist. She then erased any damage caused by you at the store."

I felt dizzy as the idea of being erased form everybody's memory sank in. I wondered if it could be reversed, but, before I could ask, Johnathen continued.

"As for the creatures that attacked you, they were goblins. A natural enemy of the fairies, so they could not have been sent by the fairies. The good news is that the fairies must think you're dead and so, for now, they are no longer trying to kill you. The bad news is; someone else in the magical world had to send the goblins. Someone else is trying to kill you. If they can control goblins the way they did, then it is someone really powerful. You are a force of power, Jack, both you and Fetch. As far as I know, in the history of dragons, there has never been another occurrence like yours. You are new. You guys changed all the rules of magic. And there are many in my realm of magic that just can't handle change."

My coffee was now cold. I hadn't taken more than the one sip from it. The sun had come up and it looked like another bright, hot, April day. It had been almost twenty-four hours since I had seen the fairy. I felt very tired. I wanted to lie down and just get some sleep. I was hungry again. I had left the bag of tacos and burritos on the other side of the pond. All that Johnathen had told me was sinking in. My world had changed completely around me. The thing that troubled me the most was that no one knew who I was anymore. My own brother didn't even know that I was ever alive. This affected me more than the news of someone wanting me dead other than the fairies. I thought of my brother. He could be in danger. If not from the fey, then from this new threat that Johnathen had just told me about.

I turned to Johnathen, wanting to understand. He sat there waiting for me to ask the question. I could tell, by the look on his face, what the answer was to the biggest question I had. I asked it anyway.

"Is it reversible? Can a spell be cast so that my brother would remember me again?"

I was something of a loner and the idea that the few friends I had not remembering me, didn't upset me as much as the idea that my brother didn't know I ever existed. Johnathen shook his head.

"It has been tried before, with disastrous results. Restoring a person's memories is a painful process that can tear a person's mind apart. Your brother would never be the same."

I looked at Johnathen in shock.

"Is he safe?"

My voice was shaking. The idea that he would never remember me hit me hard. After our parents died, he was all the family I had. I had the same feeling inside that I had when my parents had died. I no longer existed.

"I think he will be fine, Jack. I can send my bobcats from time to time to check on him if you like, but Jack, I would advise you to not see him. If your enemies found out that you were seeing your brother they might use him against you."

The thought of having enemies was strange. I had people not like me, think I was weird, and possibly hate me for one reason or another. No one is liked by everyone, but I never had an enemy. It all seemed so unfair. My mind slipped back into the idea that I had been erased from my former life. It all seemed so unfair.

"So, everything I had is now gone," I said, "and now I have feys, goblins and some other creatures that can perform magic wanting me dead. I guess the thing that bothers me most is the fact that there is no evidence that I ever existed."

"Not necessarily," said Michelle.

She walked over to the front of the limo. Reaching inside she pulled out a laptop. She turned it on and attached a strange looking glowing box.

"This allows me to get on someone's Wi-Fi. It's magic so it doesn't always work. It was designed by a friend of mine. It's new. Technology is very confusing to most people born in the magic world, Jack."

I looked over at Johnathen. He had a strange look on his face. His hands were clasped behind his back as he stared at the computer. He seemed like he didn't want to get too close to it.

"That is why I am valuable to the magic community here in Tucson. I am able to get on a computer to check and see if a magic event has been recorded or reported. The pulse erases all memory and physical evidence of a person or thing, but it can't touch a recording or a mention of something once it is on a computer. That's where I come in. Me and my little friend." Michelle had a slight smile on her face as she mentioned her 'little friend'. "I find these things and my friend gives them a kind of electronic delete erasing them from the world wide web."

Johnathen grunted, giving me the idea that he didn't necessarily like this friend of Michelle's. He seemed to not like anything that had to do with computers. He was looking at the laptop with suspicion. He saw me looking at him and smiled and shrugged.

"I guess I'm just old fashioned. Can't seem to get the knack of those things," he said pointing at the computer. "If it wasn't for Michelle, I wouldn't even have a cell phone."

After tapping on the keys of her computer, Michelle handed it to me. I set it on the hood of the limo. It was opened to a login page for Facebook. I looked at Michelle a little confused.

"If you had a Facebook page, there is a chance that it is still there. I doubt Pek has found it yet."

My heart was pounding out of my chest. The idea that I still had a Facebook page was strangely scary to me. Fetch had walked over to my side. He gave me a gentle nudge. I typed my name and password in and found my Facebook page. There it was, my profile photo, my last post from the night before. A simple one of a forest painting. There were circles of colored light in the painting. I shared it off a page called 'Fantasy, Unicorns, and Elves'. I laughed at the irony of it. There was a message from my brother, dated around the time I had to be at the store buying my coffee. Right before I freaked out over Fetch hatching.

It said, "Jack, don't go anywhere tonight. We have got to talk. I have something important to tell you."

"Well," I said out loud, "I guess I'll never know what that was about."

These words really made it all sink in for me. A strange sick feeling hit me like a wave. I started shaking all over as I stared at my Facebook page. Eighty friends. Kind of pathetic really. Most of the people I knew had thousands of Facebook friends. I had eighty. I was lucky if ten would even recognize me if they saw me out on the street. In so many ways my life seemed kind of sad and pathetic. I never really pushed myself to do anything worthwhile; to meet new people or try new things. Yeah, my life had been pretty pathetic. But, at that moment, I would have given anything to have that pathetic life back.

My Facebook page began to blur as tears of regret welled up in my eyes. My body shook in rage and fury, and regret clouded all other thought. I backed away from the computer. I started walking, tripping over Fetch's tail in my mad dash to get away. I stood up clumsily, embarrassed at my display of emotion. I reached down grabbing the remaining flip flop, throwing it toward the pond, and stormed off. No one followed me as I went over to the same bench that Michelle had walked over to just a short time ago. I had to get away from everything for a while. They all seemed to understand my need to walk away for a minute.

I looked up and could see the limo. Johnathen had made no attempt to come over, giving me this time to think things through. I noticed Michelle walking toward me. At first I felt like waving her away, but I realized that she was probably the only one who could understand what I was feeling. She had to have gone through worse. I felt a little embarrassed at my outburst right now. I thought about my brother, grateful that he was alive. I owed my brother so much. He took me in and took care of me during one of the hardest times in my life. He was there for me when our parents died and when I broke my hip. How could I ever pay him back now?

Michelle reached the bench where I was sitting. She sat down next to me not saying a word. Both of us just stared at the limo. She put her hand on top of mine not speaking. This simple gesture seemed to say so much. It let me know that someone understood, at least in part, what I was going through. This simple gesture seemed to break down all barriers I was trying so hard to build up. Before I knew what I was doing I began to cry. Silently the tears poured from my eyes. I let myself feel just how lost I was. I was mourning my lost life. My own death. Michelle put her arms around me and held me for a few minutes. I could feel her gently crying too. I found myself comforted by those tears. I knew I was not alone in what I was going through, and if I had someone like Michelle as my friend, then I think I could make it. We looked at each other. Remembering what Johnathen had told me about her life, I didn't know what to say to her. She broke the silence.

"Pretty crappy huh?" she said.

I laughed a little, "Yeah, I guess that describes it perfectly."

We both laughed. We sat there, enduring another award silence. I wished I was more comfortable talking to girls.

"He can help you," she said, finally breaking the silence. "He helped me and he can help you. We both can."

I could tell she really believed that he could. I wasn't sure if anyone could help me.

"I hope so," I said.

"He can," she reassured me. "He has helped so many others who have continued on and now have great lives. I stayed with him to help with the others he finds, like you, who have had magic destroy their lives. He has asked me time and time again to leave and go on with a new life but I just can't."

I could tell the way she was talking that she was in love with him. We sat there for a little while in silence. I looked down at her tattoo. From up close it looked even more amazing. It looked like multicolored scales wrapping all around her arm. She looked over and saw me staring at it.

"It's a dragon."

She turned her hand over and I could see the end of a spiked tail tattooed into her palm. She showed me her other arm that ended with a clawed paw resting on the top of her hand. She pulled her dress over exposing her shoulder. You could see part of the dragon's mouth and one of its eyes.

"It's beautiful," I said.

"Thanks, but it can't compare to the real thing."

Fetch wandered over as we sat there looking at the tattoo. His eyes changed color rapidly. Michelle gasped at this. She was in complete awe of Fetch. I couldn't blame her, he was pretty cool. Even though he was a pain in the butt sometimes, I was beginning to think of Fetch as someone who had always been there in my life, even though he had only become a part of it in the last day. With all the things that had happened in this short amount of time, how I had changed, and how my old life had been erased, in a way, he had always been there. Fetch ducked his head down toward Michelle's hand and nudged it gently. At first Michelle was confused.

"I think you created a monster Michelle. He wants you to scratch his head."

Michelle smiled, happy to oblige. Fetch's eyes turned blue and rolled upward as he sat there really enjoying the attention. I thought of all the old stories of dragons eating young maidens and wondered of there was any truth behind them.

Looking at Fetch I knew maidens had nothing to fear from him.

Michelle made a strange sound. I looked over and saw the tears flowing from her eyes. She was lost in a fantasy. Her choice of a dragon tattoo gave me the idea of how much she loved the idea of dragons. Being here with Fetch must have been a dream come true. I wondered if she had ever seen a dragon before. She had been living in this fantasy world for a while, surely there must be other dragons around. Then the thought hit me. What about other fantasy creatures? I have already met goblins, wizards, dragons, and fairies. If they exist, then what about unicorns, griffins, dwarves . . . the list went on and on in my head. The fantasy geek in me was thrilled at the idea of it.

"Michelle, are there unicorns?" I asked.

She laughed, continuing to scratch Fetch's head.

"Anything you have ever read about, Jack, they are real. Not necessarily the way they are in the books, but they do exist."

"How have they stayed hidden all this time?"

Michelle had a thoughtful look on her face. I could tell that she had given this a lot of thought.

"Most people just refuse to accept what they are seeing. There are councils around the world, in all the different magic communities, that govern the appearance and effects of magic. You have experienced the pulse and what it does to people's minds when magic is seen."

She stopped for a moment frowning at this.

"Sometimes the magic world leaks through. A lot of writers in the past have written what they have learned and seen and that became fantasy books and novels. It wasn't always hidden, Jack. There was a time when it not only wasn't hidden, but both worlds were one. Something happened that caused the magic world to separate itself from the non-magic world. I don't know what it was. Johnathen does. I wish I could tell you more, Jack, but there is so much that I don't know myself. Johnathen has protected me from a lot of the magic world because, just like you, there are those that want me dead or at least erased from knowing that magic is real."

She was quiet for a while. I got the impression that she wasn't necessarily happy with the idea that so much seemed to be kept from her by Johnathen. I looked at Fetch. He was listening very intently to what she was saying. He was new to the world and so much seemed to be unknown to him as well.

"Have you ever seen another dragon before Fetch?" I asked this question not just for me but for Fetch as well.

He looked over at me, his eyes turning green for a second. He seemed grateful to me for asking it. He looked at Michelle while smoke poured out of his nose in different colors.

"No, Fetch, you are the first dragon I have met," she said. "Dragons have been missing in this part of the world for a while now. They have great power and anyone who can gain control over them has a chance of taking over everything. It has always seemed obvious to me that it was the fairies that did this. From what Johnathen has told me they have always tried to take over."

At the mention of fairies, Michelle's face seemed to turn dark. I thought about the fairy that had tried to kill me. I knew Johnathen must be right about the fairies, but there was a part of me that wanted to believe they couldn't be all bad.

"Do you think that all fey are bad?" I asked Michelle.

She stopped petting Fetch and turned to me, getting right in my face.

"They're all bad, Jack, don't ever think anything different. They tried to kill you and they killed my family. I have seen the damage that they have caused and the lives they have destroyed. They are a darkness in this world, Jack, and they must be stopped."

I looked deep into Michelle's eyes. I could almost feel the pain she must have gone through. But I could also see a strength in her. She looked away, staring at the limo.

"I will do anything I can to stop them, Jack. Anything! If you could have seen what they did to my family . . ."

She stopped talking. There was a hitch in her voice and the tears began to pour out of her eyes. It amazed me that someone could be so strong and confident one minute, then could begin to cry so quickly the next. She had to have gone through so much. She sat there with her head in her hands as Fetch rested a paw in her lap. She looked up at him, then grabbed him tightly around the neck, and began to sob. At first Fetch had a surprised look on his face, but slowly closed his eyes and rested his head on her shoulder. He gently wrapped his front paws around her, returning the hug. I stood there watching this exchange and I knew, at that moment, that Fetch was innocent. He was not to blame for all the things that had happened to me. I was reminded that in his own way Fetch needed answers too. I didn't want to break up this touching moment, but, looking around, I started getting nervous that someone would come into the park and see this exchange between dragon and girl.

I cleared my throat and said, "Looks like you have made a friend for life, Michelle."

She broke the embrace turning toward me. There were tears in her eyes and a smile on her face.

"Oh I hope so," she said, "I hope I have made two friends, Jack."

She grabbed me and gave me a tight hug.

"Boy, look at us," I said, "you would think there is something wrong the way we keep breaking into tears."

Michelle pulled away. Her reaction gave me the idea that it had come out wrong. I felt my old clumsiness coming out. I felt a thump against the side of my head as Fetch gave me a smack with his tail. Michelle looked at both of us and began to laugh. This made me feel better. She did understand that I was just trying to lighten the mood and not make fun of her. Wanting to keep the mood light, I thought of a trick I could show Michelle.

"Hey, you want to see something neat?"

Michelle looked at me suspiciously.

"You are gonna love this."

I jumped up from the bench with a smile. I had no idea if what I was about to do would even work, but I wanted to show off. I looked around and saw how light the park had gotten. The sun was starting to rise and soon the early morning park walkers would start to show up. With another quick look around the park to make sure no on was there yet I turned to Fetch. I raised a hand in the air looking and smiling at Fetch. He got what I was going for right away. He sent a stream of fire out of his mouth catching my hand on fire.

"Great job, Fetch," I said.

Just in the short amount of time since last night's battle, Fetch's aim had gotten better. I kept my hand up for a while looking at Michelle and smiling. She sat there with her mouth hanging open.

"Ha!" I laughed, "You should see the look on your face right now."

I put my hand down, palm up, and looked at it. I had learned to juggle when I was about seven. It had been a while since I had done it. I stood there hoping I could do this. The last thing I wanted was to send fireballs around the park, catching it on fire. I focused on the fire, trying to picture a fireball in my mind. As I stood there, focusing on the flame, I started feeling all these different emotions. First curiosity, then pride, a fondness for Michelle, and humor at a joke that I didn't seem to truly understand. It felt very strange, almost alien, like these emotions were not my own. All that was pushed aside as surprise and delight flooded my mind. I had formed the fire in my hand into a perfect little ball. I kept my eyes on it as I heard Michelle's gasps of delight. I tried tossing the ball of fire gently into the air. It landed back in my hand. Picturing an image in my mind, I lobbed the ball of fire into my other hand. It split in two. I now had two balls of fire, one in each hand. I tossed one in the air and it split again. I was juggling three balls of fire. Michelle laughed and Fetch grunted with appreciation. They were impressed with what I was doing. I was feeling pretty good about myself.

I heard a shout. It was Johnathen. Remembering my juggling lessons I had years ago, I turned slowly toward the limo. Keeping my peripheral vision on the balls, I looked over at Johnathen. He was waving wildly to his left. Out of the corner of my eye I saw a car pulling into the park. I dropped the balls at my feet. They quickly caught the dry grass on fire. I stomped quickly, putting the small fire out.

Fetch had gone into chameleon mode. Becoming the brown and green color of the ground, he was soon undetectable. You could only tell that there was something there if you happened to catch the occasional silver gleam from his scales. Michelle had stood up and was stomping the ground, helping me put out the fire. I was embarrassed at how quickly we were almost discovered.

"That was close," said Michelle. "You don't want to draw too much attention to yourself."

I remembered my battle from the night before and the people who had been filming it.

"Huh, talk about drawing attention to us, I think we need to check your computer to see if there are any videos of Fetch and me fighting the goblins. There were a lot of people there, and I know I saw someone with a camera phone taking videos."

Michelle's eyes got really big. "I didn't even think about that," she said. We walked a little faster toward the limo.

When we got back to the limo, Johnathen greeted us with a frown. I looked at him and shrugged my shoulders giving him a nervous embarrassed little laugh. He chuckled and shook his head. Michelle had gone back to her laptop. She was typing a mile a minute, talking to Johnathen the whole time.

"There is a chance that Jack and Fetch might have been caught on video. I'm checking right now to see if they have gone viral."

Johnathen gave her a look of confusion. Michelle sighed.

"To see if there is a video and if a lot of people have seen it. Yep, there it is."

We scrambled to gather around the computer.

"What? So fast?" said Johnathen.

He was looking over Michelle's shoulder keeping his hands clasped behind his back. It was like he was afraid to touch the computer. Michelle looked at him rolling her eyes.

"Honestly, Johnathen, you really need to learn how to use it. We know that magic users can. You just have to take the time to learn how. I know you would enjoy it."

Johnathen continued to look at it as if he was afraid it would shock him. I have to admit I was pretty excited to see the battle on film. Since I had never been in a fight before, I had been impressed by how well I had done against what I now knew were goblins. We all crowded around the small computer screen to watch.

There I was in the parking lot. You could see the blue ball and the goblins running around. The camera jumped around a lot, so it was hard to get a clear look of what was going on. It finally focused on me. I was pinned to the ground by Booger. My face began to feel warm as the flush of embarrassment hit me. I remembered feeling like I had done so well. There I was though, on film, flaying wildly underneath Booger. I looked like a fish flopping around on a dock. My hit that I had gotten in was nothing more than a lucky punch. The most embarrassing thing of all was I had on that stupid red stocking cap with the fuzzy ball. As I swung my arms around wildly the little fuzzy ball wiggled up and down. The camera cut away from me as a screech from one of the other goblins distracted the cameraman. The video went on showing the choppy story. You could hear the goblins chanting "Booger, Booger" and the camera focused back on me as I used him like a club. Again, I was fixed on the stocking cap and the jiggling bouncing fuzzy ball. To my right I heard the sound of Fetch laughing. I took a guess as to where he was standing and elbowed him. The way he coughed and choked, I could tell I got him in the throat. I watched the rest of the video. Both Michelle and Johnathen gasped at me catching the fire, but went silent as they watched me panic and fling it all over the parking lot. They gasped again as a strange shimmer that was the pulse gathering in me, was forced out of my body. There was even a shot of me climbing awkwardly onto Fetch's back and picking up the duffle bag. There was one more shot; when I had passed out, I had fallen off of Fetch. He had swooped down and grabbed me, by the seat of the purple sweats, with his mouth. I could see me hanging there, as we flew off, mooning the cameraman. Finally it ended. I looked and saw that thirty thousand people had already seen it.

Neither Michelle nor Johnathen would look me in the eye. I slowly moved my hand to the top of my head. I was still wearing the red stocking cap. I pulled it off feeling the strange new sensation of a cool morning breeze blowing across my bald head.

"Fetch got these clothes for me," I said. "He thought it would be funny."

I could hear Fetch laughing, Johnathen was struck with a sudden coughing fit that was not fooling anybody, and Michelle had turned her head shaking with silent laughter. I was going to get Fetch back for this. I didn't know how, but I was going to get him back.

The park was starting to come alive as the early morning walkers started to show up. Fetch was hidden, but with the limo, my tattered appearance, and Johnathen and Michelle's neat and well-pressed looks, we were starting to draw attention to ourselves. In fact I was very conscious now of how I was dressed. An elderly couple had gotten out of their car and was now giving me a strange look. Gaining some control Johnathen spoke quietly.

"I think for Fetch's sake, we should walk to the nearest ramada and continue our talk."

I knew it was for my sake and not Fetch's. After all, he was pretty much invisible with his chameleon-like abilities, a talent that wished I had at this time. The four of us walked calmly to the nearest ramada. We got a lot of second looks from people as we walked over. When we got to the ramada, Johnathen stood there, eyes closed, whispering words very rapidly. All of a sudden, a slightly dim shield began to appear from the ground. It reminded me of a tinted car window being rolled up. When it covered all four sides of the ramada, Johnathen opened his eyes and, smiling with satisfaction, said, "That will keep people from seeing us or coming over here."

As if in an answer to my puzzled look, Johnathen pointed to a couple walking hand in hand toward us. All of a sudden they stopped in their tracks, and with slightly puzzled looks, turned and started to walk in the opposite direction. I didn't know how I felt about the obvious manipulation that was used to keep them from getting too close, but I decided to keep it to myself.

"Now, let's talk about you and Fetch," said Johnathen.

Fetch had gone out of camo mode and was sitting next to Michelle. She had her laptop out, and was absentmindedly scratching Fetch under the chin with one hand, while tapping the keys of her laptop with the other.

"Ok," I said, "I have some questions I need answers to. Could it be possible that the fairy meant for me to find Fetch's egg?"

Fetch opened his eyes and stopped purring at this. He looked very intently at Johnathen. He apparently wanted answers to this question as much as I did.

"No, Jack, you must know that you picked it up randomly. There was no manipulation in you finding it. She appeared to you as soon as she felt the dragon's egg begin to hatch. If she had manipulated you into finding it, you would have been taken to a place to be watched and probably tortured. The fairies are not above experimenting on people."

I shuddered at this last statement.

"No, you found it on your own. Her presence when she lured you out into the street was a result of the egg beginning to hatch. Before that she wouldn't have been able to detect the egg at all. Dragon eggs have a natural protection about them that keeps them from being found by magic. It is just when the egg begins to hatch that it can be detected. She appeared to you to lure you into the street to kill you, and perhaps to see if the egg would still hatch from your dead body. Or, that's what I'm guessing."

"You mean to tell me that she tried to kill us both?"

Fetch sat up again growling at this last statement. Neither one of us thought of the possibility that the fairy wanted us both dead.

"It would appear so. I'm sorry, Jack, but from what I can tell, you were both just part of some sick game. Why she was willing to possibly kill Fetch along with you is puzzling to me. After you were almost hit, she must have been pulled away by some force. Perhaps whoever sent the goblins to attack you. Yes, this seems to make sense."

It was like listening to Sherlock Holmes as he started putting the pieces together. He seemed pleased with what he had figured out.

"By the time she got free from whatever pulled her away, Fetch had already begun to hatch. To cover her own tracks, she must have been the one to cast the pulse spell that made everyone forget you. I had no idea that you were alive until one of my bobcats found you. I sent them out as soon as I knew that a dragon was hatching. I was hoping to find out what was happening to the dragons and to get some clue as to who was behind the whole thing. I couldn't have been more surprised to find you in the tunnel, covered by the yoke of the dragon egg."

My face wrinkled up at the memory of the smelly, slimy stuff that I had been covered in. I always had an idea what it was, I just never wanted to admit it to myself. Fetch snorted and gave me a dirty look.

"So those bobcats, are they real bobcats?"

"Yes, I raised them from birth and cast some spells over time to use them as my eyes and ears. They can run very fast and get to places that I can't. When they found you, and I saw that you had survived, I sent for them to return to me. I knew I had to get you the money and then talk to you. I would have come myself, but, I was afraid I would draw too much attention to you, and you would have been attacked. Just my presence in certain parts of town can be felt by other wizards and magic users. I realize that my choice was rather a stupid one, seeing as how you were attacked anyway. I feel that I owe you both an apology."

"Hey, its ok," I said. "There was no way you could have known I would be attacked. I just wish I hadn't fought with Fetch and then allowed us to separate for a time."

Fetch's eyes turned green at this last statement. I smiled a little. It seemed like he thought what I said was a kind of apology. I just didn't want to get into it with him right then. After all, I would have never gotten mad at him if he hadn't picked out the God awful clothes I was now wearing. My face flushed at the thought of what I was wearing. I pushed it aside as wanting more answers from Johnathen was more important than my embarrassment right then. Johnathen was staring at me. There was a strange light in his eyes.

"Jack, I need to know what you did to those goblins in the parking lot. Catching the dragon fire was amazing enough but the magic you performed is something I have never seen before. When you told me about it, you seemed to have difficulty describing what it was."

I though for a moment before answering. "Well, I guess the best way to describe it is to call it a pulse. It kind of flowed out of me like water. But, before it did, it was building up inside me during the whole fight. At first I thought it was just excitement and fear at what I was facing. But It kept on getting stronger until I pushed it out of my body."

"Did you say anything that triggered it?" asked Johnathen.

"No, it just kept building up in my body. A tingling sensation that made me itch all over. I had to get rid of it. It was driving me crazy."

"Is that when you pushed it out of your body?"

"Yes, but it was more than a push. It felt like it wanted to stay inside of me. I had to force it out of my body, and when it left my body it did exactly what I wanted it to do."

My own words shocked me. I hadn't realized that the strange feeling in me had felt this way until I described it. Johnathen stared at Fetch for a while.

"A natural magic. A forced magic," he mumbled.

He turned back to me, a very serious look on his face.

"Jack, you and Fetch are very special. There has never been anyone like the both of you. You have survived hatching, and from what you explained, you seem to be able to do some sort of natural magic. I would advise you to use your forced magic with caution. We don't yet know what it might do to you. Your ability to catch Fetch's fire shows that you have a link with him. Fetch, your ability and willingness to communicate with us is a power in itself that no other dragon has ever had. The simple fact that you have a name and that you possess the rare ability to heal with your fire makes you very special. There are not many dragons that possess that power, and I have never heard of one that has used it on a human. You are both unique to the magic world. This makes you dangerous to people. The more they find out what you can do, the more they will want to destroy you."

Chapter 15

"I don't want to hurt anyone. I just want to live my life in peace. Maybe I could get to this council you mentioned and show them I am not a threat."

"I think you should, Jack, but not just yet. With your fight in the parking lot, and the mess it caused by being filmed, I think it would be better if you stayed hidden for a while. Just until things get cleaned up. I do have an honorary seat on the council, so I can help. But I am not always happily received."

"You should be in charge of the council, with everything you have done for them," said Michelle. "If you were, you could get that fairy kicked off."

"Wait," I said, "are you telling me that there is a fairy on this magic council? I thought they were all bad."

"It's like I said, Jack, not all people in the magic world see my point of view. The fey are clever and powerful. I have argued with the council to investigate the many rumors about fairies attacking and destroying people's lives. You, Jack, are the first victim of a fey messing with someone's life, that didn't have their memory wiped. And now with your abilities, you have the chance to be accepted by the council. You could be a voice exposing the fey for what they really are. But until I can discover who else is after you, and make sure you can keep from being manipulated by the fey, you need to stay hidden, both you and Fetch."

It was a lot to take in. I seemed to be some kind of enemy number one in the magic world. It was funny when I thought about how easily everything was taken care of in the non-magic world by simply erasing the memories and fixing a few tables.

"Why wasn't my memory erased when everyone else's was?" I asked.

"They thought you were dead, Jack. You weren't added to the spell. Besides, I have a feeling that magic like that might not work on you. I mean, our unknown enemy could have easily wiped your memory making it easy to get to you. It takes a lot of magic to convince a group of goblins to work together the way they did. I can't see the sense of going to all that trouble, unless they couldn't destroy you any other way."

"Unless they were trying to test what he was capable of doing," said Michelle.

Johnathen looked at her in surprise.

"Huh. I hadn't thought of that. Yes, I guess that is a possibility."

All of this seemed so unfair to me. After all, I never asked for any of this. Now I had wizards and goblins and who knew what else after me. I had to stop myself from falling into this kind of mind set though. I realized that thinking this way wouldn't change a thing. I had to find a way to go on with my life and I needed my new friends to help me. I truly was lost in this new world.

"Okay," I said, "all of this is getting me no closer to what I need to do. If all of this magic going around is not reversible, and it isn't the right time to meet with the council, what do I do now? Where do I go?"

"You can't return home, Jack. I hate to keep repeating myself on this, but, I just want you to understand that your old life is over."

"Yes!" I shouted, "I understand that!"

I was trying to not let it all overwhelm me. I didn't mean to yell. It was just starting to annoy me when the painful truth kept on being thrown in my face.

"We are trying to help you, Jack," said Michelle.

"I know, I know." I sighed. "I'm sorry. So what do we do?"

"Well, you need a place to lay low for a while."

"We could stay at the hotel down the street from here. I used to work there. Or we could stay with you."

I was hoping Johnathen would say 'yes'. Even with Fetch in my life, I felt very alone. Having your whole life erased, even one as pathetic as mine, can have that kind of effect on you. Michelle looked hopefully at Johnathen. She wanted us to stay with them, more for the chance to get to know Fetch better, than to get to know me, I thought. I couldn't blame her for that. Johnathen shook his head.

"If you were discovered at my place, before I had a chance to find out what the council is saying about you, it could mean trouble for us all. It was hard enough to allow Michelle to keep her memories and let her become a part of the magic community. I have still had to shield her from the fey. If the fairy on the council wasn't under a spell of silence that keeps anyone on the council from discussing what goes on in the meetings, then she would have been exposed to the fey and would be in a world of hurt right now. I know it seems harsh but the further you are from me, right now, the better."

Michelle had been digging around in a strange looking pouch. She pulled out a cell phone and handed it to me.

"Here, Jack, we can stay in touch with each other this way. Then we won't draw too much attention to ourselves using the bobcats for communication."

Remembering the bobcats, a thought entered my head.

"Are you the only one to use animals for communicating?" I asked as I put the cell phone in my pocket, giving Michelle's hand a quick squeeze to let her know how grateful I was to her.

"No, a lot of wizards and other magic folk use animals the same way. Why?"

"Do you know of someone using a squirrel that way?"

I looked at Fetch who quickly looked away. The little confrontation with the squirrel in the tunnel wasn't one of our proudest moments. In fact I had kind of skipped over the whole laughing squirrel thing when I had told my story.

"No, no one that comes to mind, Jack, but again I ask why? Did someone talk to you through a squirrel the way I talked to you through my bobcats?"

"No," I said.

Both Fetch and I were avoiding looking at anyone. I really didn't want to go into too many details about our embarrassing fight, in front of Michelle. It was bad enough that she saw my clumsy attempts at fighting off Booger and the snot brigade. The whole mess in the tunnel really wasn't mine or Fetch's proudest moment.

"What are you not telling me, Jack? Everything that has happened to you is important. It could lead to a quicker end to this mess. Please tell me."

I looked at Johnathen and could tell that he was upset. Here we were becoming friends and now I left him with the idea that I didn't trust him. I looked at Fetch. The smoke was purple but he nodded 'yes'. I felt bad that I hadn't asked him before I told Johnathen so much. After all this was just as much his story as it was mine.

"Did this squirrel talk to you?" asked Johnathen.

"No," I answered, "it didn't talk. It, uh, laughed."

"Laughed?"

"Yes, it laughed at me and Fetch when we were fighting in the tunnel."

"Oh, I see," said Johnathen. "Just laughed?"

"Yes, he pointed and laughed."

"Oh well, if that was it, I doubt it was a messenger for anyone. I'll check it out to make sure, but I wouldn't worry about it. It does bring up a point though. You will begin to see things, Jack, things that were hidden from you in the past. Now that you have been touched by magic, your eyes, mind, and, most importantly, your heart, will now see what was unseen. But, just like you will be able to see many things now, many things will notice you. Fetch will be able to hide from these things, but you will not be able to on your own. So I'm going to give you a few things to help you out."

Michelle reached into her small bag again, pulling out another small bag. She handed it to Johnathen. He reached inside it, pulling out a leather choker with a teardrop-shaped piece of turquoise tied to it.

"Here," he said. "Put this on. It will hide you from people in the magic world."

"Will it make me invisible?" I asked.

"No, just overlooked. It sends out a tiny pulse that makes anyone who sees you forget that they saw you as soon as they look in your direction. It won't work on non-magic people, but with you basically being a new person, you really won't need to conceal yourself from them. Fetch, the collar I gave you in the tunnel is designed to do the same thing. I didn't know you would have your natural talent to hide yourself."

As I tied the choker around my neck, the teardrop felt warm against my skin.

"As long as it stays warm, it is working," said Johnathen. "When it gets cold, it means that it needs time to gather more magic."

Michelle pulled out a similar looking teardrop to show me that I wasn't alone in using such magic.

"Don't bump into anyone, Jack. If you make physical contact with anyone then the spell is broken and they can see you."

"Ok," I said. "This is great, but what if someone recognizes me from the video on YouTube?"

Johnathen put a hand on my shoulder and smiled. "You need to relax. Worrying about things too much isn't going to help you. All you need is a change of clothes. In a few days, when your hair starts to grow back, no one will be able to tell that you were the one in the video."

I had to laugh just a little. I mean, after all, I had dark forces who could use magic after me.

"You really think my hair and eyebrows are going to grow back?" I asked, touching my bald head.

Fetch made a coughing sound. It was so obvious he was trying not to laugh at me. I couldn't help but wonder if it was Fetch's inexperience that cost me my hair and eyebrows, or if he did it on purpose. I wouldn't put it past him, twisted lizard.

"Sure," said Johnathen. He didn't sound too convincing. "Now, let's do something about those clothes you are wearing."

He looked at me for a few minutes. He walked all around me whispering something under his breath. I felt a tugging of the sweats, and I had a moment of panic when I thought they were going to be pulled off my body, leaving me naked in front of Michelle. But instead, they began to change. It felt like they were folding upward, a kind of waving sensation, and when it reached my neck it stopped. I was now dressed in a pair of black jeans and a long sleeved, black, button up, oxford shirt. I had on black leather boots and a leather belt with a silver buckle. Michelle whistled.

"Not bad," she said, giving me an appreciative nod.

The clothes fit well and made me feel a lot better about my appearance. I smelled a faint odor of cologne and realized that Johnathen had cleaned me up a bit, as well as changed my clothes. A part of me wondered why he couldn't have done that in the tunnel when I was left naked, but I was too grateful to him for all he was doing to say anything.

Johnathen looked at me for a moment. With another wave of his hand, and a whispered word, a bandana appeared on my head. Another wave of his hand and sunglasses appeared. I couldn't see the bandanna, but I figured it was black. It seemed to be a theme for Johnathen. He smiled, a little pleased with himself.

"Now, Jack, for some real magic," he said with a crooked smile and a gleam in his eyes.

He took the pouch in his right hand and passed his left hand over it. Reaching in, he pulled out a red box and a flat metal rectangle about the size of a credit card. The red wooden box was the amazing part of the trick. It was too big for the pouch, yet somehow, Johnathen had pulled it through. He set the box on the table and handed me the metal card.

"This has a special spell placed on it. Michelle helped me come up with it. It is a universal I.D. card. If you are ever in a place where you are asked to show your identification, hand them this. It sends out a pulse that convinces them that it is a real I.D. It will give whoever touches it a feeling of peace and will reassure them that you are ok."

"It's gotten me out of a traffic ticket or two," said Michelle.

She was holding up a similar card. She had a guilty smile on her face. I took the card from Johnathen and put it in my back pocket. Johnathen walked over to the duffle bag, waving a hand over the top. It opened and all of the money began to flow out of it. It flew around Johnathen's head before it began to disappear into the small pouch. In just a few seconds, all of the money had disappeared into the tiny pouch.

"Show off," said Michelle.

Johnathen laughed, handing me the pouch.

"Reach inside and pull out some money," he said.

I took the pouch expecting it to be heavy. It had no weight to it at all. I reached inside it. I could only get about three fingers in it. I touched the bottom of it, not even able to get my fingers in very deep. It was just an empty pouch.

"Ok, what's the trick?"

Johnathen smiled. There was a gleam in his eyes. He was enjoying showing off.

"Just picture what you want to pull out of the pouch. Make sure you have a clear image of it. It helps to close your eyes and get the image first, until you get the hang of it. Then just reach in and pull it out."

I closed my eyes for a second, getting an image of a hand full of cash. When I felt I had a good picture in my mind, I opened my eyes and reached into the pouch. My whole hand fit inside. It wasn't like the pouch had grown, but more like my hand had shrunk. It was the strangest feeling. I quickly pulled my hand out holding a wad of cash.

"You'll get used to it," said Michelle. "It's just one of the things that people use in the magic community."

I had to start getting used to all of this. It was now my life. I placed an image in my mind of me putting the money back into the pouch, and reached inside again letting go of the cash. I made a point of slowly pulling my hand out, not wanting to appear too freaked out by the strange sensation.

"Now, Jack, I have one more gift for you."

He reached over and picked up the red box. Michelle had stopped working on her computer and was watching me very closely. She seemed to have an idea as to what was in this red box. I got the impression she was very interested in my reaction to this last gift. Johnathen opened the box. Inside was a dagger. It was silver and covered with strange symbols. At the base of the hilt was a blood red jewel. The dagger was long and sharp on both sides. Lying next to it was a leather sheath.

"This is a very special dagger, Jack. It is very rare. Not many like them. This dagger is one of the few things that can kill a fey."

My heart went cold as Johnathen's words sank in. I had realized that I was in danger. I knew that my battle in the parking lot could have ended up with someone getting hurt, or worse, but what Johnathen seemed to be suggesting was a little too much for me. I backed away from the box, not wanting to touch the dagger. I shook my head to let Johnathen know I wouldn't take it. As I backed away from it, I continued to stare at it. It was one thing to defend myself against goblins and learn to protect myself from any more fey attacks. But, I felt that taking the dagger meant that Johnathen expected me to go after the fairy and kill her. Even knowing that she wanted to kill me, even knowing that my life was erased because of her, the idea of killing her was beyond me. I was not the same person I was just a short twenty-four hours ago, but I just couldn't see myself as a killer.

"Jack, this is just for your protection. Please take it. If you are ever in a situation where you come across a fairy, just them seeing the dagger will stop them from getting too close. Just touching it could kill them. Use it as a last resort and only as a last resort. Having this kind of protection will make me feel better when I'm not around."

"Go ahead, Jack. Please take it," said Michelle, "just in case. We just want to protect you. I would hate it if you got hurt."

I looked over at Fetch. He was staring at me, his eyes green. He didn't move a muscle. I got the idea that he didn't want to give me any idea as to what to do. This had to be my decision and mine alone, whether to take the dagger or not. I reached into the box and pulled it out. My heart was pounding out of my chest as I slid the dagger into the sheath, and then stuffed the thing into the pouch. I looked at Johnathen. At that a moment he looked old. It was like seeing behind the young and carefree veil he had set up in his life. I could see sadness and pain in his eyes. Only someone who has been through a lot, who has lost a lot, can have that kind of look. In that moment it struck me how old Johnathen must be. I couldn't even guess at his age, but I knew he was very old.

"I gave you the dagger, with the hope that you never have to use it, Jack. I am hoping that if you are in a situation involving the fey, you will show them that you have the dagger. Just seeing it will discourage them from attacking you."

"I won't kill anyone." I said. "I don't think it is in me."

I felt as old and tired as Johnathen looked. It was getting harder for me to accept that any of this was real. I just didn't want to accept that I might even have to look like I was willing to kill anyone. A thought of the destruction that I was a part of in the battle in the parking lot went through my mind. For the first time I wondered if I had killed any of the goblins. The thought made my skin crawl.

"Do you think I killed any of those goblins?"

"I don't think so, Jack. They are a pretty tough race. I think you hurt them pretty good. They have been used in many wars. They create chaos, as you saw. But you have nothing to feel bad about, Jack. You were trying to save yourself and all of those witnesses."

Johnathen's words made me feel a little better. But I remembered how angry I had gotten, and I couldn't get the idea out of my head that I was just lucky no one got hurt. I made a promise not to let myself get that angry again. With all I seemed to be able to do now, the last thing I wanted was to lose control. Johnathen put his arm on my shoulder. He looked young again.

"You and Fetch have been through a lot in just a day. I would like to tell you that it will all be smooth sailing from now on, but I would be lying. This is a time of change in the magic world, Jack, and you and Fetch are a big part of that change. Some people say there is a war coming. One that will shake the very foundation of the earth. I am trying to keep that from happening."

"What do I do now?" I asked, my frustration starting to show.

"For now, I think you and Fetch need to find time to get used to your new life. Check into a room at the hotel. Michelle and I will keep in touch. We need to go for now. At times I am watched and I don't want them to figure out that I have found you just yet. We will find time to go out and see just what you can do with your forced magic. For now just try to enjoy yourself a little. Take some time to observe the new magic world around you. The teardrop will allow you to do this unseen. I promise you both that I will find a way for you to become a part of the magic world, without people fearing you. Don't worry yourself over the unknown person that sent the goblins to attack you. The teardrop will protect you from them as well. You have a very unique opportunity to observe and learn without being seen Jack."

I felt a rush of gratitude for both Michelle and Johnathen. They had already done so much for me. I was grateful. It seemed like they were taking a big risk in doing all of this.

"Now that you have changed your clothes, Jack, you really can't tell you are the same person as the one in the video," said Michelle, "and with a little visit to a friend, it will be off the web and considered a fake in no time."

I smiled in gratitude. I was very tired and hungry, so it was getting a little hard to concentrate on what she was saying. Fetch had stayed quiet during all of this. His eyes had stayed green and he had watched all of us in turn. He seemed to be studying us, trying to get his own grasp on everything that was going on. I looked at him and realized that decisions were made and plans discussed that involved him, without any of us asking his opinion. For all I knew, Fetch might not want to hang around with me anymore.

"So, Fetch," I said, "you want to hang around with me? At least until we get this mess cleaned up?"

Fetch looked at me for a second. He walked around me like he was giving me the once over. I knew he was just showing off for Michelle. He sat in front of me and with a much exaggerated sigh nodded his head 'yes'.

A feeling of relief washed over me. Even though it had only been a day since I had known him, and all the mixed feelings I had about his involvement, about how my life had been turned upside-down, at that moment I couldn't imagine going through any of this without him.

"Great," said Johnathen. "Well, I guess we had better get started now."

With a wave of his hand, the field around the ramada dissolved. The sun was nice and bright and made me squint. I saw a small child playing catch with his dad do a double take as Fetch went into camouflaged mode. He didn't time it right, and, judging how the boy was pointing and jumping up and down, I had the idea that he had seen a glimpse of Fetch. I nodded my head in the kid's direction.

"Should you pulse him?" I asked, hoping that was the right terminology for erasing someone's memory.

"No, it was just a glimpse. He will remember this day and, who knows, he might write about it and become the next great fantasy novelist of his generation. That is something that has happened throughout time, Jack. Even the greatest of magic users, and the most powerful spells, can slip at times. I think you might be surprised as to who have seen glimpses of the magic world. As long as stories are perceived as fantasy or fairy tales then it is usually allowed."

"But there have been times in history when man has believed in magic. There has to be a time when both worlds were aware of each other."

"Yes, but that time passed. A terrible spell was cast that caused a lot of things to die. It was a long time ago and that was when the magic world started to separate itself from the non-magic world. It's a long story. I will have to tell you about it sometime."

We had been walking up to the limo while we were talking. I could hear birds from the zoo and smell the different animals as they began their early morning stirring, waiting to be fed. As we approached the limo, the sound of the animals died down. I wondered how those animals would react if they could see or sense Fetch. I made a note to myself not to visit the zoo with Fetch.

We walked the rest of the way to the limo in silence. This was going to be goodbye for a while, and I wasn't ready for that. It was a little strange to me how, in just a short amount of time, I felt so close to these people. I was closer to them than people I had known my entire life. After all, now that my life had been erased, these new friends were the only friends I truly had now. This thought weighed heavy on my heart as we all stood in front of the limo. People were looking at us. After all, you don't see a stretch limo at the park in Tucson a lot. I wondered where Johnathen got the limo. With his gift to me of seven million dollars, it seemed obvious that he was rich. I had no idea what a wizard could do to gain such wealth, or why he would even need it. I didn't feel this was the time to ask.

"Well, Jack," said Johnathen cheerfully. "I guess this is goodbye for now. I know you still have a lot of questions, but they will have to be answered over time, as my questions will have to be answered over time. Fetch, take care of our friend."

Michelle wrapped her arms around me, kissing me on the cheek.

"I'll text you with my number. Let me know what room you are in. I'll stop by tonight and we will go out to dinner."

I smiled as a feeling of relief washed over me. I was not expecting to see her so soon. Fetch's silver scales shimmered for a second and a puff of purple smoke floated upward. Looking at me, Michelle spoke to Fetch.

"I would give you a hug, Fetch, but I am afraid that would draw too much attention to you."

She let out a little gasp of surprise as Fetch, unseen, moved over and nudged her hand gently with his snout. She reached over and petted his invisible head. She had tears of joy in her eyes, and a smile that could light up a room. I looked at her tattoo again and knew how much meeting a dragon must mean to her. She turned around going to the front of the limo and got in the driver's seat. She started the car and waited for Johnathen to get in.

Johnathen shook my hand while looking me in the eyes. "You truly are unique, Jack. The both of you will change history in the magic world."

I let go of Johnathen's hand and dropped my eyes to the ground. I didn't want that kind of responsibility. Once again I found myself thinking of how unfair this all was. I never asked for it.

Johnathen smiled. "Don't get too down, Jack. I know I painted a pretty dark picture. But there is a light at the end of the tunnel."

"Yeah," I said. "A light and a laughing squirrel."

Johnathen burst into laughter at this. He opened the door to the limo.

"Michelle will see you tonight. I will have to wait until I am sure someone is not watching me. If you need to talk, let Michelle know and I will send out one of my bobcats. Keep thinking positive thoughts. Good thoughts have a strength that most people are not aware of. They can help you with your magic."

He got into the limo and Michelle pulled slowly away. She had rolled her window down and was waving frantically at us. I stood there watching the limo drive away and soon it was out of sight. I stood there staring at the road it had gone down and felt alone. Fetch nudged my hand letting me know that I wasn't.

"Well, Fetch, first things first," I said trying to sound cheerful. "I'm hungry. Let's get something to eat."

A growl from Fetch, followed by a flash of scales, led me to believe that he was hungry too. We walked slowly out of the park.

Chapter 16

Growing up in this area gave me a good idea as to what was around here. We had crossed a street to a fast-food place. I could smell the sausage biscuits and fresh brewed coffee, making my mouth water. Fetch had stayed on the ground, walking by my side, the whole time. I was grateful for this. As long as he was around, I knew I wouldn't feel completely alone. I whispered to him hoping that no one else would hear.

"You want some sausage biscuits?"

A gruff 'Huh' sound let me know he did. Fetch stayed outside as I walked in. I felt a little exposed at first, but, I noticed no lingering looks in my direction as I walked up to the counter. I knew that my all black look would draw a little attention to me. The head band and sunglasses had to make me look like a guy who might try to rob the place. I thought about taking them off, but I remembered my eyebrows and decided to leave them on. Ignoring the looks I was getting I walked up to the counter.

The girl behind the register smiled at me. This helped me relax a little. I smiled back.

"May I help you?" she asked.

I froze. I had no idea how much Fetch could eat. I realized that this was going to be something I was going to have to think about from now on, unless I depended on Fetch to get us food. I still hadn't figured out how he was doing that task without drawing too much attention to himself.

"Uh, this is going to be a big order, " I said. "I'm getting food for a lot of guys."

As soon as I said it, I knew I was going overboard with my explanation. This was still new to me. I really didn't know how to handle ordering food for a dragon. I figured ordering twenty sausage biscuits would be a good start. If we were still hungry after that, then we could go down the road a little way and get more food at another place. I ordered the twenty biscuits and one cup of coffee. The girl gave me a surprised look. I just glanced at her thinking what would happen if I tried to explain why only one drink with such a big order. I wondered to myself if Fetch would drink coffee. Something else to discover.

It didn't take as long as I thought it would for the order to be ready. I had reached into my pocket, and into the pouch, keeping an image of a hundred-dollar bill in my mind. I pulled it out pleased with myself at how easy it was to do this. I paid and, not waiting for the change, walked out the door. I tried to decide if we should go back to the park or sit at one of the tables outside the restaurant. I didn't want people seeing food just disappear as Fetch ate in camouflage mode.

Fetch was growling. I saw the ripple of his silver scales and I knew he was trying to warn me. I looked all around, expecting to see Booger or another blue ball that would transport more nasty's to attack me, when I spotted it. It was the ugliest thing I had ever seen. It was grey all over and fat. Large boils were covering its body, all of which seemed to have a white pus-filled head. It sat on its enormous butt, its feet sticking out in front of it. It didn't have any clothes on. I dropped the bag of biscuits and reached for the turquoise necklace. I hoped it hadn't noticed me yet. Fighting Booger was bad enough, but the thought of touching this pus-filled monster was enough to make me sick. As I touched the stone, I felt a tingling sensation all over my body. I prayed that this meant that it was working.

Blobby was sitting next to the dumpster. It was twice as big as the dumpster and smelled twice as bad. It was reaching inside the dumpster and absentmindedly pulling out handfuls of garbage, stuffing it into its mouth. It reminded me of someone watching a movie and eating popcorn. It never bothered looking to see what it was eating. It just kept stuffing its mouth with whatever it pulled out. It stared off into space and every once in a while its bloodshot eyes would roll back in its head giving me the distinct idea that it was really enjoying its meal. If I wasn't so shocked at the very sight of this thing, I would have been sick.

Thinking that I couldn't be surprised anymore, I got another shock as a little creature with big pointy ears and a tail stepped out of the bushes. It was wearing an oversized purple sweat shirt with a hood. Its tail dragged along the ground and its face reminded me of 'Droopy Dog'. It shook its head, obviously upset at the sight of the blob. It started to make a hissing sound waving its arms from side to side. It couldn't be more than two feet tall. Blobby could have squashed it like a bug but instead it continued to move toward Blobby hissing and waving its arms. Blobby started to eat faster still staring off into space. As Tiny got close Blobby stopped eating. Looking at Tiny waving its skinny arms in the air, Blobby let out a big sigh and slowly got to its feet. Looking down one last time at Tiny, Blobby let out another sigh and surprisingly, for its enormous size, quietly walked away. Tiny watched Blobby walk away and then turned and started to walk back to the bushes. It stopped for a second looking in my direction. It blinked its enormous black eyes and shook its head like it had seen me for a second, and then with a sigh as big as Blobby's turned and disappeared into the bushes.

I stood there for a second, not even daring to breathe. Fetch nudged my hand, letting me know I could move again.

"That was the freakiest thing I have ever seen," I whispered to Fetch.

There was a little puff of purple smoke from Fetch's nostrils as an answer that he agreed with me. Somehow, I had kept from spilling my coffee. I picked up the bag of food and started walking down the side of the road, choosing to go in the opposite direction from Blobby. I remembered that Johnathen had told me I would be seeing things from the magical world now. I realized once again how much my world had changed. I pulled out the phone that Michelle had given me and texted a simple message.

"U wouldn't believe what I just saw...I don't even know how to describe it."

She texted back, "try me☺."

After I texted a brief description, she texted me, "Troll, they like garbage, gnomes, they are like the janitors of the magic world. Any damage caused by magic, they are the ones that clean it up."

"Well that explains why there was no damage at the store."

"Did you use the stone to hide?"

"Yes"

"Good. Get used to this Jack. You have been touched by magic. You will start seeing all that was hidden before. Welcome to the magic world hope you enjoy the ride. ☺"

We made our way over to the hotel near the park. It was a strange experience standing there looking at the hotel. I had worked there a few years ago, and, as I stood at the lobby doors, I had a pang of regret for the loss of my old life. For the first time that day, Fetch took flight as I walked into the lobby of the hotel to check in. I didn't want to take the chance of him bumping into someone or someone bumping into him in the lobby. He grumbled and growled a little, not wanting to leave me alone, but he understood why it was necessary.

Once again, it struck me how young Fetch really was. He had hatched only the day before and was already doing amazing things. In a way, he seemed to be much older than I. It was a strange thought to grasp that we were so close. I guess in a way I owed him my life. I knew that it wasn't his fault that he hatched, using me as an energy source to come into this world. I didn't fully understand that whole thing. The thought that he was supposed to eat me seemed ridiculous to me now. Fetch and I were connected.

All these thoughts ran quickly through my mind as I walked up to the counter. The man, checking people in, gave me a strange look. Walking around dressed the way I was, all in black with a bandanna on my head, is one thing, but, in a place like this hotel, I must have looked a little intimidating. Once again I wondered if people thought I was going to rob the place. I knew I was going to have to get new clothes to wear soon. I took a chance whipping off the sunglasses. The man immediately noticed my lack of eyebrows. He placed a hand under the counter. I figured his finger was on some kind of silent alarm button. I couldn't blame him, the way I looked. Adding the fact that I was about to ask for a room by the pool for a week, without having any luggage, and the alarm bell might go off in my mind too.

I didn't think he was going to get me a room until he asked to see my driver's license. I handed him the blank plastic card that Johnathen had given me and watched as his eyes glazed over when he looked at it. His whole face relaxed and he smiled pleasantly. He took back the clipboard with the information card on it that I had yet to fill out. He glanced down at it as if I had.

"Welcome, Mr. DeWitte," he said pleasantly. "How long will you be staying with us?"

I told him a week and paid cash for the room. He gave me the hotel spiel and told me if I needed anything to let him know. He handed back the card and for a second had a confused look on his face. His eyes glazed over again and he smiled and asked if I needed any help with my bags. I told him no. I looked at him for a second, not knowing if he was going to be ok or not. I told myself I would come back later and check on him. There was more to that plastic card than Johnathen had told me. That seemed to be the norm for him. I felt uncomfortable manipulating anybody the way the guy behind the counter was. It didn't seem right. If this was what magic was all about I wasn't sure I wanted any part of it. I knew a thought like that was silly. I was now a part of it whether I liked it or not.

I went outside and met Fetch. He flashed his silver scales to let me know where he was. He seemed to be getting better at controlling when his scales would flash. We walked around the hotel to our outside room by the swimming pool.

I was glad that Fetch was only the size of a German shepherd. Any bigger and I don't think we could have maneuvered around to our room, without knocking something or someone over. When we got into the room, Fetch got out of camo mode and stretched. He looked tired. As far as I could tell, he hadn't slept at all since he hatched. I at least had passed out a few times. Not necessarily a good night's sleep, but it was something. I stretched myself and felt a familiar twinge in my hip.

"Well what do you know?" I said. "I still have my hip problems. Guess your fire couldn't heal previous injuries."

Fetch just gave me a tired look and yawned, showing rows and rows of sharp teeth. I lay down on the bed taking out the cell phone. I texted my room number to Michelle. She responded with a smiley face and a promise to see me tonight.

I was hungry again. This worried me a little. I seemed to get hungry frequently. I had never been a big eater but now I couldn't get enough. Ordering room service, and a couple of large pizzas from a nearby pizza delivery, barely seemed to fill me up. Fetch had drifted off to sleep and now, with a little more food in my stomach, I decided to join him. Lying on top of the bed, not even bothering taking my clothes off, I drifted into a much needed dreamless slumber.

Chapter 17

I woke up to the sound of someone knocking on my door. I jumped up and, stumbling over Fetch's tail, made my way to the door. I looked in the spyhole and saw it was Michelle. I felt like I had just shut my eyes, but it was already night and Michelle was at my door. I opened it and she quickly stepped in giving me a hug and a kiss on the cheek.

"You look like you just got up," she said with a smile.

She threw herself on the bed. Fetch had woken up and was enjoying being scratched under his chin. I yawned and stretched. I caught a glimpse of myself in the mirror. My bandanna had fallen off and my bald head seemed to glow in the light of the hotel lamp. I put my hands on my head as my face got red. Michelle had thrown the bandana at me. I caught it, let out a little "thank you" and began to put it on my head.

"You know. I think you look better without it," she said.

"Really?" I couldn't think anyone would be serious about me looking ok without hair. My head was shaped a little weird. One of my nicknames growing up was peanut head. The idea that I looked good bald was one I wasn't sure I wanted to believe.

"Trust me."

She got up and walked over taking the bandana out of my hands. She stuffed it into her pocket. I looked at myself in the mirror. I figured she knew what she was talking about, besides, I had to get used to the idea that I might never have hair again. I forced myself to look away from the mirror and the shiny head that seemed to stare back at me. Michelle had pulled out her laptop.

"I wanted to show you guys something. There has been a lot of talk about your fight." She motioned me to come over and sit next to her. Fetch sat on one side and I sat on the other. The video was playing, to my embarrassment, but then the headline appeared over it.

"Trying to find the film maker of this new popular video. People want the creator's new special effects system."

I looked at Michelle. "Everyone thinks it's a fake?"

"Yup. We are still working on getting it taken off completely, but it seems like people are not taking it too seriously."

It was the best news I could think of, one thing I could check off my list to not worry about. Fetch blew purple smoke in mine and Michelle's faces, showing that he was pleased too. The smoke made Michelle cough a little. I breathed it in with no problems. In fact, I realized that Fetch's smoke never bothered me. I had always been sensitive to smoke. If I was around people smoking long enough, my eyes would begin to water and I would definitely cough. I wondered if it was just Fetch's smoke now or all smoke no longer bothered me. Just one more change in me. I was beginning to feel like a superhero. This was my origin story and Fetch was my sidekick. No, wait, not my sidekick, my partner. This thought made me smile.

Seeing the smoke curl up from Fetch's snout got me a little worried. I jumped up and looked around the room. I spotted the smoke detector on the wall over the television. I jumped up on the dresser and removed the battery before it could go off. Michelle smiled.

"Good thinking, Jack."

Fetch nodded his head reluctantly. I was getting the impression that he was not happy with the attention that Michelle was giving me. After sitting around for a few minutes in silence, Michelle spoke up.

"Hey let's go down to the restaurant in front of the hotel. I saw it had a patio so Fetch can easily sit out there and we can enjoy it together."

"Sounds great," I said.

It didn't matter to me if we stayed in the room or went out. In fact, I was enjoying being able to sit in the room quietly. It was a new experience for me to have a friend like Michelle, who I felt comfortable enough with to sit in a room without saying anything, but Fetch's tail was twitching at the idea of getting out of the room. He was only about the size of a German shepherd and the room was really big, but with all of us in there it seemed a little cramped. I wondered if Fetch would get any bigger. If he did, we wouldn't be able to stay in hotels for long. I looked at myself in the mirror, mostly at my bald head. I guess I looked ok. I mean, I still had no eyebrows, but, without the sunglasses and the black bandanna, I didn't look as intimidating. I didn't want to deal with people wondering if I was going to rob them every time they looked at me.

We walked around the outside of the hotel and around to the patio of the restaurant. Choosing a table in the corner, I sat down with Fetch as Michelle went inside to let them know we were there.

"It's nice to have a friend like her," I said to Fetch.

His scales flashed silver in agreement.

Michelle came back with some menus, and a waiter in tow behind her. At the sight of me, the waiter's face fell. I guess he was expecting another girl out here instead of me. Boy, I thought if Fetch showed himself to this guy he would really be disappointed. I looked at Michelle and began chuckling. She began to laugh too. She must have gotten some idea as to why I was laughing. Soon we were both laughing uncontrollably as the server stood there with a puzzled look on his face. We got ourselves under control and looked at the menu. In the silence that followed, Fetch let out a loud growl just for fun.

"My," said the server, "someone here is hungry."

Of course the sound of the growl could have been confused as being some other sound than a stomach. His face was red, giving away his thought process. This got us laughing again and soon the server himself had joined us. I could hear the gruff laughter of Fetch and his all too familiar "huh" sound that seemed to come with his laughter.

We calmed down and decided to order. We got our drinks first. The server got the strangest look on his face when I ordered three sodas at one time. I was obviously ordering for myself and Fetch. This sent Michelle into a fit of giggles. She ordered an ice tea and asked for five straws, which got Fetch and I laughing again. The server left to get us our drinks as we continued to giggle and chuckle. I was afraid he wouldn't come back, but soon he appeared with our drinks. He made sure there were five straws in Michelle's ice tea.

Ordering appetizers became a bit of an ordeal. Michelle left the ordering up to me as I was not just ordering for me, but for Fetch as well. I read down the list of appetizers to see what Fetch might like, reading the description of the ones that Fetch might not know. He would let me know what he wanted in true Fetch form by smacking me in the back of the head with his tail. It had to be the strangest sight; me reading the menu out loud and my head bobbing forward before I ordered something. I was enjoying hearing Michelle laugh and giggle too much to be really upset at Fetch. After ordering three orders of boneless wings (hot, mild, and barbeque), two orders of cheese sticks, and a super nacho with extra chicken, I turned to Michelle, and, as straight faced as I could, asked, "What are you going to get?"

This started her giggling again. The server gave us the 'heard that one before' look, which quickly turned into a look of surprise when Michelle ordered a small cheese crisp. After another surprising order of two double bacon cheeseburgers with fries and a side of coleslaw, a large chicken finger basket, and a chicken Caesar salad, the server turned and slowly walked away.

"We're never going to get our food," said Michelle. "Did you see the way he was looking at us?"

"Nah, we'll get it. He's already got a great story to tell the rest of the servers. You wait and see, he'll be sending out other servers to look at us. It's kind of the way it is with servers. I used to work in the restaurant in this hotel a few years ago. They had a contest over who had the most interesting table. I have a feeling, on a slow night like tonight, we are definitely in the running."

"That's right. I remember you saying something about growing up around here."

"Yeah, I went to elementary school not too far from here. I wasn't very well liked."

I flashed on the memory of my nightmare. In real life, Ms. Rose stopped the others before they peed on me, not the best memory of my childhood. Michelle reached out and grabbed my hand.

"What's it like, Jack? What's it like when you use your magic?"

I was relieved by the change of subject. It was still too early to talk much about my past. My life had already changed so much in just a day. I wasn't ready to really chase the past.

"It feels like an itch that you just can't get to," I said, trying to get a clear image of what it was like. "When it is released, it really takes a lot out of me. It is almost like it's torn out of me, but it has to go somewhere. The feeling as it builds up is just too much, too uncomfortable to stay, so I just force it out of me."

I realized how the explanation sounded, but it was very hard to explain what it was like. Johnathen had called it a natural magic, whatever that meant. All I knew is that it wasn't the most pleasant feeling. I could tell that Michelle was expecting more of an answer.

"Sorry," I said, "it's all new to me. I wish I could explain it better, but that is the best I can do."

She shook her head. I could tell that she understood, but I also saw her disappointment at the lack of explanation.

"You want to hear a secret?"

I looked up to see a mischievous look on her face. There was a gleam in her eyes and the way she asked the question had Fetch and I, both, leaning in closer to her. Fetch bumped the table causing one of the sodas to fall. Michelle twisted her hand and said a word under her breath. The glass stopped in midair and all of the soda filled up the glass again. It hung there in the air for a second and then Michelle grabbed it and set it back on the table. Fetch went visible for a second before getting control over himself. Michelle put the glass back on the table. She had a proud smile on her face.

"Not necessarily the way I wanted to tell you, but, as you can see, Johnathen has been teaching me magic."

"But, I thought that people from the non-magic world couldn't do any real magic."

"Most of the time that is right, but, Johnathen figures I have elf blood in me from a long ago ancestor, that gives me a chance to do magic. It was a one in a million shot that I would be able to do it, but, as you can see, I can."

I wondered why Johnathen didn't tell me about Michelle learning magic. In fact, the way he talked, it was like an impossibility. This made things more confusing than ever.

"So, you were actually part of the magic world, but you just didn't know it?"

"Yeah, funny huh? There are a lot of people out there that are part elf or dwarf or even fairy."

At the mention of the word fairy, Michelle's face went dark for a second. She snapped out of it, smiled, and went on talking.

"Most can't do magic. That is why they are kept from the magic world. Johnathen fought to get me into the community. It wasn't until later that I discovered that I had magical ability. I'll never be as great at it as Johnathen or you, but I can do pretty well in my own right. It was my magic that helped develop the box I use to get Wi-Fi on my computer. I have to keep my magic abilities a secret. The council would never allow it. They barely tolerate me as it is."

I had so many questions to ask, but, before I could, our appetizers came. I looked up as a pretty girl was serving the food. I knew her. I used to work with her at the hotel.

"Jenny!" I said. "Wow. You're still here? How are you?"

Jenny looked at me blankly. For a second I had forgotten that anyone who knew me before, now had no memory of whom I was. She smiled and gave a nervous little laugh. Obviously our server had told her about us crazy people on the patio.

"I'm sorry, do I know you?"

"No, I guess not," I said.

Jenny gave another nervous laugh. She was so nice to me when I worked there, always smiling and giving out hugs. She even tried to set me up with a friend of hers, once. She was going to be one of the people that I was going to miss not knowing me. I had to get used to this.

Jenny made a hasty retreat from the table. I looked down at the food. All of a sudden, I didn't seem so hungry anymore. I looked up at Michelle. She had tears in her eyes. I realized she was the only person in the world who could possibly know what I was going through. She began to speak.

"I was just a little girl when it happened. I was out at the mall. It was the first time my parents let me go on my own. I met my best friend, Lisa, at the mall. My parents' tattoo shop was across the street. We were going to get some makeup. There was a loud explosion outside and from the doors of the mall you could see smoke. It actually blew out a couple of windows. I remember my friend screaming my name as I ran out the door. I knew, somehow, I knew that my family was in trouble. I ran out into the parking lot and saw that the whole row of buildings across the street was destroyed. I ran to the rubble that used to be my parents' shop screaming for my mom and dad, for my brother. I don't even know how I got across the street. I ran up to the shop, still screaming and saw their bodies." She choked on the word 'bodies'.

"Please, Michelle," I said. "You don't have to tell me if you don't want to."

"But, I do want to tell you, Jack," she said. "I want you and Fetch to know. When I found their bodies, and tried to get to them, there was a terrible sound, like glass breaking, and a blinding flash of light. I felt a strange pain behind my eyes and I passed out. When I woke up, Johnathen was holding me. The store and the other buildings were repaired and I had a broken arm. My head hurt and I had trouble focusing. You should have seen Johnathen then, Jack. Long hair, full robe, he even had a staff. He looked like a wizard out of a book. I guess you could say I changed him. He wanted to be a part of the regular world. He didn't want there to be any separation between the two. He feels that if both non-magic and magic users were aware of each other, then tragedies, like what happened to my family, would become a thing of the past. I saw my friend, Lisa, a few weeks later. She didn't know who I was. That was one of the hardest things I went through. I know what you are going through, Jack, I really do."

She had tears in her eyes. I wanted to know more but I didn't want to push her to talk. I was embarrassed at how I had been acting and feeling. She had been through so much. In the end, I really didn't have much to complain about.

"Come on, Jack, let's eat. Fetch is getting hungry."

In response to those words, Fetch grabbed a chicken finger and smacked it down in one bite.

The rest of the night was dedicated to laughter and fun. We talked about the city that we both grew up in and all of our favorite places to go. We watched food and soda disappear into the air as Fetch ate and drank in camo mode. I found out that Michelle went to school and graduated at fifteen and that her tattoo was a gift from Johnathen.

"I have been going in and getting it worked on for two years," she said. "I am almost done."

I started to spread the money around that Johnathen gave me, tipping every server that came out to refill a drink order or clear a plate. One server dropped a tray of drinks as Fetch, trying to get Michelle to laugh, picked up a glass and drank down the soda with a straw. I quickly explained to the server that I was an amateur magician and handed her a fifty-dollar bill. She smiled and made a quick retreat.

We ended the meal with chocolate malts. I ordered one and Fetch let me know he wanted one by slamming his tail on the table. This made the server jump. We got the malts and were quietly enjoying them, when I spotted the bobcat. It was across the street, on the bike path, at the park. It was just sitting there staring at us. I pointed at him and Michelle waved. I waved too and Fetch flashed his silver scales. The bobcat did a double back flip in response to our waving and disappeared into the park.

"He told me he would be checking up on us," said Michelle.

"I wish he could have joined us," I said

"Me too, but he is so busy. He never seems to sleep. He is constantly trying to find the missing dragons and he can disappear for days at a time. I can honestly say that I know him better than anyone, but at times he is a mystery to me. He can get in these dark moods and go for a day or two without saying a word. But, I think me being around him for the past ten years or so have loosened him up a bit. You should have seen the look on his face when I bought him his first pair of jeans. He wanted to start interacting with the non-magic world and I told him that he wasn't going to get very far wearing robes and carrying a staff. There are those in the magic world that have changed with the times and adjusted to styles and some technology, but Johnathen had to be dragged into a T-shirt and jeans, kicking and screaming. I introduced him to Heavy Metal music and he really liked that, but he still is very resistant to computers. I have almost talked him into a Facebook page."

"Why do people in the magic world have such a problem with technology?"

"Not all tech is confusing to them, but computers are. I think it's because it is in a state of constant change. For centuries they have been using magic the same way. A spell that a wizard cast two hundred years ago, to make a light, is the same one used today. I think, for a lot of them, it is a tradition thing and they are just being stubborn. But, I have found a few people that can do it. It at least gives some of them a means of communicating behind the backs of fairies and other traditionalists who won't even look at a computer."

At the mention of fairies Michelle's face went dark again. It seemed to be a trigger word for her.

"So, what kind of magic people have you met?" I asked, wanting to keep her away from the dark mood that even mentioning fairies seemed to put her in.

Her face lit up a bit at this. "I have met a gnome or two. I have seen trolls. For a while, when I was younger, I had a golem nanny who took care of me when Johnathen wasn't around. I saw a unicorn in Johnathen's courtyard and I have taught basic computer skills to a few elves. Johnathen has kept me away from a lot of the magic world. There are those who, I guess, don't want me around. But, now that you are around, the people like me, the forgotten ones with magic ancestors, have a better chance of being accepted. If I can be accepted, I can go to the council myself and plead my case and get those responsible for my family's death brought to justice."

There was a fiery gleam in her eyes as she said this.

"I have been sheltered from the magic world in a lot of ways, Jack. There has been a time or two that I have wanted to take off my teardrop and expose myself to the magic world, just to see what would happen. But, that might undermine all of Johnathen's work. It's not so bad, though. I have free reign in the non-magic world, and, with the magic that I am learning, it is like a dream come true."

It was easy to see how happy Michelle was to have someone to talk to about all of this. I guess she never had anyone to whom to tell her story. I was beginning to have my doubts about the magic world. It seemed that there were prejudices against non-magic people. I hoped that I could meet and get to know other magic creatures and talk to them one day. I wanted to do more than be an observer and keep hidden all my life. After all, with the memory of anybody knowing me erased, there wasn't much of a chance of me fitting back into the real world, especially if Fetch was going to hang around with me.

With a loud slurp Fetch finished his malt. The server came back to the table with the check and after paying, and leaving a hefty tip, we started to walk back to the room. I was very tired by then. It was hard to wrap my mind around the fact of how much my life had changed in just a little more than one day. We made it back to the room. With a quick hug and a kiss on the cheek for me and for Fetch, Michelle said her goodbyes.

"I'll come back in a few days, Jack. I know that Johnathen wants to take you out to the desert, to see what you can do, and to see if you have gained any new abilities. You should rest up, both of you."

It felt good to have a friend that seemed to care so much for me. I gave her a hug and a returned kiss on the cheek, earning me a smack with Fetch's tail. I didn't care though, it was worth it. After reassurances, to both of us, that she would be fine, and a promise of a text from her when she got home, we watched her walk away. When she was out of sight, we went back into the room.

It really hit me how tired I was when I walked in the room. I plopped down on the bed and turned on the television. I scanned the news for any mention of the YouTube video. Nothing was said about it. I knew I needed to get a computer so I could keep track of those kind of things. A seed of an idea was forming in my mind, and I knew I needed a computer to get it going. I also needed to get more clothes. I couldn't keep wearing the same dark clothes Johnathen had made for me. I was making a mental list of what to get tomorrow. There was an excited element to all of this. How many people get the opportunity to change their lives overnight? Add a magical element to that question, and I was sure that everyone out there, at one time or another in their lives, wished or fantasized about something similar to what I was going through. Yes, there was sadness, and a definite element of danger, but still, here in my comfortable hotel room, fed and relaxing on the bed, I couldn't help but feel the adventure. And, to top it all off, I had just had dinner with a very pretty girl. I knew that I could never have a relationship with Michelle, but it was enough that she was a friend, closer to me than any friend I had ever had.

A loud banging sound got my attention. Fetch had found the TV remote and was watching an animated movie about a dragon. He was laughing at it. I turned out the light and lay back down on the bed.

"We have got some pretty good friends, Fetch."

Fetch stretched his long neck around to look at me. His eyes were glowing green. He made a 'huff' kind of sound in agreement.

"I'm glad Michelle is our friend, and I'm glad you're my friend too."

Fetch stared at me for a few seconds, then shoved my foot gently to let me know he felt the same way.

"Good night, Fetch. Try not to eat me in the middle of the night."

Fetch laughed and made a smacking sound with his mouth. I laughed too. As I drifted off to sleep, I had a thought. "What if this is all just a dream?" Then I fell asleep.

Chapter 18

I woke up to a buzzing sound. It was my phone going off. Michelle had sent me another text. I was fuzzy headed and it took me a few minutes to focus on the words of the text. I could hear Fetch snoring at the foot of the bed; deep in-and-out loud breaths. I was glad to see that fire didn't shoot out of his snout in his sleep. He would have burnt the place to the ground that way.

"ur video taken care of.. More people calling it clever fake. No 1 can trace it back to source. Me and Johnathen bz now text u l8tr. Big things happening!!!:)"

This put my mind at ease a little. Some of it seemed vague but I was happy about the video. I thought it was good no one knew about the magic world. If I could be attacked the way I was, then anybody could be. I texted back a simple "K" and told myself I would let them know where I was and what I was doing later. It hurt a little that Michelle didn't ask me about that now, but I shrugged it off. Fetch had left the television on and, by what was playing, I could see it was early the next day. I had slept in my clothes. They seemed to be tight on me and my muscles ached. It felt like I had a really hard work out. I figured that my muscles were catching up to what I had been through the previous day. With a snort from Fetch, who was still sleeping on the floor at the foot of the bed, any thought of it all just being a dream left my head. I thought I better get the "Do Not Disturb" sign on the door or the maid would walk in to a surprising sight of a sleeping dragon on the floor. I took off my shirt and rubbed my bald head and got a pleasant surprise. I could feel the start of hair growing on my head. Feeling my face, I could feel eyebrows starting to grow in and a thin beard covering my face. I made a mental note to get some shaving cream, deodorant, and a toothbrush, along with clothes and a computer, today.

It was going to be a busy day. I got up quietly, not wanting to disturb Fetch, and headed for the shower. I walked by the big mirror leading into the bathroom and took a good long look at my face. In the middle of the night Fetch had found a marker and had drawn a beard and eyebrows and even squiggly hair. I could see the shadow of hair growing underneath Fetch's art work. I heard a 'huh' sound behind me and discovered that my dragon friend was not asleep after all. He was up and laughing at his little joke.

"Laugh it up you stupid lizard, I'm going to get you back for this one."

Fetch just continued to laugh. I turned back to the mirror and got a shock. I didn't recognize myself.

It was more than Fetch's art work. I was buff; really buff. I looked like I had spent months working out in a gym. Lean, powerful looking muscles were popping out all over my torso. I even had six-pack abs., something I had never been able to accomplish. I felt strong and now realized why I was so sore. My new body grew overnight. That also explained why I had been so hungry. I needed the calories to grow into my new body.

This was yet another transformation. I was elated! I was Spiderman discovering my new found powers. It was like I was a super hero. I picked up the phone to text Michelle to let her know about this new change. I left her a text that simply said, "New changes" accompanied by a photo of myself in the mirror.

Michelle texted back, "WOW! I really like the mustache and beard (lol), but really Jack, you weren't this big last night. I'll show this to Johnathen and see what he has to say."

I stripped off my jeans and headed to the shower. This was too awesome for me to be concerned about. I had tried every kind of workout program for years and never got the results I wanted. The best shape I had been in before was when I was riding my bike to work every day. When I got hit by the truck, that stopped me from working out at all. This overnight success was incredible. Fetch not consuming me had turned me into all I could ever want to be. I was beginning to enjoy my new life. How could I not? It was every comic book and fantasy lover's dream come true.

I stood there in the shower, letting the hot water massage my sore muscles, and I looked down at my leg. On the spot where Fetch's egg had attached itself, there was a strange spot. It looked like a bruise. It was in a perfect square and was purple, green, and had a strange white bump. I didn't like the look of it. I touched it and discovered it had a strange smooth feel. When I pressed on the small bump it felt hard, like a smooth callus. I really didn't want to worry about it. I felt too pumped and excited about the transformation of my body. Well, I couldn't expect not to have some kind of scar there, after all, I had just had a dragon rip through that part of my leg. I'm lucky I didn't have a scar across the whole side of my body. I told myself that I would show it to Johnathen the next time I saw him and see what he had to say about it. I jumped out of the shower and wrapped a towel around my waist. I went back to the mirror to get another look at myself. I looked down at the scar again. I was beginning to think of it as some kind of battle scar.

Fetch was sitting on the bed watching "The Price is Right".

"Hey Fetch," I said "take a look at my leg."

I pointed at the strange mark. He leaned in and studied it for a while. He took in a short breath and breathed a small line of healing fire, but it didn't do anything. He sat up, looked at me, shrugged, and went back to staring at the TV. He didn't seem to be too concerned about it.

I was acting like a little kid, flexing my muscles in the mirror, showing off in front of Fetch. He continued to watch TV, ignoring me. I could still see a faint outline of the artwork Fetch had done on my face. Then it hit me.

"Fetch, where did you get the markers to color on my face?"

Fetch turned to me and smiled a big toothy grin. I guess it would have to remain a mystery along with how he got food. The way he just sat there and smiled let me know that I wasn't going to get an answer out of him. My stomach growled. I had to get something to eat. Fetch seemed to like those sausage biscuits had gotten yesterday so I figured I would make that the first stop of the day.

I got dressed and grabbed my teardrop choker and phone and checked that I had money in the pouch. As I headed for the door, "Come on Fetch," I said "let's start the day." He turned to me and with the end of his tail shut off the TV. Going into camo mode he followed me out the door.

The next two weeks were spent in shameless excess. I bought clothes and a laptop computer. I strutted around town enjoying my new body. I texted Michelle as much as I could and she kept on saying that she would meet me soon. I tried calling her but would only get her voice mail. From time to time, I would see one of Johnathen's bobcats watching me from a distance. I wondered why the teardrop choker had no effect on them. I guessed that it was because of some spell that kept them from not seeing me. I was a little annoyed at the idea of always being watched that way, but I knew it was just Johnathen's way of watching out for me. I was starting to get a little hurt that neither one of them had come to see me or Fetch. Fetch was getting grumpy. He missed Michelle. I could tell he was down, because he wasn't bothering to play any tricks on me. We spent a lot of our time walking around town. We stayed outside as much as we could. During that time I was learning about Fetch. We found a stretch of desert where Fetch could fly around. He had to stay low and in camo mode because it was close to the Air Force base. It was out in the Vail area, not too far from my brother's house. I thought about going to see him, but I realized this was a bad idea. He didn't know who I was anymore. I waited one day, until he left for work, put fifty thousand dollars in an envelope, and stuck it in his mailbox. I left a note with it simply saying "Accept the blessing." I hoped he would keep the money and spend it on something he wanted.

I never had a lot of money before and I was quickly discovering how intoxicating it could be. I am ashamed to say that I lost my head for a while. I strutted around town enjoying my new found wealth and my new body. I had a new confidence I had never before experienced. Since nobody knew who I was, I could be whomever I wanted to be. My new found physical strength made me feel I could take on the world. Only the familiar twinge of pain from my hip let me know that I wasn't indestructible. I talked with people I would never talk to before. I flirted with girls with a new confidence. It was, in a way, the best time of my life.

I was starting to become lazy. I spent a lot of time out by the pool. With my teardrop choker, I had no fear of the magical world discovering me, and was beginning to think that I had nothing to worry about. I would wake up in the morning, muscles aching. A text from Michelle, containing a message from Johnathen, suggested that I start working out. It would help my body adjust to the changes it had undergone. I made it a habit to go to the small gym at the hotel every morning and then swim in the pool once in a while. It helped and I stopped feeling sore.

It was getting harder and harder to keep Fetch from being discovered. He was starting to grow and I realized he would soon be too big to stay in the room. On the second night we were there Fetch had plopped himself on the bed and refused to budge. Not wanting to get into it with him, it became an unspoken agreement to take turns with the bed. One night I would get it, and the next Fetch would. I didn't want to argue with him about this.

From time to time, Fetch and I would come across something from the magical world. Most were hidden from everyone who was not touched by magic. I began to see magic working all around me. I never let myself be seen by these gnomes. It took me a while to realize that it was the same funny little fellow who was doing the entire cleanup around the hotel and park. He seemed to always follow the giant troll, cleaning up after him. It amazed me that no one but me, and of course Fetch, could smell that troll. There was one day, as I sat out by the pool, that the little guy looked in my direction. I grabbed the choker in my hand as the little gnome stared in mine and Fetch's direction. We didn't move a muscle. A girl, who was staying at the hotel with her family, noticed how still I was sitting, and how I was staring, and came up and talked to me.

"Watcha doing?"

She couldn't have been more than four. I didn't want to respond to her, afraid that would let the gnome know that someone was here. I still didn't know who sided with the fairies and who didn't, and there was the chance that whoever sent the goblins to attack me would strike again. The gnome eventually sighed, not really paying attention to the little girl, and went on his way. The mother called the little girl over telling her not to bother me. I glanced over and saw her give me a worried look. Even with my new look and confidence, I seemed to be a little intimidating to some. My hair and eyebrows had grown in pretty well, but I was still a little scary looking to some people. I stopped sitting by the pool for a while. I was starting to get frustrated and I wasn't alone. Michelle had said she would see us in a few days but it had been longer. We had already extended our stay at the hotel and I didn't know how much longer I could stay there. I had the idea of getting an apartment, but I wanted to wait until I got the "ok" from Johnathen.

Fetch was getting extremely antsy. He was growing and was now about the size of a pony. If he continued to grow at this rate, we wouldn't be able to stay in hotel rooms anymore. He started going off on his own at night, and I figured out he was hunting. Sometimes he didn't get back until morning. I was concerned about what he was hunting and I made him promise not to eat anybody's pets. I kept my eyes open for any fliers of lost dogs or cats. His abilities continued to improve. The thing that was amazing to me was Fetch's dragon fire. We would go out and practice with it from time to time. It never burned the same color but would change with his mood. When he was angry, it would burn red or white. When he was happy and having fun, it was purple. When he was sad, it would be blue. I began to notice that it was blue more and more. Fetch was lonely. We did have each other, but there seemed to be no other dragons around. I had people to talk to from time to time, but Fetch had no one but me to relate to. I had to remind him to stay in camo mode from time to time, and, I could tell by the look on his face, he was beginning to resent this. He wanted to see another dragon. Knowing what they would do when they hatched, I wasn't sure if I wanted to meet one.

It was on one of Fetch's hunting nights that it happened. I went down to the pool, sure I would not run into my little gnome friend. I had never seen him at night and so I figured it would be safe. There was a family at the pool, but the hot tub was not being used. I sat in the hot water, enjoying the bubbles, when I spotted it. It was a goblin. He was hiding in the bushes, looking at the family. They had a stroller with them. Dad played with two older kids in the shallow end of the pool, while the mom stayed with the baby. The goblin was staring at the stroller. I froze, not knowing what to do. I knew the goblin couldn't see me. If he could, there might be trouble. But, by the way he was staring at the stroller, I knew I couldn't just sit by and do nothing. I hoped the thing would just go away. I made a note to myself to tell Fetch about this, and see about taking turns keeping an eye out for the little creeps. Before I could decide what to do next, the goblin made his move.

Darting out of the bushes he grabbed for the stroller, knocking the mother to the ground. She screamed as the goblin took the entire stroller, jumped over the fence, and took off. I jumped out of the hot tub in pursuit. I was thankful for my night vision as I could see the little creep. I was stronger than the last time I had to face one of these little beasts, and I was not about to let it get away with that baby. I could feel that funny, itchy, feeling again as I ran after the goblin. I let the magic build up inside me as I quickly caught up to the creature and grabbed it by the foot. It dropped the stroller, which landed on its wheels, and I could hear a frightened cry coming from it as I pulled the goblin away. The little slimy beast squealed in surprise. It wasn't Booger, but, by the way it looked at me, I could tell it was one of the snot brigade from the parking lot, and he knew who I was. I took a swing at his head and knocked him to the ground. I kicked him in the face with my bare foot and I could feel the sting of his acid spit on my toes. I began to wish Fetch was there.

The little beast was staring at me in shock. It must have been quite a surprise to him when I appeared after grabbing his foot. I took complete advantage of his surprise and dragged him away from the stroller and the crying baby. The magic continued to build up inside me. I forced it out and sent a wave of power through the goblin and out toward the stroller. The goblin went limp in my hands, and, as the wave passed the stroller, the baby went quiet. My heart went cold. I didn't mean for the magic to affect the baby. I looked down at the now limp form of the goblin. Terror flooded my heart! If I had killed the goblin, then surely I had killed the baby. The goblin let out a snort. I looked down at him and discovered that he was sleeping, just sleeping. I dropped him and rushed over to the stroller. I looked inside and saw the baby. It was sleeping peacefully. My forced spell had just put them to sleep. I made a promise to practice my magic and get a better grip on it.

I could hear the frightened voices of the parents as they ran in our direction. A flash of pain hit me in my bad hip as the goblin had recovered quickly, blindsided me, and smashed into the hip. I crumbled to the ground. The goblin was on top of me, sneering, as he looked in the direction of the voices.

"That was my snack you just took from me, Flap. No worries though, there are plenty others out there. You can't be everywhere at once, dragon survivor."

With these words a blue light appeared behind him. He flipped over backwards and disappeared into it with an insane little giggle.

The mom and dad came rushing up going straight to the stroller, and found their baby sleeping peacefully. They helped me up, thanking me over and over again. I could hear the siren as the police got closer. The acid was burning my foot, and the blow to my hip made it too hard for me to just run off. That was when the gnome showed up. He stood there as the mother and father screamed in terror. She clutched the baby to her chest and the father stood in front of her, protecting them both. Then, with a wave of the gnome's hand, a pulse went out. As it washed over the parents, a strange confused look came over their faces. They got the stroller, and, without a second look at me, walked calmly back to the pool. I sat there in the grass not wanting to move. The little gnome looked around as if he was looking for something. I realized he was looking for me. After a few seconds, he moved in the direction of the approaching sirens. As he walked off, I got up and quickly went back to the pool.

The family was still there getting their stuff. They seemed fine, as if nothing had happened. I wanted to get a look at the baby to make sure it was all right. Mom decided to change him before they went back to their room, so she unwrapped the little guy from his blanket while cooing at him. I sat down at a table nearby not wanting to be noticed for staring. The baby wasn't crying, so I didn't think it was hurt. The mother changed his diaper and tickled his little feet. I could hear him laughing and cooing. Tears of relief flooded my eyes and I sat there quietly and watched the family leave. They really didn't pay any attention to me, except for the little girl. She was holding her daddy's hand, and, pulling on his finger, pointed at me.

"Daddy, that's the man who jumped the fence when the green monkey got Joey."

The dad looked at me with a little embarrassed smile. I smiled back, the tears still streaming out of my eyes. The pulse had no effect on the little girl. She remembered everything. I said a little prayer in hopes that she didn't have nightmares from it for the rest of her life. The family left and after a few moments I got up and limped back to my room. I was hyper aware of every sound and shadow as I made my way back. I was sore and stiff. My hip hurt and there was still a burning feeling on my toes, but I was all right. The thing that bothered me the most, was the words of the goblin, that there were others. I had to find a way to stop this from happening again.

Chapter 19

I walked into the room and saw Fetch sitting on the bed. He was watching some reality TV show. He had gotten some burgers and bottled sodas. I picked up a bottle and threw it at the side of his head. It bounced off and hit the floor.

"Where were you?" I shouted at him.

He slowly turned to me. I could tell he was ready to retaliate until he saw the look on my face. He could tell that something had occurred. I sat on the bed next to him and told him what had happened. His eyes shifted colors as he sat there listening to my story. We had sat around long enough, now we needed to start acting. There seemed to be too many magic creatures that were victimizing non-magic people. It had to stop.

"We've got to tell Johnathen about this, Fetch. We have to do something."

Fetch nodded his head in agreement. I texted Michelle telling her I needed to see her, right away. When I received no immediate response to the text, I called.

"Look, Michelle, I need to talk to you. Something bad has happened and I need to talk to someone about it. You said you would see us in a couple of days and it has been weeks and I REALLY NEED TO TALK TO SOMEONE NOW!!! "

I hung up the phone and put my head in my hands. A few minutes later I heard a scratching at the door. Fetch and I both jumped up ready for an attack. This thing had scared us both and we were now ready for anything. I put out my hand and Fetch shot a burst of flame into it. I walked up to the door keeping to one side. There was another sound of scratching. My senses seemed to intensify and it felt like I had two, strong, fast beating, hearts in my chest as I got ready to open the door. Fetch planted himself squarely in front of the door going into cameo mode. He let out a little "huff" to let me know he was ready. I flung open the door to the surprising sight of one of Johnathen's bobcats. It quickly slunk in and, jumping over Fetch, sat on the bed. Its mouth opened and Johnathen's voice came out.

"Michelle said you were very upset. I sensed a pulse of magic at the hotel. What happened?"

I told the whole story again. When I finished, Johnathen's voice came through the bobcat again.

"They are getting bolder and out of control. For one to act on its own that way, means that things are getting bad."

"Wasn't it sent by the person trying to kill me?" I asked.

"No. I don't think so. If it was, it would have attacked you directly. Besides, there would have never been any way to tell where you were. You have been wearing the teardrop?"

"Yes, and Fetch has stayed out of sight."

I didn't want to tell Johnathen that Fetch had been going out on his own to hunt and fly around. I didn't want to be a tattle tale. Besides, I was upset that Johnathen and Michelle had blown me off.

"Did you hear all of that, Michelle?" said Johnathen.

"Yes" said Michelle's voice out of the bobcat.

It sounded like it was coming from a long way off.

"Jack, I'm almost there."

I sat down in a chair again, my head in my hands. I was relieved that Michelle was coming. The bobcat jumped down off the bed and came over to me, putting a paw on my lap. Johnathen spoke again.

"I'm sorry, Jack, it was my fault that Michelle hasn't been around. It's just that things have gotten dangerous. Somehow word has gotten out about you. You are something of a celebrity, Jack. People are concerned that you might cause trouble. I am trying to get you an appointment to see the council. They are being stubborn and there has been more than one incident over goblins and other creatures openly attacking non-magic people. I am trying to explain that you really don't have anything to do with it. I was afraid if Michelle was seen with you, she would be in trouble herself."

"What?" I said. "Tell her not to come here then. I don't want her to get in trouble."

There was a knock at the door.

"Too late," said Johnathen.

I jumped up and opened the door to see Michelle standing there. She looked concerned as she stepped in and gave me a hug. Fetch bumped me out of the way to get one too.

"Well," said Johnathen, "I will leave you all now. Jack, I will be coming to see you myself soon. I still want to see what you can do."

With that the bobcat headed for the door. Michelle opened it and the bobcat ran off.

"He seemed upset," I said. "Is he ok?"

"He got mad when I demanded to come see you. He is just worried."

I could tell that there was more to it than that, by looking at her face, but I didn't want to push it. I was just glad to see her.

"You shouldn't have come. If I had known you could be in danger, I wouldn't have sent you that message."

"It was my decision to come, Jack. I did tell you I would see you in a few days, and I can make up my own mind and take care of myself."

In that short sentence I could tell what kind of conversations Michelle and Johnathen had been having lately. Again, I didn't want to press it. My mind was in a whirl. I knew in my heart that I couldn't be there to keep every goblin or fairy from attacking, but I felt that I needed to do something. I had an idea, something I had been thinking about for a while now. I wanted to run it by Michelle.

"It is Johnathen's ultimate goal to get the word out about the magic world right?" I asked Michelle.

"Yes, you know it is."

Michelle was looking at me while absentmindedly scratching Fetch's head. She seemed upset. I knew it had to do with Johnathen but I didn't want to push it. I had to tell her my idea though, so I walked over and got my computer.

"Let's go down and get some coffee."

Fetch perked up at the idea of coffee. His mood was beginning to mirror Michelle's mood. I wanted to make them both feel better. If I was right, then this just might do it.

We walked down to the little coffee shop. They had great mocha lattes, something that I discovered was a favorite of Fetch's. It was a big shop and was usually not very busy at night. With a little clever maneuvering, Fetch could sneak inside, and we could sit at a corner table, away from the cameras, and drink a few in peace. They had Wi-Fi there too. Not something I usually concerned myself over, but tonight it was important if my idea was to work.

We got lucky and found an available corner table. After placing our drink order I got my computer started. I kept looking over my shoulder, expecting to see a blue ball and an army of goblins appear. I was sure the last one had to have told some of his little snot buddies about me. I was beginning to think this was a bad idea, going out of the room. Michelle grabbed my hand. I looked her in the eyes and I saw strength in them. She had been through so much.

"You can't live in fear, Jack."

I knew she was right. After everything that had happened, the worst thing I could do is live in fear. I squeezed her hand as I smiled at her. I felt Fetch's paw on top of both our hands. I was a little overwhelmed for a second. In all my life I had never had friends like this. Not ones that I could truly count on. The closest thing I had would be my brother. He was the only person from my old life that could match the closeness I had for these two. I took a deep breath and a sip of my coffee and began.

"Ok, creatures in the magic world have a problem with computers. You told me that some can't use them and others just won't try. We now have a connection to the magic world but we are still able to use computers. Why don't we use this technology to tell the world about magic?"

Michelle I gave me a blank look. "What do you mean? Like a blog or something?"

"Well, yeah, eventually I guess. I'm not the best with computers. In fact, if I hadn't had help I probably would never have gotten a Facebook page."

I turned on my computer and found my Facebook page. It was still there. It hadn't been deleted yet. I had posts from people who really didn't know who I was. Most people never checked their Facebook friends list and so it was conceivable that people would keep me without knowing who I was.

"Here, let me show you what I mean."

I wrote a message on my Facebook wall, "Not many people know this but dragons love coffee! :)" I showed it to Michelle. She still looked puzzled.

"I have seen a little girl who was not affected by the memory pulse. There have to be people out there who have experienced magic, and, because they either didn't recognize it, or were afraid someone would think they were crazy, they didn't say anything about it. I was thinking of keeping my Facebook page and seeing if I could find out if anyone else has seen or experienced anything to do with magic. I know there are a lot of people out there that talk about magic, but I figured if I kept it simple and even a little funny at times, I might get some responses that could help us discover who knows what. We could also use it as a way to get the word out there that the magic world does exist."

Michelle's eyes lit up. "Ok, I see where you are going with this. The benefit is that the council would have no clue as to what we are doing, and before they found out, the word could already be out there."

"Yeah, I mean, I could put little things out there like 'Don't pick up any cool looking rocks, they could be dragon eggs.' and see what kind of response I got. I mean I thought I would keep it simple to start, just to see who would respond and why. This could be a great tool to get the word out there as to what is going on. The more people are thinking about it and keeping from getting pulsed, the better. Johnathen wanted to get the word out about the magic world, why not use computers to do it?"

"I think that is a great idea, Jack! I don't know why I never thought of it myself. I mean, I have been teaching computers to the magic world and I never thought to use it this way. It's a great start, Jack. I can start monitoring stuff more and I will make sure your Facebook page stays open. But, there are those who are learning to use computers. You need to keep it simple, Jack. Keep it light, just like your post, for now. If you say or do too much, it could draw too much attention to you. You don't want to get in trouble with the council before you see them. This could really work."

Michelle sat there looking at me for a few minutes. I could tell she was trying to decide something.

"Let's not tell Johnathen about this, at least not for a while. I think he would try and put a stop to it, but if we could get more people thinking about the magic world, then it would help in the long run. It might even prevent a few tragedies."

"I thought it would be a good way to find those with magic ties too. Like you and your elf blood, we could find others with connections to the magic world and help them."

Michelle smiled. "By the time you go before that council, Jack, you are going to have more support than you know."

"That's another thing I wanted to talk to you about. I think we need to show ourselves to the magic world."

I said it all in a rush, not knowing what her response would be. Most of what I was saying sounded like betraying Johnathen. Michelle sat there staring at me. I couldn't read the look on her face. She had been protected from the magic world for a long time. I really didn't know her whole story about what she had to do for the magic community to accept her. I had a feeling that Johnathen had introduced her to just certain creatures of magic. What I was proposing was to expose myself and Fetch to the whole magic community.

"I would keep Johnathen's name out of it, Michelle. I wouldn't want him to get in trouble. But, if Fetch and I were to show ourselves, then it could keep him from getting into trouble for hiding us."

"I can't tell you what to do, Jack. But, I will ask you to wait before you do anything like that. You have to remember that Johnathen is trying to protect you. He is trying to protect us all. Exposing ourselves slowly on the web to the non-magic world is one thing. But, to reveal yourselves to the magic community, before Johnathen is ready for you to do so, is dangerous. You don't know what he went through for me. Please, Jack, just give him some time before you do this. It is only fair to him."

"Ok, I will, but you need to understand that I don't want someone to get hurt because of me. You guys keep telling me how special Fetch and I are, and all I can think of is someone getting hurt because of that. I want you and Johnathen to be safe too. The only reason I would expose myself to the world, magic or non-magic, is because I want you all to be safe. I don't want another baby kidnaped because of me."

I hoped what I said made sense to her. I wanted everyone to be safe. All the positive feelings I had because of the physical changes I had undergone were fading fast. I was back to being frustrated and confused. I felt guilty about what almost happened to the baby today.

"Jack," said Michelle, "you can't blame yourself for what happened today. It was just a renegade goblin causing trouble."

"Yeah?" I asked. "Then why did it attack at the hotel where Fetch and I were staying? Do you really think that was just chance? I feel like someone is manipulating me, and, if it isn't the fairies, then who else? Who sent those goblins to attack me?"

"I don't know, Jack. Johnathen is working on it right now. Please don't freak out on us. Just please give him more time. Give us more time. Your idea with the Facebook is a good one and I have another idea for you. Let's go back to the room and I'll show you what I mean."

When we got back to the room, Michelle pulled out her computer. She had her little magic box attached to it and ran a wire to my computer. She got on my Facebook page.

"Jack, you need to write your story."

"What? No, I'm not a good writer."

"I think you are, Jack, and besides, if my idea works, you won't have to sit there and type everything out. The magic will do it for you."

"I don't understand. You mean let the magic tell the story?"

"Yes, from what you have told us about your forced magic, it seems to be a part of you. You wanted to stop the goblin but you didn't want to hurt the baby. The magic put them both to sleep. I think on some level you have complete control over the magic. You don't want to kill anyone, so the magic won't. It has built up inside you and it has to come completely from you. That's why it is uncomfortable for you to release it. It is a part of you. If my hunch is correct, you can use it to write your story. We can get it online and people will be able to read it. You can get the word out about magic to the non-magic world."

"How would I do this? I have only been able to use my magic when I am fighting or in some sort of danger."

"Have you tried? I mean, have you concentrated on something and tried to use the magic to make it happen?"

"No, I guess I haven't done that. I don't really know where to start. I don't think I can do this."

Fetch came over to me, sat in front of me and just stared. His eyes stayed green and he put a paw up onto my computer. It was obvious what he wanted me to do. I had his vote and also his faith. If I did this right I could help change the world and warn them about magic elements that might affect their lives. People had to know that their fantasy book could come to life. I thought about my nightmare vision, the one that Johnathen seemed to dismiss. I wouldn't wish another person to go through that. Not even my worst enemy. They had to know about not picking up something as simple as a sparkly rock. It could actually kill them if it were to turn out to be a dragon's egg. It had to stop, and if this could stop it, then I had to do it. All I could do was try.

I closed my eyes and tried to remember what the magic felt like when I had used it before. I needed to find a way to bring it out of me when I wanted it to, not just when I was in danger. I stood there for a long time. I could hear Michelle and Fetch breathing in and out, in and out. At first it sounded like two separate breaths, but then it seemed like they merged together and were breathing together. I could feel their presence, almost as if they were pressing in on me and trying to share their strength with me. I felt a small tugging in my stomach, and then the familiar itchy feeling slowly started to come over me. As it grew, I tried to control it. It was like trying to hold onto sand. I seemed to get a grasp of it. I pictured myself balancing a broom stick in the middle of my hand. I had to make sure that I kept concentrating on keeping the magic still in my body until I was ready to release it. I slowly opened my eyes and stared at the computer screen. I put a hand on Fetch's neck.

"This is as much your story as it is mine, Fetch. I wish you could put yourself into it as much as I am about to."

Fetch let a small jet of flame pass in front of my eyes. He kept the flame burning. It was his healing fire. I watched it slowly change colors. When I released the magic, it would pass right through Fetch's flame. He would be a part of this story. I was nervous. I figured Fetch was too. We were pretty much winging it and I hoped that our computer wouldn't blow up in our faces. I thought about that first day. Picturing it in my mind, trying to imagine it as words being typed on a computer screen. I knew I had to start with a warning, hoping to grab the full attention of whoever read it. Then I pushed. I felt the magic forced out of me. I could see a glimmer as it passed through Fetch's flame. When it touched my computer the screen went black. Then all of the colors of Fetch's fire began to pop up on the screen. It went to a blank white screen and just stayed that way. At first I thought that it didn't work, but then I saw words appear. They didn't type themselves onto the page, they just appeared on the screen. They were the first words of my story, "Do you believe in magic?" I watched as mine and Fetch's story began to appear on the screen. It wasn't all at once but in spurts. I believed it was coming from my head, but it was something more. It had to be Fetch's twist on the whole thing. At times it wasn't all that flattering to me. It was showing the real me. Michelle sat next to me and the three of us continued to read the story. I didn't even think of it until that moment, but Fetch can read. Just another thing he seemed to be able to do. I wondered if it was part of the magic of all dragons, that from their birth they seemed mature and able to do so much immediately, or if this was just unique to Fetch? I wondered if I would ever know or would it remain a mystery like how Fetch got takeout food from restaurants.

We continued to read until it came to the nightmare I had. I didn't want to read that and was trying to figure out a way to erase it. So much of what is now my life seemed to be coming out on the page. It was embarrassing enough when it mentioned that I was naked for so long in the tunnel, this dream was too intimate. It exposed fears and regrets of my life that I wasn't ready to share. I reached to shut my computer off but Michelle grabbed my hand.

"Don't hide this, Jack. The world needs to see as much as they can. This could end up helping a lot of people. Even if it only keeps people from picking up a shiny rock that ends up being a dragon's egg, it is important. This could save lives, Jack."

"Ok," I said, "but we have to agree not to read this ourselves. You are a part of this story too, Michelle, and what you have told me will also appear on the screen. Are you ok with this?"

Michelle kept looking at the screen. I could tell that this was something she hadn't counted on. She let my hand go and closed the computer.

"It has to be ok. It has already started."

I could tell what was bothering her. Since the story was being written in my words, she would be able to see what I thought of her. I wouldn't be able to hide it. My feelings for Michelle were a little confused. I really didn't know how I felt about her. She was my friend and I cared about her. I didn't know if I felt anything more than friendship. I was unclear on her relationship with Johnathen, and, if she read something in my story that suggested that I had any strong feelings for her, then it could cause a strain in our friendship. I was beginning to regret my decision to do this.

Michelle gave me a level look and said. "Let's agree not to read this ourselves for a while. When it gets ready for the public to see, then we will go over it, but, for now, let's trust that the magic will write the story the correct way."

This sounded fair to me. After all, I really wasn't sure how I felt about Michelle. I would have hated to have tension between the two of us over any mixed feelings. I knew that she had strong feelings for Johnathen, even though she might not admit it. And, the way Johnathen acted tonight, I didn't want to cause friction between the two of us either. It was funny to me. Here I was, my life turned upside-down because of magic, and my biggest concern at that moment was a possible crush that sounded like an old high school style drama. What a mess! There was a part of me that wanted to undo the magic and forget the whole thing. But the idea of warning people, any way I could, about what could happen with magic was too important.

I wanted to talk to Michelle about feelings, but it just didn't seem the right time. She sat uncomfortably on the bed. I could tell that she was not ready for that kind of talk. She looked different. She was wearing a pair of jeans and a long-sleeved red blouse. Her long black hair was back in a ponytail, and all that could be seen of her tattoo was the tail and claw on her hands. She seemed tired and a little thin. Almost like she had been working too hard. I felt bad that I hadn't noticed before and I felt even worse at my outburst voicemail I had left earlier. I should have realized that the reason she hadn't been in contact with me was that she had been working hard with Johnathen, probably over something for me.

The silence between us had stretched to an uncomfortable amount of time. I didn't think either one of us knew what to say. The silence was broken by a familiar scratch at the door. We both seemed to start to breathe again. I went over to the door and opened it. Instead of the bobcat Johnathen stood there.

He had his crooked familiar grin. He stood there with his hands in his pockets. He had a sheepish look on his face as he walked in. He seemed a little embarrassed. He wouldn't look either of us in the eye and Michelle just looked up at the ceiling, not wanting to look at him. I grabbed his arm and smiled at him. I was just glad to see my friend. I hadn't seen him since the park and I could see a little grey in his hair. There were also faint dark circles under his eyes. He seemed tired and had a stretched-too-far look to him.

"I would like to apologize for earlier. I shouldn't have been so short with you both. I was being silly and I should have known better."

He shook my hand, not really taking his eyes off Michelle. I had the feeling that he was apologizing more to her than to me. I didn't mind. He walked over to Michelle and put his hand on her knee. He looked at her until she dropped her head down and looked him in the eyes.

Johnathen repeated, "I'm sorry."

I could see Michelle break down and melt at his gaze. She put her hands on his cheeks and smiled. He opened his arms and engulfed her in a big hug. It was that moment that I truly realized the affection and love that these two had for each other. I had the feeling that the fight they had was a lot more than Michelle had suggested. Over Johnathen shoulder I saw Michelle's closed eyes tear up. She was in love with Johnathen. Really in love with him. I had no idea if he felt the same way.

They finally came out of their hug and Fetch came over to Johnathen. He had been waiting until there was no tension between Michelle and Johnathen, before he would even acknowledge Johnathen at all. I had to keep from laughing as Fetch pushed his head into Johnathen's chest playfully. It almost knocked Johnathen over.

Laughing, Johnathen pointed at him and said, "Careful, I am a wizard you know."

Fetch stretched his neck up to his full height. He was now taller than Johnathen. He blew purple smoke out of his snout. With a flick of his head the smoke made a ring around Johnathen's head. It looked like a crown. My jaw dropped and Michelle gasped in amazement. The smoke just stayed there floating around Johnathen's head. It almost looked solid. It was just out of Johnathen's line of sight so he had no idea what we were all staring at. He turned and looked into the mirror. It was his turn to look shocked. He reached up and touched the ring of smoke. It slowly lifted into the air and dissolved. The last part of it took on the form of a small dragon before it flew into the ceiling and disappeared. Fetch chuckled at his little joke, pleased with all of our reactions.

Johnathen turned to Fetch, "Long ago I had the opportunity to work with the dragons. I saw many amazing things. I have a deep respect for them all, Fetch, but during all the time I was with them, I never met one as amazing as you my friend. You are truly one of a kind."

Fetch's eyes changed colors rapidly. He bobbed his head slightly as Johnathen's words affected him greatly. I tended to forget how alone he must feel at times, never seeing another of his own kind. He had to feel lonely.

Johnathen reached into his pocket and pulled out his pouch. Reaching into it, he pulled out a bottle of wine and four glasses. He opened the wine and handed a glass to each of us.

"I thought a little wine was in order," he said.

The wine was a deep red color that shimmered in the glass, almost like a light blinking on and off. I could have sworn it was making a humming sound. Johnathen caught me looking at the wine with a strange look on my face and laughed.

"It's called 'Wizards Celebration'. The grapes are cultivated by gnomes. They sing and perform magic on them before they are pressed into wine. That humming you hear is part of the song they sang. Once you take a sip of the wine the humming will change. The gnomes claim the song you hear is the song of your true self. Each one is different. Crafty magicians, the gnomes, they have cleaned up magic messes for centuries. They were never asked to do it nor were they ever ordered to do so by any council. They have just always been there to do it."

"I've seen one around here," I said. "There have been a couple of times that I would swear he can see me with the teardrop on."

A shadow seemed to pass over Johnathen's eyes when I said this.

"Was he the one you saw tonight?"

"Yes I think so, unless they all wear the same kind of purple sweatshirts with hoods."

"No, they don't. Be careful around him, Jack. If he keeps being around wherever you are he might sense you. He has to have some idea that you are around, especially after tonight. You don't realize it, Jack, but you demonstrated yet another new ability. You worked magic tonight, magic that has never been done before."

"What? New magic?"

I was keeping myself from looking at Michelle. It seemed that Johnathen had known about my little bit of magic I used to start my story. This was something we didn't want Johnathen to know about yet. I figured playing dumb would be the best thing to do. It wasn't that I didn't trust Johnathen, I just didn't want him to be worried about it. After all, we did kind of go behind his back and get the whole thing started.

"You don't have any idea what you have done, do you? Jack, you were right there when the gnome sent out a pulse. It had no effect on your memory. It had to have passed right through you and it didn't affect you at all."

I hadn't thought about it until that moment, but he was right. The little gnome was just a few feet away from me and his memory spell had no effect on me. I thought about the little girl who was unaffected as well. I wondered what that meant. Johnathen had made it out to be a big deal that the spell had no effect on me.

"There was a little girl who wasn't affected by the magic as well," I said.

"Really? It was a powerful pulse and for a human to not to be affected by it is rare. Do you think you could point her out to me if you were to see her again?"

"Her family is staying here at the hotel so unless they leave tonight, I think I could."

"Good, we will check for her tomorrow. I think it would be a good idea for us to stay here too, Michelle. I have already gotten rooms for us. I have neglected you for too long. It is time to really see what you can do. First of all we need to see if you can perform your forced magic in conditions that aren't necessarily dangerous."

I nodded my head and looked at the wine. I was starting to feel guilty for keeping the writing a secret from Johnathen. It was quiet in the room for a few minutes.

"Are we really going to stay here for a while?" asked Michelle.

I could tell that she was desperately trying to change the subject. I had the feeling that she wouldn't be able to keep our little secret for much longer. I hoped by the time she revealed it, the writing might have already done some good and Johnathen wouldn't be too upset.

"Yes, we need to see what Jack and Fetch can do. The best way to do this would be to stay close. Look at us, just standing here with wine in our hands! Let's have a toast and a drink. To new and best friendships. May we all find our way to make this world a better place."

If anyone else had made that toast, I would have thought it corny, but just looking at the gleam in Johnathen's sad tired eyes when he said it, let me know that he meant it. He wanted a better world. I made a promise to myself to help him achieve that goal.

I took a sip of the wine. It tasted wonderful! The humming did change. Each of our glasses started to make a new music. Johnathen's tune sounded like an old madrigal number I sang in high school choir. It was strong and sweet with a proud undertone to it. There was a strange weight to the music that could only be described as determination. Michelle's song was much sadder. It had a driving beat to it and the melody flowed from one style to the next. It seemed to say that she was accepting of change and could adapt to any situation. Fetch's tune was loud but lighthearted. At times you could hear a sad lonely melody attached to it. It was a little jangly but it stayed together and would eventually get on track. My wine sounded much different from the others. It was a messed up mix of melodies and sounds. It never seemed to stay with one melody or sound for very long but jumped around. Loud one second, soft the next, the best way to describe it would be like members of a giant orchestra were given different pieces of music and they played them all at the same time. This was very disturbing to me. It seemed to say that my life was a mess. I mean, I knew it was a mess, but for it to be brought before me like this was not a good moment. It was a noisy room for a bit until Johnathen motioned us to quickly finish our glass. When we all drained our glasses the sound stopped. Johnathen brought out a bottle of what he called 'Dwarf Ale' and gave each of us a pour from the bottle. With just one sip the world became a happy lighthearted place. My doubts and concerns over my music were pushed aside. An old memory of a friend of mine, whom I had not thought of in years, and how we had, on a dare, mistakenly mooned a cop, came to mind. I shared the story and we all had a good laugh. Our mood became happy and relaxed. We did this so quickly that I didn't have time to even think about why my music was so chaotic. Soon we were laughing and just enjoying each other's company. Michelle shared a story of a guy sitting on an ice cream cone, and Johnathen shared a tale of a dwarf and an elf having a burping contest that was interrupted by a troll who didn't understand the rules and farted knocking both contestants off the stage. We laughed some more. Fetch laughed the loudest and, as always, caused me to laugh even more.

Our little party went well into the morning hours before we finally decided to end it. Michelle and Johnathen left for their rooms, and, after a brief wrestling match for the bed, I pulled the top cover off the bed and drifted into a satisfying slumber.

Chapter 20

I woke up the next morning stiff and sore. I hadn't done my usual work out and ended up paying the price for it today. Fetch was already up watching TV. I lay there remembering the roller-coaster night I had last night, from the fear and anger of an attacking goblin, to a bonding moment with a wizard and an up-and-coming witch. You definitely couldn't call my life boring. I thought about how mine and Fetch's story was now being written; magically. I wondered, if something were to happen to me, would it continue writing? Then I remembered all of the things I had been thinking about Michelle. Those words would go on the computer soon and Michelle would be able to read them. I had to find a way to edit it. My face went red with the thought. I felt a sharp pain on the top of my head. Fetch had seen me just sitting there staring at the ceiling and had thrown a bottle top at my head. Before I could retaliate, my phone rang. It was Michelle. She said that we should meet them down at the pool in about twenty minutes. I jumped up and headed for the shower.

"We've got to get ready to meet Johnathen and Michelle by the pool Fetch. You should do something about your breath. It really stinks."

I slammed the door to the bathroom before he could respond. I took a quick shower and wrapped a towel around my waist, and then I cautiously opened the door expecting Fetch to retaliate over my comment. He was sitting on the bed still watching TV. You could see the bed sagging from his weight. I grabbed my bathing suit and slapped on some deodorant. I turned to the vanity area to brush my teeth and saw the toothpaste squeezed out and my tooth brush mangled and twisted. I looked over at Fetch who was sitting on the bed looking at me. He was smiling a very big toothy grin.

"Ha Ha, Lizard, very funny."

I brushed my teeth with my finger and in minuets headed out the door. I saw Michelle and Johnathen sitting in lounge chairs. Michelle was wearing a two-piece suit. I could see more of her incredible tattoo, which seemed to cover most of her body. I had to admire her commitment to get that much work done. It had to have taken a lot of time and effort. Johnathen was in a pair of shorts and, of course, a black T-shirt. He was having an animated conversation with a little girl, the little girl from last night. I walked up as the little girl was talking to Johnathen about the green monkey that took her little brother. I saw her parents giving Michelle the once over. They seemed to have a problem with her tattoo. They didn't give Johnathen a second look as he continued to talk to the little girl. When Johnathen saw me, he smiled and said.

"Hello Jack. I would like you to meet Brittney."

The little girl turned around and her eyes got really big when she saw me. She ran up and gave me a big hug.

"This is the guy who saved my brother," she shouted.

I looked over at her parents. They continued to look at Michelle who was effectively ignoring them. It seemed strange to me that these parents were not worried about Johnathen or me talking to their little girl. I patted Brittney on the head. She let me go and went back to standing in front of Johnathen.

"This is Michelle's and my friend, Brittney. His name is Jack."

She ran back to me giving me another hug. "Hi, Jack! I'm four. How old are you? Did you get that green monkey and kick him when you saved my brother?"

Johnathen laughed at Brittney's rapid way of talking. Michelle looked over, smiling at the whole exchange. She got up and moved toward us. I could see a look of concern from the parents, then, when she got about five feet away from us, a strange glazed look came over the parents' faces and they both went back to their books as if they had never noticed her at all. Johnathen had taken Brittney's hands. Michelle sat next to Johnathen. Brittney kept on staring at Michelle's tattoo. She wasn't scared at all. Michelle smiled and Brittney climbed into her lap. I glanced over at her parents, but they didn't even seem to notice. It had to be a spell. When someone got close to Johnathen, it was like they were forgotten and not seen anymore. They would look over at their daughter, smiling and waving, but it was like they didn't see any of us. I sat down on the lawn chair across from Johnathen, Brittney, and Michelle. I had mixed feelings about this kind of magic. It seemed so manipulative, so controlling. Both Michelle and Johnathen were ok with it. I could hear Fetch grunt and was sure he didn't like it either. I gave Johnathen a questioning look. He nodded his head letting me know he understood.

"Brittney is a very special little girl, Jack. She can see things that others can't see. I want her to understand that she should never talk to these things, because they might not understand why she can see them, and they might get a little scared." He had something in his hands that glowed. "Did you know that Jack is friends with a dragon?"

Brittney's eyes got big and her mouth dropped open. "Really? Can I meet him?"

Before I could say anything, Fetch appeared. He was sitting next to me, his eyes blue and his smoke purple. Brittney jumped up and wrapped her arms around Fetch's neck. She kept hopping up and down excitedly, laughing. Again her parents looked over, smiling, but not concerned. Her mother had picked up her little brother and was taking out a bottle to feed him. Fetch blew smoke under Brittany's chin and she squealed in delight and giggled. Johnathen took her hand for a second. The glowing thing went from his hand to Brittney's hand and then went out. Brittney didn't seem to notice. I wasn't sure how to feel about all of this. I was about to say something, when Michelle caught my eye. She was nodding her head, so I stayed quiet.

"It was nice to meet you, Brittney," said Johnathen. "I think you should go back over to your parents now."

Brittney looked at Fetch. She was disappointed that she had to leave. With a sigh she gave him another hug and a kiss and gave one to me and Michelle. She turned to Johnathen and whispered.

"Is this when I pretend not to see you?"

Johnathen nodded 'yes'. With another sigh and a sad wave, Brittney turned and went over to her parents. I sat there watching her for a while as she tried to pretend that she didn't see us. But she would look over at us and smile and give us a wave when she thought no one was looking. Her parents would smile and shake their heads. I had a feeling she saw many different things at times and her parents had dismissed them as imaginary friends. I hoped she would learn to not tell people about what she saw.

"What was that Johnathen, the glowing thing you put in her hands?"

"It was a spark of magic. She will pass it to her brother and the rest of her family. It will keep them safe from anyone who might realize that she can see into the magic world. When she is older and ready, I will come see her again, and teach her some magic if she wants. She has elf and gnome blood in her. That makes her very special. Her brother is the same and I have a feeling that is why the goblin attacked. You were right to be suspicious, Jack. There are forces in the magic world that seems to be getting ready for something, and I think that the same ones who sent the goblins to attack you are the ones who kidnaped that baby last night. We need to find a way to stop them, Jack, or more children will be kidnaped. These things happen from time to time, but it is too much of a coincidence that they took a child with such strong magic potential for this to be random. I didn't like to manipulate her parents that way, but I had to talk to her without them around. The spark will help her, if they get too worried about her telling them about the things she sees as she gets older. If her brother sees things too, it will also protect him."

"What do we do then?" I asked. "How can we stop it?"

"It might take some time, Jack. You have to be patient. I am trying to discover who our mystery enemy is. I have been able to cast a spell of concealment, so that I won't be detected for a while, but I can't do it forever. For now, Jack and Fetch, I think it is time for me to see what you can do."

We went back to our rooms. I realized that Johnathen wanted us to go to meet them by the pool, to show us what he did for Brittany. It was strange to me that he felt he had to do that. Before going back to our rooms, we had discussed going out to the desert and showing our abilities. Fetch seemed eager to show off, and, even though I didn't want to admit it, so was I. This was more than for Fetch and me though. Michelle would be given a chance to show what she could do as well.

I changed into a pair of jeans and a black T-shirt. I gave myself a good look in the mirror and rubbed my head. My hair was coming in nicely. It was much lighter that it was before, in fact, I began to wonder if I might end up being blond when it grew out. My goatee had red in it as well as some brown and a little grey. I kept it trimmed and wondered if I would eventually have to shave it when more of my hair grew in as it didn't seem to match the hair on my head. Fetch smacked me in the head with his tail. He was right. I was spending too much time looking in the mirror. We left the room and met Johnathen and Michelle out front. This time they had a jeep and Michelle drove. It seemed to me that Johnathen had a problem with any kind of technology; even how to drive a car seemed hard for him to grasp.

Chapter 21

We drove out to the spot in the desert, where I had gone with Fetch to practice. I didn't bother telling anyone that it was close to my brother's house. I had the urge to spy on him a little bit, but thought better of it. When we got out of the jeep, Fetch, who rode on the top of it the whole way, jumped into the air, flying in great big loops. He was out of cameo mode. I wanted to tell him he better not fly too high or someone might see him, but he looked so happy that I didn't have the heart to say anything.

He dove toward the ground, scooping something up with his hands. He landed next to me.

"What's that?" I asked.

Fetch showed me what he had in his hands. It was a tarantula. My stomach dropped to my feet and my face went cold. I was never a fan of spiders, but ever since my dream in the tunnel, I hadn't been able to even look at a spider on TV, let alone one up this close. I backed away from Fetch. The tarantula was wiggling in his hand trying to get away. Fetch looked puzzled at me backing away. He shrugged and popped the thing into his mouth and crunched down on it. He gulped and smacked his lips and looked around for another. I felt sick. I had never seen Fetch do anything like that before. Michelle looked a little green. Johnathen seemed the only one, besides Fetch, who was unfazed by the little snack.

"There are properties of the tarantula that are good for digestion. Besides, Fetch picked one that was obviously stung by a wasp and was dying. He did it a favor by eating it instead of letting it suffer. It really is a balance in nature."

I shuddered and stood there for a second, trying to get the image out of my mind.

"Heads up!" shouted Johnathen.

I opened my eyes and caught a sword that Johnathen had thrown at me. It had a blue fire burning around the edge of the blade. Johnathen stood about twenty feet away from me, with one that had red flame surrounding it. Before I could ask what we were doing, Johnathen charged. He moved so fast that I barely had time to react. He moved twenty feet in milliseconds, with the sword over his head. He swung it down toward my head. I thought he had lost his mind and that I was a goner, but, as the sword came racking down it made a ringing sound as it struck my sword that I had raised up to block his blow. Before I could even be surprised, I blocked three more swings he made at my body.

He smiled,"Good, good, I had a feeling that you would be able to do this. You see, Jack, even your clumsy attempts in the parking lot showed that you had gained an ability to sense where a blow would land. The magic that is now a part of you protected you from harm."

Four more blows came from Johnathen. I managed to block all of them. Two more and Johnathen managed to hit me in the ribs with the side of his sword. I felt a crunch as at least two ribs broke. I crumpled to the ground as tears of pain blinded my vision.

"Stay where you are, Fetch," said Johnathen. "You can't heal him every time he is hurt. He needs to recognize pain and overcome it himself. If you come to his rescue all the time, he will remain weak."

These words seemed harsh from Johnathen, harsh and unfair. He was implying that I had never been hurt before. Even before I got into this life I now had, I had survived being hit by a truck. How could he say that I was weak? I looked up at him. He was standing over me leaning on his sword and was looking down at me with a look of impatience on his face. I heard Michelle start to say something.

"Stay out of this Michelle."

He swung his sword in an arc over his head. I barely had time to block it. I was seeing stars from the pain in my ribs, but I was starting to get mad and I didn't want to give Johnathen the satisfaction of knowing how much pain I was in. After scrambling backwards, I got up and waited for the next blow to come. Johnathen just stood there looking at me. He didn't move a muscle, just stared. Out of the corner of my eye I could see Fetch. He was swinging his head back and forth between Johnathen and me like it was a tennis match. My ribs hurt. It was hard to breathe. Johnathen continued to stare at me. I had no idea what he was doing. It was like he was waiting for me to do something, but I didn't know what it was.

"Do I have to explain it to you?" he said.

There was anger in his voice. I had never seen him like this. I reminded myself that he was a powerful wizard. He probably could wipe me out with just one wave of his hand. A strange shadow seemed to cross over him and his whole body seemed to glow with power. I heard Michelle try to say something again. Johnathen cut her short.

"You insisted in coming out here with us, Michelle, on the condition you wouldn't interfere. Stay out of this."

It was hard to believe this was the same man who was talking so sweetly with Brittney just a few hours ago.

I crouched low to the ground. My mind was in a whirl over what was going on. I couldn't figure it out. Johnathen stood there like a statue waiting for something. Fetch continued to look back and forth between us. Why wasn't he helping me? Johnathen flicked a finger in my direction. I felt a scratch across my face, not too painful just annoying. He flicked his finger again and my arm turned red with the scratch. This was starting to make me angry. Then it dawned on me. Any time before I started the writing, my magic only surfaced when I was in danger. It seemed like I could only use it when I was angry or in danger. Johnathen was trying to see my magic, to test it and see its limits. He didn't know that I had found a way to use it when I was not in any danger. He waved his hand at me, knocking me to the ground. I felt like I had been stung by something and I felt my cheek swell up. My ribs exploded in pain as I fell backwards. I had to use my magic to get him to stop. I could feel it building up. Fetch's eyes were on me. He seemed to know what was happening. He wasn't helping because he knew I needed this. I needed to learn to attack and not just defend. I would be knocked down every time in a fight if I didn't learn to attack first sometimes. That was what Johnathen was trying to teach me. I let the magic build as I got to my feet. I could tell the forced magic affected my ribs, not healing them, but numbing the pain, helping me focus. I wondered if I would ever be able to heal myself. The itching sensation continued to build and now my body was buzzing with controlled power. Johnathen flicked a finger at me again. I could tell where it hit me, but I no longer felt pain. I waited for another minute. Johnathen's lips were moving and I had a feeling he was taunting me, but I couldn't hear him over the roar of my heartbeat and the strange pulse of the forced magic. I waited another second and then I charged. I ran so fast that I surprised myself. I was almost upon

Johnathen, and, as I released the magic in front of me, I jumped into the air and swung the sword down. This time Johnathen barely had time to get his sword up. He blocked my blow, but he had no time to react to the magic. It hit his body full force knocking him backwards. I heard a 'wuff' sound come from his body as he flew backwards. He landed about ten feet away. I sank to my knees as the magic left me. The pain in my ribs seemed to have tripled and I tasted blood in my mouth. I was weak from my attack. I needed to learn to control the force of the magic when it left me. I was too vulnerable this way.

Johnathen's body twitched. He wasn't getting up. I hoped that I had just knocked him out. I tried to stand up, wanting to walk over to him and see if he was alright. But, every time I tried to stand up, the pain in my ribs kept me down. I heard Michelle yell. She was running toward Johnathen. His body continued to twitch like he was having some sort of seizure. Before she could get to him, a strange light came out of his body. It looked like someone had turned on a klieg light. Along with this came a wind storm. It poured out of Jonathan's chest, picking up dust and debris from the desert. It hit Mitchell first, lifting her up in the air. Fetch flew up and caught her before she was flung into some cactus. The wind hit me knocking me backwards. I managed to stay on the ground by grabbing at the desert floor, digging my fingers into it to try to keep from being blown away. Fetch and Michelle were out of sight. I hoped they were safe. Slowly the wind was pushing me away from Johnathen. It built in intensity and when I felt I couldn't hang on any longer it stopped. It was like someone had turned off a giant fan. The silence following the sound of the wind was almost painful. I started to stand up. I was looking around trying to spot Michelle and Fetch. Out of the corner of my eye I saw Johnathen twitch again. I prepared myself for another wind storm but it never came. Instead, out of Johnathen's chest grew a troll. It looked like it was made of rocks and grew about thirty feet tall. It never detached itself from Johnathen. It roared and beat its massive arms on the ground and thrashed around like it was throwing a massive tantrum, whipping and flinging itself around, destroying whatever was too close to it. I was glad that I was too far away. With my ribs the way they were, I doubted I could dodge those massive fists for very long. My breath was coming in short spurts. Every gulp of air was a stab of pain.

The troll spotted me and raised its fist above its head and crashed them down in my direction. I was far enough away that it couldn't reach me. The massive arms hit the ground and sent a shock wave that knocked me off my feet. My ribs exploded in pain and I almost blacked out. I scrambled up painfully to see the troll flailing its arms around as it slowly shrank back into Johnathen's chest. As soon as it disappeared, fire shot up from his body. It formed into a dragon of massive size. Just like the troll, it stayed connected to Johnathen, its tail never completely leaving his chest. This beast had a longer reach and moved toward me with purpose. I knew I was a goner for sure this time. Fetch came out of nowhere. He roared and shot a red flame directly at the fire dragon. He was furious. The flame connected with the red fire dragon and, in a burst of pure energy, they became one. I couldn't tell where Fetch began and the fire dragon ended. The sky lit up and I was grateful that this was in the middle of the day. If it had been at night, then the fire would have been seen for miles around. I had a feeling that there would be some reports of a strange fire ball seen by someone. I figured the gnomes would be busy wiping the memories of people. Michelle came up and grabbed my shoulder. Over the roar of the fire, she yelled in my ear.

"We have to see if Johnathen is ok," she said.

I could see the fear in her eyes. I don't think she had ever seen anything like this before and it scared her. I shook my head and turned to yell at Fetch. I tried to spot him in the flame but all I could see was a big ball of fire. I was quite sure that Fetch couldn't be killed by a flame like that, but I wasn't positive. Then, just like with the other creature, the fire dragon disappeared. Fetch was left in the sky circling around. He was mad. This whole thing had sent him over the edge. Johnathen had almost hurt Michelle and that was something that he would not put up with. I saw Johnathen's body spasm again. Air, Earth, Fire, I had a feeling what was going to happen next.

"Fetch!" I yelled. "Get us!"

I had no time to explain but Fetch understood. He swooped down and grabbed Michelle and me with his back claws. I felt my ribs move, groaned in pain, and coughed up blood. Michelle reached out to me, realizing for the first time just how hurt I was. She said something to me but I never heard it. The last element shot out of Johnathen. It was a stream of water. It shot out of his chest with the power of a tidal wave. When it reached a height of about sixty feet, it crashed down toward us like a giant whip. Fetch swerved and barely missed being hit. The wave of water crashed down on the desert floor. There was a loud booming sound as the water hit the ground with enough force to send a shock wave through the desert.

This was power. This was Johnathen's magic. He came out here to test my abilities and I ended up learning about his. The water whipped along the ground as if it was trying to find us. Fetch remained airborne until the water, like the other apparitions, disappeared back into Johnathen's chest. Fetch swooped down and gently set us on the ground. I collapsed completely as the last of my reserves gave out. I kept coughing up blood. As I lay there, face down in the dirt, I could hear Michelle sobbing and calling my name. Then I felt the warm healing fire as Fetch began to heal me. With that fire came an overwhelming feeling of rage, fear, and confusion. At first I thought they were my emotions. Then slowly, as my ribs snapped back into place and I felt my strength returning, I realized I was feeling Fetch's emotions. I could feel his surprise as he realized that he could feel my emotions too. I guess we both always knew, in a way, that we were doing this, but it took the extreme outpouring of emotion to kick in the idea that we were reading each other's thoughts. It was incredible! The longer Fetch used his healing flame, the more we felt each other's thoughts. I felt his loneliness of being the only dragon around. He felt my frustration and sorrow of losing my brother to the memory pulse. My thoughts of being sure that Johnathen didn't mean for this to go as far as it did calmed Fetch down a bit. I was excited to tell Michelle about this. I could feel Fetch's reluctance to tell her. Even though he had a great amount of affection for her, this one thing seemed to be very personal, something he wanted to keep between just the two of us. It made sense. I realized then just how much Fetch and I were connected to each other. I wondered if he could do this with anybody else. Then Fetch's thoughts faded away. The healing was complete. Michelle was looking at me with tears in her eyes. I had been rolled over onto my stomach. I must have passed out for a second. I heard Michelle talking to Fetch.

"Let me go!" she was saying.

Fetch had his tail wrapped around her waist. I guess when he had started to heal me, he had kept her from running over to Johnathen. She didn't look too happy about this, but I felt, just as Fetch must have felt, that it was best not to rush over to Johnathen until we could be sure it was safe.

I heard a groan coming from Johnathen as he sat up. He had a hand on his forehead. Michelle grabbed for Fetch's tail and frantically tried to pull him off of her. I put a hand on Fetch's side. He looked over at me and I nodded. I could tell he wasn't happy with the idea, but he let her go. She ran over to Johnathen and knelt next to him. I got to my feet, and, with Fetch at my side, went to join her.

Johnathen had a confused look on his face. At first I didn't know if he knew where he was, but when Michelle grabbed his hands, he looked at her and realization came slowly in his eyes. He looked around the desert near him, seeing the destruction his elemental magic had caused. He put his head in his hands and began to cry. Through his hands he began to apologize over and over again. I could see his hands shaking. Michelle took his hands and gently pulled them away from his face. He looked at me, wracked with guilt. All I could do was look at him. I wanted to tell him it was all right. No one was hurt. But, after such an impressive display of power, all I could manage to say was "Wow, Dude, wow."

Fetch huffed in anger at my lack of words, and in true Fetch fashion slapped me in the back of the head with his tail. I could tell that he was still upset at Johnathen, but I had a feeling that what we witnessed was a defense mechanism of some sort, that an unconscious Johnathen had no control over. I wondered if he was even aware of what he did at all.

"I'm so sorry, Fetch," said Johnathen.

It was pretty obvious that Fetch was the one who was really upset.

"Please, it was my fault. I underestimated Jack and in my impatience to see what he could do, I almost destroyed us all. I was careless and I beg your forgiveness."

Johnathen's voice was shaky and weak. I didn't like to see him this way. It didn't seem right for someone with such power to appear to be so vulnerable. After such a display of power I felt very uncomfortable by his display of such raw emotion. Fetch turned to look him in the eye. His eyes were rapidly changing color as he stared Johnathen down. Finally they went to green again. He reached out and took one of Johnathen's hands. He took his tail and smacked Johnathen's hand, like you would a little kid's hand after he reached for the cookie jar after being told no cookies before dinner. Johnathen laughed shakily at this.

"Point taken," he said to Fetch.

Michelle let out a little hiccup laugh as tears ran down her face. Johnathen put a hand on the side of her face and the other one on my shoulder.

"Look at the four of us. What a team we make. If we are not careful, an emotion pixy could take us out with one swoop."

We all laughed at this. I wanted to ask what an emotion pixy was, but I thought it could wait for another time.

"What was that?" I asked. "Those things that came out of you, are they part of you?"

Johnathen smiled a little at this. "A long time ago, wars were fought in the magic world. They were pointless battles and there were no real winners. I cast powerful spells that would protect me if I was ever hurt, or knocked out, on a battle field. I've had them in me for so long, I pretty much forgot they were there. Your attack triggered them, Jack. You are a very powerful magic user, and you are becoming an excellent fighter. I only wanted to help you bring out your full potential, but I went too far. I can never apologize enough for what I did. I just felt that there was no other way to test your abilities. I thought you had to reach a point of pain and hurt that would release the magic, without any real focus to it. You are much better than I gave you credit for, Jack."

"Tell that to my ribs."

Johnathen's eyes got wide.

"I really did hurt you, didn't I?" He looked over at Michelle again. "I could have killed you all. This was stupid. I should have known better. You are such an enigma, Jack, both you and Fetch. Your power is so different from anything I have ever seen. I should have taken it slowly. Again, I'm sorry."

He hung his head down, not wanting to look at us. Once again, I saw just how old he must really be. There was a burden of responsibility he seemed to think he had to shoulder. Most of it seemed to center around Michelle and me. Truthfully, all he wanted to do was teach me how to better use my abilities, but it seemed that my magic was different from anything he had ever seen before. He just didn't know how to fully test or train me. I felt bad that he had put so much pressure on himself because of Fetch and me. I had to find a way to relieve some of that pressure. It wasn't fair for him to take responsibility for me. It wasn't his fault that Fetch hatched on my leg. It wasn't his fault that I picked up Fetch's egg to begin with. I had to find a way to help him. I somehow had to introduce myself to the magic world. I had to do it on my own. Not because I was being impatient, but because I didn't want to be a burden to Johnathen, Michelle, or anyone else again. I needed to take responsibility for my own life, no matter the cost.

Chapter 22

Johnathen got up and sent a pulse out, just in case someone saw any of our battle. Michelle was going to check online later for anything that mentioned a possible sighting of fire balls or jets of water. It was confusing how some magic, like the gnomes cleaning up messes, could stay hidden and how others, like attacking goblins, could be seen by everyone. It had to be a constant undertaking to keep it cleaned up and forgotten. With the lack of computer and technology experience, I wondered just how much got past the magic world on the Internet. Michelle had mentioned someone who was good with computers, but they couldn't stop all of it could they? There just seemed to be too much of it.

I pushed aside these thoughts for now. We spent the remainder of the day practicing and showing off what we could do. Johnathen stood there and watched for the most part. Michelle found a way to roll up dirt in a tight ball and threw it at Fetch as he dodged and swirled to avoid the missiles, smacking them with his tail. We all laughed and continued to act like we were having a good time, but there was a tension in the air. We all found out new things about ourselves that day. Discovery can leave you feeling strange sometimes. I know that Johnathen didn't mean to hurt me or anyone else, but in his speed to discover new things he seemed to get a little careless.

We left as the sun went down. Johnathen must have cast a spell that kept people away from that spot. We ended up making a lot of noise and for us not to have drawn any attention to ourselves seemed impossible without magic. I drove the Jeep back to the hotel and I don't like to drive. I never really owned my own car, but that didn't mean I couldn't do it. Besides, if I was to ever own a car, it would be a Jeep. Michelle sat next to me and Johnathen stretched himself in the back seat. He looked exhausted. I was a little worried about him. So was Michelle. I could hear Fetch scrape the hard top as he settled himself down on it. He was still a little moody over the whole day. He had forgiven Johnathen, who continued to apologize for what happened all day, but I had a feeling it was going to be a while before he trusted him again. It was a strange awesome display of power, and I think it bothered Fetch that Johnathen went as far as he did when trying to provoke me into using the forced magic that was part of whom I had become. We drove in silence for a while. We were all tired and seemed at that point of trying to find something to talk about to keep our minds from wandering. Michelle broke the awkward silence.

"Next time, I want to show off a little bit myself. You boys got to play. All I did was throw dirt balls at Fetch."

I laughed at this comment. I appreciated her attempt to make light of what happened that day. Johnathen was silent for a while, then, after a few minutes, he spoke.

"No. I don't think it is a good idea. You need more time to practice before you attempt any spells. It's too dangerous."

"I need to try and see what I can do, Johnathen. It isn't right to teach me how to use magic and then not let me use it."

"It's too dangerous and I forbid you to use it! I wish I had never taught you any of it."

There was a long tense silence as we drove down the road. Michelle stared ahead, frowning. Her jaw was tense and she seemed to be clenching her teeth. I had the feeling that this was an argument that the two of them had before. I couldn't think of a thing to say to break us out of this moment. I looked in the mirror. Johnathen was lying down so I couldn't see his face, but, by the tone of his voice, I could tell that the shadow that seemed to pass over his face when he was upset was back.

"You know why you taught me magic, Johnathen. You know that it's right for me to learn it. Without it I would be an outcast. I would have no way to be fully accepted in the magic world. You know that."

"I could have protected you. I could have sent you into the non-magic world with money and a life, and erased all memories of what happened to you, but I chose to keep you close. When I discovered the elf blood in your veins, I gave you the opportunity to learn magic and be a part of finding those who destroyed your family and bringing them to justice. Sometimes I feel that I was foolish. My need to see change made me careless when it came to you. I should have known better."

This whole conversation was intense. I wanted to lighten the mood. I was all right, Michelle was all right, and Fetch was fine too. We needed a way to get over this or things could fall apart very quickly.

The sun was going down and the road in front of us stretched for miles and miles. I wanted to say something but I couldn't think of anything. Fetch was moving around on the roof of the jeep. I knocked on the roof hoping he would get the message and stop moving around up there. I was afraid he would scratch up the roof. Then he did it. As the sun began to set Fetch slowly peeked over the front of the car, his head was on Michelle's side. He slowly slunk down like a snake. When he was half way down, he stretched his neck out turning his head to look at Michelle. He took turns looking at Michelle, me, then Johnathen. When he was sure we all saw him, he got the most satisfied look on his face and, with a little nod, gave us all the biggest, toothiest grin a dragon could give. We all busted out laughing. It was exactly what we needed. I don't think I was ever more grateful for Fetch's sense of humor. I turned on the radio. 'Twist and Shout' was playing. Fetch must have been able to hear it. You could hear his tail thumping to the beat. I started singing and by the end of the song we all had joined in.

We pulled into the nearest fast food drive thru. Just the idea of having a dragon on the top of the jeep was a story to share with the grandkids one day, but to order food for one was a whole other adventure. The girl's voice through the speaker sounded board and tired. This just made the situation even funnier. I hoped Fetch remembered to go into camouflage mode. It struck me as funny that most people never spotted Fetch in cameo mode. It didn't make him completely invisible. He just blended in. It had to be like the trolls I would see from time to time. They weren't hidden and non-magic people seemed to ignore magic most of the time. It just didn't register in their minds. Maybe that was why it was so easy to erase their memories when they were affected by magic. Maybe the pulse just gave them the nudge to get them back on track, back to what they saw as normal.

I ordered myself a number five. Fetch's tail thumping on the roof indicated he wanted one too. This started Michelle giggling. I asked Johnathen what he wanted. He responded by thumping the roof with his hand.

"Ok three number fives. And you Michelle?"

She thumped on the roof too, still giggling. Johnathen was beginning to chuckle and soon we were all laughing. When the laughter died down a bit, the girl read the order of four number fives back to us. She asked if we needed anything else. Fetch thumped his tail again. It took a little time to figure it out, but by the time the ordering was done, we had seven number fives, three fish sandwich meals, two special order number sixes, and ten apple pies. Michelle and Johnathen couldn't stop laughing and the look on the girl's face when we pulled up just made it worse. When we finally got all the food double checked, to make sure we got everything, and all of the drinks checked out, I handed the girl some money. She smiled, looking a little puzzled. I looked at her straight faced and said in the calmest voice I could.

"This isn't all for us. Most of it is for the dragon on the top of the Jeep."

This sent Michelle and Johnathen into peals of fresh laughter, as I pulled away from the place. Fetch was banging his tail. He was hungry. As I pulled out onto the street, Michelle rolled down the window. She had a fish sandwich and a double cheeseburger in her hand. After reaching up to the roof, her hand came back empty. Man, was my life different. We drove back to the hotel. I decided it was time to change rooms. Fetch was careful not to do any damage, but I felt the less we stayed in the same room, the better. Johnathen and Michelle checked out that night. I could tell there was still tension between the two of them. I hoped they could work it out.

The next few weeks were spent in working on improving what Fetch and I could do. We would meet Johnathen every other day, down in the lobby, then go into the desert, or up on Mount Lemon, to spar and train. I began to feel like a soldier getting ready to go off to war. I didn't like the feeling, but knew it was necessary if I was to discover my potential and my limits. Fetch began to show some amazing flying abilities and a new level of control of his fire. Johnathen cut his hand on purpose to see if Fetch could heal it. It slowly healed and left a scar on his hand. Fetch's ability to heal had its limits. We figured that because Fetch hatched from my leg, his magic worked better on me.

We had agreed to keep our mind link through the fire a secret between the two of us. It wasn't a trust thing. It was just that it seemed so personal.

The more we used it the deeper our thoughts would combine. It was kind of entertaining. Fetch discovered things about me I had never shared with anyone, and, I in turn, learned new things that he would never share with anyone else. Fetch was more than a friend to me now. He was like a brother. Our uniqueness kept us separate from both worlds, and that gave us a bond that couldn't be broken. I couldn't imagine my life without Fetch now, even when he would smack me with his tail.

We didn't see Michelle during this time. Johnathen told us that she was busy working on a project that the two of them started a few years ago. I had the feeling he kept her away to keep her from getting hurt. The training never got as intense as the first time, but I think Johnathen was worried about what could happen. I would call her and check up on her Facebook page to see how she was. She sounded a little tired at times. I noticed on her Facebook page that she had more friends from different tattoo shops in town than she had before. I had the feeling she was searching for information that could lead her to answers about her family's deaths. I hoped that she wouldn't let this drag her down.

Johnathen was not looking his best during these times either. He looked tired and stressed and, on more than one occasion, he would stop what he was doing and just stare off into space. The last time I caught him doing this, he was looking up into the clouds. His lips were moving and, after a quick debate with Fetch, I decided to walk over to him. When I got close to him, I heard what he was saying.

"Watch the clouds. Watch the clouds," he was repeating over and over.

I put my hand on his shoulder, and his body jerked a little. I immediately let the forced magic form in my body. I was ready for another defense attack, but Johnathen just shook his head and yawned like he was just waking up.

"Ah Jack, sorry. I'm a little tired today. Would you mind if we cut it short?"

"No, not at all," I responded. "Are you ok?"

"I'm fine, Jack, just a little tired that's all." He smiled at me and patted me on the arm. "Let's get back to the Jeep."

We walked through the desert toward the Jeep in silence. Fetch stayed in the air, flying low. He was just as concerned about Johnathen as I was. Right before we got to the Jeep, Fetch let out a little hiss. I looked up and saw him hovering in the air. He had a snarl on his face and was staring at a point over the Jeep. Hovering above the Jeep was a blue ball of light. The goblins had found us.

Chapter 23

Johnathen spotted them at the same time he mumbled a word, sending a flash of what looked like lightning at the ball. He missed. I could hear squeaks and growls coming from the ball as if the goblins were running down a long tunnel toward us. The magic building up in me jumped into overdrive. As I saw the first arms and faces of the goblins start to come out of the ball, I sent a pulse of magic toward them. Fetch sent a burst of fire at the pulse. This always seemed to strengthen my magic. As more of the pulse left my body, I wondered if I would ever get used to the feeling of it leaving me. It always felt as if part of me was being torn apart when I forced the magic out of me. It was an uncomfortable experience every time I used it.

My forced magic hit the goblins as they came out. It pushed them back into the ball. Johnathen had recovered from his earlier attempt and sent another flash of lightning. This one hit the center of the ball. With the frightened squeals and grunts of the goblins the ball imploded on itself. There was a pop as air whooshed back into the space that the ball had left. I was seeing spots before my eyes.

"Jack. We have got to move. Whoever is trying to destroy you has discovered you again. There were too many goblins coming out of that hole to believe it was just a random attack. We have to get back to the hotel."

We jumped into the Jeep and sped off down the road. Fetch stayed in the air while staying in cameo mode. He sent a spark of fire that landed on my pinky as we sped down the road, that way I could tell what he was doing. Johnathen was too focused on looking at the sky to notice.

"You focus on the road. I'll keep an eye out for more portals."

As I drove down the highway, I was looking through Fetch's eyes as well as my own. I was grateful that the road was empty during this time of day. I might have gotten distracted and caused an accident otherwise.

Fetch spotted a glowing ball. He sent a blast of red fire into it and it closed immediately. Johnathen shot another one that shrunk with a pop. One more appeared and Fetch got that one too. Whoever wanted me dead or just captive didn't seem to want to give up.

"How did they find us?" I asked.

"They found me," said Johnathen. "I let my guard down and they found me. Whoever this is, has figured out that I know you, Jack. They must have figured wherever I am you would be there too."

Another flash from Johnathen's hands blew up another ball.

"I've been careless, but now you can see why I kept you away from me and Michelle. They would have eventually traced you and Fetch to me at my place."

Johnathen mumbled a few words and a whistling sound came out of his fingers. A strange dome appeared in the sky over us for a second and then faded.

"There," said Johnathen. "That should keep them away."

Fetch flew in close keeping an ever watchful eye on the sky.

We made it back to the hotel. We hurried into our room and shut the door. Johnathen sat on the bed with his head in his hands. He was stressed. There was a slight tremor in his hands and he was breathing heavily. I felt bad. He seemed to be doing so much for me and Fetch. It looked like it had taken its toll on him.

"Hey, are you ok?" I asked again.

"No! I'm not ok!" he shouted. "I'm getting nowhere with the council, Jack. They stubbornly believe you two are a threat. Now they are convinced that since you are hiding and not showing yourself that you have some plot to destroy their precious way of life. I have made so many bad choices when it comes to you and Fetch, Jack. I don't know what way to turn these days."

I could hear the heavy burden in his voice. I looked at Fetch. His fire on my finger had gone out, but I didn't need it to tell he was feeling bad too. He nodded at me, and I knew he knew what I was about to say. He came over and stood next to me as I spoke.

"Maybe it is time for us to show ourselves to the magic world. If they can see that Fetch and I are not dangerous then they will accept us. At the least maybe they will leave us alone."

Johnathen looked up at Fetch and me. He seemed to be struggling with this idea. Finally he spoke.

"It seems to be the answer, but please, Jack, give me a little more time. I know this whole thing is unfair but if I can just persuade the council to see you, I know they will see the light. Then you will have all their protection and we can stop whoever it is that is trying to kill you."

I was getting tired of hearing about this council. It seemed like every time Johnathen mentioned them, I felt a little more annoyed by them. Why were they so afraid of change? What did they have against someone who was different? I was beginning to feel that I didn't want to have any part of the magic world, if I had to follow along with the guidelines of this council. I reminded myself that Johnathen and Michelle were the only friends that Fetch and I had. I nodded my head. I would wait a little longer, but not much longer. Johnathen looked to be in bad shape and, if anything, I wanted to help him. I felt in my heart, if I exposed myself to the magic world, it would relieve some of the pressure that was on him. I would wait but not for much longer.

Chapter 24

The next couple of days went without any excitement. Johnathen left that night, after I agreed not to reveal Fetch and me to the magic community yet. We stayed near our room, ordering room service. I had called and texted Michelle several times in those few days. She had heard about what happened from Johnathen, but was anxious to hear mine and Fetch's side too. She told me that she was busy with a project, but wouldn't give me any details. She said that she would love to show me instead later. I sent her a text explaining Fetch's mood. I asked if she would come see him, knowing that would cheer him up. I wanted to see her too. I had a feeling that she would say 'No' and that Johnathen would keep her from coming for her own protection. But, to my surprise, she responded saying she would love to see us. We decided to meet at the ramada in the park, that night around ten. When I told Fetch, he perked right up and snorted a bright purple flame. It was worth the risk to see Michelle. I held the teardrop and felt its warmth, knowing that it would protect me.

That night Fetch and I walked to the park. On the way, I saw the same gnome as always. He was fixing a pot hole in the street that looked like a giant troll footprint. I kept myself hidden from him as I walked by. He was wearing the same purple sweatshirt that he wore the first time I saw him.

Fetch and I were across the street from him, and, as he had done before, he glanced in our direction almost as if he could see us. We stood perfectly still, and for a moment I had the crazy idea that I should just let him see us. I remembered my promise to Johnathen to wait, and just watched him look in our direction. After a few seconds, he went back to his work. It was a very comical thing to watch as he performed magic to fill in the hole. He kept shaking his head and clicking his tongue. He had walked out into the street, focusing on the work at hand. He was so involved with his work that he didn't see the car heading straight at him. The driver certainly didn't see him. He was going to get hit. I couldn't let that happen. I shouted, running toward him. He looked up to see where the sound was coming from and finally noticed the car barreling down the road toward him. He looked like a deer caught in the headlights, completely frozen and unable to move. Running at full speed I grabbed him by his hood and pulled him out of the way, just in time. The car never even slowed down. It just honked as it sped down the road. The gnome squeaked and hung there, limp in my hands for a second. He blinked, shook his head, and gave me a surprised look. It was apparent that he could see me now. Fetch came bounding up behind me, his cameo mode forgotten. It was already dark and I had the idea that Fetch didn't always like having to stay hidden. I didn't think too much about it at that moment as I was more concerned over the little guy. He saw Fetch coming and his eyes got even bigger with surprise. I gently set him down.

"Are you ok?"

"Oh, yyyyes," he stammered. He kept moving his head back and forth between me and Fetch. "Thththank you for saving me," he squeaked.

"No problem," I said, trying not to laugh.

He looked so comical standing there, head bouncing back and forth.

"Just be more careful next time."

He stopped moving and stared at me for a second. All of a sudden his eyes filled up with tears and he started breathing rapidly. I was a little concerned that he was going into shock when he reached out and grabbed my hand.

"It's true! You really do exist," he said. "Everyone is talking about you, but here you are so it must be true. You saved me! Oh, thank you! Thank you!"

He was really starting to get worked up. I didn't want to leave him like this, so I sat down on the curb next to him. Fetch had gone back into cameo mode, but, as the sun was going down, I could see in the gloom the orange smoke of concern that was pouring out of his snout.

"Hey guy," I said, patting him on his shoulder. "You're ok. Calm down now. My name is"

"OH! I know who you are," interrupted the gnome, "You're the dragon survivor."

He pointed in the direction of Fetch's smoke and in a whisper said, "And this is the dragon with a name. You are the protector. You fought off the goblins and won."

With these words I now knew just how far my story had traveled, and, with a rush of concern, I also realized that by saving this little guy I had my first exposure to the magical world. How would I explain this to Johnathen?

It was the second time I had been called the dragon survivor. I couldn't think of anything cornier to be called, but the way it was said by this little guy, let me know just how serious it was to him. The way he was looking at me made me feel uncomfortable. I didn't really know how to respond to him. He looked as if he was able to see right through me. His dark little eyes seemed to twinkle in the disappearing light of day. I hadn't thought about it for a while, but I was glad for my ability to see in the dark. This guy seemed harmless but I didn't want to take any chances.

The way he was talking, I surmised people in the magic world were talking about me and Fetch. I liked the idea. The more people knew about me, the better. That way when I revealed myself it wouldn't be such a shock to them. I realized I wanted to be accepted in the magic world. I didn't want to be this mysterious thing that creatures like this little guy thought of as a savior or a protector. Is that what Johnathen was training me to be? How could I be any kind of a protector?

I looked down at this funny little guy. He was looking at me with a look of awe. Johnathen would look at me like that sometimes. I wanted him to stop looking at me that way. I stuck out my hand again and said.

"I don't really think I am anything like you just described. My name is Jack. This is Fetch. What's your name?"

His eyes got bigger with surprise at the gesture, and slowly a smile started to appear on his face. Grabbing my hand, he pumped it up and down. It surprised me how much strength he had as he squeezed my hand.

"Jack and Fetch," he said with just as much enthusiasm as his handshake. "Thank you for saving me." He spoke clearly without the stammering. "My name is Smith. That's my whole name, not my last. Gnomes don't really have last names, so it's just Smith. "

He threw back his head and laughed. It reminded me of a groundhog jabbering in the park. I wasn't sure if I understood what was so funny, but, seeing what I thought was a sad sack type character laughing this way, I couldn't help but join in. From his cameo hidden mode I heard Fetch laughing too.

Smith motioned for us to follow him into the park. We walked a little way in and he stopped at a bush. He put his face up to it and blew on one of the leaves. The bush shook a little and split apart, revealing an opening to what seemed to be a tunnel. Smith motioned for us to follow as he walked into it. We still had time before meeting Michelle, so with a look in Fetch's direction, I shrugged and followed Smith into the hole with Fetch at my side.

We entered the tunnel by crawling and, to our surprise; it opened up into a big room. It was the most fantastic and strange room I had ever seen. First of all, it was enormous! There was a mishmash of magic items and non-magic items. Smith had planted himself on an overstuffed couch in front of a big screen TV. On a table next to the couch was a small cauldron, bubbling and popping with some sort of potion. It smelled like a tennis ball and cinnamon stick. There was a toy plane flying overhead being chased by what I thought was a silver ball at first, but, when it hovered in front of my face for a second, I could see that it was a quarter spinning in the air. The room seemed to stretch all around us, with broken toys and little gizmos tweeting and hooting as they chased each other on the floor. I realized that these little things were playing tag. They stopped playing as Fetch came into view. They slowly moved over to him. Before long, he had a whole group of them just sitting there staring at him. One little car moved up and started crashing into his back paw over and over again. Fetch bent down and, with an amused look on his face, he blew purple smoke in the toy's direction, sending them all running behind the couch, accompanied with squeaks, whistles, and buzzing sounds. After they all disappeared, one little stuffed mouse stepped out from behind the couch. It shook a tiny fist at Fetch, squeaking and hooting. You could tell that he was really chewing him out. This was more like the magic world I had fantasized about.

I glanced at a workbench that was cluttered with different objects. In the middle of this table was a laptop computer. I looked back over at Smith. I was in full geek mode again. It felt good to have these familiar feelings. So much had changed for me that a familiar excitement was a comfort.

Smith had a can of soda and was loudly slurping it down. He patted the seat next to him and waved us closer.

He burped loudly saying,"Please sit. I'm sorry the place is such a mess. As you can see, I have been busy with a few projects that have gotten away from me."

He smiled and his eyes twinkled. I couldn't believe that this was the same little guy who seemed so meek just a few moments ago. Here, in this cave, he seemed to be in his element. I had a feeling that the meek little guy was more of an act and this confident little fellow was more like the real Smith. He handed me a soda and offered one to Fetch. He stared at Fetch with a look of curiosity and wonderment.

"Amazing!" he said. "You have to forgive me for staring at you, Fetch. I have never seen a dragon up close before. I've cleaned up after one that has caused trouble, but even that has been while ago."

Fetch seemed a little bothered by this last statement. Once again word reached our ears that dragons might not have been seen for a while. I wondered if Smith knew anything about the dragon eggs that had been spread around. I thought I would see what he knew about dragons.

"What do you mean it's been a while?" I asked.

Smith looked at me with a blank look on his face. "Don't you know?" he asked. "Fetch is the first dragon to be seen in this area for twenty years. That's why everyone is talking about you. When you were seen on YouTube together, it got everybody in a dither. First, there was Fetch hatching, and then choosing not to take your life force, then the two of you fighting together. Why for years now there have only been rumors of other dragons hatching, but no evidence, only trace magic of an essence exchange, a smell of magic gone dark and nothing else. Just the fact that you are both alive is a great mystery. You see Jack, if Fetch didn't consume your essence, then he shouldn't be alive. That your life force wasn't consumed, whether Fetch wanted to do it or not, is just as big a mystery as what you have become. You both are forces against the very nature of magic."

He reached for another soda, giving us time for this to sink in.

"There are many stories about you. It is believed that a wizard is helping you. If I may be so bold as to ask, would this wizard's name be Johnathen?"

My stunned silence was enough of a reply

"Ah, yes. He has always had a connection to the world of humans, and for years he has been trying to discover the mystery of the dragons. His past is a tragic one full of misery. No one knows his full story. He is very mysterious and there has been talk that the council has not agreed with what he does. He is a wizard with great power. He keeps them on their toes. Wizards have a way that can keep others guessing about their intentions. Johnathen is a good man and a better wizard. It is just hard to read what his intentions are sometimes. We gnomes have a saying, 'A wizard's glass is always half full, but you never know what it is full of.' Smith laughed at what he seemed to think of as a good joke. I didn't know how to respond to this. I took a drink of my soda and glanced over at Fetch. He sat there listening to every word trying not to look too interested. I felt a little uncomfortable at how the conversation seemed to be going. It seemed like our new little friend knew more than it had first seemed. After a short pause and a long drink of his soda, he continued talking about Johnathen.

"He has had a lot of difficulties with the Fey. Many a time he has accused them of causing trouble. There was one incident that involved a little girl, but no real strong evidence has surfaced. Some say it is because a Fey sits on the council. Have you had any interaction with the Fey?"

I looked him in the eye at this comment. There was that little twinkle. I wondered just how much he really knew about me and what had happened. I wrestled with the idea of saying 'No'. I looked over at Fetch and saw his eyes changing colors rapidly. They stopped on their neutral green color, giving me the idea that he seemed to think it was ok to answer truthfully about my run in with the fairy.

"Yes. Just before Fetch hatched, I saw a fairy. She tried to kill me."

At these words Smith's eyes got big and round. He sat there in stunned silence.

"Tried to kill you?" he asked.

I nodded my head 'Yes'.

"How?"

Again I looked at Fetch for some guidance. He nodded his head 'Yes'. I felt that I needed to tell my story. It could be helpful and I was in too deep as it was. I was taking a chance telling our new little friend as much as I was, but it was my story. I wanted to get the word out, so I went for broke. I described how it all happened in as much detail as I could remember. I wished I had my computer with me so I could read the whole story to him. I finished up to the point when Fetch began to hatch. I didn't want to go any farther than that for now. Smith sat there rubbing his chin. I felt something bumping my foot. I looked down to discover the little toy car that had bumped into Fetch was now trying to get my attention. In fact, all the toys had gathered around me. I guessed that they had been listening to my story.

"Did she use magic to lure you out into the street?" asked Smith. "Did you feel a tug or lightheaded? Are you sure she cast a spell to lead you into the street? The fey are trying to find all of the scattered dragon eggs, it is true, but to lure you out into the street so you were almost hit by a truck, and risk damaging the egg, seems strange to me."

"Yes. I mean, I think."

I was trying to remember exactly how I felt. I always thought it was strange that she would risk damage to the egg that would become Fetch. I remember feeling lightheaded, but was that because of the shock of seeing a fairy, or because she cast a spell? When I took a moment to really think about it, I wondered why she would do that. I was beginning to have my doubts.

"Ah, my young friend, I can see that you are troubled. I just wanted to learn more about you. You are the biggest mystery that the magic world has had in a long time. There are things that have happened to you that make you an enigma. For instance, I saw your battle with the goblins on YouTube. You were very brave."

"Do you know who sent the goblins to attack me?" I asked.

"Yet another mystery," said Smith. "There have been rumors that someone has been controlling them for a while now. They have attacked others and caused trouble, but I wouldn't worry about them now. They are a very cowardly lot. You beat them pretty badly."

I didn't want to go into the other encounters with the goblins. I was beginning to feel I had already said too much. This little meeting left me feeling strange. After a while Smith broke the silence.

"Now Jack, I have a question for you. The lead goblin that attacked you is a chief leader of his people. I recognized him by his always present cigar. His name is Pockhammer. He is considered very cunning and has a fearful reputation. In the goblin community a name is very important. A nickname can destroy the reputation of a goblin, so I need you to be completely honest with me. Did you really call him Booger?"

I nodded my head 'yes' and shrugged. Smith threw back his head roaring with laughter. After a few minutes, he sat up with tears of mirth in his eyes.

"Goblins and gnomes have been at odds for generations. For that insult you have given them, you have earned our friendship and respect."

He got to his feet and walked up to me. He motioned for Fetch to stand next to me and asked us to kneel down closer to him. He took his thumb and licked it and wiped it across our foreheads. He smiled and with a look of satisfaction said. "There! You have now both been marked as friends of the gnomes. When you see one of us, ask for what you need and we will help. I must get back to work now. No telling what Tolback has done now."

The droopy dog look had returned to Smith's face. I realized that Tolback had to be the troll. It seemed that Smith took on the job to clean up after the hulking beast. He showed us out of the tunnel and closed the bush behind us. I felt a little dizzy by all that had happened.

Looking over at Fetch I said "Well pal. I guess we are unique. I don't know about you but I just want to know what we are."

Fetch nodded his head, and, as a car's headlights went by, quickly went into cameo mode.

Chapter 25

We walked quickly over to the Ramada. We were both anxious to see Michelle. I didn't know if I should tell her what I had found out about Fetch and me or what Smith had said about Johnathen, and I knew I couldn't say anything about the fairy. I had the feeling that Smith was trying to convince me that the fey might not be bad. That I might have just wandered out into the street on my own. The whole meeting seemed a blur, and the fact that it ended with Fetch and me now being friends to these little gnomes seemed strange. I did want to let the magic world know about us and I guessed that being friends to the gnomes didn't hurt. I began to wonder if it was an accident that I stopped him from getting hit by that car. I remembered all the times I would see him looking in our direction, and wondered if his sensing we were near staged the whole thing in some way so that Fetch and I would expose ourselves to him. I checked the time and discovered we had been in there for a lot longer than it seemed.

We walked up to the Ramada and saw the silhouette of Michelle standing there. Fetch threw caution aside, got out of cameo mode, and ran up to meet her. I ran after him and approached Michelle.

She had her arms around Fetch. In one of her hands was a white light that she let go. It floated up about four feet and cast a light on us all. I got my first look at Michelle. She looked terrible! Her eyes were sunken in and her face was pail. She looked up at me and said in a weak voice. "Hey Jack, it feels like it's been forever." Then she fainted.

I leaned in to see if she was still breathing. I took her hand in mine and felt how cold she was. There was a grayness to her face and even her tattoo seemed faded. Her eyes were rolled back in her head and she wasn't responding to any attempts to bring her around.

"Fetch, breathe your fire on her," I said.

Fetch, who was obviously very agitated by the state Michelle was in, looked at me with a concerned expression. I backed up and let him get close to her. His healing flame had not worked as well on others as it had on me, but, with her ragged breathing and glazed half lidded look in her eyes, I was afraid Michelle was going to die. Nodding in encouragement Fetch sighed and turned back to her. Leaning in he gently breathed a thin jet of multi colored flame that caressed her face. At first it didn't seem like it was working, but, with a gasp, Michelle opened her eyes in the light of the floating ball. I watched as the color returned to her face. I was impressed by how much control Fetch had now with his flame. After a few minutes, Fetch stopped and Michelle looked much better, but I could tell by the way she was breathing that she wasn't completely healed.

I was angry, angry that Johnathen had allowed this to happen. What did he do to her? She looked at Fetch and said in a ragged voice, "Hungry, so hungry." Fetch looked at me I nodded at him knowing what he was going to do. He jumped into the air and flew off. He was on his way to get food. I took off my shirt and made a pillow for her head.

"What happened? " I asked. "How could Johnathen allow this to happen?"

She put her hand up to my lips making me stop talking. "Not his fault. Tried a spell before I was ready. Not his fault. He didn't know I was coming. I used a new spell to transport myself here. I guess I'm not that good at that type of spell."

Fetch returned with his customary bag of burgers. He gently raised her up and got behind her, supporting her head. She leaned against him as I fed her a burger. After eating half way through her second burger she started to get a little stronger. She finished and grabbed for another one under her own power. After that one, she started to talk again.

"I'm sorry. I got cocky. Johnathen has been teaching me how to use this kind of magic. It takes a lot of strength if you're not born with the ability. It took a lot out of me." She said in a horse whisper.

She wouldn't look me in the eye, and this gave me the idea that she might not be telling the whole story, but I didn't want to force the issue just yet.

"We need to get you out of here," I said.

I thought about finding Smith and getting her to his tunnel, but I didn't want her to know about my new little friend just yet. Her feelings about the fairies might cause trouble if the subject came up.

We stood her up slowly to see if she could stand on her own. She was shaky and weak but she made it to her feet. Fetch stayed to the right of her while I stayed on her left, wrapping my arm around her waist and walking slowly. We made it halfway through the park before she collapsed. I didn't wait for her to try to stand up again. I scooped her up into my arms, and, at a quick pace, made my way through the park. She weakly protested that she was fine, telling me to put her down. I just ignored her and kept walking. I had made up my mind to call for an ambulance when we got back to the hotel. I had no idea what I would tell them. I just wanted to get her help. Later on maybe Johnathen could cast a pulse making those that helped forget. I was upset at Johnathen and myself. Things had been getting increasingly strange with Johnathen. I should have guessed he wouldn't let her take a car to see me. I shouldn't have asked her to come.

Chapter 26

We made it back to our room at the hotel and went around the back way to avoid anyone seeing us. Fetch, in his worry for Michelle, couldn't keep his camouflaged mode on. He would click back and forth like a light bulb, his silver scales flashing. It was a miracle that we were not spotted. When we got to the room, I gently put her on the bed. She was looking better, much better. Fetch laid his head on her lap and was humming softly to her. She was scratching his head letting him know she was ok. She looked at me and smiled.

"It was my fault," she said. "I know you want to blame Johnathen, but it wasn't his fault. I tried to do a spell before I was ready, and it took more out of me than I thought it would."

Michelle sat up a little bit. She was about to say something when there was a loud banging on my door. I rushed over to open it, thinking that someone must have spotted us on our way here. I looked though the peephole and saw Johnathen on the other side. I opened the door and Johnathen pushed past me, knocking me over, to get to Michelle. Grabbing him by the neck, Fetch growled, letting Johnathen know he was upset.

I got up and went over to Johnathen who was at Michelle's side. I reached up and put a hand on his shoulder. There was a white flash of light and I found myself in the corner of the room entangled in a heap with Fetch. Michelle had jumped off the bed and crouched down next to me and Fetch and looked us in the eyes.

She said, "Please don't do this. Please don't fight over something that I did. It was my stupid mistake. Not his, so please stop."

Johnathen stood there staring at us, ready to cast another spell if he had to. Michelle was breathing heavily and her face was going pale. This was too much for her right now. We untangled ourselves from each other and helped her back into bed. I propped a pillow behind her head.

I looked over at Johnathen. He had a strange look on his face. It was the same look he had on his face in the desert that day. It was if he was not really there. He seemed to be fighting with his emotions. Not wanting to risk being blown across the room again, I kept my distance and asked"Are you ok?" He looked at me and slowly the glazed look in his eyes faded. I was really becoming more worried about him. His display gave me the idea that he might not be in his right frame of mind.

He reached into his pocket and pulled out a small pouch. "This will help her," he said in a flat monotone voice. I looked down at Fetch. He was not too happy with Johnathen and didn't look like he wanted to let him anywhere near Michelle. Michelle spoke to him from behind us on the bed.

"It's all right, Fetch. He wants to help me."

Fetch looked at her, then me, then back to Johnathen. He moved around to the other side of the bed and put his head on Michelle's lap. He never took his eyes off Johnathen, giving him the message that even if Michelle allowed him to help, Fetch was not going to trust him.

Johnathen went over to the sink. Filling a glass with water, he opened the pouch and took out a powder which he sprinkled into the glass. The water turned red for a second and then was clear. He brought it over to the bed, and, kneeling down, gave it to Michelle to drink.

"I have to apologize to you. I have let myself get too busy again. Things have escalated since our little goblin encounter the other day. It is a dark time for people in the magic world. The two of you have put it on edge. I know this is not your fault but there it is."

Michelle had drunk the potion and almost immediately started to look better.

"I have been trying to block the magic council in their attempts to find you. Everyone wants to meet you. Some want to study you, others want to destroy you. It has been a constant trial. I got home from yet another debate with them and found a note from Michelle. The transport spell is one that she was not ready for and I had a feeling she would come here."

He said a few words over Michelle as he waved his hands. She moaned softly, her eyes starting to close. Fetch growled softly at Johnathen. He looked over at Fetch and his eyes seemed over bright.

"Do you really think I would hurt her?" he said in a soft voice.

Fetch stopped growling, his eyes turned blue, and he looked down. Just the way Johnathen had said it made us both realize that he would never hurt her. I felt bad. He had been working so hard trying to give me a great start in this new world I had been thrust into. I couldn't even remember if I properly thanked him for the money I now seemed to take for granted. I felt like it was my fault. I didn't know how to apologize for all of this. I hoped that this wouldn't ruin our friendship.

Michelle opened her eyes. She grabbed Fetch's claw and Johnathen's hand pulling them across her stomach till they were touching. Michelle reached out her hand to me. I stepped forward and grabbed it. She then put it on top of the other's hands and then placed her hand on the very top, squeezing hard.

"I can't think of anything cornier to do than this guys. I'm sorry for what I did. Can we get over it and move on now?"

We all laughed a little. It seemed to lighten things up. We pulled our hands apart and Johnathen went over to a chair by the window. He pulled the curtain open a little. We could hear some kids out at the pool splashing and playing.

"I want a better world, Jack, a better place for all of us, one without war or poverty. Magic can help the world be a better place. I know it can. It makes me angry when those who believe they are in charge just don't listen. Can you imagine a world where a child will no longer get sick? Where there is no cancer? Where everyone goes to sleep at night with food in their stomachs?"

"Can magic do all of that?" I asked.

"I believe it can. It just needs time and the right way to set it in motion. I think I can do that, Jack. I stumbled across some magic about fifty years ago. Magic the likes this world has never seen. It has taken me years to possess it, to harness it. I am almost ready to use it, and, when I do, I believe this world will be paradise. But the council and their backward thinking has stopped me at every turn."

"There has been a great upheaval coming in the magic world. It was gaining strength before you and Fetch appeared, but it has gained even more strength since then. If I could convince the council that you have adjusted well to magic, that you are not controlled by the power, but have control over it. If I could show them you and Michelle and many others that have a spark like you, then we can show them the truth. If we can change the way they think in this part of the world then we can put a stop to all the feuding and fighting. We can stop the fey and their evil little tricks."

He paused and looked at Michelle. She had fallen asleep. She let out a little sigh, her face frowning for a moment like she was dreaming. It was good to hear her breathing easily.

"I need to keep you and Fetch safe from the magic world for as long as I can. I think it's time for you to go into complete hiding at my place. The council is asking too many questions about you, and it has now reached a point that you need to understand I can't protect you. You have become too powerful. There are those who are using you as a symbol."

I thought back to what Smith had said about the rumors concerning Fetch and me. I didn't want any of this. I had to get a grasp on all of it.

"I don't want to hide, Johnathen. I'm tired of hiding. I'm tired of waiting to see what will happen. I never asked to be a part of this world. If magic can do all the things you a say it can, then I want to be a part of that, but I can't spend my life hiding. Maybe if I show myself to the magic community they can see that I mean no harm. Maybe if Fetch and I can show them that we aren't dangerous then the council will have to accept us."

Johnathen looked at me, that dark shadow that passed over his face again showing just how old he really was.

"It would be risky, Jack. They call you dragon survivor and Fetch is a dragon with a name. No dragon would ever take a name that people could call it with. A name is a secret thing to a dragon and only shared with other dragons. This makes people believe that you have some control over him, Jack."

At these words Fetch scoffed. He had lifted his head up and his eyes glowed red.

"You know I don't control Fetch," I said. "I could never control him. I would never want to control him. Everything he does is his choice. I never forced him to do anything."

Fetch put his head in Michelle lap at this comment. His eyes glowed red still. I knew Fetch wanted to show that he was independent, that he had free will. I knew that even if I didn't show myself to the rest of the magic world soon, Fetch would do it on his own soon enough. I couldn't help but feel that there was more to the story than Johnathen was telling. That there was something he was keeping hidden. To protect Fetch and me? Possibly. To protect Michelle? Definitely. I thought back to my new little friend Smith and what he said about wizards. I realized he was telling me that wizards were not always what they seemed to be. They kept things hidden. I thought of Smith and how I misjudged him. How, until I met him, I thought of him as some sort of janitor, cleaning up magic messes, but, I realized he was so much more. I realized that I wanted to learn more about the creatures in the magic world on my own, even the fey. Smith had put the doubt in my mind about the fairy luring me into the street. Could the idea that all fairies are bad be wrong? He even mentioned that a fairy was on the council.

"Tell me more about the fairies," I said quietly to Johnathen.

A moan came from Michelle's lips as she slept. Even when she was asleep it seemed that the very word 'fairy' seemed to affect her. Johnathen looked at Michelle with concern on his face.

"What else can I tell you that I haven't said before? They are bad, evil. They are a hidden force representing all that is bad in the magic world. They have many believing they are innocent when they are not. They hold themselves apart from the rest of the magic community. They believe themselves superior to everything else. They ignore and cast out those who have impure fairy blood in them like they were animals, and they will destroy anyone who gets in their way. If you want a comparison, they are like the mafia of the magic world. You have to believe me and accept this or when you do present yourself to the magic world they will either try to control you or destroy you."

"But are all of them evil? There has to be some that are good. They can't all be bad."

"They are, Jack."

It was Michelle. She had woken up. The color was back in her face. She still looked weak but she definitely looked better. She stared at me with tears welling up in her eyes.

"You asked if I think they are all evil? Yes Jack. They are," she said in a shaky voice, "and you better start believing it too, or they will kill you and your brother the same way they killed my family. You think your brother is safe from them, Jack? You start to believe some are good and they trick you into telling them about your life. They will discover the feelings you have for your brother and manipulate you, through him, to do what they want. Then they will destroy you, Fetch, and your brother the same way they did my family."

Fetch, who had been sitting at her side this whole time, looked at me. Yellow smoke was coming out of his nose and I could see how confused he was about what Michelle said. As much as I cared about Michelle, and, even knowing that she believed the fey wanted to control or kill me and possibly my brother, I still didn't want to believe they were all bad. After talking to Smith I couldn't help but feel that they couldn't all be bad. This was a terrible time for this kind of debate. I knew, if I continued, I could lose the two closest friends Fetch and I had. If I risked telling them what Smith told me, I could lose them both. I had to find a way to get Michelle over to Smith. He seemed to be able to explain things better than I could. I hated to admit it, but, the only reason Michelle felt the way she did is because Johnathen told her the fairies killed her family. I couldn't shake the feeling that there was more to that story than Johnathen was telling. But, why would he lie about the fey? I was more confused than ever. I glanced at Fetch and saw the same look of confusion on his face.

"I'm sorry," I finally said. "This is all too confusing and frightening. I feel like I am going to lose you guys because I just don't understand. I want to believe I am in a world of great possibilities. I guess the glass is half full. I'm just not sure what it is full of."

The words were out of my mouth before I realized what I had said. Fetch tensed up for a second but I don't think anybody noticed it but me. I looked over at Johnathen, trying to keep my face as neutral as I could. I had just quoted a gnome expression about wizards. I wondered if Johnathen knew that and would catch on that we had made a new friend. Johnathen stared at me, his eyes narrowed. He was trying to get some sort of read on me. He heard me use the expression and was trying to decide if it was a fluke that I used it or if I had heard it from a gnome.

He opened his mouth, ready to say something, when a high pitched humming suddenly filled the room. It was like a smoke detector going off. I turned to Fetch to tell him to stop blowing smoke, when I remembered I had taken the batteries out of the smoke detector. I was about to say something, when Johnathen jumped up. He had a snarl on his lips. I saw the reason why. At eye level in front of him was a familiar blue ball. It was already growing and getting brighter. This time I was ready for it. I quickly jammed my hand into the light. I hit something solid and without thinking about it I pulled it through. I had a goblin by the throat. I took him by surprise so he just hung there in my hand. I recognized him immediately. I smiled and said through gritted teeth, "Hello Booger so good to see you again."

As soon as I pulled Booger out, Johnathen had put his hands on either side of the ball and simply started to squeeze. It began to shrink and as his hands got closer together the ball started to glow brighter until with a loud pop it disappeared.

Booger started to struggle and squeal, but, before he could cause any real damage, Fetch whipped out his tongue and hit him on the forehead.

Booger went limp. It seemed Fetch's tongue had an anesthetic effect on Booger.

"That's a new one," I said to Fetch.

He looked as surprised as I did at this discovery. He kept shaking his head and whipping out his tongue, trying to get the bad taste out of his mouth. I guess it was pure instinct that caused him to try that. Part of me was worried. Now that Fetch knew how to do this there was no telling what was in store for me. Judging by Fetch's wicked sense of humor and his continuing battle to keep me humble, I wondered if I would ever learn all the fantastic things he could do.

Returning my full attention back to Booger, I kept a firm grip on him as I went over to the table and slammed him down out on top of it. He was squeaking and his eyes were looking around wildly, but he was unable to move. I was glad it kept him from spitting acid everywhere.

"You like your new name, Booger?" I said through gritted teeth.

I really didn't like this little monster. He had broken my nose and caused me a lot of pain. It was all I could do to keep from smashing my fist into his ugly little face.

"You Flap!" he screamed.

I heard Johnathen mutter a word and felt a strange tingle.

"No one can hear us. No other portals will appear. I'm sorry. In my haste to get here, I forgot to put up any concealment spell to keep anyone from knowing I was here. I was careless, but we are safe now. Booger? I like the name. It suits him."

I looked at Johnathen. He had an amused look on his face and motioned to me.

"Please continue," he said.

I looked back at Booger as he continued his rant. "You are troll fung. A pile of gnome snith. You have ruined me you Flap." He screamed.

I just smiled and said, "Booger."

He made a choking sound in his throat and spit at me. I guess I was wrong about him not being able to spit. Before it could hit my face, Fetch shot a thin flame at it and it sizzled in the air and evaporated. I was impressed by Fetch's aim. He was really getting good at it. I gripped Booger's neck a little tighter.

"Try that again and I will squeeze your head and pop it like a zit. Hey, maybe that's your new name. Zit. You like that?" I asked.

He focused his eyes on me when he spoke. I saw the calculating beast from the parking lot in that stare. "No, please not another name, "he said, sounding like a twisted little squeaking mouse. "It's hard enough going around being called Booger. Haven't you done enough damage already? "He began to whine and choke and I almost found myself feeling sorry for him. Almost.

"All the damage I caused?" I said, shaking him just a little.

It was hard to control myself around him. It was like his very presence was making my blood boil. I remembered how mad I was when Booger and his friends attacked us in the parking lot, and how I used him like a club to hit the others with. I had to fight the urge to pick him up and do that again.

"You attacked me!" I shouted in his face. "You broke my nose and tried to kill me! Why shouldn't I return the favor, Booger? I should break your nose. Or maybe I should just let Fetch eat you."

Booger squealed like a pig and a gagging noise came from his throat

I felt a hand on my shoulder and turned to see Michelle standing next to me. She was looking at me with fear in her eyes. She had to know they were just empty threats. I really wouldn't kill him and feed him to Fetch. But, as I looked into her eyes, I realized that I didn't know that for sure. I really hated this ugly little thing and it took all my willpower to not smash its ugly face in. This scared me a little. I don't think I truly ever had those kinds of feelings before. I heard Fetch growling somewhere behind me, ready to attack just as soon as I gave the word. I looked at Michelle. Confusion filled my heart. What was happening to me?

"Jack, "said Johnathen, bringing me back into focus. "I believe he will tell us what we want to know. If he doesn't, then I believe Fetch can eat him. "

Johnathen had that twinkle in his eyes that he had when I first met him. He looked more like his old self. I hadn't seen him look that confident in the past week. It helped relax the anger toward my little friend here.

"I'm sure Fetch is hungry."

He gave me a little wink of encouragement. I wondered if he saw the same fury in me that Michelle had seen.

Fetch moved over to Booger's face, opening his mouth and snapping it closed inches from Booger's pig like nose. Booger squealed in terror. It seemed that Smith was right in saying that goblins were cowards.

Fetch stayed close to Booger's face for a while, growling and snapping. I wanted him to think we were serious about letting Fetch eat him. Booger continued to squeal in terror and he began to sniff and hiccup. It was hard to imagine, but this ugly, smelly creature, that so viciously attacked me in the parking lot, looked like he was starting to cry.

"Ok, Ok!" he sniveled. "I'll tell you what you want to know. Just please don't let him eat me."

I stayed silent for a few more minutes, letting Booger sweat it out. I looked over at Johnathen like I was trying to decide what to do. I shook my head and sighed.

"Ok, this is against my better judgment, but we'll let him talk."

Booger began to giggle with relief. He took in great big gulps of air and his ugly little face relaxed.

"You guys mind if I smoke?" he asked with the same growling bravado he had at the parking lot.

I squeezed his throat a little and Fetch growled. Booger squealed again. Even though I had calmed down, and had the upper hand on this goblin, the last thing I wanted was to lower my guard around him too much.

"Who sent you to attack Fetch and me?"

"Attack you and...?" started Booger. His eyes got really big. A smile formed on his lips and he looked at me in surprise, as if he was just now realizing something.

"The dragon has a name?" he squeaked. "There were rumors but no one believed it."

Fetch rolled his eyes at this. He moved in closer and continued to growl. He whipped his tail around, smacking Booger on the side of the head. Fetch was getting a little tired of everyone being surprised he had a name. Booger snarled at Fetch, showing teeth. I reached over and forced his mouth closed.

"No snarling or spitting or I will break your jaw."

Booger looked me in the eye. He sighed and mumbled something that sounded like an 'ok'. I let go of his chin.

"Man boss, you have gotten stronger," he mumbled.

I guess he was right. I had changed quite a bit in the time since I fought him last. In a strange way, I wanted to fight him again, to show him I wasn't the clumsy doofus that had barely got away the last time we fought.

"Look, we are getting tired of this," said Johnathen from behind me. "Just answer the question."

Booger looked around at all of us with a wild look in his eyes. He took a deep breath and with a pitiful look on his face said, "I don't know."

Fetch let out a short burst of flame to show his anger. Booger squealed, throwing up his arms. We all noticed this but Booger didn't seem to realize that he could move yet.

"No. I swear man. I don't know. We were pulsed, all of us. We found a bag of money and directions on where to find you. It was nothing personal man. It was just a job. We were just doing a job. The only time I even came close to finding out who it was that kept us going on these raids, was a glimpse of him on a mountain top. All I could see was a shadow of this guy. But the shadow was kind of like this inky smoke that kept moving around. It gave me the creeps. It was all I ever saw of this guy. He kept on giving us money and leaving us notes as to who to attack next."

Johnathen put his hand on my shoulder. "I think he is telling the truth, Jack. Goblins are not the most trustworthy of creatures. It makes sense that whoever hired them to attack you, would pulse them into forgetting or hide themselves in some way. The thing is, it is very hard to pulse a goblin. They have very sharp, clever minds."

"A goblin don't forget easy," squeaked Booger.

He giggled that insane little giggle again. I kept my hand on his neck. There was something about the way he described the inky black smoke that sounded familiar. I thought back to that dream I had in the tunnel. Could it be connected somehow? I let go of Booger's neck. He sat up realizing that he could move now, but Fetch remained close enough and ready to paralyze him again if he made any sudden moves. Michelle, who had been quiet this whole time, finally spoke up.

"Do you think it was someone from the council?" she asked.

Booger had moved a little to get a better look at her. He licked his lips greedily and reached behind himself, pulling out one of those cigars. He popped it in his mouth and prepared to light it.

"Why don't you leave with me when we are done here?" he asked. "We could have a good time before I eat your face, pretty girl."

This was supposed to scare her. Michelle just opened her hand and closed her eyes. She muttered a few words and a small flame appeared in her hand. She blew the flame in Booger's direction. It landed on his eyebrows, which quickly disappeared.

"Hey!" he squeaked, beating his face to get the flames out. He sniffed the air when he put out the flame out, his eyes narrowing. "You weren't born with it girl. You're not supposed to do magic."

Johnathen sent a ball of what looked like raven feathers into Booger's face. They slapped him silly for a few seconds before disappearing.

"That is none of your business," he said. I could tell that Johnathen didn't like how smart Booger seemed. He stared at Booger for a few seconds, his eyes flashing. He was angry. You really don't want a wizard to look at you the way Johnathen looked at Booger.

"Ok, I get it. You all hate me. So what's a guy to do?" He started to light the cigar.

Fetch grabbed it out of his mouth, leaving just the tip between Boogers lips. Fetch quickly chewed the cigar and spit it on Boogers face. It stuck to his cheek. He had a look of shock and hurt on his face that made it hard not to laugh.

"Ok dragon," he said. "You can eat me if you want, but don't destroy the stogies. That's just harsh."

Shaking his head, Johnathen walked over to the mini bar. He reached inside, grabbed a bottle of soda, and handed it to Booger. Without even thinking about it, Booger opened the bottle and in one gulp drank it down, never taking his eyes off of Fetch. He stuffed the bottle in his mouth, chewing loudly, and swallowing hard. Johnathen leaned down looking Booger in the eye.

"I think we need an inside man to keep an eye on things for us. Someone who can discover just who we are dealing with. And you, my friend, will do nicely."

Booger's eyes got even larger at this comment. "No! No way! This guy finds out I'm working against him, no telling what he will do to me. He is powerful. He has a magic I have never seen or smelt before." At this last statement, Booger looked at me. "It's close to yours, but darker and twisted."

Booger shuddered at this last comment. It had to be pretty bad for a creature like a goblin to shudder that way. I went to the mini bar getting a soda for myself.

"Do you think we can trust him?" I asked Johnathen.

"No," he laughed. "But I can put a spell on him that will dissolve his head if he betrays us."

I really didn't think Johnathen would do that, but, it didn't hurt our situation to let this guy think that he would.

This was becoming quite an interesting situation. What an opportunity to fall in our laps. As far as I knew, this was as close as Johnathen had got to finding out who was attacking me. If we could keep Booger in line, we just might have a shot.

I turned back to Booger and got down close to his face. I knew this was risky, but I wanted to let him know that I had no fear of him. I felt a pounding sense of urgency. I had pushed down all the fear and concern over this unknown enemy. I felt closer to answers than I ever had and I was not going to let this opportunity go. As I stared at Booger, fear dawned on his face. He seemed to see something in my eyes that frightened him.

"What are you?" He asked in a shaky voice.

I had no idea what he saw when he looked at me, but I seized the opportunity to use this little coward's fear to my advantage.

"I am your personal worst nightmare. You will never be able to hide from me or from Fetch." I sniffed the air, closing my eyes for dramatic effect. "I've got your scent now. You turn on me and I will hunt you down. I will make you pay for any kind of betrayal, and when I am done, you will beg to have your head dissolved by Johnathen."

My heart pounded in my ears as my own words frightened me. The silence in the room was intense and heavy. I stood up after a while, still looking down at Booger.

"I'm counting on you, Pockhammer. Whatever Johnathen asks you to do, you better do."

The room was completely silent. Everyone was staring at me. I turned around to look at Booger and saw an evil grin on his face, his eyes narrow.

Something had happened and for a second Booger had lost the fear that I had given him.

"You've been making friends," he growled. "I thought I smelled gnome on you."

I realized what I had done. I had called him 'Pockhammer'. I had called him by his true name. How would I know this?

Johnathen walked over to Booger and above his head made a green ball appear. It floated down, covering his head, and grew until it covered his entire body. I could see him inside it, yelling and screaming. He was really angry.

"I think it is best to keep him with me for now."

Johnathen looked over at me. There was anger and hurt in his eyes. He had heard what Pockhammer had said, and all he had to do was look at me and he knew it was true.

"Johnathen," I started, "let me explain."

"Explain?" he interrupted. "What's to explain? You obviously have been making friends despite my pleas that you stay hidden."

"You don't understand," I started again.

Johnathen just raised a hand. "Now is not the time or place for this, Jack. Whatever happened, it could cause serious problems. All my work over the last few months could be compromised. I don't pretend to have any control over your actions. You are free to do what you want. I just hoped you would listen. You betrayed me, Jack. Both you and Michelle."

Michelle sat up. She was starting to look a little pale again. She looked confused at his words. She must not have heard what Pockhammer had said. Johnathen turned to her.

"Michelle, you took a great risk using that spell. I asked you to keep it simple and stay safe. But you went ahead and took the risk that could have killed you. I wish I had never taught you magic. You betrayed me as well "

"Jack, it seems the magic world is already forming their opinion of you and Fetch. You can't hide forever. You seem to have already found a gnome and made a friend. That means that your story is being spread even more. Please be careful. It is hard for you to believe, but I do have your best interest at heart. I don't know how to fix this. It changes everything."

Once again Johnathen got that faraway look. We had hurt him deeply. I wanted to explain what had happened, but I could tell he was in no mood to listen. Fetch sat there, his eyes changing color rapidly.

"Michelle, I think you should stay here for now and recover. You have had quite a shock to your system and it is dangerous for you to move around too much. Please do not attempt any more magic for now." He put his hand up to his forehead. "I really have been working too hard. This changes everything. I need to go now. I will be in contact with you soon. Within the next couple of days I think."

He got that faraway look again. He reminded me of a guy I knew in high school who was addicted to meth. He had that same faraway look.

"I would ask you to stay here and not leave this room until you hear from me, but I don't think that would do any good."

He looked as if he was about to say something more, but then changed his mind. With Booger flung over his back, still swearing at all of us, he opened the door and left. In the silence that followed Michelle began to cry.

Chapter 27

I felt terrible. I didn't mean to meet Smith, it just happened. If Johnathen had only allowed me to explain. He looked so hurt and upset at all of us, but the one thing that was nagging me was how completely worn out he seemed, almost a shadow of his former self. It looked like he was getting worse and worse every time I saw him. I couldn't shake the idea that it was because he was working too hard to hide and protect Fetch, me, and Michelle. There was still so much I didn't know. I was beginning to think I would never know. But, I felt I needed to take more action; more than the writing that was still going on in my computer; more than the Facebook postings. A seed of an idea was starting to form in my head. I hoped Michelle would go along with it. She continued to cry, unconsolable. I kept my distance, feeling she needed to cry this out. Fetch laid his head on the bed next to her, letting her know he was there for her when she was ready. The affection Fetch had for Michelle was touching. After a while Michelle stopped crying. She put her hand on Fetch's head and sat up.

"What happened, Jack?" She asked.

I told her the story of how we met Smith, trying to stress to her that I had no choice. I could tell that she was not upset. I knew she felt that we should show the magic world who we are. She was already known, but her ability to use magic was not. Too many secrets seemed to be flying around.

At the end of my story Michelle sighed, "You have become more of a part of the magic world in a few months than I have over the past ten years. I know he is upset but Johnathen is wrong to keep you hidden."

At the mention of Johnathen's name, tears welled up in Michelle's eyes.

"I'm so worried about him, Jack. I'm worried and scared. He will disappear for days sometimes, and, when he comes back, it's like a part of him is gone or changed. I don't know what kind of magic he is doing but it is taking its toll on him. I'm sure it is to help you, to keep you hidden, to keep us both hidden. We have to show ourselves for what we are, Jack. All three of us. Even if it means Johnathen would be mad at us. I am afraid of what will happen if he keeps on going like this. We have to help him.

It's time for us to show the magic world who we are. If he keeps this up, I'm afraid he will die."

She put her face in her hands. It was amazing to me that a person as strong as I believed Michelle to be could cry the way she did over certain things. I reminded myself of everything she had been through and how much she loved Johnathen. I knew the idea of going against his wishes was hard for her, but she already showed that she wanted to break away from him a little too, even if it was to protect him. I wanted the same things too. I was glad that she felt this way. I decided to tell her my plan.

"How are you feeling?" I asked her.

She shrugged. "I'm ok, just a little tired."

She smiled an encouraging smile to let me know she was fine.

"You think you would be up for a little adventure tomorrow night? I have an idea, but, for it to work, I need you to meet a friend of mine."

She sat up and smiled even wider.

"Ok," she said.

"Then I want you to meet one of the only friends I have in the magic world." I said. "He can help us. It would be the magic world equivalent of networking."

Michelle would amaze me at times. She was pretty much raised in a magic world, but had an understanding of the non-magic world. She was incredibly smart. The magic she used seemed to require words and gestures that I didn't think I could ever master. Her friendship was something I would always cherish, no matter what. My feelings for her grew stronger all the time. I tried not to think about them too much. I was afraid it would jeopardize our friendship. Besides, it was obvious how she felt about Johnathen. I knew how hard it was for her to go against him. I also knew that deep down she was doing it because she believed it would help him in the end.

I realized that I had been staring at her for a while. She smiled and threw a pillow and the bedspread at me.

"Sorry guys, but I need some beauty rest and this girl don't sleep on the floor."

I had to stop myself from saying something stupid like "You don't need any beauty rest."

"Good night," I said turning out the lights in the room.

Fetch curled up at the foot of the bed, laying his head on the end so he could keep an eye on Michelle. I sat in a chair and wrapped myself in the blanket. I planned to go outside in a little while to take a look around for signs of any more goblins. I felt bad that I didn't get a chance to explain to Johnathen about Smith. I hoped I could tell him about it soon. I lay there staring at Michelle as she drifted off to sleep. I remembered that my magic journal was writing this all down. If I didn't find a way to edit it, Michelle would read all of this one day. I closed my eyes for a moment and when I opened them it was early the next morning. I guess I was more tired than I thought.

Michelle slept the better part of the next day. Neither Fetch nor I wanted to leave her alone, out of concern that someone or something might attack. I wanted to move to another room, feeling that we had stayed here too long. Then the idea occurred to me that Johnathen might have placed some sort of spell around us to protect us from harm. Looking at her sleeping, I began to have second thoughts about going to see Smith. She had been through so much and I didn't want to push her. When Fetch saw that I was up, he went over to the door. He opened it, going into camouflage mode and closed the door behind him. He returned a little later with breakfast, doughnuts and large coffees. We stayed quiet so we wouldn't wake up Michelle. I grabbed my computer and got on Facebook. I wanted to say something, but didn't know what to post. I watched Fetch drink his coffee. His eyes rolled back in his head a little. It was quite obvious that he enjoyed the coffee very much. I posted on Facebook; "I don't know if anybody knows this, but dragons Looove coffee☺." I waited to see what kind of response I would get. After a couple of likes I logged out and put my computer away.

Michelle woke up a few minutes later. Fetch sat there with a bag of donuts in his mouth so he would be the first thing she saw when she woke up. She opened her eyes and smiled at Fetch's eager face. He could really be a dork when it came to Michelle. She laughed and scratched his head, took a donut and a big sip of coffee.

She looked much better than she did last night. She still had the dark circles under her eyes and I didn't want to push her too much, but she insisted that she was fine and got up.

"Do you have something I can wear?" she asked with a mouthful of donut.

She had slept in the clothes she had on last night. They were worn out and very dirty. I remembered how Fetch had healed her last night and noticed that her clothes weren't burned. I wondered if this was because Fetch had gained more control over his flame or he had burned my clothes off on purpose. Knowing his sense of humor, it wouldn't surprise me at all if he had.

"Uh, sure," I said, "nothing that will fit you though."

She smiled and there was a twinkle in her eyes as she said, "I don't think that will be a problem. A simple spell should change that."

"Do you think it is wise for you to do magic again so soon?" I asked.

"Oh, I won't be casting the spell, you will."

I looked at her in surprise. I never thought of using my Forced magic that way. I guess that it wouldn't be any different from the way I used it to start the journal. But it would be directed at another person this time. I shook my head.

"I don't think I'm ready for anything like that. I could hurt you."

"I don't think you will. Your magic seems to be tied into who you are. The simple fact that your magic comes from inside you the way it does, means you couldn't hurt me because it is just not in you to hurt me."

I thought back to when I had knocked out Johnathen. I was about to remind her of that.

"I know what you are thinking, but that was when you were defending yourself. Johnathen didn't give you much of a choice. I still don't know what he was thinking when he pushed you so hard. You have to learn to accept your magic, Jack. You can't be afraid of it. You won't hurt me."

I looked in her eyes and was a little overwhelmed by her confidence in me. She really believed I could do it. She smiled and gave me a peck on the cheek.

"I won't take 'no' for an answer, Jack. Besides, Fetch will be right there with you the whole time."

I looked over at Fetch. His eyes were the steady green that showed his confidence in me.

"You really think I can do this?" I asked him.

He rolled those green eyes and smacked me with his tail.

"I'll take that as a yes," I said, rubbing the side of my head.

"Ok. How do you think I should do this?"

Michelle jumped up. "Give me a sec."

She grabbed some towels and headed for the shower. This gave me a few minutes to think of how I was going to do this. I had no idea! I paced back and forth in the small hotel room. Fetch watched me going back and forth. He was sitting on the bed with the TV remote in his hands. After a while, he got up and stood in front of me. He pushed on my chest with his head trying to make me stop. With a great shove he knocked me back into a chair, flipping it over backward. I heard a laugh and saw Michelle standing there fresh from the shower. She had a big towel wrapped around her body and another one on her head.

"Thanks a lot you stupid lizard," I said to Fetch. "You pushing me doesn't help me get in the right frame of mind."

"Ok, Jack," said Michelle. "Time to stop playing around. I want you to look at me. Get a good mental image of me in your mind."

I got up off the floor and looked at Michelle. She stood there wrapped in the towels, hands on her hips. I could see the design of her tattoo curling around her body. I had to admire the time that it must have taken to get such a design. I got a little distracted at the thought that she was standing in front of me wearing nothing but a couple of towels.

"Relax Jack," she said. "It's just me. You can do this. The human mind has a better understanding of things than we give it credit for, Jack. I know you're not aware of it, but you already have the idea of what size I am. If you think about it, it was a mind, just like ours, that came up with the idea of numbers and languages, a mind like ours that created pyramids and The Hanging Gardens of Babylon. Those things were created by the strongest magic of all, Jack. The human imagination. It is what I believe fuels your magic, Jack. There is no way you can hurt me, because you choose not to. It is the choice we all have. It's what keep us human and not some kind of beast, the simple fact that we can choose who we are and what we do. I have confidence in your forced magic, Jack, because I have confidence in you. Think about me, Jack, the magic I can do. If I can learn to do magic, then you can do this. Once I realized that I knew I could perform magic, it was just the right words and a little practice and I transported myself across the city."

"Yeah," I mumbled, trying not to get distracted at her standing there in the towels. "But that didn't turn out so well did it?"

"This is different, Jack, now do it."

She stood there not moving. I knew she would stand there all day if I didn't do something. I nodded 'ok'.

The idea was for me to change the towels around her so that they became clothes. I was going to accomplish this by imagining her in a certain outfit. I wouldn't be making something out of nothing. I would just change the towels into something else. I just hoped I wouldn't change Michelle along with the towels. I closed my eyes and got a good mental image of Michelle. I remembered the black dress she wore when I first met her. I played that day over and over in my mind. I wanted to make sure I got the right image. When I was sure I had it clear enough, I searched my mind for the forced magic. It was a little harder to find but soon I found the spark. At first it didn't want to grow. The thought process I had behind it was different from what I had before. Even when I had used it to start the journal, it was different from making clothes. Finally it started to grow. That uncomfortable itchy feeling spread through my body. When I was sure I had the image of that dress in my mind, I began to rip the magic out of me. As it started to leave my body, that first time I met Michelle became crystal clear in my mind. So much so that it felt like I was standing there, almost reliving that day. I saw Michelle and I even saw myself for a second. The magic left me almost reluctantly this time. My vision blurred for a second. I heard a little gasp from Michelle and a strange grunt from Fetch. I opened my eyes and saw Michelle standing there in the same black dress that she was wearing when I had met her. The towels were gone. I had changed them. Michelle stood there, her hair and even her makeup done exactly the way I remembered it being that day. She turned to look in the mirror.

"Wow, Jack! You did good. This is just how I looked that first day, isn't it? Wow! All you need is a little more focus and it would be flawless."

I was confused at her last statement.

"A little more focus? But you look fine. Wait, did I hurt you, are you ok?" I asked.

Michelle turned back to me and looked like she was about to laugh. I heard a strange snort coming from Fetch. I looked over to see him on his back on the floor. He was holding his chest and his great big snout was wide open. For a second I thought he was in pain, but I quickly realized he was just in the throes of silent laughter. Michelle was unable to restrain herself from laughing any longer. I was confused. What was so funny? I glanced down and got the answer. Yellow flip flops, purple sweatpants, and blue T-shirt. A quick look in the mirror and I discovered I was wearing the same thing I had on that first day, right down to the red fuzzy stocking cap. I whipped it off, relieved I still had hair and eyebrows. I turned to look at my two closest friends who were laughing like hyenas.

"Don't laugh too hard, Michelle. With one stray thought you could've been wearing this and I could be in the dress."

Fetch found this really funny and started to snort purple fire. He got ahold of himself, picked up the fuzzy stocking cap and handed it to Michelle. He sat there in front of her. He looked from the hat to Michelle over and over again.

"Oh all right, you overgrown lizard," she said.

She put the stocking cap on, pulling it down until it covered her entire head. We all laughed at this. I thought back to all the times I had enjoyed laughter like this with my new friends. They were the best times I'd had in years. This, more than anything, strengthened my resolve to help Johnathen by showing myself to the magic world, whether he wanted me to or not.

I grabbed some clothes and a few towels and announced I would be taking a shower myself. I closed the door to the small bathroom to the sounds of Michelle and Fetch's laughter. As I stood under the water, I felt a strange tingling sensation on my leg. I looked down at the strange mark left from Fetch's hatching. It itched a little. I touched it and felt its strange roughness. If it wasn't so high up on my thigh I would have shown it to Michelle to see what she thought, but I figured that would be a little embarrassing. Fetch had enough to laugh at, without me adding an awkward exchange like showing a mark on my leg to Michelle. I dried off and put my clothes on in the small bathroom. I was feeling a little raw at the idea of Fetch always having a laugh at my expense. I could still hear the two of them laughing in the next room. I wanted to get Fetch back. After all, it was because of him that I was ever in the purple sweats and blue T-shirt combo. An idea was beginning to form in my head. With my new discovery of what I could do with my magic, a trick I could play on Fetch was forming in my mind. Something that might even make him think twice about playing another trick on me. I sat down on the toilet lid and concentrated on an image. I knew he had to be close to the bed, so I knew I could use one of the pillows. I let the magic build in me. It was easier this time. It was as if the magic just had to get used to the idea of what I was doing for it to work. After I was sure that I had a clear image of what I wanted, I pushed. From the next room I heard a yelp of surprise from Fetch, followed by a shriek from Michelle, which was quickly followed by peals of her laughter. I had a feeling that was a good sign. I walked out of the bathroom to the funniest thing I could possibly imagine. The magic had worked better than I had expected.

Fetch stood there with a surprised look on his face as he stared in the mirror. On his head, attached by a bright yellow bow, was a twirly beanie cap. The propeller was spinning and whistling a happy little tune. He had a pink T-shirt with gold letters saying 'I'm a widdle dwagon' across the chest. Slowly Fetch turned to look at me. I knew I was in trouble. I didn't care. I was laughing too hard to care. Whatever he was going to do, it was worth it. He got up in my face. Then, with all the pomp and drama he could master, bowed down to me. He continued to keep bowing in front of me, admitting that I finally got the best of him. I know he picked up on the bowing thing from some movie he saw on TV the other night. We all laughed at Fetch scraping the ground in front of me as the beanie continued to twirl and whistle. This was turning out to be a great day.

Chapter 28

We spent the day in the room, ordering room service and watching whatever was on TV. I hoped Smith would be home. I was sure I could find the bush and I made a hopeful guess that, now that Fetch and I were friends of the gnome's, we would be able to get into his tunnel. I hoped Michelle would be able to also. Another guess made me believe that as long as she was with us she would be able to enter the cave. The day stretched out like a day will when you are waiting to do something. Finally it began to get dark and we decided to go.

After getting some food, and asking Michelle if she was ok about a hundred times, we left to go see Smith. As luck would have it, we didn't have to try to enter on our own. I found him trimming the bush where he lived. His face lit up when he saw me and Fetch. He waved to us enthusiastically. He opened the tunnel and before we went in I told him I had a surprise for him. We went into the tunnel and Michelle touched him, allowing him to see her. He was love struck immediately. He took her hand and patted it muttering "My, my, what a beauty, what a beauty."

I let out a little sigh of relief that he was so accepting of Michelle so quickly.

"Hello. My name is Michelle," she said with a little giggle.

It was plain to see that she liked Smith right off the bat.

"Of course you are, my dear. I knew it the moment I saw you," said Smith as he led us down the tunnel never taking his eyes off of her. "Pek has told me all about you, though he never said you were so beautiful."

"You know Pek?" asked Michelle.

"Of course I do my dear," answered Smith, proudly pointing to his laptop.

"Who is Pek?" I asked.

The name sounded familiar but I couldn't place it.

Smith waved a hand in a dismissive way toward me and, never letting Michelle out of his sight, said, "All in good time my boy. You will know all in good time."

He reached above his head and pulled on a long root that was protruding through the roof of his home. He pulled it all the way through the ground. It made a popping sound and Smith was standing there with a bunch of flowers in his hand. They were roses in the process of blooming. They bloomed in his hands and changed colors. When they were fully bloomed, they gently shrank down to buds and started to bloom again.

They were beautiful and strange, and Michelle loved them. She leaned in and gave Smith a kiss on the cheek, thanking him. Smith's face turned beet red and he touched his cheek like he would never wash it again. Fetch, not liking all the attention Smith was getting from Michelle, came up and stood between them. Smith put his hands on his hips and, looking like an old teacher about to scold a mischievous student said, "Well my friend, we are just going to have to fight for her."

They glared at each other eye to eye. Both Michelle and I froze. We didn't know how serious this was. I knew that Smith seemed timid and weak, but looks can be very deceiving. I had a hunch there was a lot more to Smith than was apparent and that was why I wanted to come see him.

After a few tense moments of glaring at each other, Smith threw back his head and began to laugh his chipmunk laugh. Fetch joined in the laughter. Michelle and I started breathing again.

Smith threw his arms around Fetch's neck like you would to a long lost friend.

"Imagine me, challenging a dragon for the honor of a beautiful lady."

He shook his head. I still had a suspicion that he could handle himself a lot better than he was letting on.

"You will just have to get used to having two suitors who obviously adore you Michelle. I don't think Fetch could survive the fury of a gnome attack."

With this comment Fetch and Smith roared with laughter again.

Michelle and I glanced at each other. Neither one of us fully understood the humor. We started laughing anyway. We were of this magic world and more of the non-magic world seemed to be a dream. I thought about my brother and hoped he was ok. His life had changed so much, affected by magic without him being aware of it. I made a promise to do everything I could to keep that from happening again. It was wrong to manipulate people. All this talk of keeping the magic world secret from the non-magic word was untrue. As long as the fairies were allowed to affect people's lives there was no true separation. Only deception. It had to stop. People had to know the truth in both the magic world and the non-magic world. I hoped that Smith was the one that could help with accomplishing that.

Smith was wiping his eyes and breathing heavily from his and Fetch's little joke. He looked at all of us with gratitude.

"Friends," he said, "I am so grateful you are here. It can be so lonely out here in the park. Gnomes often spend their days alone, rarely communicating with each other. I was always a different kind, wanting the company of others. Oh, don't get me wrong, we are very social in our own right, it is just hard for us to interact with other magic folk. For so long we have done the work of cleaning up after the magic mistakes and disasters. The gnomes are a reminder of those little mistakes people make in the magic world. Let's face it; most people don't like to be reminded of their mistakes."

"But, please, forgive me for going on. You have the look of those who have questions that need to be answered. But, first things first, as Jack here is a little befuddled right now, let me introduce myself to you, Michelle. My name is Smith and it would be my honor to call you 'friend of the gnomes'."

Michelle looked at me like she was expecting me to say something. I shrugged and gave her a reassuring nod. I was a little embarrassed that I didn't introduce her to Smith, but, the way he lead her in, ignoring Fetch and me, I hadn't known when to speak up. I didn't really blame him though. Michelle was one of those types of girls that commanded attention when she entered a room, whether she meant to or not.

Michelle nodded at Smith. Motioning her to kneel in close, like he was about to tell her a secret, Smith kissed her on the forehead.

"Now Michelle, you are friend to the gnomes. If ever you see our kind and need help, you have but to ask. Oh, this is wonderful! You are just as much a legend in the magic world as Jack and Fetch are. I have secured a place in the history books by proclaiming all three of you 'friends to the gnomes'."

Michelle had a strange look on her face. I didn't blame her. The way Smith was talking, it sounded like there was some sort of price to being a gnome friend. I hoped we hadn't gotten into some kind of situation we would regret later on.

After a few moments of awkward silence, where Smith stood there smiling at all of us, he spoke.

"Now my dear friends, even as delighted as I am for your visit, I have the feeling that you are here for more than my famous hospitality."

Michelle and I just looked at each other. I knew this was when I had to put my idea into effect. Before I could say anything, Michelle spoke up.

"We are part of the magic world. I have been a part of it for much longer than Jack. Fetch is completely lost to how he is supposed to be and we are all tired of hiding. We're ready to take the risk of being seen. Can you tell us where there are more magical beings like yourself?"

I looked at her in surprise. She must have picked up on my idea and she definitely said it better than I could. Smith walked over to his fridge and took out four sodas, handing one to each of us.

"Are you sure you want the entire magic world to see you?" he asked staring down at his unopened can of soda. "There are those who might not accept you as easily as I or the other gnomes would. I know that the elves already consider you a friend in some circles, Michelle, but there is no guarantee that they would accept Jack, and the very different nature of Fetch scares some people, and there is the issue of the Fey."

Smith looked at Michelle at this last statement. Michelle, as usual, had that same dark look in her eyes at the very mention of the fairies. It hit me at how quickly her mood would change whenever the fey were mentioned. It was kind of weird how quickly she would react. Smith opened his soda and took a sip. Just for something to do to break this tense moment, I moved over to sit next to Michelle. Fetch moved next to her other side. Michelle was fighting to keep the tears from streaming down her face. She tried to look as normal as she could as she opened her soda and took a long drink. She was shaking a little. She was afraid. She wanted to show herself to the magic world, but she knew she had to expose herself to the Fey as well. She was afraid of what would happen if she met a fairy. Not necessarily what they would do to her, but what she would do to them. I thought back to her reactions to the very words fairy or fey and realized how deep her feelings were involving them. I put a hand on top of hers and her thin barrier of emotions broke.

Smith stood up and came over to stand right in front of her. He motioned her to kneel down. He put his hands on either side of her face and looked deep into her eyes. His eyes welled up with tears.

He smiled a sad little smile and said, "Some believe that gnomes have magic that can see into the hearts of people. You have been hurt deeply. Someone has used magic against you and now you are looking to get even. Feelings like resentment and hate have a very powerful effect in the magic world. Feelings like that can eat you alive, Michelle. In fact, in the magic world they often do. Learn to forgive. You may discover a new truth as to what happened to you and what the windows of your soul tell me about your family. Magic can be harsh and, like anything else in this world, can be turned to evil. Please let your heart heal, Michelle. Let your spirit mend."

Tears were streaming down Michelle's face, tears of release. She held my hand tightly as the tears seemed to wash away some of the pain she had felt over the years. I didn't expect her to be completely better, but, since Smith's words gave me reason to rethink my opinion of my fairy. Maybe it would give her something to think about as well. She gently turned her head away. Not willing to forgive just yet, but at least think about forgiving.

We sat there in silence for a while. The little toy mouse came from behind the couch. It walked across the floor, passed us all, picked up a rubber ball that was almost bigger than it was, and carried it over until it was standing right in front of Fetch. It picked the ball up over its head and with surprising strength threw it at Fetch's head hitting him right between the eyes. You could hear the other toys from behind the couch cheering. The mouse turned and walked away with a proud swish of its tail. It had obviously won some kind of bet and showed his fellow toys who was the bravest. Michelle laughed a little at this. She looked better and even had a peaceful look on her face, like she was finally starting to come to terms with things.

Smith drank down the last of his soda and encouraged us to do the same. He got up and grabbed another one.

"There is a place where magic folk gather," he said, "a club that is downtown. I can introduce you to folks, only those whom you find worthy of meeting, but, promise me dear Michelle, that you will not give your heart to another. I don't think Fetch or I could survive the experience."

"I urge you both to wear your teardrops at first, my friends," said Smith. "Walk carefully among the folk to determine whom you can trust and whom you cannot. Trust your hearts and realize that at this place once you reveal yourselves to one, you will eventually reveal yourselves to all. Take care and remember, even though you are part of the magic world, you are also part of the world of non-magic. You are still affected by it and, as I hope you both know, it can be very dangerous. Over confidence can destroy you just as much as a bad spell. Stay safe and I will meet you there. I feel we should do this tonight. Strike while the idea is fresh."

"I will go on ahead and see who is there. If I feel there is someone there you shouldn't meet, then I will warn you when you get to the club."

He gave us directions to the club. Surprisingly it was a popular night spot I had been to myself. Smith saw the look of surprise on my face and smiled.

"Yes, it is the same club you probably know of. Magic folk gather there too. You will see when you get there how it works."

With those words he showed us on our way with a few hugs and kisses on the cheek from Michelle. She looked happy. This short visit to Smith seemed to really help her. I figured it must be the simple fact that she got to hear another person talk a little about the magic world, other than Johnathen. I felt a little pang of guilt as I thought about Johnathen. I was sure that he wouldn't be happy about what we were about to do. I reminded myself that we were doing this to help Johnathen.

Chapter 29

We went back to the hotel to get ready for the club. I sat in the room absentmindedly scratching Fetch on the ridge between his eyes. I was letting Smith's words sink in. It had been a few months since I had walked out my brother's door and into this crazy world of fantasy. I had changed so much since then. I was no longer the same Jack Dewitte that had walked that street a hundred times before. I was still trying to figure out why that fairy had appeared to me when she did. I was no longer sure she was just playing a cruel game that would have ended up with me being dead or some victim of cruel magic. If I believed Smith, then she might not have been trying to kill me but perhaps warning me about Fetch's egg in my pocket.

I looked at Fetch. I wondered if I was supposed to find his egg after all. If it was just a random, thing then why did he choose to go against his very nature and not destroy me? Would this affect him in some unknown way in the future? Would the changes that have happened to me continue? What was I becoming? The thought thrilled me and terrified me at the same time. I thought of Michelle and how she was convinced that the fairies had killed her family. She had never said that she saw them herself.

I had the feeling that if we could meet more magic folk then we would be able to understand things better. How were we to be accepted if we didn't try to acclimate ourselves? It was like going to a different country and expecting everyone to speak English. You had to learn to speak their language or you wouldn't be able to get around. This brought a new question to my mind.

"Michelle," I said, "Are there other languages in the magic realm? Everyone I have come across speaks English."

Michelle looked up from the small notebook that she had been writing in. It was full of spells and chants to help her work magic. I wished she wouldn't use magic the way she did. We were not born into the magic world and we really didn't have a full understanding of what would happen if we went too far. In a tired voice Michelle answered me.

"Yes there are many different languages, but Johnathen told me that most creatures of the magic world have a natural ability to understand any human language. It takes training to understand the languages of the magic realm. For instance a fairy might not be able to understand what a gnome is saying in its own language and vice versa. So if you wanted a fairy to not know what you are saying you would learn how to speak gnome. Weird huh?"

"Yeah," I replied. "There is so much to learn. We really need to understand who would be against us and who wouldn't be."

"With me it is easy," said Michelle. "Anybody who is against someone using magic when they weren't born to it is someone I have to watch out for. You, I'm not sure. So far everyone in the magic world that interacted with you has been amazed that you even exist. You and Fetch are enigmas, Jack, and that scares people, magic or not. The simple fact that you can perform a spell the way you did, without even looking at an incantation or the right wording, is unheard of in the magic world. Magic needs a command or a request to be effective. You manipulate it without either one, and very well I might add," she said referring to her clothes that she was still wearing. "You conjured these up in a way that would make even Johnathen jealous."

Fetch and I sat there in stunned silence. I don't think she realized she had mentioned fairies. It was the first time we had ever heard her say the word 'fairies' and not have a strong negative reaction. Usually she would get that strange dark look on her face that seemed to indicate she was thinking of her family and their tragic deaths. I looked at Fetch and tried to remember a time when she didn't act that way at the very mention of the fey or fairies. Smith's little talk seemed to have helped a lot.

I could tell that she was having doubts about some of the things that Johnathen had told her. This was painful to her. She owed him so much, but didn't like the idea that he was keeping her from so much of the magical world. I remembered Smith and her talking about this Pek. He seemed to be the only other one, from the world of magic that Michelle had ever associated with. She was determined to find out some things on her own, even if she wouldn't like what she found out.

As Michelle continued to get ready, I let my mind wander. I looked at Fetch. Everything that we had heard about dragons pointed to the fact that Fetch was unlike any of them. The simple fact that he had a name seemed beyond the comprehension of anyone we had met so far. How everyone referred to him as 'the dragon with a name' showed me how different he was. After the time I had spent together with him I couldn't picture him being any different. Michelle was finally ready. She had me make another set of clothes. It took me five tries before I finally got what she wanted. She looked amazing.

We decided to take a cab downtown. It took us both to convince Fetch that this was the best way. He could fly above us as the cab took us downtown. Once there we would conceal ourselves with magic and walk the rest of the way into the club. Fetch would have to stay outside flying around until we were sure it was safe for him to join us in the club. Michelle had purchased a cell phone at a convenience store and tied it around his neck. Another little odd magic box plugged into it and activated it. When we thought it was safe, we were going to call it and let him know he could join us. I hated the fact we were going in there without him, but it would be hard enough just keeping people from bumping into us in the crowded club.

The plan was that we would mingle, undetected, and hopefully learn about magic folk. With the teardrops we would be invisible to everyone. We could hear conversations and see what people were saying about me and Fetch. If it seemed that too many people were going against us, we would call the whole thing off and think of something else. It seemed sneaky, but there was still so much to learn about who would support us and who would destroy us. Smith had told us the best way to learn about magic folk was to listen and observe. Even Michelle, who had been learning from Johnathen about the realm of magic, had limited knowledge. Only what Johnathen had told her. I thought about Johnathen and wondered what he would think about what we were doing. Would he think of it as a betrayal? It was something I had to put out of my mind for now.

After a quick goodbye to Fetch as the cab pulled up, we climbed in and went downtown. After arriving we got out and started walking to the club. I looked over at Michelle. She looked worried and I could tell she was having second thoughts about the plan. I grabbed her hand.

"Look," I said. "We don't have to do this if you think it's not a good idea. We can go back and forget the whole thing."

She looked at me with a grim determination in her eyes.

"I love Johnathen, Jack, but I can't help feeling that he is keeping things hidden from me. There are questions I have about the night my family died. Every time I ask him about it he skirts the issue and tries to change the subject. All he has said is that the fairies did it, but there has to be more to the story, Jack. I believe he is trying to protect me from something. He is very powerful and sometimes that power scares me, but I really do love him. I think he would accept that we are doing this. He wants the chance for both magic users and non-magic users to know about each other. He has been protecting us and now it's time for us to protect him, even if it is from himself."

We walked down the street for a while, both of us silent.

"We seem to be between both worlds, Jack. " said Michelle. "You even more than me. It is our

responsibility to let them know that we are not
dangerous and we can learn from each other."

Chapter 30

It was very late when we arrived and the streetlights gave off a thin light as we walked down the alleyway that led to the club. We made sure our teardrops were working, then, walking with caution, we made our way to the door. I looked up at the dark skyline, visible between the two buildings, and saw the familiar flash of silver that let me know that Fetch was there. I looked over at Michelle, gave her hand an encouraging squeeze, and together we pushed on the double French doors that led into the club. As a blast of loud music hit our ears, we were greeted by the most incredible vision I had ever seen. It was like an explosion of all the fantasy books I had ever read. Everything from unicorns to pointy eared elves were there. The loud music would go up and down in volume and I realized it was a spell that allowed people to talk without yelling. When you got close to someone, the music would get quieter. When you began to talk to someone, the music around you would automatically go down in volume, allowing you to have a conversation with that person without having to shout. If you got too close to people as you walked by, the volume would go down. It was a strange experience walking around with the music getting louder and softer like someone playing an annoying joke. It really threw off my equilibrium for a few minutes. After a while I began to get used to it, and, after my eyes adjusted to the light, I looked around at this new incredible environment.

Every place I looked created a new experience of amazement. From the unicorns and pegasi that roamed around having genial conversations with each other, to the sprites colorful drinking games where the loser had to dive into a mug of ale and drink their way out. It was a fantasy geek's dream come true. To explain all I saw in that club that night would take years. I looked at Michelle and the amazed expression on her face let me know how fantastic this whole place was. There was a purple troll with a basket collecting all electronic devices that the few non magic folks had. Anytime a cell phone was brought out to take a photo or a video, he was there to take it away. Looking closely at them, you could see a glazed, glassy eyed look on their face. I watched one girl in particular who was staring at a blue unicorn. After a few minutes she shook her head and whispered to a friend about the place getting to her. She and her friend left a few minutes later. Another guy was busy trying to pick up what I could only describe as a pixy in human size. She turned to him with a ball of what looked like lightning in each hand. A purple troll pulled him away just as she tossed the balls of energy in his direction. They left a deep hole in the floor where he had been standing. The troll escorted the guy out as he shook his head the same way the girl had just moments ago. It was obvious to me that there was magic designed to manipulate the human mind. Looking around I could see several magic creatures pleased at the non-magic people's eventual, fuzzy headed exits. I overheard two pointy eared elves in Armani suits making bets as to who would be next to leave. Michelle had pulled her hood up. We had discussed how we needed a way to disguise our appearance in case we got bumped. Touching someone or bumping them could break the teardrops' spell and it was inevitable that we would be bumped in here. We didn't know if anyone would have an idea who we were, or if we would be recognized, but we didn't want to take any chances.

Pulling my hood up I signaled to Michelle that we should split up. I headed toward a particularly loud group of dwarves as Michelle headed toward a group of well-dressed elves. I know she was looking for fairies. I had been looking around trying to spot some myself. They would possibly have the answers we needed. I hoped I would see them first. I didn't know what Michelle would do if she saw one. I wanted to signal Fetch and find a way to sneak him in, but I just didn't know how. I looked around for Smith, but I couldn't spot him either. It didn't go unnoticed by me that out of all the fantastic creatures attending, there wasn't one dragon to be seen.

The club was enormous and as I walked around I heard little conversations. I thought I heard someone say something about 'the dragon survivor', but when I got close to the group, of what I can only describe as air mermaids, the conversation had changed to the color of their hair.

I walked up to one group that had gathered by a back wall of the club. They were thick and strong looking. The tallest of them was no more than five feet tall. The men had thick beards and the women had long thick hair. The women were exceptionally beautiful and were just as loud and rowdy as the men. As I got close to the group, I saw what they were all yelling about. There was a young woman in a wheelchair. Her hair was blond and in a thick braid down her back. She had piercing green eyes that could stare right through you. She was concentrating very hard, lost in thought. She was very beautiful, and, judging by all the looks she was getting from the dwarves gathered around her, had many admirers. Standing facing her was a particularly fierce looking dwarf. He was firmly planted a little to her right. His eyes were tightly shut, as if he was bracing himself for something. The young woman had a little crooked half smile on her face. She sat there patiently waiting for some kind of signal from the dwarf. He took a few deep breaths, opened his eyes, and nodded. The whole group of dwarves quieted and stared at them both. They just stood there looking at each other, then, almost faster than I could see, the girl pulled her fist back and swung at the stomach of the dwarf. She hit him so hard that he was sent flying backwards, doubled over. He hit the wall that was thirty feet away from the girl. It exploded into rubble with the dwarf disappearing in a cloud of dust .There was a pause for a few seconds, as the dust settled, and then slowly the dwarf emerged. He was covered in dirt. He shook his head like a wet dog, stood there on shaky legs, and then, with a wave of his hand, and a bow toward the girl, admitted his defeat.

"See! I told you!" said a gray-haired dwarf to another. "She is truly strong. The dwarf blood is thick in her veins. She belongs with us. The council has to listen."

Another mention of the council, the all-powerful group that decides the fate of so many. I wanted to hear more of this story, but something caught my eye from across the club. It was a group of fairies sitting quietly at a table. There were five of them, two males and three females. The one in the middle was my fairy. There was no doubt in my mind. My heart began to thud loudly in my chest. In my mind I replayed that day. The scar on my leg from Fetch's hatching burned and itched as I stood there looking at her. She was as beautiful as she was that first day. Part of me wanted to just rush over there and reveal myself. Just to show her I was there, and demand answers to questions I have had from the beginning, but I knew this was not the best idea. I had to get closer to them and try to listen to what they were saying. I stood there for a while trying to decide whether or not I should go over there. From my vantage point I could see most of the club. What I saw made me realize I needed to get to the fey as fast as I could.

Michelle had spotted them too. All the years of frustration and hate for the fairies seemed to be on her face. In her hands was a dagger just like the one that Johnathen gave me in the park, the one he told me would kill a fairy even if they just touched it. I hadn't even thought about mine in over a month. My stomach fell into my shoes as I realized I wouldn't be able to get to her before she got to the fairies. I didn't want to believe it, but the way she moved toward them with the dagger in her hands gave me the idea she was going to kill one, and I couldn't stop her.

It played out in front of me like a slow-motion film. I made my way across the club as Michelle came up behind the fairies with her dagger raised in her hands. She stood there panting heavily, and, even from the distance I was from her, I could see her shaking in rage. She moved right in front of them. Her teardrop kept her hidden as she stood there in front of my fairy, ready to plunge the dagger into her heart. Her face was a mask of rage and pain. Her eyes were wild and I knew that she was going to do this. I rushed across the club, not caring if I would be revealed. I had to stop her from doing this.

Then slowly I watched her face change. The rage melted away and was replaced with a look of confusion. She looked down at the blade in her hands. She seemed surprised that she was holding it at all. She shook her head like she was trying to clear her mind and stood there staring at the fairies. They were having a very animated discussion. She heard something that they said and looked over at me. I finally reached her. She was staring at me as if I wasn't real, like she was seeing me for the first time.

The dagger never made it to the floor. Smith had appeared at our sides, seeming like he had just appeared out of nowhere. He caught the dagger as it fell. Without looking at it, he quickly concealed it in the sleeve of his purple sweatshirt. He looked at me with concern on his face, and gently led Michelle away from the fairies and over to the bar. I started to follow them when I overheard one of the fairies say the word 'dragon'. I looked over at Smith and Michelle. Her head was in her hands and I could tell she was crying. I made a move to come toward them and Smith signaled for me to stay where I was. He motioned to the fey and pointed to his ears. I got the message. As much as I wanted to be there for

Michelle, this was my chance to get the most information I would probably get on the fey. Michelle looked up at me, nodded her head and pointed at the fairies herself. She gave me a smile, through her tears, to let me know she was ok and again pointed at the fey. She would never forgive me or herself if I let this opportunity pass.

I looked over and realized I was right behind the fairy who led me out into traffic. The one who stood over me staring after I broke my hip. A strange phantom pain shot up my leg as I stood there looking at her. The whole exchange went unnoticed by the group of fairies. Somehow we had both made it across the club without being revealed. Our concealment had not been blown. They would never know how close they came to being killed.

I stood there just a few feet behind them. I could smell her. She smelled like the desert after the rain. Then she spoke.

"We have to find them. They can't be left alone. There are too many things that could happen. There are already people talking about them, and, if we don't find them soon, no telling what could happen."

"It is not our responsibility to protect them," said one of the male fey.

They were all hovering above the ground, their wings creating a cool breeze behind them. As perfect and fragile as they looked, there was a power that radiated around them making it very clear to anyone near them that they were not to be messed with.

"That's not fair, William," she said. "They never asked for any of this. He has already been forgotten by his family and friends, and no telling what the dragon is going through."

I realized with a shock that they were talking about Fetch and me. They had been looking for us. The other female fairy was bobbing up and down with an excited look on her face. She spoke in a high voice so different from the rich alto voice of my fairy. I found myself wanting to know her name, hoping that someone would say it. The excited fairy was an ebony skinned beauty, with a blue glow that radiated a few inches from her body. With every word she spoke her blue glow would get brighter.

"It is obvious that someone is concealing them from us," she said. "Perhaps whoever has spread the dragon eggs around is the one hiding them."

"Please Molly, keep your voice down," said another fairy. "If word gets out that there are more dragon eggs out there, just scattered around, it could cause a panic."

It was one of the guys that spoke. Both the male fey were dressed in what looked like very expensive suits. One had dark brown hair and dark tanned skin. The other had hair that looked almost white with skin to match.

"I don't care," replied Molly. "There is someone who is using the essence of hatching dragons to gain power, and I feel that it is up to us to warn the public, magic and non-magic."

"Not until we find the 'dragon survivor' and the 'named dragon'," said my fairy.

Those words used to describe me sounded too much like a title. I wasn't sure I liked that. When you had a title, there were always people expecting certain things from you, and I had no idea what those things were. Fetch and I deserved some freedom. We never asked for this life, but it was still ours, and I didn't want to lose it. It was time to get

Fetch in here. I realized I should have had him there from the very beginning. I felt trapped. I wanted to stay and hear more, but I wanted to get Fetch in here to hear it with me. It affected him too, and it was only fair that he heard what was being said. I looked around for Michelle and Smith. I finally spotted Smith sitting at a bar stool. He was looking right at me with a concerned look on his face. Michelle was nowhere to be seen.

I left the fairies to go ask Smith where she was. When I reached him, he had tears in his eyes. In his hand was the dagger that Michelle almost used on the fairies.

Chapter 31

"What's going on?" I asked. "Where is Michelle?"

Smith looked at me and said. "Your blade, I know you have one as well. Let me see it."

At first I didn't know what he was talking about. Then it hit me. Michelle must have told him about the dagger that Johnathen had given me. It was identical to hers. I reached into my pocket and pulled out the pouch that Johnathen had given me. I wasn't concentrating hard enough and as I pulled out the dagger money spilled out of the pouch too. I quickly handed the dagger to Smith and bent down to hastily pick up the money and stuff it into my pockets. I stood up and saw Smith sitting there with tears streaming down his face. He was looking at the blades in his hands and nodding his head.

"Of course, it is all making sense now."

His hands began to shake and he shut his eyes tight. When he opened them again, he began to speak to me in a low voice, completely unlike anything I had heard from him.

"I was there, Jack. I was there the night Michelle's family was killed. I had a feeling that she was the girl that survived, but I had to be sure. There have been many attacks on places like the one Michelle's parents owned. Magic attacks that needed to be cleaned up. No one knew who was involved in those attacks. The only clue found was these daggers. Do you know what they are used for?"

"Johnathen told me they could destroy a fairy," I answered.

A chill was going up my spine. I had a feeling where this was all going and I didn't think I was going to like it.

"They disappeared after I found them. It was the only evidence that the fairies might have something to do with the attacks. I was told they were concealed to protect the fairies on the council. Their magic is strong and can harm a fairy at a distance if in the wrong hands. I had no idea they were given to Johnathen. Why he gave them to you is another mystery. When I mentioned that they were found at the scene of the attack on her parents, Michelle cast a spell, keeping me here, and ran off saying she would get answers from Johnathen. These blades have a magic attached to them, Jack, a dark magic. If a fairy was to just see one, it would mean their end. If Michelle had revealed herself to them without even stabbing them, just them seeing the daggers could have taken their very life force from their bodies."

He looked around and quickly concealed Michelle's blade up his sleeve. He handed the other back to me. At first I didn't want to touch it.

"It was given to you, Jack. I'm sure Johnathen had a reason to give it to you. I imagine for protection. It is said that if a fairy were to even suspect someone had one of these blades they would retreat and leave whoever had them alone. With Johnathen's belief that the fairies have been behind so much trouble in the magic world, I'm sure he meant for you to have it for protection, you and Michelle. She is so confused right now. I wish I could have stopped her, Jack. She seemed to be realizing that not all fairies are bad. There is trouble brewing and I think Johnathen suspects someone on the council is the cause. Michelle is in danger now. Running after Johnathen the way she just did can lead the unknown enemy to him. On her way out she bumped into a goblin. I was unable to move because of her spell or I would have stopped him. As soon as she revealed herself, the goblin got a wicked look on his face and disappeared. I am afraid that she is in serious danger, Jack."

I ran for the door cursing myself for not having Fetch with me the whole time. He might have been able to stop her from leaving. I hoped he saw her as she left and was with her outside right now. I knew that Michelle was dealing with conflicting emotions and wouldn't do anything foolish. As I ran for the door, I bumped into a unicorn. It was blue with a red mane. As I was revealed, it jumped back in surprise

"You are the dragon survivor!" it shouted.

I ran for the door bumping and brushing up against all sorts of different things. I heard many different magic creatures yell and gasp in surprise as I was revealed to all that I happened to touch on my mad dash for the door. I could hear the unicorn still yelling that he had just bumped into the dragon survivor as I made my way into the alley.

I looked up for a sign of Fetch. I wasn't paying attention to what was around me. I was about to call out to him when it happened. Something hit me on the back of the head. It was some sort of club and I could tell that it was meant to keep me from getting up. I went to my knees wondering if Booger and his friends had pulled a sneak attack. Whoever it was kept on hitting me. I was in pain and shock but somehow I managed to stay on my knees. I refused to go down all the way. I could hear the heavy breathing of my attackers, and, through the haze of pain, I was amazed at how much I was taking without going down. I had become stronger. Finally a blow to the kidneys brought me down completely. My attackers continued to hit me. I couldn't see who they were. I had covered my head for protection and tried to call upon the forced magic. That first unexpected blow kept me from concentrating enough to get it to work. I was not doing well.

"Where is Fetch? "I thought.

If he was overhead, he would have been here by now. I was lying face down on the street as my attackers continued to beat on me. I cursed myself for not calling him on the cell phone tied around his neck, as my attackers continued to beat me to a pulp. As I lay there, I began to feel the first spark of the forced magic as it started to build in my body. I found the strength to push myself up which only made them beat on me harder. Another blow to the kidneys turned me around to finally face my attackers. They were ordinary people. Three guys with hoodies and bandanas covering their faces beat on me brutally with baseball bats. They stopped and looked at me for a second. One of them spoke up.

"Man, I don't know what you are on dude, but I want it. I saw you drop a wad of money in the club and I'm gonna get that too."

He and his two friends continued to beat on me as if they felt they would get nothing from me until I was dead. This struck me as funny. Here I was being so cautious about the magic world that I forgot about the non-magic one. I began to laugh. I could taste blood in my mouth, and, in spite of the changes my body had undergone, I didn't think I was going to survive this. How could I have forgotten about this world, the one I grew up in? Had all the things that had happened to me changed me so much that the normal world I had been a part of became completely foreign to me? Was this going to be the end of it all? "No!" said a voice in my head. I refused to let this happen to me. I had fought off goblins and even knocked out a wizard in a duel. This should be nothing to me. I was stronger than this. I was stronger than they were. There was no way they could win this. I just let them surprise me, but that was never going to happen again. I felt a surge of strength and I began to stand up. The blows kept coming from these guys but I barely felt them. I grabbed one of the bats, twisting it out of my attacker's hands. I heard the snap and the screech of pain as my grab cause him to break his wrist. I broke the bat in two, and grabbed the next guy by the throat. I shoved him backwards into a wall. He sank to the ground and just lay there. I turned to my last attacker and received a new surprise. He had a gun. I heard the shot go off and felt a strange tearing sensation in my shoulder. I ran at my attacker and smacked the gun from his hand. Even though I could feel no pain, the loss of blood from my shoulder wound was making me strangely dizzy. My attackers must have been on something. Two of them started hitting me again with their baseball bats. The lack of blood made me sink to my knees. I began to crawl toward the club door. These guys weren't giving up. They followed me step by step in some sort of drug induced fury. I could see the purple troll doorman looking at these guys. He looked confused. Because of the teardrop, he couldn't tell what they were doing. I imagined that it looked like two guys beating the road with bats. The third one stayed crumpled by the wall where I had thrown him. A wild thought entered my mind. Where were all the creatures from the club? The ones who saw me? Why hadn't they come out?

I continued to crawl toward the troll. I thought that if I could get to him and touch him, he would see me and then I could get some help. Not the way I wanted to reveal myself but I didn't feel like I had too much choice. I heard a commotion at the door of the club. The troll had barred the door keeping everyone inside. He must have thought he was protecting the club goers from the crazy guys hitting the ally floor and shooting in the air. This thought struck me as funny. I started to laugh which just made these guys madder. I continued to laugh as I crawled. Blood was now pouring out of my mouth, and these guys were screaming in rage that I was not dying. As I reached the troll, who, not wanting to get involved with these crazy humans if he could help it, had flattened himself against the wall next to the door, I reached out and was able to touch his big

toe. I heard a grunt when I was revealed to him.
That was when I heard the roar. Fetch was back
and he sounded pissed. He dropped into the alley,
completely visible to all. His face was contorted in
rage as he rushed at the muggers. Knocking them
aside, he shot a flame of healing at me. As it
engulfed me, I could feel it start to work. The bullet
in my shoulder popped out. A very odd sensation.

Fetch had turned his back on the boys and
one of them took his bat and with all his might
brought it down on Fetch's head. It was just enough
to stun him and enough to piss me off. With the
added fury of Fetch's emotion I turned on my
attackers. Hitting me was one thing, hitting Fetch
was something else. The healing flame had
engulfed me by now and I was rapidly gaining my
strength. As I stood up, the color of the flame
changed from a bright orange to a deep black with a
yellow outline. The troll and my attackers all stood
still in shock. Fetch's roar must have been heard by
all the people in the club. Out of the corner of my
eye, I could see that someone had finally broken
through the door and all sorts of creatures were
pouring out. I could hear the gasps as I stood there

covered in the black flame of Fetch's fire. I could see Fetch shaking his head trying to clear it.

The girl in the wheelchair came out into the alleyway chanting "Fight, fight, fight" and I heard more than one voice calling me 'dragon survivor'. Not the best way to announce my arrival to the world of magic, but at this point I didn't care. I was still mad and I was ready to teach these guys a lesson for attacking me.

I could feel the forced magic building up inside me. It reached the middle of my chest and forced its way out. The fire that continued to surround me added to the strength of my magic. It was now a ball of blue flame about the size of my fist. Grabbing it like a baseball, I threw it in the direction of my attackers. It engulfed them. I could hear them scream and watched as they ran down the alley trying to put out the flames. By the time they got to the end of the alley they were engulfed in it. The two who were still standing fell down and then the flames went out. I looked over at the one I had thrown into the wall. One of the fairies was kneeling down next to him, a strange light coming out of his hands. The fallen man twitched as the light engulfed him.

I was struck with horror on what I had just done. Once again I had shown that I could do amazing things, and, once again, my anger got the best of me. Putting aside my fear that I might have killed them, I rushed over to Fetch. He had passed out. He lay there, very still. I had never seen him look like that before. His breath was shallow and I was afraid he wasn't going to make it. I put his head in my lap.

"Hey Fetch, wake up," I said. "You did good pal. Come on and wake up."

His silver scales glowed and his black ones changed colors for a second, then with a sigh he opened his eyes. He looked at me as if he was trying to remember what happened. I was so relieved he was all right. His eyes drifted past my shoulder. He had a slight snarl on his face and I turned to see what he was looking at. The entire club had seemed to empty into the alley. At the front of the crowd was my fairy. I still didn't know her name. I stood up and realized that the spell had exhausted me. I swooned and then fell to the street. Fetch turned me around and was staring at me, his look of concern was matching the one I had just had for him. Other creatures came into view. I saw the purple troll looking at me and could hear Smith calling out my name. I saw my fairy. She was looking at me the same way she looked at me two years ago when I broke my hip. A strange ball of light appeared in her hand, and, before I could react, it hit me in the face. Darkness took me.

Chapter 32

There were people talking. I couldn't tell if it was a dream or not, and I couldn't tell what they were saying, but there were definitely people talking. I was sore, not in pain, just sore, like I had been working out. I remembered the guys with the baseball bats hitting me over and over again. How could I not be in pain? Fetch . . . Fetch healed me again with his flame. Why was he so late in finding me? Those guys really beat the crap out of me. Fetch. Fetch? Fetch was hurt! He had been hit! Where was Fetch?

I opened my eyes, coming out of my half sleep dream. Smith was there along with three fey. Fetch was nowhere in sight. I recognized the place as Smith's little cave under the park. When I first met Smith, I thought he was just a type of janitor for the magic world, cleaning up magic messes so the real world would not discover that magic was real. So the real world wouldn't know that the fey, gnomes and dragons were something more than fantasy. Looking at him sitting in his wooden easy chair with three fey circled around him, listening with rapt attention to his whispered conversation. I wondered again if it was an accident when I saved him. It could have been planned. I lay there as still as I could, wanting to hear what he said. I still didn't know so many things I needed to learn about this new life I was in. Smith glanced over at me and smiled.

"Ah, our good friend is finally awake," he said. "Jack, I would like you to meet some very good friends of mine. This is Molly, Peter, and I think you already know this lovely lady, Samantha."

There she was. My own personal fairy. She was as beautiful as she was on that first day long ago. She was staring at me with hands on her hips and her mouth a thin line. Molly was looking back and forth between the two of us. The male fey named Peter was standing there, not making eye contact with anyone at all. Slowly, Samantha floated across the room toward me. I sat up and tried to think of something to say. All this time I had thought that she might be trying to kill me. Seeing her here made me feel like I had been wrong the whole time. When she reached my bedside she stared down at me with her eyes narrowed. Any look of concern I remembered her having when she kneeled over me in the alleyway was gone. I had a flash of a thought of the alley, and the strange light that had knocked me out, that had come from her hand. I had a moment of panic as I started to think that maybe she had tried to kill me on the street that day. She definitely was staring at me like she could kill me right now. She was mad and I had no doubt she was mad at me.

"Uh, hi," I stammered.

I heard a familiar 'HUH' from over my head. Looking up I saw a long shelf and Fetch's snout peeking over the edge.

"Fetch!" I said in relief. "You're ok. Man, you had me worried, you stupid lizard. What took you so long to get to me in the alley? What were you waiting for? They were beating the snot out of me. Do you only attack goblins?"

I was hyper aware of Samantha and the others staring at me. I could hear Smith chuckling.

"You see? I told you," he said. "They are connected and the best of friends. All the rumors are true. I have witnessed them with my own eyes and now so have you. Now do you believe me when I say he has a name?"

Samantha looked at us in complete shock. When she noticed that I was looking at her, the look of anger appeared on her face once again. Looking at me, she spoke in a low controlled voice.

"How dare you suggest that I was trying to kill you? I was trying to save your life, you smelly Flap!"

There was that word again. I was beginning to think that it wasn't a nice word. I had to find out what it meant. I stared at her, and, to my surprise, I started to feel angry. I mean, who did she think she was talking to me that way? Gritting my teeth and looking into her blue eyes, I spoke in a low voice trying matching her fury.

"Well, what am I supposed to think? You just appeared out of nowhere and lured me out into the street. I was almost hit by a truck. In fact every time I see you, there is some sort of truck involved. The first time I saw you, I ended up with three pins in my hip. The next time I saw you, Fetch hatched on my leg. What kind of sick game are you playing with me, you fairy tease?"

I heard a strange metal sound and saw Pete with a large sword in his hand. I remembered him from the club. I didn't see the other one with the white hair. He looked like he was about to say something when Fetch jumped from his perch, and, quick as a flash, was crouched in front of him growling. Pete had a look of surprise on his face and didn't seem to want to move. Keeping his eyes on Fetch, he spoke to me.

"No one speaks that way to Samantha. She has sacrificed much for you and is next in line for the council."

These words meant nothing to me, so I just sat there staring at Samantha.

"Put it away, Pete," she said. "It is obvious that Jack here was hit a little too hard to realize what he said. I will let it go this time. His apparent stupidity is enough of an apology for now."

At these words, Pete put away his sword, and, with a puff of red smoke in Pete's face, Fetch turned his attention to Molly. He slowly crawled up to her, and, bowing just a little, put his head under her hand and gently gave it a nudge. Molly let out a little squeak and looked over at me, not knowing what to do.

Glancing at her I said, "He likes to be scratched on the head."

I looked back at Samantha. In my mind, all sorts of clever comebacks for her 'stupidity' comment were swirling around in my head, but, after looking in her eyes for a while, all I could manage to come up with was two words.

"Fairy tease," I repeated.

I heard Pete's sword come out of its sheath again. It was really odd knowing that there was a fairy, standing there in an Armani suit, threatening me with a sword. Samantha raised a hand signaling him to put it away. Fetch was too busy getting his head scratched by Molly to come to my rescue this time. Samantha turned her hand in the air palm up. A strange glow appeared in the center of her hand. It was a ball of white light. She looked at this ball then back at me. She smiled. It was a sweet smile, one that could melt your heart. I felt my own heart skip a beat and I was about to apologize for my 'fairy tease' comment. I even opened my mouth to begin to apologize, when she gently flicked her hand. The ball of light shot out of her hand and hit me square in the forehead. It knocked me back and flipped me over Smith's small bed. There was a loud clatter as I landed on the shelves, knocking down and breaking dishes and bottles. I heard Molly let out a little squeak and the familiar 'Huh' from Fetch. I was SO glad he was enjoying this. Samantha's face appeared above me. Hovering in the air, she had the same sweet smile on her face. I didn't find it so appealing anymore. It was silent in the den, and, as I lay there, sprawled in an awkward position, Samantha spoke.

"So," she said in a sweet voice, "call me a tease again, Jack. I dare you."

You could have heard a pin drop. Nobody moved. Nobody breathed. I realized that this was a defining moment for me. This would determine how the fey in this room would treat me. Perhaps it would determine how all fairies would treat me from now on. I looked at Samantha carefully.

I opened my mouth and with apparent slowness I said, "Fairy---Tease."

The air seemed to go out of the room. The look on Samantha's face made me think that she had never been talked to that way. All the color drained away from her pretty face. No one had challenged her to this point, and I had crossed some line and could not come back from it. I knew I had gone too far, but I was not about to back down now.

I felt a stubborn pride as I lay there staring defiantly into this fairy princess's eyes. Her beautiful face contorted into a mask of rage.

"This is going to hurt," I said to myself.

Before anything could happen, a high-pitched laugh rang through the air.

"Friends, friends, please," said Smith. "This must end. I don't think my home can take much more of this. Samantha, please, Jack has been through so much and you did startle him with your appearance that day. Can you blame him for thinking you might try to do him some harm? Jack, you must forgive me as well. If I had known it was Samantha that was your fairy, I would have reassured you that she meant you no harm. Now we must start over and all be friends."

Samantha backed up a little as I scrambled around trying to get on my feet. After I slipped around trying to stand, she offered me her hand. Reluctantly I took it. There is no way to describe the sensation of being given a helping hand from a fairy that is hovering in the air. As I stood up, she leaned in close and whispered in my ear,

"This isn't over, you flap."

"Not by a longshot," I retorted.

I made a promise to myself to ask Smith what flap meant.

"Now that you have met Jack, Samantha, it is your turn to meet Fetch, "said Smith.

Fetch had stayed by Molly's side during the altercation and he moved over to Samantha. She had a look of complete wonder on her face as Fetch, in what I understood as a complete, over the top, grand gesture, bowed low to her. Then, looking her in the eye, he lowered his head like he had with Molly and nudged her hand. She gently scratched his head, a true smile on her face. There was a look of complete joy in her eyes, and, once again, I was mesmerized by her absolute beauty. Mentally I slapped myself in the face. I needed to keep it cool. I knew if she ever found out how beautiful I thought she was, it would be the end of me. Smith had told me something that came back to mind 'Never make a fairy angry'. I had done just that, even though I felt that it wasn't fair. After all, how was I supposed to react to a fairy appearing in front of me in the middle of the day? I began to realize it was just my attraction to her that had mesmerized me to the point of wandering into the street.

This only made me more angry and stubborn. I made a promise to myself that I would not let her beauty affect me that way again. In my mind it was still her fault I was almost hit by that truck. It still wasn't clear why she had appeared to me that day, or why she was there the day I broke my hip. She saw me staring at her and the look of wonder left her face.

"You are a lucky person," she said. "By all rights you should be dead."

"Yeah," I replied, "that's what everybody keeps telling me."

"Come to the table, you three," said Smith. "We must plan our next move."

Fetch and I hung back for a second. Once again I had a moment of disbelief. All of this was so strange. I looked over at Fetch. He was staring at me intently. He looked from me to Samantha and back to me. He kept on doing this back and forth for a while. I knew what he was doing. I pushed his head over to the side.

"Shut up. There is no way, stupid lizard."

I walked to join them at the table with Fetch following close behind me.

"Now," Smith started, "I believe Michelle has gone to confront Johnathen. At the mention of Michelle's name, my stomach dropped to my feet. I had run out of the club to stop her. So many twists and turns in this new world. One of my best friends had told me how dangerous and evil fairies were, and now I found myself almost trusting them. I had a flash of anger as something was revealed to me about this crazy world, something that I should have been told from the beginning. Smith knew these fairies. I was pretty sure he knew they would be at the club last night. I felt I was a pawn in some sort of game and I was getting sick and tired of it.

"Michelle, I believe, is safe for now," continued Smith. "I think the best thing to do is to present Fetch and Jack to the council. They would be under their protection and it would give Jack a chance to persuade them to act against the forces that seem to want him destroyed."

"No," I heard myself say.

This was it for me. We had been lead around by all of these forces and it hadn't gotten us any closer to the truth of what was really going on. It wasn't fair for me and Fetch to have to defend our right to exist in front of a group of council members who would treat us like most of the magical creatures had been treating us so far, with fear or wonder. Why should we have to defend our right to live when it wasn't the fault of either of us that we were here in the first place?

"Fetch and I are not part of your world. We are not part of the world I left behind. From what I have learned from all of you, we are something new and unique and I refuse to allow myself to be controlled by a council that might very well decide to kill us."

There was silence in the cave. Smith had a peculiar smile on his face.

"What do you want to do Jack?" He asked. "What do you and Fetch want to do?"

I looked at Fetch. I could see a look of pride in his ever-changing eyes and I could tell that he would support whatever I had to say.

"We're gonna go confront Johnathen. Ask him what is going on. I'll go see your council after that, maybe. I'm beginning to think that Johnathen has been keeping things from me and Fetch. I hope Michelle is with him and safe. That is another reason I want to talk to him, to make sure she is safe. What Fetch decides to do is up to him. I never claimed to own him and he never claimed to own me. I hope he stays with me. With everything that has happened, he is the only one that truly understands what I am going through. I would like your help. I feel you owe us."

Pete spoke up at this point. "We owe you nothing!" he shouted.

"My brother has no memory of who I am. No one I knew before this mess knows me anymore, and, from what I understand, that is because of you fairies messing with his memories. I never asked for any of this at all. Fetch didn't either. It blows my mind that he decided not to eat me, but, in my opinion, he has shown that we all have a choice. Heck, for all I know, he is waiting to eat me in my sleep one night."

Fetch made a retching sound and covered his nose at this comment. Molly laughed a nervous little laugh at his gesture.

"Yeah pal," I said to Fetch. "I would choke you all the way down."

Fetch gave one of his usual 'Huh' sounds. Molly giggled again. I walked over to Pete and jabbed a finger in his chest.

"You owe me for erasing my life. Please help me. Let me and Fetch go to the one person that could answer our questions. Help us make sure Michelle is safe. She is just another victim in all of this and has done some amazing things to prove that she has the right to exist, either in this world or the other, with all of her memories intact. All I have seen of magic, so far, is how it is used to control and manipulate people. It has to end. It has to stop. I have a feeling that you all don't fully agree with this council, or you would have at least tried to turn me over to them. Please help me. Show me that there is some of the good that I always found in the books I've read my entire life. Show me that there are true heroes in this realm of magic."

I didn't know that this was what I felt, until I said it out loud. I wasn't sure I could trust these fairies, but maybe, if I could get them to help me go to Johnathen, I could change his mind about the fey and show him that they were not all bad. I felt like I was betraying him in some way, but so much had been said about how I was different from anything else ever seen in the magic world. Maybe it was mine and Fetch's destiny to change people's opinions of things in the magic world. I couldn't help but feel that if Johnathen was willing to accept me and help the council accept me, then maybe I could help him change his mind about the fairies. It was worth a shot.

I didn't know what Smith had originally planned, but I hoped he would see things my way. If anything, I wanted an explanation about the daggers and why Johnathen had given one to Michelle as well as one to me.

Fetch came to stand in front of me. He looked at each of them showing that he supported me. I felt a wave of gratitude for him. In a way this affected him more than me. He was part of this magic world since he was a dragon, and for some reason he chose to go against his very nature and spare me.

The many times I got mad at him, the times I tried to drive him off, and he still stuck with me. He was a victim too. From what I understood about Fetch letting me live, he may have turned all other dragons against him. Never accepted fully by his own kind, he would always be an outcast. Me, Michelle, Johnathen and Fetch, we had to help each other. We seemed to be trapped in between two worlds. Never fully accepted by either one. We were a strange family. In many ways Michelle was like a sister to me. I had to find her.

I realized that everyone was staring at me, as if waiting for what I would say next.

Finally Samantha spoke up, her voice heavy with sarcasm, "Fine, oh great dragon survivor, what is your plan? And it better be good. Anyone gets hurt, I will personally feed you to fetch."

She had a crooked smile on her face. It might have been my imagination, but I figured I might have won a grudging respect from her. I thought she might have tangled with this council on more than one occasion. I noticed that Pete and Molly were dressed in the most impeccable ways. Pete, with his Armani suit, and Molly, looking like she just walked out of a fashion magazine. This was quite different from Samantha's light summer dress. I wondered if this was her way of saying she was an individual, different and not wanting to fit into the norm.

"Great!" I thought to myself. "I'm dealing with a bad girl rebel fairy. I'm surprised she doesn't have a tattoo on her arm that says 'Born to Flutter'."

Smith spoke up. "Ok Jack, what's your plan?"

He had a slight smile on his face and a twinkle in his eyes. I remembered our first conversation and realized he was enjoying this immensely.

"Ok, we need to find Johnathen and Michelle and find out what is going on."

I paused for a second. This sounded better in my head. They were all staring at me with blank looks on their faces. I knew I needed to get in touch with Johnathen without him knowing I was on the side of fairies. I would spring that on him when the time was right.

I continued, "Does anyone know how to get ahold of a wizard or his animal messengers?"

Samantha groaned in frustration and looking at Fetch asked in a pleading voice, "Why didn't you eat him?"

"Wait," I said. "I was just asking, in case. I have a backup plan if you can't. If I could get ahold of him, tell him I need to see him, then I could find out if Michelle has confronted him yet, and we can take it from there."

At that moment I remembered my cell phone that Michelle had given me. I felt stupid for not remembering it before. I reached into my pocket and pulled it out. Molly made a little sound of interest, Pete sighed in disgust, and Samantha gave me a blank stare. I remembered that most people in the magic world were baffled by technology.

"Uh, cell phone, forgot about it," I mumbled.

"We know what it is," said Pete. "Who will you contact with it? Johnathen? He is known for having problems with tech stuff, just like a lot of us do, so you won't be able to call him."

I thought back to the times Michelle would show Johnathen something about tech stuff. He wouldn't even touch the computer when she showed him the YouTube battle, with me and Fetch against Booger and the snot brigade.

"Uh, this was given to me by Michelle," I said reluctantly.

Mentally I was kicking myself for not thinking of this sooner.

"We were keeping in contact with each other."

"You mean you had the ability to speak to her this whole time and you didn't?" said Samantha.

"So sorry, your fairy highness. Before I could use it I was shot and beaten with baseball bats, then I was passed out for a while," I said through gritted teeth.

"That's two, "she said, looking at me in a very threatening way.

"Great! " I thought, pulling up Michelle's number and texting her. "Now she's keeping track of what I do that makes her mad. I don't even have a clue what that is."

I texted two words 'U ok?' and waited. It didn't take long for the response.

"Check Facebook. Help the dragons go see Pek."

I sent her a question mark and got no response. This worried me. Obviously there was something on her Facebook page that would help us find her.

I repeated those words to the others. When I said the name 'Pek' they all gave each other a look. I knew I had heard the name before, I just couldn't remember when or where.

"I need to get to a computer," I said. "This phone can't get Internet. Do you guys know where I can access a computer?"

"Your text from Michelle has the answer," said Smith. "I think it's time you met Pek."

It hit me where I had heard the name before. Michelle had talked about him with Johnathen and with Smith. He was the elf with a knack for computers. I was about to meet this Pek.

I looked over to Smith's workbench and saw his computer was gone. I turned back to him with a questioning look.

"When we got back here, I found my computer gone. I didn't want to alarm anyone. It seems as if someone was trying to keep us from using computers, another reason to see Pek. He might be in trouble. He should be warned."

I was trying to text Michelle again as Smith was talking. I was encouraged by her message that she was still unharmed, but her lack of a response after her message had me worried. I wondered what she would think when she discovered that I was working with the fey. Still, no response.

"Ok," I said, "let's go see this Pek."

Chapter 33

We left Smith's tunnel home, walking across the park. I kept my eyes open looking for any signs of one of Johnathen's bobcat messengers. They were nowhere to be seen. Samantha had surrounded us in a cloak of concealment, allowing us to walk undetected through the park. I could see it shimmering in the dark. It surrounded us like a dome and kept up with us as we walked. We walked in silence except for Molly. Molly never stopped talking. She was fascinated by me and Fetch and was not afraid to let us know. She asked us everything from what kind of deodorant I used to asking Fetch how he got rid of evidence of going to the bathroom. Samantha had gasped in protest and began to berate her for asking such a personal question. Fetch stepped in-between them, staring at Samantha, telling her in his unique mute way that it was ok. He seemed to be in a good mood. I could tell that he felt we would soon be reunited with Michelle and was also happy that he didn't have to go into cameo mode as usual. He went up to a very full garbage can. At first I was afraid he was going to go right then and there, but, with a short burst of flame, caught the trash around it and in it on fire. Within a matter of seconds the garbage was reduced to ash. He looked at Molly who didn't seem to understand at first.

"He burns it," I said. "He lights it on fire and destroys all evidence of it."

I tried to sound casual about this, like I had known the answer all along. The truth was I had wondered that myself a time or two. There was still so much I didn't know about Fetch. I still had no idea how he was able to get those bags of food he kept showing up with.

Our short walk through the park led us to a tunnel going under the street. I looked over at Fetch. He was looking back at me with a half-smile on his face. I was sure that he was thinking about the first time we met. It seemed like forever. I was definitely a different person, and not just physically. With all that I had learned and experienced in such a short time, I had gained a confidence I had not had before. My whole life I had run away from conflict. Now I have fought goblins, faced a dragon, made friends with gnomes, and now I am leading a group of fey into what could very well be a confrontation with a wizard.

The tunnel opened up to a type of subway stop. Green balls of energy were whisking people to their destinations, yet another surprise from this realm of magic. I guessed that not all magic users could transport themselves like Michelle or even the goblins could. I looked around thinking of the goblins and looking for their blue balls that appeared before they would show up. I didn't see any.

Shaking my head to try and focus on the task at hand, I took out the cell phone that Michelle had given me. I texted her hoping for a response. I got one. Hurry Jack, Facebook important. See Pek.

Everybody seemed to be in agreement that this Pek guy would have answers for me. We all got into a bubble and started moving fast through a tunnel. I was relieved that I finally got a response from Michelle. She was ok for now, but she seemed to be running out of time. She couldn't tell me where she was. I was hoping this Pek could.

We reached a kind of station and got out of the bubble. There were too many fantasy creatures to count, all rushing around like they were going to work or heading home. If it wasn't for the fact that some were floating, seemed to be on fire, or some other fantastic magical thing was surrounding them, you could almost believe that it was just another subway station in some major city, something you would see in a movie or television show.

I saw two bobcats running through the station and wondered if they were Johnathen's. I looked around and discovered many different bobcats and other animals running around. I guessed that animals were used in this way a lot. If I could just see them, I think I could have figured out if they were Johnathen's or not, but, as quick as I spotted them, they disappeared, moving through the crowd in a flash.

We had walked from the underground station into the cool night air of the desert. Not paying attention to what direction we had been headed I had no idea where we were. All I could see was the dark outline of cacti and hear the sound of coyotes howling. As far as I knew, we were either out of the city limits in the middle of the desert or in a large vacant lot in the middle of town. Tucson is like that. You never knew what you were going to find around the next turn. Maybe that was why all the magic creatures of the world seemed to be here. There were so many places to hide.

We walked through the desert for a short while and came across a dirt road. Without any hesitation Smith began to lead us down this road. He seemed to know where he was going. As we walked, I remembered the first time I saw Smith. I wondered if he had known I was there, watching him shoo away that troll from the dumpster. I had the feeling that he did. There was definitely more to him than I understood.

We reached the end of the road. There was a small trailer with bright floodlights surrounding it. A small picket fence stretched around the piece of property. All around the yard was an assortment of different colored lights and electronic devices in an odd decorative style. Everything from Christmas lights to Halloween pumpkins and bats surrounded us as we walked through the yard. Neon signs glowing the cliché 'EAT AT JOE'S' or 'Get car washed here' littered the ground. All of them were working, blinking and shining brightly. You could probably see the light for miles and I wondered why this Pek creature didn't try to hide himself like all of the other residents of the magical realm did. It was as if he wanted to be discovered. As we walked up to the front door, we must have stepped across some kind of hidden sensor. Two of those waving things you would usually see in front of a car dealership popped up. One looked like a tin Christmas soldier. The other was a gorilla. They waved up-and-down and side-to-side like overly excited guards. Molly squealed in delight and Pete, who I guess had never seen anything like that before, pulled out his sword.

Smith walked up to the door of the trailer and knocked.

"Go away," said an angry voice from within. "I'm busy and I don't care if my Santa Claus is freaking out your dogs. I'm not turning him off."

I guessed that he was referring to the big waving Santa on top of the trailer. You could hear him 'HO, HO, HO'ing', loudly and happily. Smith chuckled at this and pushed the door open, signaling us to follow him inside.

As bright and colorful as it was outside, it was dark and shadowy inside. The only light in the small trailer was coming from a laptop computer. In the glow of the screen I got my first glimpse of this mysterious Pek.

He had a long curved nose. His greasy looking black hair hung down in his eyes. A pair of glasses hung in the air about four inches from his face. He was about two feet tall from what I could tell and I could hear his short fingers hitting the keyboard of his laptop computer at an alarmingly fast pace. Without looking up he spoke to us.

"Rude, "he said in a high but gruff voice. "After telling you to go away, you still just barge right in. So rude."

"Sorry old friend, "said Smith,"but we don't have the time to wait for a formal invitation."

At the sound of Smith's voice, Pek's eyebrows jumped to the top of his head. His ears gave a little wiggle and I noticed that they came to a point.

"Ah, Smith," said Pek. "So you have come to see me, eh? Tired of cleaning up after that Troll? Well, you can forget my vote to get you back on the council. You have made your goblin nest now, so it is your responsibility to eat in it."

"I'm not here for me," said Smith, with a little impatience in his voice. "I have brought some friends to see you. We need your help."

"Of course you do. Everyone does these days. Well what is it? Someone wants to learn how to use a cell phone? Or maybe an explanation of how a debit card works? Hmm?"

"No, no my friend, nothing like that. There is danger afoot and my young friends, Fetch and Jack need your help."

At the mention of our names, Pek slammed his fingers on the keyboard so hard that it had to have broken something. Slowly Pek's face appeared above the screen of his computer. He stared at me and Fetch. Clapping his hands together the lights in the trailer came on revealing a small table and one chair on which Pek was sitting. Nothing else was in the trailer except discarded empty boxes of to-go food scattered around the floor. Pek moved out of his chair and walked around the table. His face was getting redder by the second and by the time he had moved to the other side of the table it was reaching a deep purple.

"Fetch and Jack," he said slowly and carefully. "Fetch and Jack, here in my trailer. You have no idea how I have wanted this moment to happen. I have dreamed about it these past weeks more than any other dream I have had. You incredible, living, walking, FLAPS!" he screamed. "Do you have any idea the trouble you have caused? You stupid, airheaded, abominations! What right do you even have to exist?"

He moved toward us, getting in Fetch's face.

"You couldn't have just eaten him, huh?" he scolded Fetch. "No, No, NO! You had to choose to go against nature itself. Do you have any idea how much work I have had to do on the internet to erase your fight in the parking lot?"

He had walked back to his little table touching the back of his computer. He had a box just like Michelle had. He touched the laptop almost lovingly. You could hear him mumbling to himself. He gently shut his computer, and, to the surprise of everyone, he turned back around and charged us. His hands were claws and his face was a mask of cartoon rage.

Molly had stepped in front of us and caught him as he launched at us, murder in his eyes, his hands reaching toward us like claws, wanting to scratch our eyes out.

"Ah! "Said Smith, "Nothing like the passion of an Elf."

Fighting her, it took Molly shouting his name a few times before the little guy stopped trying to break away from her to get to us. Looking Molly in the face, he finally stopped and went limp.

"Molly, dear," he said in a wavering voice, "one of my best pupils. Please tell them to leave. Please get them away from me. I just can't help them no matter what it is. No, no, my heart can't take the strain. No, please send them away dear please?"

Talking calmly, Molly managed to get Pek to calm down. After a few angry glances and kicks in our direction and a half-mumbled promise not to charge us again, Molly let him go. He walked around to his chair again and sat at his computer, ignoring all of us.

Speaking only to Molly, "Now dear, what can I do for you?"

The emphasis on the word 'you' let us all know that he would not even acknowledge that the rest of us were even there. I looked at Fetch and could tell he was trying to keep from laughing. I didn't blame him. Pek was like a demented Christmas elf. It was hard to believe he was this computer magician everyone kept talking about. It hadn't gone unnoticed that he knew Molly. I wondered if Michelle had known that Pek seemed to be teaching fairies about computers. When I thought about it, I realized that, just a short time ago, I would not have stood here with fairies the way I was now. I had been told they were untrustworthy by one of the few people I considered a friend. I had no idea how Johnathen would react to all of this. Once again, I hoped I could change his mind about fairies. Pek, who worked with Michelle, seemed to know fairies, and, the way he was looking at Molly, was even fond of at least some of them. Could Johnathen have been wrong about all of the fairies? Maybe he had met some bad ones in the past and placed some kind of judgment on all of them. My head was spinning over all of this. I was beginning to realize that it was going to be a very hard task to convince Johnathen, and perhaps Michelle, that the fey were not all bad.

Pek continued to rant in mine and Fetch's direction. He would go back and forth from looking furiously at me and Fetch, to looking fondly and sweetly at Molly. The others he completely ignored. It looked so comical it was very hard not to laugh.

Pete was studying an empty box of chicken like it was the most interesting thing he had ever seen. Samantha had her hands over her mouth, shaking with uncontrollable laughter, while Smith looked at her with the stern stare of a teacher trying to silently warn a student before they said or did something they were going to regret. Once again I was reminded that I was now part of a world that just didn't make much sense.

Molly took over. She knelt down and began to talk to Pek, reassuring him that this was very important, or they would never have disturbed him. She was the only one of us who seemed to take this little guy seriously. I couldn't help but stare at this creature wondering what he was. As Molly began to explain how we needed his help, he caught me staring at him. He jumped up onto his chair and threw a half empty soda can at me.

"Stop staring at me! "He screamed.

I was beginning to get a little annoyed by this guy. His high-strung attitude was getting us nowhere and time started to weigh heavy on me. The longer this took, the more Michelle might need our help. I hoped Johnathen wouldn't be too mad at her. I remembered what he did to me in the hotel room. I didn't think he would ever do that to Michelle, but as strange and as tired as he had been acting lately, I couldn't be sure he wouldn't do something he would later regret.

I looked at the ceiling and tried to keep from looking at him. Pek sat back down and in a calm voice spoke to Molly.

"Now dear, please tell this old elf what he can do to help you."

He seemed to act so sweet to Molly. I wondered what I could do to get on his good side, the crusty old elf. As soon as I thought the words I berated myself for thinking that. It really wasn't fair to judge him that way. As far as I knew, he had been through a lot. His apparent ability to use computers must have made him an outcast from other magic realm people. He called Molly a pupil, meaning that he must be teaching others how to use computers, so he had to be a pretty smart guy. It was just hard to understand that, when he was chucking soda cans at my head.

"Pek, we need to access someone's Facebook page," said Molly.

Pek gave her a sad little look.

"Molly, that is the first thing I taught you how to do," he said in a trembling voice. "Have you already forgotten?"

I was about to pipe up and say that I could do it when Smith spoke up.

"This page is one of your special pages, Pek."

Pek jerked in his seat as if he had sat on something sharp.

"I don't know what you are talking about, Smith," he said in a high squeaky voice.

Obviously he was lying. I began to pace a little, trying not to let all of this get to me. I should have just gone back to the hotel room and gotten on my own computer. I started to feel this was a waste of time. I reminded myself that Michele said to come here.

"It was made by one of your favorite students, Pek," said Smith in calm, even voice. "One that you took under your wing, even though the council might have forbidden you to do so."

All eyes were on Smith at this comment and once again I was hit with the thought that there was more to this gnome than meets the eye.

"The council is not always right," said Pek. "They can be too easily influenced by fear and a lack of understanding of what is new. You, young lady, should be mindful of that."

He was pointing at Samantha at that last statement. She looked at the small elf, her face turning red.

"I have done more than you know," she said. "I have opened discussions between members of the council that have allowed you to continue your work."

"Not enough," said Pek stubbornly. "You should have stepped in between your father and Johnathen long ago."

Once again I felt like I was being left in the dark over matters involving the magic realm. How was I ever to fit in with a group that seemed to have so many rules that I just didn't understand?

"I found Jack and tried to warn him about the dragon egg in his pocket. If he hadn't been so stupid and stepped out into traffic, we wouldn't be having this conversation right now."

"Yes, perhaps not, but the problem would still be there. The council would still be arguing and we would still be learning what we need to learn in secret. Jack's stupidity may have set in motion things that needed to be set in motion. "

"All right," I said. I was getting a little annoyed at being called stupid. "Let's just move on, ok? Michelle is not going to get the help she needs if we don't stop this bickering. "

Pek had once again stood up in his chair.

"Did you say Michelle? Why didn't you tell me it was her?"

He sat down hard in his chair and began to furiously type on the keyboard, mumbling the whole time. I got a good look at his computer as he typed. I had never seen the symbol that was on the back of it before. It was not like any computer I had ever heard of. The whole thing glowed blue and would pulse as Pek typed on the keys. The design changed with every stroke of the keys. It reminded me of Molly's blue light that surrounded her. Pek must have worked some kind of magic into this laptop, something I thought was impossible to do. Where there is a will there is a way, I guess. The whole time Pek was working on his computer he was mumbling to himself. Every once in a while I would hear words like 'Flap' and 'troll dung' come out of his mouth. I figured he was talking about me. I really needed to find out what flap meant.

After a few minutes Pek let out a little grunt of satisfaction. He signaled me to come and look and I moved over to him. Fetch followed me around and Smith came over. I noticed that no one else in the room made a move toward the computer. They acted as if they were scared of it. I realized that they had the same reaction that most people would have if they were suddenly introduced to the magic world, untrusting and scared of the unknown. I needed to work on this with them.

I glanced down at the Facebook page. Michelle's smiling face was there on her time-line. All of her posts seemed to be questions regarding two things, dragons and tattoos. I knew that these were things close to her heart, but reading the questions I discovered that she was trying to get information from people about both. Questions of why people got their tattoos seemed to spread all through the page and I thought she was gathering information to give to Johnathen. But why? Why hadn't I noticed this before? What would Johnathen want with information about tattoos? I read a post where she was encouraging people to check out my Facebook page, and I realized that I needed to thank Pek for keeping it around. His face was still red and I decided to wait until he was not so angry before bringing up that little fact.

There was a blog that Michelle had written regarding the reasons why people got tattoos. I knew I was missing something, something that she was trying to tell me, something that very few people in the magic world would ever discover. Then a post popped up on her Facebook page. A simple post dated today:

"All the cool dragons meet here, even my tattoo."

There was a map that pointed to a single spot. I looked at the map. It named two streets I was familiar with. They were the cross streets where the tunnel that Fetch hatched off my leg was located.

Chapter 34

There was a loud booming sound outside of Pek's small trailer. It shook us all to the bone, vibrating through our bodies. All of a sudden the trailer was lifted into the air and then slammed down again. It was like a giant child had picked us up like a toy and then threw us down in anger. We all went flying through the small trailer. The power went out. The only light was the blue glow Molly was generating.

I could hear Pek groaning. He was hurt, but I didn't know how to get to him. He seemed to be buried underneath a pile of his empty chicken boxes. Smith was laying face down by Molly. She had her arms around him, protecting him in case another attack happened. Samantha was helping Pete up. He drew his sword, a wild look in his eye like he was ready for battle. There was a gash across his forehead that was bleeding freely. There was a strange glow to his blood. I felt a twinge in my hip as I got up. I had a strange wild thought about my hip. Even though I had gone through all of these amazing changes, I felt like one day I would still have to have my hip replaced. I looked around, and, in the low glow of Molly's blue light, I couldn't spot Fetch.

"Fetch!" I yelled "Fetch, where are you?"

He made a small sound. It sounded almost like he was groaning. I spotted him over by the small window. He was looking outside, his body was stiff as if he was getting ready to spring into action. A light had appeared outside. Fetch began to hum. The only time I had ever heard that sound before was when we first met in that tunnel. It was a sad and eerie thing to hear. The hair on the back of my neck stood up. Smith had slowly moved to a sitting position with the help of Molly. He was staring at Fetch with a look of confusion on his face. Samantha had followed Pek's moans, after helping Pete get to his feet, and had successfully pulled him out of the middle of his avalanche of garbage. His computer was clutched to his chest and he kept his eyes tightly shut as if this was a bad dream that he could wish away.

Seeing that everyone was ok, I turned my attention back to Fetch and his strange humming. I move cautiously toward him. He was seeing whatever had attacked us and seemed to be transfixed by it. I reached out to touch him and before I could ask him what was up a voice spoke.

"Come on out, Jack. You and Fetch. We need to talk."

The voice sounded familiar. At first I couldn't place it, and then it dawned on me. It was the voice from my nightmare in the tunnel. It was the voice of my nightmare brother telling me I was a burden. I didn't know who was waiting for us outside, but I knew it had to be my mysterious attacker. He knew mine and Fetch's names and somehow he had tracked us here. I wished more than ever that Johnathen was here.

I looked around at everybody in the trailer. Both Molly and Samantha had balls of attack light in their hands, and Pete's sword was glowing with a white energy. Smith had stood up and spread his arms. He was chanting in a language that was full of power. His very words had a weight to them and you could almost see them as they fell out of his mouth. Pek continued to sit there, his eyes shut.

I could hear laughter outside and again, his voice amplified, he spoke.

"It's all just empty gesturing my friends. You don't have the power to defeat me."

The trailer was picked up and dropped again, not as high as last time but enough to let us know that he meant business. Pete moved toward the window. When he was standing next to me, he tried to look around Fetch. A light of pure energy shot through the window hitting his sword. He fell back as if hit by lightning, his sword reduced to a twisted black piece of metal.

"Jack, I am beginning to get a little angry. If you don't come out now, someone is going to get hurt."

I had no choice but to do what the voice said. I walked to the door and stood there. Fetch had never stopped looking out that little window.

"Fetch," I said. "Come on."

I wanted to ask him what he saw. I knew I was about to see it myself. I didn't think this guy wanted to kill us. If he did, he would have already done it. Fetch's tail twitched and he moved over to my side. He had a look on his face that I had never seen before. It was like he was in some sort of trance. When we stepped out of the door into the unnatural light, I understood why.

It was just a silhouette standing there. It moved and twisted around and I knew what it was. It was the smoke from my nightmare. Smokey and oily, moving around like it wanted to change form. This was the thing that had attacked me in my dream. I was sure of it. Power was emanating from the smoke. Behind it was a red and gold scaled dragon the size of a house. Its long neck curved in the same 'S' shape as Fetch's. It stared straight ahead not even looking at either one of us. Ignoring us as if we were beneath its notice. Its presence radiated power and its slow breathing gave off a heat that had me breaking out in a sweat.

"Impressive, huh?" asked the voice. This is what Fetch should be, Jack. He should be like my good friend here."

At the word 'friend', the dragon glanced down at the black shadow. His eyes went from a green color to a dark red and the smoke coming out of his snout was the same color. He was not happy at being called 'friend' by this shadow. Then it hit me.

"You have some sort of control over him." I said.

It wasn't a question. It was a statement. The dragon glanced down at us as if telling us this was true. It was not happy at its situation. The shadow waved his hand in the air and a very familiar blue ball appeared. Dozens of goblins began to pour out of the orb. They were strangely quiet, just standing there waiting for an order to attack. I heard Pete rattle his sword behind me and knew that my little group of friends was behind me. The shadow laughed.

"You really think you can stop me now?" he asked. "Now? I am more powerful than all of you combined and could destroy you with a flick of my hand."

"What do you want?" I asked ignoring his bragging.

"Many things, Jack, many things, but first things first."

He threw something at me from within the darkness. It landed at my feet. It was Michelle's cell phone.

"She is mine now, Jack. I caught her just outside of the club. Did you think that you and Fetch were the only ones that were important? She should have stayed safe. By leaving Jonathan's side and going into the club to expose herself and you, she betrayed the one who would protect her from harm."

I didn't like the sound of this. He sounded crazy and I was scared he had hurt Michelle in some way. I knew that Michelle's Facebook page was a clue as to what was going on.

"It's not too late to save her, Jack. All you have to do is join me and you can save her. With your ability to control Fetch, and the changes you have gone through, I could make you the controller of all the dragons, Jack. Hundreds of them, all yours to command."

At these words, Fetch and I turned to each other and did something that shocked everyone present. We laughed, long and hard. Here we were in the presence of a power that, for all we knew, could wipe us completely out of existence, and we laughed. The dragon looked down at us with an obvious look of surprise on its face. This just sent us into more fits of laughter. Fetch took his tail, and, like so many times before, smacked me in the back of the head. I turned to him and punched him in the snout, just like I had done the first time we met in that tunnel under the street. We stood there laughing as I rubbed the back of my head and Fetch grabbed the front of his snout, tears streaming out of his eyes.

Shaking my head, I looked toward the shadow. I was scared for Michelle, but I felt that giving this thing the upper hand was a bad idea. Putting a hand on Fetch's shoulder, I spoke.

"Man, you just don't get it, dude. I don't control Fetch. Never did. He can leave anytime he wants. He is free to do whatever he wants. He hangs around because we are friends. No one understands that I have never controlled him. He makes his own choices. Sure, his hatching on me, and his choice not to eat me, has changed me and made Fetch different from other dragons, but it was his choice to do so. Even his name was his choice, not mine."

This little rant was greeted with silence. All the pieces were coming together, and if I could keep talking, I might distract the shadow long enough for

Smith or someone to find a way out of this. If I could get to Johnathen then he could help me get Michelle, but giving into this thing was wrong. I could feel it in my bones. Giving into its demands would mean terror. I could hear Smith chanting behind me and Molly whispered so no one would hear, "Stall". This thing seemed focused on me, so I had to come up with some way to keep it occupied.

"How did you do it? How did you get into my dream that day?"

The shadow laughed. There was a shimmer, and, for a second, I saw someone behind the shadow. The smoke was just a shield, a disguise hiding the person behind.

"Get into your dream, Jack? I didn't get into your dream. I caused it. It was all part of a spell. The dragon eggs, the nightmare visions you had were all part of a spell designed to gain control over the dragons, to gain part of their power. I was on my way to becoming what this world needed, a master, someone to take control and set this world right. Your nightmare was part of a spell designed to give me part of your essence and life force, as well as the essence of the dragon consuming you. I pull the host into my mind at the time the dragon consumes them. When they do a part of me is consumed as well. This part gives me power and control over the dragon. But Fetch decided to go against nature and keep you alive. It broke the spell, causing me to lose my impetus of changing this world into my design. It doesn't matter though, I have another path to power and control. This botched spell will only set things back a little bit. That's what you really are Jack, a botched spell."

This guy was a maniac. Whatever else he was, he was crazy. You could hear it in his voice. That scared me the most, power with no conscience. I thought about what he said. It seemed to make sense in some strange way. I wondered what this new power he was talking about was. I wanted to believe he was bluffing, but I wasn't sure.

"Sorry we spoiled your plans, dude." I said. "I guess I was better equipped for getting some dragon power than you were. Of course, the way you were forcing it, may have given Fetch the ability to choose."

It was a risk talking to him this way but I needed to keep him on his toes. All the talking was directed at me and Fetch, and no one else seemed to want to say anything. The dragon looked down at us at my words. For a second it looked confused.

"So what's this new thing you are talking about? You're taking snot from trolls now to make a power drink?"

I knew it was corny and taunting to say what I was saying. I was relying on my years of comic book reading for guidance. I was trying to get the villain monologue-ing. Trying to get him to give away his plans. Behind me Smith continued to chant.

The shadow laughed. "Oh no, Jack. My new powers come from ordinary people. I need no help from dragons. I found a way to take the life force of people and add it to my power. I will soon be too powerful to stop. People's emotions fuel their essence. Fear, doubt, regret, anger, happiness, love, all of the emotions, and the memories attached to them, are powerful things, Jack. I have found a way to take them from certain people. I have been working on this for a while, Jack, not ever having much success, until tonight. Not until I captured your friend, Michelle. She was the first true success. Oh, how she screamed for you and Fetch. How she begged for me to stop. But in the end, I had to take it all. She will never be the same, but you can still save her, Jack, by joining me."

During this little speech my anger and frustration were building up inside of me. I couldn't keep it all in check much longer. I was ready to attack this shadow and tear it apart. Something in its voice made me believe he wasn't bluffing. He had hurt Michelle and for that I was ready to tear him apart. But, before I could do anything, Fetch attacked. With a roar and a flash of red fire he charged. This shadow guy made a fatal mistake. He had pushed Fetch's buttons. He hurt Michelle, and there was no more listening to him.

The red dragon roared in return and blocked Fetch's fire with a red blast of his own. Smith seemed to finish his spell and a blast, of what looked like silver, shot out of his hands straight for the chest of the shadow man. As it got close, the shadow man clapped his hands together in front of him. As the silver hit his hands, he pulled them apart, splitting the silver spell in two. It went in two different directions into the desert and disappeared. The spell seemed to have an effect on him though. He staggered back making a grunting sound.

The goblins that had come out of the ball began to move on us. With one shout from the shadow man they stopped and crouched down, waiting for another chance to advance. Fetch had been knocked back by the blast from the red dragon but had recovered quickly. He stood at my side, growling, ready for another chance to attack.

"You picked the wrong friends, Jack. My, my, what will Johnathen say about you spending time with fairies?"

"What will Johnathen say when he finds out you hurt Michelle?" I retorted.

I was getting angrier by the minute. I could feel the forced magic beginning to build in me. It swirled around in my chest, gaining strength from my anger. The shadow man pointed at Smith.

"You have interfered for the last time, Smith," he said, "you and Samantha. I have decided that one of you must die."

Chapter 35

He pointed at Samantha, and, before I could react, a bolt of lightning shot from his hand. I knew it would kill her. The air around the lightning smelled like sulfur and as it flew toward Samantha it changed color from red to black. This was meant to kill on contact. Strangely it wasn't moving very quickly. It was reaching out toward Samantha like a snake moving across the ground. I shouted at her to move as it went past me, picking up speed as it went. To my horror, no one was moving to stop it as it zipped past me. Everyone just stood there frozen. I moved toward Samantha hoping that I could stop it. I knew it was too late for me to push her out of the way, but I kept on running anyway, cursing myself for not acting sooner. It seemed like time had slowed down. I could see the connection from the end of the bolt to the shadow's hand. It looked like a rope of energy. Not knowing what else to do I reached up and grabbed it.

A current of power shot through me. My whole body shook as the energy that was meant for Samantha worked its way inside me. It was growing in intensity and I knew it would kill me. I felt the forced magic fighting the bolt. It pushed out of me forcing the bolt out of my body and shot it into the air. I could almost see it as it continued to grow. As it stretched outward, it knocked everyone to the ground. I heard the shadow's scream of rage and turned just in time to see his red dragon blow a jet of red fire at Fetch. Fetch was ready this time and blew his own flame of blue fire. Both jets collided and as they did an explosion of sparks shot into the air. It was amazing for me to see Fetch, so small compared to the other dragon, fending off the attack so easily. I started to run toward him to see if somehow I could help. This was a mistake. My movement toward Fetch distracted him, and a jet of red fire broke through the flame barrier. It headed right for me. Working on complete instinct, I did what I had done with Fetch so many times before. I reached out and caught it. It wrapped itself around my hand and stayed there. It was heavy. For a second I felt the strange and alien emotions from the red dragon. It was not happy at how it was being controlled and manipulated. In a flash his thoughts were gone but the fire stayed.

Fetch's fire always seemed so light, but this flame weighed down on my hand like a fifty-pound bag of sand. It kept pulsing as if it was trying to get hotter and burn me. The longer it stayed there, the heavier it got. I swung my hand around and shot the flame back at the red dragon. It hit him in the face and caused him to stumble backward. He roared in pain and unfolded his wings. There was a whooshing sound as he beat them up and down and continued to roar.

The shadow yelled in rage. Not even wanting to know what was next, I pushed the magic out of me once again. This time the pulse went directly toward him. His spell looked like the black inky smoke from my dream. It poured from his hands, and, as my pulse hit him, this smoke wrapped itself around his head. Fetch had come to my side by this point and was standing in front of me in a protective stance. The others were still picking themselves up after my first pulse. I could hear more screams of rage from the shadow as he clawed at the black smoke around his head. The red dragon looked at him in confusion. He seemed to not know what to do. He looked over at Fetch with a pleading look, and then with another roar picked up the shadow in his front claws and took flight. They got up about fifty feet in the air and in a flash of red light disappeared. The goblins, with a chorus of squeals, jumped into blue balls and disappeared.

I rushed over to the others, Fetch at my side. I was worried that my pulse had hurt them. As I got to Samantha, she was pushing herself to her feet. I grabbed her arm and helped her to stand. When she wasn't hovering, she stood just about even with me. Her blue eyes were staring into mine with a look of wonder. She realized that I had hold of her arm and quickly pushed me away.

"Don't touch me, idiot," she said.

She looked over at Pete, who had helped Pek and Molly to their feet. He met her gaze with a blank look and made no attempt to reach for his charred sword to protect her honor. I think I had made a new friend.

"You're welcome, Princess," I said, "next time I'll let him cook you like a hot dog."

Pete smiled at this and quickly turned his attention to Molly. Samantha moved away from me. Looking around I spotted Smith sitting on an overturned trash can. He was staring at me with a look of deep thought on his face. I walked over to him.

"Are you ok?" I asked.

He looked at me for a minute. Studying my face, he began to laugh. He sat there laughing for a good while and it began to worry me. Everyone gathered around him wondering if he had lost it.

"I am ecstatic, Jack!" he finally said, "If I live another four hundred years I will never forget this day. You stopped a spell from a wizard. One who has found the ability to control dragons. You stopped him in his tracks, Jack. You have done what no human has ever done before. And you, dear Fetch, you deflected fire from a dragon three times your size! Truly the two of you are a force that the world has never seen before. You are truly a living legend."

"I wouldn't go that far," said the shadow's voice.

We all readied ourselves for another attack. The voice was coming from a small coyote sitting about twenty feet from us. It had its mouth open and the shadow's voice was speaking through him.

"Don't get me wrong, Jack, you are truly amazing, but not a legend. You took me by surprise, I'll give you that much. You will never do so again.

Remember, I still have your friend Michelle. I am gaining strength. There is magic, Jack, magic that the world has never seen before. You are a small part of it yes, a very small part though. Come see me, Jack, midnight tonight. My friend here will show you the way. You might even save Michelle. Though I doubt she will ever trust you again."

He was trying to get to me. There was a chance she was still alive. If she was, I had to play his little game if there was any chance to save her. I wanted to hold on to the hope that Michelle might be alive. I had to believe she was.

Pek spoke up, "You can't fool us. You are just trying to control Jack. He is smarter than you think and very powerful. Whatever spell you cast to control the dragons has backfired. Nature finds a way. That way is Jack and Fetch. They will stop you."

The shadow laughed, "Do you really think Jack is on your side? He is nothing like any of you. He will eventually join me. If he does so tonight he might save his friend. If he waits too long, she may die."

"Johnathen won't allow this," I shouted, "He will find you and we will stop you together."

The shadow laughed, "By all means, if you can find him bring him along. It would be a most interesting meeting. I will send my messenger back for you, Jack. Until then, try to consider what you are doing. Without my help you are truly alone. Your new friends will never fully trust you. Look at them, Jack, even now they fear you. You will never fit in the world of magic the way it is now. Your only hope is to join me. "

The coyote turned and disappeared. I was standing there staring at the spot where it had been. I looked at the little crew of people I was with now. Any thought that these fairies were trying to kill me left. They had every chance to destroy me tonight, and instead they stood their ground with me. But still, I could see something in their eyes. They were afraid. They had no idea who or even what I was. They didn't fully trust me. An old familiar feeling came creeping into my heart, the same feeling I have had my entire life. I simply didn't fit in. I was different. Every day I seemed to change and those changes took me away from the world I grew up in and kept me distant from the world of which I was now a part. I was truly alone now, a complete misfit.

I felt a gentle push on my hand. Fetch had come up to join me on the small hill. I looked down at his bowed head as he nudged my hand. He had grown since that first day. He was about the size of a pony. His snout had grown hard ridges of silver all around it and the two small bumps on his forehead had gotten bigger. I wondered if they would become horns one day. He moved his head up toward my face and looked me in the eye. His eyes were changing colors from red to blue to green to purple. He had a look of confusion on his face. He had finally seen another of his kind. One that commanded power, even if it was being controlled by a wizard. But, just like me, he was left with more questions than answers. To my surprise a big white tear rolled out of Fetch's eye. Some kind of silent communication had gone on between that dragon and Fetch. Even if it was controlled by the shadow, there was still a nobility to it. I remembered feeling what it felt and I wondered if I could use that to our advantage.

I looked at Fetch and thumped him on the forehead. Fetch had refused to destroy me. He had refused to take my life essence, and, because of that, he would never be fully accepted by other dragons. He was a misfit too. I wasn't alone.

I put my hand on the side of his face and looked him in the eye. I said the one thing I should have said in the tunnel when I first realized he was not going to kill me.

"Thank you."

He looked surprised at first, then simply nodded. I smiled at him. Leaning in and talking quietly, so the others wouldn't hear, I whispered to him.

"Who cares, Fetch? Who cares what they all think? We will find Michelle and get her out of this mess. We will live our lives the way we want. I have always been a misfit, so why not keep on being one? The way they treat us, we can be a mystery to them. All we have to do is look wise and act like we know more than we are telling. I'm done trying to fit into any kind of mold that people think I should fit into. You should feel the same pal. You just beat that big dragon like it was nothing, and I just had a standoff with a wizard, so let's keep playing the part.

They want to be afraid of us, let them. Who gives a flap?"

Me, using the word 'flap', made Fetch laugh a little. He looked at me with defiance in his eyes. I knew a lot of what I was feeling was bitterness from the life I had always lived. I wasn't mad at everyone. I was hurt. But, I was going to do things my way. If I had to play the role of a powerful enigma, then I would. I looked behind me and saw all of them staring at me and Fetch with the same look of wonder and apprehension I had seen on their faces before. What was I supposed to be to them?

I started walking toward them, not looking at any of them. I needed them to believe I knew what I was doing. They needed to tell me everything that they knew. If they didn't, then I was ready to strike out on my own. I really had no desire to go before this council they kept on talking about. Not if I was going to be judged by them as a threat. As far as I knew this council was not in the right. From what I had heard, they might not have mine or Fetch's best interest at heart. I kept from looking at Samantha. She affected me in a way that made it hard for me to think straight. I really had to focus around her to keep her from affecting me too much. I walked up to them.

"Is everyone ok?"

They all acknowledged that they were fine.

"Ok. I'm sorry about your trailer, Pek. I had no idea that you would be attacked. It was this shadow's plan all along to use Michelle's cell phone to lure me here."

I reached into the pouch that Johnathen had given me at the park and pulled out handfuls of money. Not bothering to count it, I handed it to Pek.

"If you need more, just let me know. All I want is to get Michelle out of this mess she is in. I hope she is still alive and I think she is. We are the victims in this. Neither one of us asked for this life. We both wanted to go before this council and get their approval. At this point, I don't care what they think. This mixed up world you live in is way too complicated for me. I hope, if I can stop this crazy guy, everyone will see that Fetch and I are not a threat and just want to live in peace. I just want to save my friend. We are making the best of what has happened. We deserve to live our lives the way we choose. Fetch should be allowed to live the way he wants. His choices have kept me alive so far. He is just as much a victim as any of us."

I was tired and I had no idea where all of this was coming from. All I knew is that I wanted a normal life, well as normal a life I could have now. I was scared and tired, and I couldn't see any other way out of this but to go up against this shadow wizard and get Michelle back, or die trying.

"Now I realize you weren't trying to kill me that day, but could you tell me just what you were doing by appearing to me?"

"I'll tell you what I know," said Samantha, "the rest will have to be filled in by the others. If you haven't pieced it together by now, someone has been spreading dragon eggs around the entire city."

I already knew this but I didn't want to interrupt her as she talked.

"The Fey have known for some time that someone was doing this. We didn't know why until now. This shadow wizard has obviously found a way to take part of the essence that dragons create when they are hatching and use it to control them. I was In search of one of those eggs that day when I first saw you. A dragon's pulse had been felt in the area, and I was trying to locate it before it disappeared. There is a pattern to dragons hatching. They will always hatch in threes. You can't detect a dragon until it has hatched. A magical barrier protects them from being seen, but the last dragon pulse we felt was in that area. When I appeared on the road that day, it was because I was searching for that dragon. I just happened to be there when a spell was cast that destroyed my magic that had kept me from being seen. When that happened, I realized that you had a dragon egg with you." She paused for a moment. "Why did you have Fetch's egg with you anyway?"

She was looking at me with those blue eyes and before I could stop myself I blurted out.

"It looked like a cool rock, so I picked it up for a lucky charm."

I could feel my face get red as soon as I said it. Samantha looked at me and shook her head slightly.

"You really are an idiot. I can't believe that you are the key to getting to the bottom of all of this. Fetch I can understand, but you?"

I heard Fetch snicker and I made a promise to myself to make him pay for that later, if we survived all of this.

"Could you just explain what happened please?" I said through gritted teeth, "Just tell me why you lured me out into the street."

"I didn't lure you anywhere, you stupid flap," she shouted, "You just walked out there when I was trying to tell you that you had a dragon egg in your pocket. It was like you were in some kind of trance. I was just trying to warn you so I could get it from you. I was trying to save your life."

When I thought back to that day, I remembered how shocked I was at her appearance. It did make sense now, that I could have just walked out into the street out of shock from her appearance, but I wasn't about to let her know that.

"If dragon eggs are hidden from magic, how did you know that I had one in my pocket?"

Smith interrupted then, "Samantha is very skilled in detecting the magic that surrounds all living things. She has a sensitivity that has not been seen in a millennium. It was the simple fact that she could not sense magic around an egg that allowed her to tell where a dragon egg is located."

Samantha looked at Smith in surprise. "Yeah," she said with some hesitation, "that is the best way to describe it."

This was a little confusing to me, but I wanted Samantha to go on so I kept my mouth shut. I wanted to know more.

"Ok. So you were just warning me, wanting to get Fetch's egg away from me. But why did you disappear when I was almost hit by the truck? Why didn't you reappear and help me out?"

Samantha sighed and looked down at the ground. She was trying to figure something out.

"I don't know," she finally said, "I saw you walking out into the street, and then I saw the truck bearing down on you, but then something happened. It felt like I was yanked away from the area. I found myself in Marana, unable to use any magic. By the time I could use it again and return, you were gone. I saw the damage at the store and figured that you had been destroyed by then. My presence and being seen by you triggered the hatching. I searched the area, trying to find Fetch before he disappeared like the other dragons. I couldn't find anything. Not one sign. So I pulsed a spell making sure no one would miss you and left. It wasn't till Molly had shown the YouTube video to me, that we found out you were even alive."

"Wait," I interrupted, "You were the one that cast the spell that made my brother forget me?"

There was a silence that could be felt in the air. Samantha had looked up in defiance and stared me in the eye. This time I felt nothing in the pit of my stomach. She saw the look of angry hurt on my face. Slowly the tears started to run down her face.

"I didn't know," she said softly, "I thought I was keeping those who knew you from going through the pain of your loss. I didn't know you were still alive."

I felt betrayed, even though I had only known her for a short time. Even though we spent more time telling each other off, here was the one person that had changed my life, even more than Fetch had. I stared at her. My hands clenched. Ever since this whole, wild, messed up adventure had started, the one thing that had continued to upset me the most was the fact that my brother had no idea who I was anymore. With all the fantastic gifts I now had, I would have traded it all just so he could remember me.

"You took my life, Samantha," I said.

I didn't have to say anything else. The tears were running down her face. I knew it wasn't her fault, that she was only doing what she had thought was best, but I didn't care.

"It wasn't much of a life, but it was mine!"

Samantha turned and slowly walked away. Fetch had walked up to me and was standing at my side. Before I knew what he was up to, he had whipped his tail around and smacked me in the back of the head. Before I could even react to the stinging blow, Molly had flown up to me and got in my face.

"Samantha was right. You are a flap. You have no idea what she went through when she found out you were alive. She searched for you for days after the video had come out, and, if you hadn't been hiding yourself from us, you would have found out what she had done for you. She even went against her father's wishes and pled with the council to spare you from having your memory erased. There were those that wanted you dead, Jack, and she was the only one that said you were worth sparing, both you and Fetch. I'm sorry about your brother, Jack, but for you to be mad at Samantha for all that has happened to you, makes you a world class idiot."

She had said this all in one breath. The blue glow around her lighted up as she spoke and was flashing in my eyes like a strobe light. I felt like a jerk. I know I had crossed a line and had to talk to her. Pete had gone over and was having a discussion with Smith and Pek. The conversation looked pretty serious. I figured it had something to do with me. But I had to deal with one problem at a time.

I walked in the direction that Samantha had gone. I realized that she wasn't hovering. She had been walking and staying on the ground ever since the attack. She was looking out at the desert. Off in the distance I could see the lights of a football field. You could hear a crowd of people cheering some event that was going on. I realized that I wasn't too far from a ranch where I had spent a summer working. I probably would never do anything like that again. Samantha had stopped on a small hill looking in the direction of the lights. She was beautiful.

There was a faint glow that made her visible. Her delicate looking wings were folded neatly across her back. I could see now how easy it had been for me to believe she could cast a spell that lured me out into the street. I stood next to her. I could tell that she had been crying.

"I'm sorry," I mumbled, "I know, I end up sounding like a broken record most of the time. All of this is so new to me. Every time I find out something new about what has happened, it just seems like everyone is out to get me. I understand that you were just doing what you thought was right. What I said to you was unfair. Can we start over?"

"Starting over," said Samantha, "what a typical human thing to say. We fairies see things a little differently. We move on. It is the strongest argument against erasing people's lives after magic has affected them. We are a proud race, Jack, a proud race that, for too long, has held ourselves above others. When we discovered that you were alive, I realized what a terrible mistake I had made in erasing your existence. Until then I was a firm believer in keeping our true existence from non-magic people. Why should we expect others to live in ignorance and in a haze of forgetfulness? We need to find a way for people to accept that there is magic in this world. We need to stop referring to it as two different worlds, Jack, you helped me realize that. I am truly sorry that your life has been erased. I would feel anger if the ones I loved couldn't remember me. The solution to a mistake like that is usually more memory manipulation. You seem to be immune to such magic, Jack, but there are so many more out there who are not. Michelle should not remember anything that happened. Johnathen has cast some sort of spell that protected her from this form of magic, and, from what I understand, she has come into her own magic. I feel that she should be allowed. Most on the council would agree, but not enough."

We stood there in silence for a while. She had spoken with so much passion that my heart was pounding. I was sure that Samantha could hear it. So much was going on around me. I was part of a game I never asked to play. I was a piece of a puzzle that did not quite fit. I had to play a part. After a while I spoke.

"Ok. I understand that there is more to all of this than I thought. This shadow guy needs to be stopped. I am still going to do things my way. I will not allow this council everyone keeps talking about to control me. Fetch and I will remain free, and if you don't agree, tell me now."

Samantha turned and looked at me. Her blue eyes had that same fire they had when she first met me.

"If I had planned to turn you over to the council, I would have already done so. "

She looked toward the lights again, keeping silent. There didn't seem to be anything left to say. A thought popped into my head.

"Can I ask you a question?" I queried.

"Yes, Jack you can. I might not answer, but you can ask."

I looked at her trying to determine if this was a joke or not. Finally I asked.

"If it was a random thing that I found Fetch's egg, and you were not watching me before this, then why were you at the scene of my accident a few years ago?"

Samantha turned to me with a puzzled look on her face. "What are you talking about? I never saw you before that day. What accident?"

I couldn't figure out why she would not admit that she was there. I remembered it so clearly. Her face was the last face I saw before I passed out, after breaking my hip. I was positive it was her. I could never forget a face like hers. Why would she lie?

"The day I broke my hip two years ago, you were there. I saw you."

She looked at me narrowing her eyes. Speaking slowly, like I was an idiot who didn't understand what she was saying, she said, "No. I never saw you before that day, Jack. What accident? What are you talking about?"

"Oh!" I responded, "Ok. You must not have realized it was me, but two years ago I was hit by a truck and broke my hip. You were there looking at me. It was one of the reasons I thought you were out to get me. You must not have realized that it was me."

Samantha just stared at me, her mouth slightly open and her head shaking. Fetch, who had been quiet this whole time, let out a soft 'huh' sound as a warning to me that I was treading on dangerous ground again.

"Let me get this straight, " she said, "You seem to think that I was there, at the scene of some accident you were involved with two years ago? Did you think I caused that accident?"

"Well, yeah, at first."

Fetch let out a grumble and began to walk away. He smacked me on the side of my head as he moved away from this scene, letting me know I was on my own. Turning back to Samantha, I tried to better explain my situation.

"Look, I know now that you didn't cause the accident. I was just wondering why you were there."

A familiar ball of light knocked me to the ground.

"I was never there. I was not there! Why do you keep saying I was?"

She stormed off, leaving me more confused than ever. Could I have been wrong? All this time I had seen Samantha's face in my dreams. I had seen her at the accident, but why was she denying it? Could it have been someone else, and my mind just placed her face there, after seeing her across the street that day? There were similarities to that meeting and my accident two years ago, so it was possible that I could have imagined it was her, when it was someone else all this time. But I was sure it was her. I had dreams about her so many times after that moment that I know it was her. She had stormed off down the hill, calling me a 'fat flap' and other names that I couldn't even begin to pronounce. I stayed there on the top of the hill just looking up at the stars. Slowly Fetch's face came into view. He was looking down at me with a big smile on his face.

"How come every time I seem to get close to her liking me, I have to put my foot in my mouth and ruin it?" I asked him.

Fetch just shrugged his shoulders. Looking at him, I rubbed the spot where her ball had hit me.

"You sure it's too late to eat me?"

Fetch just laughed.

We walked back to the trailer and saw everyone gathered in a tight circle. They were talking in low voices, and, as soon as they saw

Fetch and I walking up, they stopped. They were all looking at us in an uncomfortable way. They seemed to have come to a conclusion, and I could tell from their body language that I wasn't going to like what they had to say.

Pete was holding his sword in his hands, and Pek was looking everywhere except in mine and Fetch's direction. Smith had a determined look on his face, and I had the feeling that he had been arguing with everyone else. Samantha was glaring at Pete, obviously not happy he had his sword out, and Molly had a protective hand on Pek's narrow shoulder.

"What's up?" I asked, in what I hoped was a calm sounding voice.

Smith spoke up, "We all agree that it is not a good idea to try to rescue Michelle, Jack."

Fetch stepped in front of me and sat on his curled up tail. It wasn't a threatening move, just one that showed everyone that he didn't agree with them.

"Fetch thinks I should," I said in a calm controlled tone.

"Please Jack, you need to understand," said Smith, "You have a great power and we just want to protect you. Pete has volunteered to go and rescue Michelle if he can. We need to get you some place safe and figure out what our next move is."

"Our next move?" I interrupted, "what do you mean by that?"

I looked around at the small group. No one seemed to want to look at me or Fetch.

"You want to take me before this council, don't you?"

They all stayed silent for a minute.

"We all understand now that some kind of conflict is definitely coming, Jack," said Molly. "We need to know whose side you are on."

This last statement hit me hard. They were afraid of me. They were afraid that I might join the shadow wizard in this crazy thing. Once again, as in so many times in my life, I felt like an outsider. I sat down on the ground. I just sat there, staring at the ground. Would I ever truly fit in anywhere? Was I always going to be some sort of outsider? These people, who I thought would stand with me, even loosely, were now afraid of me joining this shadow maniac on his mad quest for power. All I wanted to do was to find Michelle, my friend, and rescue her if I could. If I could only see that she was ok, then I would let it all go. My plan was to just leave with Fetch. If I were to survive this, I would just leave. I prepared myself for a confrontation with them, to let them know that I would not accept this. Michelle was my family and I was going to be the one to find her. Me and Fetch. But before I could say anything, the shadow wizard's voice spoke.

Chapter 36

"Well," said the coyote, "Looks like everyone is showing their support for you, Jack. I knew it was just a matter of time before their true colors would shine through. I bet they want to take you to the council for your own protection. The ancient Philosophers with backward thinking. They will destroy you in the end, Jack. You know that."

I didn't respond to what he said. I had no way of honestly saying that they wouldn't destroy me. I was not supposed to be alive, according to them. I was something different. Well, I had always felt different, so in a strange way I found comfort in being that way.

"Is Michelle alive?" I asked.

"You will have to meet me to find out, Jack. You and Fetch. Oh by the way Fetch, the dragons wanted me to kill you. They think you are a freak and should be destroyed. Quite frankly they are surprised you are alive. If you join me, I will protect you from them, and maybe we can find the cure to your small, dwarf size. There is so much more to being a dragon, Fetch, things that you will never discover in your present form."

I looked over at Fetch. He was staring at the coyote with a look of confusion on his face. I could tell that there was an inner struggle going on inside of him. I didn't blame him for wanting to be normal. He had obviously given up a lot when he refused to take my essence. Finally he looked up and growled. It was a defiant sounding 'no'.

"Very well, Fetch, but mark my words, in the end both you and Jack will join me or you will die. This has gone on long enough, Jack, time for my friend here to lead you to me. I will give you a few moments to say good-bye."

The coyote closed its mouth and sat there, bobbing its head up and down, showing its impatience in waiting for me and Fetch. I turned to everyone who was standing there quietly.

"This is a mistake, Jack," said Smith, "You will not survive this."

"You don't know that for sure. If you did, I doubt that you would all be so afraid of me."

The silence that followed let me know how they all felt. A strange black door had appeared by the coyote. Before anyone could say another word to try and stop me, I took off at a full run toward the door. Fetch was right at my heels and I could hear the others calling out to me to stop. When we got close to the door we sped up, and before I could stop myself, we jumped through the dark door into a nightmare of a scene.

There was the shadow wizard at the top of a tall hill. All around me were pine trees. It was cooler here than Pek's yard and I figured that we must be in the mountains somewhere, possibly Mount Lemon. In the dark I could see many different shapes moving from tree to tree toward me and Fetch. We stood there and I noticed that they wouldn't come into the light. We walked toward the shadow. As we got close to him, he waved a hand in the air and the trees disappeared. What I saw moving around were Goblins. Hundreds possibly thousands of them slowly corralled us toward a valley.

From behind him came a rumbling sound and slowly the head of the dragon that was with him earlier appeared. Then, from all around the little valley that we had been corralled into, we heard more rumbling. With a burst of flame, dragons all along the valley were revealed. They formed an outer circle in back of the goblins. We were trapped!

I had a feeling we would not survive this encounter. This was the twisted black army of the shadow wizard and it was either join or die. A hot rush of wind caught me in the face. It was the breath of the dragons that now surrounded me and Fetch.

The shadow wizard was now floating above the ground. His arms spread out to his sides, ending in two fists of crackling power. His head was tilted back. He was wearing a black robe that collected energy out of the air. It would shimmer and hum at times, and would move as if it was a living creature reaching out and grabbing at invisible threads of power. I recognized the robe as the force that had tried to pull me into itself in my nightmare. I understood that it hadn't been a dream, but a vision of how it was using the dragons hatching as a way to gain power. The darkness that was the robe reached out, whispering to me as it did in my dream, bragging about how it was done. It would pull peoples' life force toward itself at the moment the eggs were hatching. He used their pain and fear to feed that dark force, and then after it was saturated in pain and fear, he would release it back for the dragon to feed on, with the life force now surrounded by his spell. Once consumed by the dragons, he would have control of them from their first moment of life. They were consuming a life force that had been dipped in pain and fear, but something went wrong when Fetch hatched. As my life force was being pulled into the blackness, Fetch refused to consume me. He chose to go against all of his instincts and spare me. The shadow wizard was not prepared for this and had to release my life force before it was surrounded by his spell. The protection that all dragon eggs have, then surrounded my life force and became a part of who I was. Fetch was a free dragon controlled by no one, and I was now something different never seen before. All this was whispered to me as the shadow wizard floated down to where I was. I looked at Fetch and could tell by the way he was shaking his head that the voice whispered to him too.

The wizard stopped ten feet in front of us. He was laughing quietly to himself. He spoke and when he did his voice was the same as the darkness.

"You see, Jack, you are nothing but a spell gone wrong. You and Fetch are mistakes. That is how everyone sees you. You are freaks to them and you will never fit in. You belong here with me. I can help you. It was my spell that created you. I can find a way to help you, Jack. You are becoming something else. You're still changing. I can cure you. I can give Fetch the full life of a dragon."

Fetch and I looked at each other. There was a moment of silence on the field, as if all the creatures there were holding their breath waiting for our response. Either 'yes' or 'no' was expected. We either join or fight. We laughed. We laughed long and loud. We laughed at the fact that this wizard here expected us to believe he could change us? It was long and hysterical laughter. It was like a private joke between me and Fetch. No one had asked us if we wanted to change, if we wanted to be normal. Fetch had really known nothing but who he was. It was like asking a fish who had always been a fish if he would like to be a squirrel. Fetch didn't care about the other dragons accepting him. He was who he was, and that was fine with him. And as for me? Yes, I had regrets, but at the heart of it I was a comic-reading, fantasy-loving geek who had been given incredible powers. My body was now in the best shape of my life. This was a geek's dream come true. I knew that I couldn't explain this to the wizard. He was born into this world of magic, governed by rules of magic's nature. So what if this world saw me as a freak, I didn't really plan on being a part of it.

"No," I finally said, "No, I will not join you. I can't speak for Fetch, he is free to make his own choices, but my answer is 'no'." There was a stirring on the hill as the dragons seemed to react to something I just said.

"I don't know why you continue to play this game, Jack. Fetch is yours to command and I grow tired of this game."

A bolt of energy shot out of his hand knocking me backward. Another one wrapped around Fetch, tying him to the ground. This was not the same wizard I had fought earlier today. He had gained in power and it was different from before. But, even as I struggled against this new powerful wizard, I realized something. He didn't want the dragons to know that Fetch was free. He didn't want them to understand that I had no control over anything that Fetch did. My statement had scared him and I think I knew why. His spell must depend on the dragons thinking they had no choice. Fetch's very presence proved that wrong. By my saying he had a choice, I was showing the dragons that they had a choice too. His spell over the dragons might not be as powerful as he played it up to be. This must be the key to so much of his magic. Trust, and the belief that he was powerful, gave him more power. My being immune to so many of his spells was causing him a lot of trouble. A plan was forming in my mind.

The spell that had knocked me down was keeping me there. I could see Fetch struggling to get up from his own rope bond. Each rope of energy was directed from each hand of the shadow and had a different color. Mine was red and Fetch's was purple. Fetch was blasting his rope with fire over and over again. I kept forcing the magic that was in me at my own rope. In a wild second of inspiration I called out to Fetch.

"I need fire!" I yelled.

Fetch shot a flame the same color as my bonds. I caught it in my hands and grabbed the ever tightening rope. As soon as I touched the rope, it burst away from my body like a water balloon popping. I sent a wave of forced magic toward Fetch's bonds and they shimmered and disappeared. We were both on our feet now and ready to fight. The terrifying thing for me was the absolute lack of knowledge as to how my magic even worked. I just seemed to force the magic out of me and it gave me what I needed. It was almost as if it had a mind of its own. When I used it, I could feel it building up inside of me and then I would just push or force it out of my body. I knew if I got out of this fight alive, I would have to learn some kind of control over this ability.

The shadow had been pushed back from mine and Fetch's attempt to throw off his spell. I pushed another wave of magic at him as Fetch shot a burst of fire in his direction, but we had hesitated too long and he stopped our attack with a shrug. I saw a strong green shield form in front of him as our combined attack ricocheted away from him. We stood facing each other on the field. Finally I spoke.

"If we are going to do this, please stop hiding. Just show us who you are."

In my heart I already knew who he was, I just didn't want to admit it, but all the signs pointed to one person. With a laugh and a wave of his hands, the dark shadow shield melted away and we saw our attacker for the first time. It was Johnathen. It had been him all along. There never was another wizard attacking us or trying to kill us. It had always been Johnathen.

Chapter 37

He threw a flashing ball of fire at me and Fetch, and we barely jumped away in time. This was nothing like it was in the comics or fantasy books I read and loved. The fight seemed slow and clumsy. Johnathen had a strange look on his face, and for a moment I saw how haggard he looked. He had the appearance of a worn out drug addict, hyped up on meth. He was not aware that whatever new magic he was working, was taking its toll on him physically. When Fetch and I stood up, he was breathing hard. A strange smile crossed his face and sweat poured off his body.

"It worked!" he screamed, "I knew it would. I was right. Oh Jack, you have no idea what I have done. The power I am beginning to possess. I knew it was possible and I have Michelle to thank for this. Too bad she is dead now."

A roar of absolute rage came from Fetch. At the pronouncement that Michelle was dead, he snapped. I joined him in his roar, as rage swelled up inside me. This was the answer I was looking for. This was what I was afraid to ask this whole time. Michelle was gone, and it was Johnathen's fault. I felt betrayed. In my life I had read many stories about people being betrayed. I had people who had lied to me and tricked me in one way or another. The closest way to describe it, is feeling every emotion you have ever felt for someone, all at the same time. The like, dislike, love, hate, anger, happiness, and sadness. Every single emotion you can have, balled up inside you at the same time. That is the closest description to betrayal. That is what I felt about Johnathen right now.

We ran at him, with both my forced magic and Fetch's fire raging at full power. I couldn't stop myself, I was in a towering rage and the magic had taken me completely over. All I wanted was to destroy Johnathen, to tear him apart and completely obliterate him. I was dimly aware of light and the sound of explosions going on around me as I ran at him. Before I could get to him, I felt the stinging spit of the goblins as they joined in the fight. Strong hands reached for me and pulled me down. I could hear Fetch struggle and I knew they had him too. Johnathen walked up to me, confident that my magic could no longer hurt him. Blinded by rage and sorrow, I couldn't focus enough to get the goblins off me. I could feel their acid spit burning my skin down to the bone. Johnathen walked up as the goblins beat me to my knees.

Tears were blurring my view of him as he walked up and kicked me in the face. Pain exploded through my body as I felt my nose break for a second time. I could feel the blood slowly running down my face. It trickled into my mouth full of broken teeth and I began to choke. My vision swam in and out as Johnathen kneeled to look me in the eye. He grabbed my face with his hand and began squeezing it. I could feel the bones shift as Johnathen's unnatural strength began to crush my face.

"You will die tonight, Jack. Before the sun comes up, you will die. Yes, I killed Michelle. She turned her back on me, and, in the end, was the victim of the very magic I would have shared with her. I had plans for her that would have placed her in the history books when I took over. There is a new world dawning, Jack. A world of peace and harmony. I will rule that world and destroy all who stand in my way, Jack. Even though you are a mistake, I would have gladly shared it with you. I considered you a friend. But now, you must die as an example to any who try to stand in my way. How could you side with the filthy fairies? They are what is wrong with everything in the magic world. You turned your back on me the minute you stood with them. Now I have to kill you."

"As for Fetch, I will let the other dragons tear him apart. It will be the last thing your broken body will witness."

He reached his hand up and his voice amplified across the valley.

"Destroy the dragon with a name!" he said.

All was quiet. The goblins had put their hands over my mouth to keep me from yelling. I was in too much pain. I was hurt and my forced magic seemed to have left me. I was helpless. I couldn't see or hear Fetch. I wanted to tell him to get away. I couldn't.

I could feel the bodies of the goblins holding me down begin to shake. They were afraid of the dragons. The goblins that had Fetch pinned, whined a little, not wanting to bring too much attention to themselves. The red and gold dragon that was with Johnathen before, swooped down from its spot at the top of the valley. It landed next to Johnathen and looked at him. Johnathen pointed toward Fetch, and the goblins holding him, overcome with fear, ran squealing into the darkness. Fetch didn't move. He stayed there steadily looking at the dragon. I wanted to shout at him to fly away, but I realized that the dragon would just catch him in the air. Slowly the red dragon lowered its head and met Fetch's level-eyed stare.

I could see a thin trail of smoke coming from Jonathan's robes. It reached up to the head of the red dragon and circled it like a crown.

"Kill him!" said Johnathen in a commanding tone.

The dragon didn't move.

"Kill him now!" he repeated, his voice showing a little hesitation.

It was an emotionally draining experience to hear Johnathen talk this way. He had fooled us all. How could he have hidden the monster he was from Michelle for so long? The tears continued to fall from my eyes.

The red dragon lifted an enormous claw in the air. I struggled against the goblins as I felt a new ball of magic form in my body. The pain of their acid spit made it hard for me to concentrate. The hurt of Johnathen's confusing betrayal kept me foggy and unfocused. So much didn't make sense. So many questions formed in my head.

My forced magic continued to form in my body. It kept on growing since it did not have any push from me to force it out. I thought I would explode if I couldn't force this magic out. I was in a panic. Frustration and rage was all I could feel. This rage fed the magic growing inside me, but I had no focus to release it.

The red dragon stood there with its paw in the air. It was hesitating like it was not sure what to do. The inner struggle was apparent on its face. Johnathen shot a ball of power at it and hit it on the side of its face. The dragon roared, and, in its moment of pain, swung its paw to the side, ripping at Johnathen's black smoke robe.

Johnathen screamed in pain and the smoke attaching itself to the red dragon blew away. Its eyes glowed and rapidly changed colors. It had broken Johnathen's hold, and before Johnathen could get it back, the dragon blasted him with a cold green fire. Finally, the goblins nerve broke, and, letting me go, they scattered in all directions, squealing and running into the darkness of the night.

Johnathen had a strange wiggling field surrounding him, protecting him from the dragons fire. The magic inside me continued to grow as I tried to stand up. A burst of light hit my eyes as Fetch's healing flame surrounded me. I started to recover from the damage that Johnathen and the goblins had caused. Then Johnathen reached through the field of protection surrounding him and grabbed me by the throat. He was strong and I could feel my throat begin to close up, when he let me go and screamed again. Another dragon, this one purple and yellow, had slashed at his robes. The dragons were freeing themselves from Johnathen's control. The field lashed out and something in the pattern of it looked familiar. It whipped around like a living thing, grabbing at the two dragons that continued to slash at the black robe. It began to fall apart.

By this time, the magic in me had reached a point of having to be released. With all the strength I could muster, and fetch's thoughts of confidence in me pounding in my head, I pushed it out of me. It was a painful experience. I could feel it tearing itself from my body. I fell back down to my knees, still surrounded by Fetch's healing flame. Fetch had joined the other dragons in their quest to tear apart the smoking robe. He was in the air, fighting part of the strange field that was surrounding Johnathen. A red and yellow part of the field had broken off and was squeezing Fetch around the neck. I sent a pulse of magic toward him, sending the wraith like thing back to the original field protecting Johnathen. He was trying to stop the dragons from tearing his robe apart. My first pulse was still hanging in the air pushing against the field. It buckled and then the pulse broke through the barrier. It went through Johnathen, causing him to gasp in pain. He fell to his knees while the two dragons continued to tear at his robes. I started to move toward Johnathen when I was blindsided by a goblin. They were finding the courage to return, and, once again, I found myself being pummeled by these hateful creatures. This time I was ready for them. I let my sorrow and anger wash over me as I tore into them. I could hear their squeals of pain and outrage as I lashed out like a madman. I don't know how many I hurt, or even if I killed any of them.

There was so many of them. I was slowly being overwhelmed. One had a club and hit my hip. I screamed in pain and crumpled to the ground. They had found my weakest point and they were beginning to exploit it. It was amazing at how many fists continued to hit me in the same spot on my hip. The protective healing fire was the only thing that was keeping me from being burned by their acid spit. I kept on fighting through, trying to make my way to Johnathen, to help Fetch and the other dragons. I saw a dragon swoop toward me. Its roar sent the goblins scrambling away. I was relieved at its presence, thinking that this one would tilt the scales in mine and Fetch's favor. The dragon swooped down, and, before I realized what it was doing, sent a burst of fire right at me. It was bright orange in color and it weighed me down to the ground. It burned away Fetch's flame and started to crush the life out of me. Remembering how heavy the flame was when I caught it at Pek's trailer, I was afraid I wasn't going to make it this time. I could feel the weight of the fire pressing down on me as the dragon moved closer. I couldn't tell if it was doing this of its own free will, or if it was being compelled by Johnathen, all I knew was that I was not going to make it.

A blue light appeared above my head. It flew directly into the eyes of the dragon. It roared in annoyance as the light buzzed around its head. It swatted at the light like it was a fly. This made it stop the continuous flow of fire in my direction. As soon as the flame stopped, I rolled away and took a deep breath. I pounded the ground in frustration. I was way over my head here. I didn't know what I was doing. Michelle was dead and now Fetch and I were stuck in chaos. I didn't see how we were going to get out of this. The dragons seemed to be fighting each other and I had lost sight of Fetch. This strange power that Johnathen had seemed to compensate for the power he was losing from the dragons. It dawned on me that I had no idea where that blue ball of light had originated. I heard a screech coming from a group of goblins and saw the reason why.

It was Pete. Somehow he had found us and was joining the fight. He was surrounded by goblins. He was swinging his sword around slashing at them. There was a sick, green, wetness covering him and I realized it must be goblin blood. This was a real battle. There were things dying. I saw a flash of blue light out of the corner of my eye, and saw that

Samantha was distracting the dragons still fighting on Johnathen's side. Again I couldn't tell if these dragons were controlled or just chose to stay on Johnathen's side.

Samantha looked at me from across the battlefield and smiled. That was when the goblin attacked. He jumped out of the darkness, grabbed her by the throat, and spit in her face. I yelled for Fetch as I ran across the field, everything else forgotten for a moment. The only thought in my head was her safety. I had lost Michelle. I was not about to lose another friend.

Fetch appeared in the air to my right. He shot a stream of flame at my hands. Catching it I continued to run shooting flame at anyone who got in my way. My hip pounded with pain with every step I took. Goblins were screaming in pain as the flame from my hands hit them. Fetch would pick them up and fling them to the ground biting and slashing at them. I felt the splatter of blood hit my face as I finally reached Samantha's side.

She was struggling to catch her breath. Her face was nothing but a bubbling mass of raw and burning skin. You could already see a circle of bone through her forehead and her hair was almost all melted away. Her eyes were undamaged and she stared into the night gasping for air. There was fear and confusion in those eyes.

Fetch knelt down and gently sent a blast of healing fire to her face. Her breathing slowed and her eyes focused on me. I could hear Pete, now at my side, slashing at any goblin that dared to get close. A hand touched my shoulder and Smith whispered in my ear.

"It's pretty bad, Jack. I don't know if Fetch's flame can cure her completely. We have to get out of here now."

"No," I heard myself say, "I have to stop him. Get her someplace safe."

I stood up shaking in rage. It was all I had left. Johnathen had taken everything away from me, and hurt and killed the people I cared about. I was going to stop him. I had to stop him. I could feel the magic building up inside of me. This time I was going to let it build up until it would explode out of me. I didn't care if I lived or died, I just wanted to stop Johnathen. Fetch crouched, ready to run by my side, and let out a roar that matched my rage. I began to run.

All the pain I felt was pushed aside. Goblins tried to grab us spitting and snarling. I tossed them aside like they were nothing. The dragons were now busy with their own battle above us. Only one was by Johnathen's side. His robe was in tatters and he stood there waiting for me to reach him. His shimmering patterned shield still surrounded him. I continued to make my way over to him when Fetch was knocked back by a blast of black fire.

One of the dragons, still on Johnathen's side, had attacked. Before it could move in for the kill, a shining blade, thrown by Pete, landed between the eyes of the attacking beast. I kept running toward Johnathen. When I reached the shield, I dove through it. It felt like hands as it grabbed at me, trying to pull me back. I fought my way through the shield, finally standing before Johnathen. The man I trusted. The wizard who destroyed everything.

"How could you kill her? She loved and trusted you and you killed her."

There was a fury in my words. In spite of the power Johnathen seemed to have now, he took a step back from me as I spoke. For a second I saw a look of confusion followed by sorrow. Johnathen shook his head slowly. Then the light went out of his eyes and the snarling beast that Johnathen now was returned.

"There is always a sacrifice to be made in any war, Jack," he said nonchalantly, as if it was nothing to kill someone you were supposed to love.

I stepped up to him and he took another step back. He was still afraid of the power that had kept on building up inside me. I remembered how I had surprised him in the desert. He seemed to remember that too. I took another step toward him.

He smiled weakly and said, "You can't win, Jack. You won't join me. I know you will continue to refuse, and I will kill you and Fetch. Just like I killed Michelle."

His voice wavered a little at this statement.

"Look, he is already dying."

He pointed behind me. I wanted to turn around and see if he was telling the truth. But I didn't dare turn my back on him. He smiled again, realizing that it wasn't going to work. It was a standoff. I didn't dare move toward him out of fear that he would unleash an attack, and he didn't attack for fear of me unloading my unpredictable magic on him. His new power could affect me and so my previous ace-in-the-hole was gone. The strange field surrounding us both was keeping all sound out as the fighting continued around us. Out of the corner of my eye I could see flashes of fire explode in the air as the dragons continued to battle over our heads. I smiled at Johnathen.

"Looks like you lost control of the dragons, dude. Sucks to be you."

"It doesn't matter now. By the time I am done, I will be able to destroy them all."

He looked happy as he said these words, a manic joy in his eyes. He stood there staring calmly at me. We could be meeting each other for coffee instead of facing each other in a struggle for life or death. I felt a strange pulling at my feet. I looked down and saw the smoke that came from his robe wrapping around my ankles. Before I could move I was transported back to that nightmare world I had to fight my way out of in the tunnel.

There was my brother, hanging from the rope around his neck. He had begun to smell bad and one of his eyes had fallen out of his head. I felt the pain in my hip and my hand had curled up as if the bone had never been set those many years ago. With the sound of my mother screaming in my head, my brother spoke to me again.

"Hello loser, back for another tour? "

"You can't fool me this time, Johnathen. I know it is you."

"Is it? Are you sure? I mean, for all you know you are still in that tunnel. Or you could be in a mental hospital awaiting shock treatments."

Black blood was pouring out of his mouth with every word he spoke. My hip throbbed and for one second the thought that none of this was real came into my mind. My nightmare brother reached out to grab my arm again. This time I was ready.

"You always were a disappointment, Jack, always a complete loser."

The rope broke and my brother landed on his feet. His head rolled around with no support as he began to walk toward me. I could smell his breath as he moved in close. I was unable to move. He reached out to grab my face. That's when I forced the magic out of me.

It had been building up inside of me all this time. Even through the haze of pain and sorrow of this vision controlled by Johnathen, I could feel it pulsating to be released. I took a chance in believing that this moment, during the vision of my brother, was the right time to release it. It ripped out of my body causing real pain. I was shaken out of the dream as the full force of the spell, fueled by my own doubts and fears, my anger and sorrow, went through Johnathen like a blade.

He gasped in pain and his barrier fell apart. The sound of the battle raging around was overwhelming. I fell to the ground completely exhausted. Pain throbbed in my whole body from head to toe. A blast of green fire hit me from a passing dragon and I lay there unable to move. I could do nothing but stare at the sky. I was not happy with the fact that I couldn't see Johnathen anywhere. If my blast of magic hadn't stopped him, then I was a sitting duck.

Fetch appeared above me. He blasted me with his healing fire and the green flame was wiped away. I lay there, still throbbing in pain, when a strange numbness started creeping up the right side of my body. It started at my hand and quickly spread down to my leg and up the side of my face. I thought I was having a stroke. The vision in right eye went black and my ear was buzzing. I still was unable to move. Fetch stood over me, protecting me from the battle that seemed to rage on. I was just beginning to believe we were going to die, when a blue ball appeared above me. It got bigger and slowly started to sink down. I tried to warn Fetch but he was too busy fighting off a group of goblins trying to spit on me. The ball engulfed me and Fetch, growing brighter. My last thought was about Samantha. I hoped that Fetch's healing flame had been enough to save her. And then, I passed out.

Chapter 38

I woke up with a start. I sat up too fast and a pain shot through my body. I was no longer numb on my right side, which I took as a good sign. I let my eyes adjust and noticed some familiar graffiti. I was back in the tunnel. Back where it all started. I lay there and my body slowly drained of pain. I had no idea how I got back to the tunnel. A thought crossed my mind. What if this had all been a dream? What if I had fallen into this wash and crawled into this tunnel with some sort of concussion and imagined it all?

The sound of a match being struck shook me from my thoughts. In the light of the match I could see Booger's face. He was lighting a cigar.

"Hiya boss."

He took a big hit off the cigar and blew smoke in my face. It smelled terrible.

I backed myself against the wall of the tunnel ready for another fight. I felt the magic building in me along with a tingling sensation down the right side of my body.

"Whoa boss, wait, I'm on your side now. If I wanted you dead, I wouldn't have pulled you out of that fight. At the least I would have already killed you."

In a strange way, that made sense, but, I was nowhere near trusting this guy. Remembering the ball engulfing me and Fetch, I looked around to find him.

"Where is Fetch?" I asked.

Letting the magic simmer in my body, I moved my hand and felt a strange sensation.

I raised it up to my head and felt a bandage across my face.

"Been hurt, boss," explained Booger, "Face and your arm. Heck pretty much your whole right side."

I didn't care about me. I needed to know if I was the only one to survive.

"Where is Fetch, Booger?" I repeated.

In answer to my question I heard a strange gagging sound. I looked over and saw Fetch. He was facing away from me. He sounded sick. I got up and went over to see if he was ok. When I got to him and touched him he moved away from me. He kept his head down. I was relieved he was ok, but puzzled at why he moved away from me.

"Hey. You mad at me?"

Fetch looked back at me with a strange look of guilt on his face. He coughed and blood came out of his mouth. I rushed over to him. He was not doing so well after all.

"What happened?"

My throat was dry and sore and it hurt to talk.

"The battle was going badly. You just lay there as Fetch was fighting to protect you. Whatever you did to Johnathen really knocked the wind out of his sails. The goblins got smart, and, except for the twenty or so that was trying to get you, they took off. The dragons split. Some stayed with Johnathen, others sided with Smith and the others just flew off, not wanting to get involved. Johnathen was in a rage. He was trying to stand up, and I knew if he saw you laying there hurt the way you were, he would kill you, so I got a bubble going and got you and Fetch out of there."

"What about the others?" I asked as I tried to check and see how bad Fetch was hurt.

He hung his head down, not wanting to look at me.

"Don't know," said Booger lighting a second cigar, "That elf got Samantha out of there and the other fey were still fighting. Smith told me to get you to his place, but instead, we ended up here. Funny thing, huh? This is it though isn't it? The place where it all started?"

I was confused. Why was Booger helping me? How did he know Smith? Once again this strange world I lived in was twisting in a way I didn't understand.

"Why are you helping us?" I asked.

Booger just puffed on his cigar for a while.

"Got my reasons," he said.

He didn't say anything else about it. I turned back to Fetch too tired to question it now.

"Been here a while now, boss. Fetch was blasting you with that fire of his over and over again. I finally convinced him to stop. Wrapped your arm and head myself. You're a little messed up right now."

I ignored this last comment. I wasn't concerned about myself right now. Fetch looked bad and I needed to find a way to help him. I remembered that Smith had told me about a group of fairy healers.

"Booger, can you get us to the fairy healers?"

"Don't think so. Been trying to teleport you guys out of here and haven't been able to. I think your magic makes mine not work too good. Besides, I doubt I would be accepted by the fey, boss. They don't like goblins much."

I stood there scratching Fetch's head as best I could with my bandaged hand. I wondered what kind of damage it had suffered. I wasn't feeling any pain from it right now, so I didn't think I was burned. It just tingled. I figured it just took longer to heal this time because Fetch was obviously hurt. I figured that if I could get Fetch some help, he would be able to help me. I was trying to stay positive. The thought of losing Fetch was too much, especially after losing Michelle. I had to get some help.

As I stood there, I saw a familiar sight that filled me with dread. A bobcat was sitting at the mouth of the tunnel staring at us. Fetch spotted him and sent a small burst of flame in his direction. We had been discovered which meant that Johnathen, if he was able, was on his way. Sure enough, blue lights were beginning to glow all around the tunnel.

"Go boss," said Booger, shooting a strange green dart at one bubble that had a green hand reaching through feeling around for us.

"I'll hold them off. Just get on Fetch. Fly northwest out of town into the desert. When you get to the desert, the fairy healers will find you."

I wanted to say something to him. It was very confusing to me that he was helping.

"Thanks," I said.

He sent another bolt at another ball saying, "Don't thank me yet. Get going."

I looked at Fetch and asked, "Can you fly pal?"

He straightened up and shook out his wings. The proud fierceness in his eyes told me he could. I hoped we wouldn't half to fly too long. I didn't want to hurt him any more than he already was hurt. I jumped on his back and we took off into the night air.

I could hear the squeals as more goblins poured into the tunnel. I found myself hoping that Booger was going to be ok. It was hard for me to believe that he was a friend now. Well, if not a friend, at least he was on our side for now.

Just being in the sky seemed to make Fetch feel better. He shot a stream of purple fire into the air. It flew back at me and flowed around us. My hand went up and touched the bandage on my face. I wondered how bad it was. I wasn't feeling any pain in my face or my hand. I decided to take a chance and see the damage for myself. I reached up and began to unwrap my head. Fetch looked back at me with concern on his face.

"Relax," I told him, "it can't be that bad. Your fire has never failed to heal me yet."

He turned back around and continued to fly. Every once in a while he would glance back as I continued to unwrap the bandage. When it was completely removed, I just sat there letting the wind touch my face. It felt great.

All of a sudden Fetch stiffened. His head began to move from left to right, then up and down. He smelled something in the air and was very excited about it. With a roar of joy he began to dive down. I almost fell off his back as he flew to the right going more north than west now.

"Easy, you stupid lizard," I said as Fetch dipped toward a building.

I recognized it as a hospital. Fetch was flying right for it and he was not bothering to cloak himself. He landed at the front entrance sending people screaming and running. I started to get down, aware that the police could show up any minute. In fact, they might already be inside. After all, it was a hospital and there were usually police inside a hospital. Before I could get completely off of Fetch, he had bounded toward the doors and knocked me backwards. Healed or not, I was still a little weak and it took me a second to get up. I ran in calling for Fetch. There were people crouching on the ground, their hands over their heads. A small boy was standing on a chair, bouncing up and down, pointing at the doors leading out of the room.

"Dragon, Mommy, dragon!" he was saying over and over, very excitedly.

I ran in the direction he was pointing, startling people as I ran past. Some were hidden under chairs they were starting to peek out from under. Some screamed as I ran past them. Surprisingly, Fetch caused no damage as he ran through the hospital. I was unable to catch up to him, just catching a glimpse of his black and silver tail as he would turn a corner. Listening for the sound of screams, I finally caught up to him as he was pushing at a closed door to a room.

I ran up shouting, "Fetch, you stupid lizard! What are you doing?"

The door slammed open and he ran inside. I ran into the room unprepared for what I was seeing. It was Michelle. She was alive!

Chapter 39

She had her arms wrapped tightly around Fetch's neck, sobbing uncontrollably. Her eyes were shut tight and I could see her sunken face. Whatever Johnathen had done to her, had to be bad. She looked like she hadn't eaten in weeks. The way she looked made me think he had left her for dead, but she had managed to survive. I was filled with joy. Tears stung my face as I rushed up to throw my arms around both of them, just happy she was alive. I began to cry in relief, sobbing and saying over and over again "Are you all right?" I could hear a commotion down the hall as police were trying to hunt down the source of the disturbance. Michelle was whispering in my ear.

"He took it from me, Jack, he took it."

I looked at her. Her eyes were still shut tight, her body so frail. I knew I had to get her out of here. I would take her to the fairies and have them heal her. I would let Fetch do it, but he seemed so weak himself that I didn't think he could.

"Hang on Michelle. We're gonna get you out of here."

I went over to the door and peeked out. Two policemen were attempting to get a nurse to calm down and point them in our direction. It would be just seconds before they arrived. I turned to Fetch to see if he could bust through the window and fly us all out of here. Michelle was staring at me. She was shaking and her hands were curled up like claws on either side of her face. She screamed. It was a long and loud scream of absolute terror. I swore to myself that I would make Johnathen pay for what he had done to her. I didn't even have time to ask Fetch if he could get us out of there. The police ran into the room, took one look at me and fetch, yelled and pulled out their guns. I didn't think they would open fire, but I didn't want to find out. I pushed some magic in their direction sending them flying out of the room. I turned and shot another spell at the window. It flew outward in one piece, crashing and breaking on the ground outside. Michelle had fainted and I grabbed her, holding her tight. I picked her up and jumped onto Fetch's back. She was so light, as if there was nothing to her. She was so thin and frail, I prayed I didn't hurt her when I picked her up. I ducked down close to Fetch's back as he clumsily made his way out of the window. He took off into the air as shouts were coming from the room behind us.

This time he remembered to cloak himself as we made good our escape. There was something different about Michelle. I couldn't quite put my finger on it, but it was more than just her now ravaged body. Johnathen had damaged her in a way that I couldn't explain, but it was serious. She whimpered in her sleep, mumbling over and over. "He took it. He took it." I held her tightly in my arms using just my legs to hold on to Fetch. He was shaking under me. This was really taxing his strength. I hoped we would reach the healing fairies soon.

We landed roughly in the desert. There was nothing in sight. I carefully got off Fetch's back, still holding Michelle in my arms. I was weak from hunger and the battle with Johnathen. The last twenty-four hours had taken a lot out of me.

I called out, "Hello! Help me please!"

Michelle moaned in her sleep. I wondered what she would say when she found out I had brought her to the fairies. She had to realize by now that they had not destroyed her family. But, years of mistrust and hate were hard to overcome overnight.

I would deal with that later. Now I just needed to get her some help.

Suddenly out of the darkness the fairies appeared. They rushed over to Fetch who was coughing up blood again. He was totally exhausted and just lay there breathing heavily. The fey were keeping their distance from me and Michelle, staring at us with fear in their eyes. I figured we were the first humans to find them.

"Please help us," I said, my words slurred strangely in my mouth.

I started feeling lightheaded. My lack of sleep and hunger finally caught up with me. I sank to my knees, still holding Michelle to me. Finally the fairies came to our aid. They took Michelle away from me. They helped me to my feet.

"Please," I said, "you need to find my friends. We were attacked by a wizard."

An older looking fairy with white hair spoke up.

"We know all about it, Jack. Your friends are safe and on their way here."

Relief washed over me. They lead us to a grouping of tents. Separating us, I was lead to one tent as Michelle was carried off to another. She continued to moan in her sleep. There was something different about her, besides how ragged and thin she was. Johnathen had changed her somehow. I just couldn't put my finger on what it was.

Inside my tent was a simple bed made of different colored pillows.

"Please," I said, "you have to help Fetch."

"We are attending to him now," the white-haired fairy said. "Please drink this and rest."

He handed me a cup of blue-green liquid. It reminded me of 'Kool-Aid' and tasted like honey. I felt better and lay down. The fairy stared at my face, studying it carefully. I wanted to ask him what he was doing, but, before I could, I fell asleep.

Chapter 40

I woke up slowly. My eyes opened just a crack and I could see the sunlight of an early morning sunrise. I had been wrapped tightly in a blanket, from the top of my head to the bottom of my feet, like a giant baby. It felt comfortable, and, in spite of the fact that I was anxious to find out how Fetch and Michelle were, I found myself reluctant to get up. I looked over at a small table next to the bed. There was my laptop. It was open and my story was writing as I lay there. It had almost caught up to the current time, as I saw the description of how Johnathen looked on the mountain.

"Well, it looks like he is starting to stir," said a familiar voice.

I turned to see Smith sitting at my side. Next to him was Samantha. Smith had his usual smile, but Samantha was keeping her head down. I was relieved to see that Samantha's face was as beautiful as it had always been. Fetch's fire had done its job and healed her.

"Hey," I said, "I am so glad you are ok. I thought you were dead."

"Well, my boy, as you can see, we are fine," said Smith.

"You are a hero, Jack," said Samantha, "both you and Fetch. You prevented Johnathen from destroying our whole way of life. Thank you."

She was treating me nicely. This had me worried.

"We managed to stop Johnathen, though he did escape." Said Smith. "The last thing he said was to look to the skies. Very cryptic of him, if you ask me. I'm afraid he is still growing in this strange new power he has found. It is a mystery where it came from. We are hoping to get some answers from Michelle when she wakes up. We won this battle but I feel there is more to come. You should have seen the fairy army, Jack. They just appeared on the fields. Why, the very presence of them sent the goblins in all directions. Not many were hurt except for . . . "

Smith paused there. The way he just blurted everything else out, made me think he was trying to hide something.

"What's going on?" I asked.

Smith's face sank into that familiar, droopy, sad look. He looked at me and in a shaky voice said.

"There is no easy way to tell you this, Jack. Fetch is dying."

I bolted up, not wanting to believe it. "How do you know?"

"He is spitting up a lot of blood and he gets weak. They think it is because he didn't devour your life force, Jack. He is also not maturing the way other dragons do, and without a full life force he cannot survive for very much longer."

I was in shock. I couldn't believe what I was hearing. How could this be happening?

"What can we do?" I asked, "There must be a way to save him. It can't end this way. "

You and Fetch are enigmas, Jack. There has never been a dragon who refused a life force before Fetch. We have no idea what to do. With your abilities and the changes you have gone through, we are concerned about how it will end for you.

"Do you mean I am dying too?" I asked.

"We don't know, Jack, but that isn't what I meant. You don't know it yet but you have cha . . . "

Smith never finished his sentence. A blood curdling scream came from the tent next to mine. It was Michelle. I jumped out of my bed and ran over to the next tent. There was Michelle, with Fetch resting his head in her lap.

"Why am I here with fairies?" she screamed.

She looked over at me in shock. Fetch had buried his head in her lap. All the anger she had directed at me drained out of her face.

"Oh Jack, I thought it was a nightmare. I'm so sorry."

I thought she was delirious. I had no idea what she was saying. She reached out to me and I finally realized, in horror, what was so different about her. The words she kept repeating over and over again last night made sense to me now. Her tattoo was gone. Her skin was red, scratched and swollen. Johnathen had taken her tattoo away. With how weak and sick Michelle looked I figured that it wasn't a pleasant experience.

I started to cross the tent to go to her when I caught a glimpse of my reflection in a mirror. I looked at my reflection not believing I was seeing what I thought I was seeing. My heart was beating so hard and fast it felt like it was about to explode. My face was a hideous mask. The left side looked as normal as ever, but the right side was covered with a jagged line of green and white scales. The hair on that side of my head was gone and my right eye was now bigger and was rapidly changing color. My mouth drooped down in an arc that went back to my jaw line. My ear came to a point. It was a twisted horrific face out of a nightmare. I raised my hand toward my reflection, as if I could touch the mirror and change it. My hand had changed too. It was two times bigger than my left hand and it curved slightly inward like a claw. The green and white scales went up my arm. I tore open the thin cloak they had put on me in my sleep, and saw that my chest on the right side was covered in scales too. I looked down at my clawed, scale-covered foot, and realized that this stuff covered half of my body.

I had become a monster, a freak, I was now a vision of horror.

TO BE

CONTINUED

Made in the USA
San Bernardino, CA
02 February 2017